MW00616666

THE BETTER ANGELS
Published by *The Bitter End Publishing*

978-1-7351306-1-3

This is a work of fiction.
Printed in the USA.
TimeLight Photographic; picture of the Victorian Dressmaker

Cover Design and Interior Format

THE
BETTER
Angels
HEARTS TOUCHED BY FIRE, BOOK 4

Gina
DANNA

Readers Discretion Advised

This book is historical fiction of the American Civil War. It is written to be as historically accurate to the period in description and language. It is a story of the War and of the people who lived it and contains adult content. Readers Discretion is Advised.

The Living Historian's Creed

WE ARE THE PEOPLE TO whom the past is forever speaking.

We listen to it because we cannot help ourselves, for the past speaks to us with many voices.

Far out of that dark nowhere which is the time before we were born, men who were flesh of our flesh and bone of our bone went through fire and storm to break a path to the future.

We are part of that future they died for.

They are part of the past that brought the future.

What they did—the lives they lived, the sacrifices they made, the stories they told and the songs they sang and, finally, the deaths they died—make up a part of our own experience.

We cannot cut ourselves off from it.

It is as real as something that happened last week.

It is a basic part of our heritage as Americans.

~ *Bruce Catton*

Acknowledgements

THE 4TH BOOK IN THIS series could only be made possible by the strong support from a team of people. I'd like to thank my editor, Louisa Cornell, who wades through my massive script without killing me. To JJ Jennings, who is my Civil War reference point when I hit a snag. To Bob Peternell who took me to Mines Run Battlefield, which doesn't appeared to have been traversed since the 19th century. To my co-workers who find me dragging my computer to work, some wanting to be in the story without understanding the dangers that can bring, though some do fine themselves here in the past. To all, I say thank you!

"WE ARE NOT ENEMIES, BUT friends. We must not be enemies. Though passion may have strained it must not break our bonds of affection. The mystic chords of memory, stretching from every battlefield and patriot grave to every living heart and hearthstone all over this broad land, will yet swell the chorus of the Union, when again touched, as surely they will be, by the better angels of our nature."

—Abraham Lincoln's 1st Inaugural Address, March 4, 1861.

Before Abraham Lincoln took office in 1861, South Carolina, Mississippi, Georgia, Florida, Alabama, Louisiana and Texas had seceded from the Union and formed the Confederate States of America. The world waited for Lincoln's response. His speech was aimed to reconcile with these seceded states in a desperate attempt to avoid war.

"My plans are perfect and when I start to carry them out, may God have mercy on General Lee for I will have none!"

—General Joseph Hooker,

The Battle of Chancellorsville, May 1863

Prologue

Virginia, November 1863

THE GIGGLE WAS FAINT, VERY feminine, and without opening his eyes, he grinned. He had always loved her laughter. Light, airy, the sound drifted and he remembered the first time he heard it. He believed he fell in love with her at that moment, not so long ago, when it was summer in Louisiana.

"Francois, Francois," she coaxed him.

He didn't want to answer, for that meant he'd have to open his eyes and at the moment, he realized his eyelids were so heavy, he doubted he could. Instead, he'd lounge here on this rattan settee in his mother's rose garden and wait for her to get closer.

"Francois, darling," she whispered into his ear. "It's time to wake up."

"No, ma chère, non." He'd snuggle into the cushions more if they weren't so hard. That confused him. His mother never allowed sturdy furniture frames out on the balcony...Plus the birds were overly chirpy, starting to grate on his nerves. He refocused on her.

"Francois, my love," she cooed again, singing into his ear. "You'd better wake, darling."

"Non, ma chère, come back to me," he begged. He'd put out his arms to take her into his embrace but he discovered he couldn't. It was like he was far under water, trying to build a house, as sluggish as he was. He frowned.

"Francois…." Her voice faded. No! She couldn't leave him again! The birds around him seemed to multiple, busily squeaking louder and louder. He tried to get up, to go after her but the world began to swirl and he stopped, still feeling trapped and realized he'd gone no where. In his mind, he searched for her but his vision filled with smoke and the acid taste of gunpowder and sulfur burned his throat and clouded his vision.

"Francois! Wake up!" She screamed with a panic tone.

He twisted. In a split second, a stabbing pain shot into his foot, at his ankle, as if he was on fire. He roared in agony, reluctant eyelids splitting wide open. The shock of what he saw made him want to flee. He was lying with other men moaning and groaning. The men upright walked about at a hurried pace, their white coats stained in red along with more men in blue hauling some in and taking others out. The whole area smelled of blood, urine, sulfur, sweat and vomit, wafts so overwhelming, he held his breath, despite his own agony.

The commotion drowned out his pain for the second until two rough hands yanked his wounded leg to the side and repositioned it, the movement set off another cycle of pain. Another man walked up, his white coat not as dulled by red splatters as the rest. He wore a pair of spectacles on his nose and a weary look across his face. He yanked out a long metal rod, the end coated in white.

"Let's see what we got, shall we?" the man said, taking Francois's foot and twisting it.

Francois couldn't stop the cry of agony evoked by the manipulation of his foot. The dull hurt of before turned drastically sharper. Confused, Francois tried to retrace where he was and how he was wounded when another series of lightning bolt pains shot up his legs to his hips, back, shoulders and head, settling into his ears. Unfortunately, the sheering sting didn't stop the man in the white coat from prodding his ankle.

"Reed! Bring me that bag," the man called. "Need to amputate this…"

Amputate? Francois blinked hard, the scene around him blurred. They'd take his foot?

"Emma!!!"

"Bury your poor dead and say nothing more about it."
—General Robert E. Lee's response to Lt. Gen. A.P. Hill's report of the slaughter of his men at Battle at Bristoe Station, VA, October 15, 1863

Chapter 1

October 1863

FRANCOIS FONTAINE TIPPED THE GLASS up, pouring the whiskey down his throat, the flavor skating over his taste buds to carve a burning path down to his stomach. He closed his eyes, relishing the flavor, hoping it would send him down the road to forgetfulness once more. Swallowing the end of that shot, he refilled the glass.

"My darlin' Francois, you plannin' to spend another day downing my liquor, or will you spend time with me?"

Francois smiled slowly. The seductive purr from across the room came from the only woman he knew who could put him in his place, and he'd love every minute. He glanced up and found LaJoyce giving him one of her warm and inviting grins.

"No, ma'am, I hadn't plan to do so," he drawled, putting the shot glass aside. He stood, circling around the table to meet her. "That is, if I could get a chance to show you what you've been missin', of late." He smiled, hoping he wasn't as tilted as he feared he was getting.

She stared at him, a slight curve to her lips capturing his attention. "Thinkin' you best sit down before you fall," she commented, walking away.

LaJoyce was a beautiful negress. No, he corrected himself. She was a freewoman with one of the best reputations in the area. Her house was clean, her clothing exquisite and those lips ruby red and inviting. Short enough, she was easy for him to pick up and carry to bed. High cheekbones on a full face, her dark brown eyes gave a glimmer of her strength and her capacity to love deeply. He respected her, which was a rare emotion to pass through him. LaJoyce had seen him through his younger years, when he was a strapping boy, trying to control feelings and fears that popped up as he grew. She was the first woman who taught him the ways of love and how to bring a woman pleasure with the reciprocal measures. The fact she wasn't Delilah, the lady of ill repute his father or brother visited, gave him the silent joy that LaJoyce was all his.

"Instead of drinkin' my cupboards dry, I think you need to go find yourself a pretty little white girl to marry," LaJoyce continued, closing the bourbon bottle near him.

"Why, when I have such a lovely woman as you?" he countered.

LaJoyce grinned. "I know you favor a darker hue, but a paler version is all your family would approve of. And you ain't going find that sitting here all day, not even enjoying any of the finery."

Francois snorted. It was that just that issue that drove him here. He needed to find a way to escape, to forget about the one woman he could never have. After all the bottles he'd consumed and intercourse he'd had, she still haunted his dreams. A flare of frustration raced up his spine and his fingers tightened around the glass. In a flash, he downed the fiery liquor, trying in desperation to drown the vision that hovered in his mind, of a beautiful Southern belle who would never be his…

"Fontaine, been lookin' high and low for you! Dang-naggit man, you ever not goin' drink?"

Francois glanced up at the man whose shadow clouded his view. It was Randolph Morris, from the Pear Plantation, just down the river from Bellefountaine, Francois's family estate.

"Randy, don't you have something else that's needs harassing?" Francois snorted, grabbing the wrist of the ebony girl who passed him. He pulled her into his lap, enjoying the lilac scent on her skin and the ivory cotton lace-trimmed chemise that she wore, with the ruffle from her pantalets peaking under the hem. She was bare-armed, no stockings and scrumptious to hold. When she giggled, wiggling in his seat, Francois grinned.

LaJoyce swaggered over to him, the curve in her hips and the sway of her silk dress beyond enticing. She hadn't looked interested before, the reason he grabbed Lucy but the shooting glare from the woman towering over him told him that was the wrong decision.

"Lucy, I believe Mr. Fontaine has company," LaJoyce stated firmly. "And I do believe, Mr. Cartier has just arrived. I think you remember him well, as it were."

Lucy scrambled out of Francois's embrace. "Yessum, ma'am." And she darted for the hall in the front of the house.

Francois gave his mistress another glance. "You appeared busy, ma'am."

LaJoyce shook her head in apparent disbelief. "Gentlemen, I fear running a business like a bordello requires a great deal more attention than you might conceive."

Francois chuckled. "Well, my dear, yours is one of the best."

"Merci. 'Tis truly amazing, considering the Yankee presence." She shook her head and leaned closer. "Monsieur, I believe you better pay your rather long tab and find another place to hide. Those bluebellies been ramblin' to the girls about another round of arrests for any secesh."

Randolph snorted. "They done gone through here a parcel ago, ma chère. We all lay low."

"It was just a warning, sir." She winked at Francois, the hint deep. He dug into his waistcoat pocket and took her hand, pressing the gold coin into her palm.

"I think that'll cover anything you deem I owe."

LaJoyce smiled broadly, tucking the coin into her bosom. "I ain't joking about the blue coats." She caressed his cheek with her fingers. "Prison wouldn't sit well with you. So go."

He finished his drink and put the glass down, swooping his hat up. "You heard her Randolph. Let's be on our way." His friend hollered but Francois only pasted a smile on his face as he kissed LaJoyce good-bye.

She was right. Louisiana was suffocating in blue. He needed to find the war. Alcohol hadn't deadened the pain in his chest so the next solution was to fight. *God help him....*

Virginia, October 1863

For October, the temperature was way too warm and inside the tent, the temperature continued to climb. No memories of Pennsylvania or New York were ever this hot in the fall. Ada Lorrance swallowed, stiffening as another drop of perspiration dripped down her back in a river that had dampened her chemise and her corset and dress since the morning parted to noontime. Not only was she perspiring under the heat, she was thirsty to the point of anger and refused to give in to snapping at the next orderly for doing a job they didn't want to do nor were trained to do while suffering the same as she. Blinking and hoping the droplet on her brow didn't fall into her eyes, she took note that her charge was finally resting on his cot. She prayed gratitude to God for the man's slumber and the escape of his pain and took the damp rag in her fist, to stand up. Despite the corset stays, her back was tight and the change in her position from sit to stand caused a chain reaction of cracks down her vertebrae, the pressure released in a combination of pain and relief. She was convinced that stool she sat on would break her back one day.

Her thoughts were interrupted when a cool tin cup was shoved into her grasp.

"Here, drink this."

She frowned but the whisper of cold from the metal gave her a respite from the heat and gladly she held it. The liquid inside was marred in color by the dark shade of the inside of the tin.

"Its not poison," the man hissed. "Though God knows, it'd be a blessin'."

She laughed but took a sip. It was tepid water with raspberry vinegar and honey laced through it. It was the perfect blend for a hot and humid Virginia day.

"Thank you."

"Don't be," the man guffawed. "When Major Winslow finds his favorite refresher is low, there'll be someone's butt to pay."

"And I'd bet Doctor Leonard will be no where to be found when that man throws another tantrum." Ada laughed. She'd known Will Leonard for years, growing up with him in Philadelphia and schooling later. Will had a penchant for deviousness to make one's skin itch but it was never spiteful, and besides, Winslow's short temper and foul language made him one of the most disliked officer in the Union army despite his wealth that brought commodities to camp, like the supplies to make an elixir like this.

Will shrugged but a grin tugged at his lips, making her laugh harder.

"I think I'll take a walk," she stated, trying to calm the inner voice that screamed for her to run, but the issue was, run from what? The wounded or Will? She didn't wait but caught his nod as she sneaked out of the tent.

The air was hot and muggy, the sun bright and blinding but the stench of sweat, vomit and urine was lacking. She inhaled deeply, a refreshing moment as she walked toward the stream. Further from the camp, fewer soldiers lingered at the water's edge and the horses were yards away, so she found a spot, among the grass and sank to the ground. She closed her eyes, letting the moment of peace seep into her. Peace in a world of hate and bloodshed. The reasons for the war she pushed to the back of her mind, refusing to let it crowd her thoughts because she saw the result of it in the medical tent almost daily.

She yanked her handkerchief from her pocket and bent, plunging it in the water, dampening it to bring it to her forehead and squeezed. The cool water poured over her eyes and cheeks, down over her jawline to her neck and the bodice below. The worn cotton absorbed all and it clung to her skin, the slight layering of it and the chemise beneath gave her a breath of coolness that nothing outside of jumping into the stream could clear. Was that a slight breeze cooling her? She closed her eyes and settled in the quiet.

Her mind cleared so she squeezed the rag again, the water dribbling down her neck and into her bodice. The touch of the liquid reminded her of his touch, the gentleness of his fingertips and the burning path it left on her emotions, sending errant messages to her body. Slowly, as the memories budded, images appeared. She was back to home, in Pennsylvania, before the war. Back to a time she could never forget…

Spring was in the air, light breeze drifting through the open window of his bedroom. The lighter-weight warm-weather cotton drapes stirred and the birds chirped a May song. It was peaceful and her heart swelled with pride and love at the man lying next to her. He smiled, his infectious grin made her insides bubble, despite the dire consequence of the afternoon. He reached out, gently playing with her curly hair that was now a mess from their afternoon play.

"You know, my darlin', I must go." He kissed her nose tip.

"I know." She simmered, furious he had this much control over her because despite his situation, she still prayed he wouldn't answer the call to arms Lincoln had put out. "Isn't there some way you can stay?"

His fingertips traced down her neckline, his gaze following their path, making her shiver. His smile broadened as he cupped her breast and bent to suckle on the pearled tip, setting off a storm of tingles that spread throughout her body, reigniting the fire below. The fact that the man could so easily distract her with his touch was unnerving but at this moment, she relished every second, committing to memory each flash of excitement.

"You know I can't. It is my duty to go and serve." He flipped her underneath him, spreading her thighs to nestle his hardened

member.

Again, he had brought her to craving him, her body responding to his need. The cool breeze that hit her exposed core reminded her how wet she was, so ready to receive him.

"I want to remember every touch, commit to memory the feel of you as I enter, and how wet you are for me."

She lowered her hips against the feathered mattress and he slid into her slick core. Her body was full, he filled her completely and she hugged him, tipping her body up as he pushed. Back and forth they moved, dancing in the oldest rhythm of time. The rush overwhelmed her and the pressure continued to build until he thrust one more time, and the world shattered inside, stars bursting across her vision as her core hugged him tighter, sending triggers of excitement racing through her veins.

In the midst of her sudden death, she knew he came too. His member vibrated inside her sheath and she burned that feeling to her soul for the days to come, when he was gone…

He collapsed on top of her then rolled to the side, tugging her into his arms.

"I love you, Ada." He kissed her shoulder.

She grinned but it was a lazy moment as she drank him in…

"Ada! Ada!"

The male voice broke her thoughts and she blinked repeatedly, the sun blinding her. She was confused, distorted thinking about where she was and who was calling, and realized her bodice was soaking, as was the top of her skirt from the wet rag. The tingles that branched out from her nipples down to her core came from that man and it irked her at the same time she was annoyed how an outsider interrupted her memory of that day. She'd groan, but feared it'd come out more like a bedroom moan so she stifled it and scurried to make herself presentable.

"Yes, Will! I'm over here!" With a heavy sigh, she stood, shaking out her skirts and prayed there wasn't a tellin' sign what she'd been dreaming of. Unfortunately, she was too late.

Will stared at her and she thought she saw his hands tighten along with his shoulders. Rage or anger consumed him.

"What are you doing?" he hissed. "Remembering that bastard?"

She gathered her skirts and aimed to go around him. "Will, don't start."

As she pushed passed him, she heard his boots grind as he spun and followed. "That man is a scoundrel of top core! He left you, high and dry, for his own self but you? You work like a slave and still fall apart if given leave to think!"

"Will," she warned. "This is not the time or place for this."

"Ada, Ada, please." He was at her side but she refused to slow down and face him. "He's not worthy of you. He's frankly not even as good a doctor as you." He touched her shoulder gently. "I wish you'd forget him."

Inside, her heart heaved, the hole left in it still bleeding but she'd had a year to practice schooling her features, stopping the pending tears in their tracks. She stopped, bit her tongue so the sharp pain would override her breaking heart and painted a smile on to cover her emotions.

"As to who is the better physician, that is hardly the issue but that is why I'm here. To offer my skills to help our soldiers, even if regulated to a nurse, and bury the dead."

Will's frown deepened, but instead of launching another attack on the scamp who stole Ada's love, he cocked his head and gave her a tense smile.

"Then you may want to return to the hospital tent. That sergeant you were convinced was ill due to nothing more than eating molding food, has now progressed to dysentery."

Her shoulders slumped. "Bloody stools?" At his nod, she hissed and stormed back to the tent. The war was the one thing she could count on to distract her and bring her back to what was needed. Despite being a medical doctor, the Union Army only let her aid the Medical Department as a nurse. She steeled her shoulders, knowing the next battle was only a few hundred feet in front of her—a skirmish with the ranking medical officer who would deny her practicing, even if it meant death.

Tis no easy task, but I am endeavoring to bear everything as well and cheerfully as possible. Sometimes I fail entirely, but in a short time find myself persevering again in the struggle and may yet come out victorious.

—Elodie Todd, sister to First Lady Mary Todd Lincoln, in a letter to her husband, Confederate Officer Nathaniel Dawson, August 4, 1861, Selma, Alabama

Chapter 2

Virginia

"SO, YOU TORE YOURSELF AWAY from your *plantation* now to join the fight?" The sergeant glared at Francois from behind the makeshift ply boards that had been nailed to wooden legs. His face was leathered and dirt outlined the ridge of the creases in the sun burnt skin around his eyes and along his forehead and cheeks only to disappear in his mustache and goatee. It was amazing to Francois how a man so rugged as this, in a filthy uniform and skin so leathered, could keep such neatly trimmed facial hair…

The man tapped his pencil across the enlistment pages on the desk, waiting impatiently for an answer. Francois shifted on his feet, fighting the urge to tighten his fists and wipe the smug expression on the soldier's face, to eliminate that accusatory look.

He'd ridden across the torn countryside, pell mell to join the illustrious Army of Northern Virginia, as a recruit for the Louisiana Tigers. To be cast as a shirker, using the slaveholding act as the excuse not to fight, rubbed him wrong and this soldier's face, which reflected the man's disgust, only irritated Francois further. But his gentlemen's upbringing made him force a smile.

"As I recall, sir, the Confederacy needed soldiers. If I am indeed wrong, I'm sure I can find a way to give aid." The smile ached, but he was determined to maintain a modicum of calm.

The sergeant's brows furrowed as he gave him an assessing perusal, resulting in a snort of disgust before he turned back to his forms and scribbled, the lead pencil scraping across the paper. The sound grated on Francois's nerves but he managed to refrain from shifting or registering his impatience on his face—a practice he was well accustomed to back home, when his father's anger flared or his mother questioned him over issues he wanted to avoid.

"Slater, just finish! He's right and a true son of the South! Lousianian born and bred!" Randolph Morris blurted.

Sergeant Slater stopped and glanced up. "Fontaine?"

"Yes, he is," Morris continued. "His daddy runs that plantation, not far from St. Joseph's parish. Bellefountaine."

Slater frowned. "I've heard of it," he drawled. "Heard you all be planters up there abouts."

The tone made Francois give him a tweek of a smile. *Planter, hey?* "Sugar growers."

"Uh, huh." Slater went back to work, not before giving a snort. "Well, then, *sur,*" he slurred the word with a tinge of ridicule. "You'll find yourself right at home with the others in Hays troop." He shoved the halfway folded sheet to him and then quickly dismissed him by his demeanor, returning to other papers on his desk.

Francois held the page and frowned. He opened his mouth to say something but Morris yanked him away.

"I told you, you'd be sent with me to Hays!" Morris spring stepped as they crossed the field.

Francois noticed the men at the camps scattered about. The stench of boiled acorns and trace of coffee mixed with the scent of burned fat, a layer of horse manure and urine drifted throughout the camp.

"So this is what war does? Eliminate any and all manners?" He quickly saw the pile of horse dung before he stepped into it.

"You mean Slater? Nah, that man done have his gut all twisted over having to have his corps of Tar Heels under the command of the Tigers." Morris spit. "Heard once we arrived that the last run in with the Feds at the Rappahannock was a hell on fire. Damn Yankees bested the Tigers in a surprise attack on a ridge. Numbers cut back from injuries and some troops captured." He gave Francois a hard look. "Fresh troops are sorely needed. You'll find the welcome you want soon enough." He laughed.

Francois frowned. From the appearance around him, the war was just as ghastly as his brother had implied. He had assumed Jack's description bordered on the insane, an attempt to keep him at Bellefountaine, so it was disheartening to realize his sibling wasn't crazy. This mob that eyed him and Morris was the Army of Northern Virginia, led by the famous, according to the papers, General Robert E. Lee. Francois refocused, though, as they neared another set of tables and men around them that bore more stripes and feathers than sergeants.

"General Hays, sur," Morris said, stopping their progress back. "Look who arrived, newly recruited!"

The dark haired general with a drooping mustache gave Francois a quick look and snorted. "Why, if it isn't Francois Fontaine indeed! Glad to have you with us, son."

Francois returned the grin. He knew of Hays from days of old. "Yes sur. Hear your Tigers are kicking up dirt out here. Figure it's time to come see for myself…and add my efforts to the cause."

An older officer's eyes narrowed as he silently watched the exchange. Something about this white-haired aged man spoke volumes on how he commanded those around him but Francois wasn't sure who he was. It was a problem coming in late to the war, he speculated.

"General Lee, let me introduce to you another fine planter from our state, coming to help us whip those Yankees." Hays slapped Francois on the shoulder and it took a firmly planted stance to not move.

Lee's brows rose. "Fontaine, you say? From Louisiana?"

"Yes, sir." Francois replied.

"Once schooled a Fontaine, years back, at The Point. If memory serves well, he was from Louisiana. Any relations, Private?"

"This boy, I reckon, will serve as a corporal, general," Hays corrected.

Francois wanted to grin and found his lips tugging upwards to do so but he figured now was not the time to gloat over his sudden promotion, one coming without a single order being given. "Yes, sir. My brother, Jack, attended West Point before the hostilities commenced."

"Ah, yes, I do recall well. And where does he serve now, lad?"

Francois shifted. "He stayed with the Union, General."

Lee nodded. "To be expected, as I remember. Each has had to decide their own path in this divide. Glad to have you with us. Fresh faces are what we need to continue our mission."

Mission? He thought this was war, and as he opened his mouth to voice that, Morris butted in.

"General, we'll be headin' back, get him all settled."

"Good. Drill will be soon," Hays stated.

Francois nodded right as Morris pulled him away but he heard the General of the Army of Northern Virginia add, "Corporal Fontaine, I hope for you, that you won't find yourself facin' your brother on the field of battle."

"Yes, sir. I hope so too." But as he walked away, the devil inside him smirked. *Ah, but yes, if Jack fell……*

The cool air whisked through the slits in the tied tent flaps, its chilled temperatures whizzing around the few patients. It woke Ada up, and she startled when a flash of ice snaked down her spine. A crash hit the ground, the thud buffered by the dirt floor. She blinked hard, struggling to recall what she was doing and where she was. But when the stench of urine, vomit and other bodily emissions, seeped up her nostrils, reality struck hard and she jumped. The camp hospital. How could she forget?

Reorienting herself, she glanced down at the dirt floor around her and found the book she'd been working with, along with the writing instrument, sat askew near her dark wool dress hem and she sighed, bending to retrieve it. But as she scooped it up, the tent flap blew open and Will rushed in.

"Brrr! It's gettin' downright chilly out there!"

Ada snorted as she searched for the page she'd been at before she'd dropped it. "It is November, after all."

"Yes, well, that is true. But we are in the South. They're not to get as brisk as we're used to up North, and, well," he shrugged. "I'd gotten used to it being warmer now."

"Oh, so now you consider yourself a Southerner?" She couldn't resist the urge to tease him, but she buried her nose in the supply book to hide the smile that threatened.

"Hardly. I'm a Union man, through and through!"

The laugh escaped despite herself. "I see, well, good. I doubt your parents would wish to lose you to the dying cause, as it were."

Will stood quiet, and that let her know she'd won the argument. He was never good at admitting defeat.

"What task have you set for yourself?" He peered down at the pages.

"My job, that's what I'm doing," she complained, more angry with herself for allowing her time to be spent this way over tending patients. "Have you finished going over your patients?"

"Did that before the noontime sun. But you've resorted to supplies?"

"At the request of Surgeon Letterman," she stated, bringing her seat straighter, shoulders back.

"Yes, well perhaps as well," Will started. "Word has it that General Meade has another attack in order."

"Another? The wounded here have not yet recovered." The thought of another march and more wounded made her head spin. "The longer the line he creates, the harder it'll be to care for them."

"We'll have to pray for the best, then." He went to the surgeon kits and eyed the four sitting on the chest. Selecting one, he pulled and opened it.

"What do you think you are doing?" Ada asked, crossing her arms. She'd just inventoried those kits and wasn't about to let him rummage through them, no matter how close a friend he was.

"I'm heading along with the corps, as medical stop one." He yanked another satchel, one used by the hospital stewards, which held medicine and supplies.

"You?" She had to bite back the jealousy that threatened. "Since when did you get such preference?"

"Tsk, tsk, love," he corrected. "I'd say that green monster in you is pushing at the gates."

"You'll be there, at the front lines! Its—" She hated it, because he knew her that well. "Its dangerous out there. And you'll be pressured to do too much, or too little. You know the results of that." Curbing in her envy was harder than she imagined. As a way to control it, she flattened her palms against her skirt and waited.

"Yes, Ada, you are correct. But perhaps, with my knowledge of that, I'll put a stop to that mismanaging."

The nerve in her jawline, just left of her lips, twitched, like it did when she held herself back. The words to put him in place, to remind him she was better at medicine than him, came rushing to her and as she stepped closer, wound up to spin, he gave her a shake of his head.

"Ada, don't—"

"Miss Lorrance, Dr. Waxler…oh, my, pardon me!"

Ada's heart stopped for a second. Maybelle James, another nurse, had rounded the corner of the tent, turning past the crates to find her and Will inches apart. Too close for professionals, but not for soldiers who knew each other well. The flash of surprise in Maybelle eyes told Ada the woman obviously considered them in a tryst and it took all the energy she had not to snap. Her heart was already taken, and not by Will.

"It's all fine, Miss James. You were saying Dr. Waxler has?"

She unclenched her hands that had fisted.

Maybelle's gaze was still fixated on Will and it took her a moment to break it. "Dr. Waxler has asked that we prepare for possible arrivals and move our sick back to the barn."

Ada's brows furrowed. "Those boys would not fair well in that old barn. The cold will whip through there like no tomorrow!" The two dozen ill lads did have a couple of malingerers among them, those who refused or were afraid to fight, so they came down 'ill' and while their claim of sickness might be made up, she was sure they were not that far being under the weather. The fear in their eyes of possible gunfire and being on the front lines wasn't produced. Though there were three of them who were simply shirkers and those she put to the work of cleaning slop buckets and changing sheets.

"General Meade is poised to have his attack on Lee," Will added. "According to the aide I heard, he's got his plan to move across the river." He ran his hand through his hair, a habit Ada noticed he did when his worry built. "We'll have our hands full."

Maybelle pardoned herself and moved past them to talk to the two shirkers that had just brought back clean buckets. Ada bit back a smile because she could hear the nurse tell them to get the barn ready and they nearly jumped with joy, anything to escape cleaning soiled sheets.

"Ada."

She looked up, tipping her chin to see Will.

"I know, when it gets tough from all the wounded coming in, don't encourage Waxler from ordering you out. You know that old curmudgeon doesn't care for Dragon Dix's staff, and not for nurses who push doctors to use other methods."

Her anger stirred. Will was right. The head surgeon,

Waxler, did hate women nurses and Dorothea Dix who founded the nursing staff for the army, and especially ones like her that talent surpass simply nursing guidelines. "Half of their prognosis doesn't hold well. Most of these men do not need to have all their limbs removed." She stood, forcing her hands not to clench, and turned away from her friend.

"Ada, please. We need all the help we can get. That's Lee across that river. Richmond isn't that far away. It's going to be hell here and soon. Promise me. I know I need you here. You're one of the best nurses we have. Don't do anything foolish."

Ada glared, steeling her jaw shut. One of their best nurses. Her nerves prickled as the anger raced through her blood. She wasn't the best nurse. She was one of the best surgeons and Will knew that. But the US Army refused women surgeons, so she'd swallowed her pride and gone to enroll in the nursing corps that Dorthea Dix hired for the Army.

Staring at Will, she managed to put the humiliation of being regulated as a woman, and not of much use outside aiding the male doctors as a nurse, aside and sighed. He grinned, knowing she'd behave.

But one of these days, they'd regret throwing another qualified surgeon aside, simply because she was a woman.

Giving him a return tight smile, she pivoted, grabbing her notebook and stormed off to pack up the sick and gather strength for another round of war.

In every battle there comes a time when both sides consider themselves beaten. Then he who continues the attack wins.

—General U.S. Grant

Chapter 3

Rappahannock Station
November 6

IT WAS THE CRISP COOL air of the morning that greeted Francois as he dragged himself out of sleep to answer the army bugle call. Damn army kept such ungodly hours, he groused to himself as he leaned over to spit at the empty fire pit. He rubbed his eyes again, his cheeks stinging from the brisk air and he fought the urge to shiver. Virginia was too cold for his liking.

"I'd be guessing you ain't used to rising at this hour." Morris laughed as he rolled up his wool blanket and tarred lining.

"Waking at this hour is good for priests and slaves," Francois grumbled, but added a lazy smile. "Not for a good southern gentleman."

"Whoa boys! Seems we got us a prince here!" another soldier shouted, his jovial look didn't reach his eyes, which glared at Francois.

Morris's lips pursed. "Don't pay no never mind to him. Ronnie is typical of half the Tigers, men from the dregs of Nar'leans. Most of them no better than cutthroats and thieves."

"Yeah, well, we're the best out here on this field, you have no doubts on that now, do ya?" Ronnie shot back. He aimed his spittle at the ground and stormed off toward the source of the chicory that was brewing. Even Francois caught a whiff and his stomach rumbled.

"So I take it, these men despise the planters?" Francois hadn't seen much of the camp, having arrived late with Morris and, after their frantic pace to get there, it didn't take long for him to fall fast asleep. He considered it a good night, as Emma only invaded one dream, which should have relieved him, being better than haunting him all night, but it didn't. Before he could think about that further, Morris jutted in.

"Most think we are a bunch of lazy rich boys with too much time on our hands, never understanding the large amount of what we do is run a complex system, as plantations go." He shook his head. "But give them time. They'll warm to ya, as long as you don't prove yourself a coward, which I know you're not."

Francois frowned as he stuffed his rolled bedding into a looped piece, tied at one end, imitating Morris's, who wore his like a slash over his shoulder. "I see I haven't missed much, being out here."

Morris smirked as he led the way to the line. Francois looked up and down the soldiers near him. The Tigers made the news in what few papers they got since the war began and supplies for things like newspapers fell, with the Union blockade stifling all trade. LaJoyce told him all she knew, since her brothel catered many from the Crescent City, how the ruffians from the wharves swarmed to take up the fight against those Yankee aggressors. The rest he gleaned from print, and none of it was pristine. News spread how the Tigers were fierce warriors and how they also took their trade of stealing to the front as well, raiding more than the enemy. Yet somehow, the Tigers hit a chord inside him. These were his people and he'd fit right in...

"The Federals are just across the water. We're to hold, and send them straight to hell if they try to gain any hold here. So Tigers, man your posts!"

A roar ripped through the lines as the regimental leader finished his commands, more than most of it Francois realized he hadn't paid one wits attention. Inhaling deeply, he straightened his shoulders and fell into line as the Louisiana troops marched to the earthworks near the Rappahannock River.

Morris stood next to him. "Francois, I'm not sure what demons you be running from, but you better pay attention here. Us Tigers have a reputation to uphold."

Francois snorted, readjusting his rifle as he shouldered it to march. It was awkward, not anything he was used to. It's balance, combined with the wool rolled blanket and the leatherworks that held his ammunition, caps and food with the tin cup bouncing off the tie to the haversack, made him feel bulky, everything shifting as he walked. The rough leather brogans were uncomfortable, even with the wool socks, but it was the uniform and he fit in with the rest. Days of riding across green fields and managing a plantation now just a distant past. Emma, though, wasn't.

They marched over the rise then sank into the pit on the backside, every soldier settling in.

"Them Yankees won't be messing with us here," one man boasted. "If their scouts be any good, they've seen us and won't go against the Tigers!"

A mumbled agreement filtered down the line. Francois

sank down, putting the rifle down and yanking the roll off his shoulders. He needed to feel that locket in his pocket. The boiled wool of the grey-brown jacket was thick so he reached inside and searched the inner breast pocket till he found the oval shape. Relief flooded through him as he pulled it out, rubbing his thumb pad over the gold cover.

"I'd be keepin' an eye on that piece, if I was you," Morris whispered. "Gold is scarce around this place."

"Anyone who even thinks of takin' this will soon find himself without any fingers," Francois threatened softly. With practiced ease, he flipped the lid back so he could see his ladylove. It was a small portrait, painted years before the war, he reckoned, but still, he could see the beauty that captured his heart. She'd given it to him when he'd wooed her and he thought it odd she'd never asked for it back, though the unexpected return of Jack no doubt pushed any thoughts of him aside...

"Who's that?"

He closed his eyes as he slowly shut the pendant and slid it back inside his jacket, to the pocket over his heart. "Emma."

"She is waiting for you?"

Morris was a damn bit too nosey, Francois wanted to grumble. Instead, he sighed and uttered the worst word of them all. "No."

His friend frowned. But before he could mutter a word, a hail of gunfire exploded from across the river.

She was convinced she was lying to herself. The post came and she rushed to the poor corporal who had the terrible position of distributing the parcels. What should be a wonderful moment was always laced with dread simply from the prospect not everyone got a piece. The waiting soldiers often stormed the poor man. For those poor souls with no mail, this was the worst, for they appeared forgotten in this hell they lived in. Ada tried to convince herself she was more worried about them than whether or not she got something. Walking away empty-handed was never her fate, thanks to Dragon Dix and her constant reminder of reports, but what she desired was a letter from her beloved, something that rarely happened…

Already she was devising a distraction along the lines of rearranging the medical storage in search of another easier method and burying her heart beneath a crate or two. But this time, her luck changed.

"Nurse Lorrance!"

She darted her way through the throng and reached for the post. Four envelopes, three of which had Dix's handwriting, but the fourth was only addressed to her and in a masculine script. Could it be? Did she dare hope? With a deep gulp, she pulled the edges apart.

It was him! Her beloved! She devoured every word of this very short note, written two weeks past. It was the last line, though, that made her stomach flip.

It has been unsightly here. The wounds that never stop, the saws that never rest. Rosecrans attempts to beat Bragg has become a bloodbath that trails from Atlanta back to here in Nashville. As I scribe this, I find my own strength taxed so apologies for the shortness. Just assure me that you are far from this madness and you risk nothing to get closer to me. We shall reunite when we've won, or they have their independence, for at this point, either is possible from what I see at the surgeon's view.

Your humble and obedient servant, always,

Colonel Richard E. Peregoy
Medical Dept
United States Army

She pressed the letter to her breast, a surge of relief from hearing his words raced through her veins. He'd finally replied to her correspondence and it made her heart sing, despite the rather cool closure. But he no doubt wrote it with little care, pressed by the war, like they all were. He'd made the leap to staff surgeon and was fully encompassed with the Army of the Tennessee. At times, it made her wonder whether he remembered who he was writing to, but his advice to be cautious she didn't think was for another. Despite its rather cold signature, signed in military style and missing any endearments her heart longed to hear, she'd hold onto the hope that he was alive, thinking of her and the hint of seeing her again…

"Ada."

She blinked hard, realizing she was standing awkwardly still, in the footpath of the hospital row, clutching the letter as her eyes pooled with unreleased tears. Blinking furiously, she cleared her vision to find Dr. Letterman before her. The great surgeon and instigator for advancement here, on the battlefield for the wounded, surprised her.

"Yes, sir," she replied, sliding the letter into her skirt pocket.

"Are you all right, madam? Perhaps you should go inside and take a seat." A concerned looked etched across his forehead. He motioned toward the tent behind her.

"No, I am truly well. It was news from a close and dear friend. I'd been worried about him, being with the Army of the Tennessee."

"Ah, yes. General Rosecrans's venture. Bloody affair

through and through!" Letterman shook his head.

The silence that followed made her frown. "Sir, how may I help you? For I doubt your visit here is simply to inquire after my health."

Letterman nodded. "It has come to the attention of the staff that some of our physicians are not performing to their best, while there are others who do more than required." His gaze at her narrowed. "In fact, they are found stepping into a position they are not qualified for."

Her heart skipped a beat. "Major Letterman, I do the best I am allowed to do." Had Will reported her acting as a doctor? A position that, despite what the Union Army proclaimed, she was more than qualified for. Anger sparked in her blood.

The doctor snorted with a half a smile. "Madame, I have no desire to upset you. I know you are a graduate of the Pennsylvanian School of Medicine. In fact, I've been told you out rank some of our stewards, and perhaps a physician or two, in your knowledge and skills, but I must remind you that the Army will not let you practice on any of our men."

The words still stung. They had been repeated every day, she swore, since she entered the college. But she held herself still. "Sir..."

"No, let me finish. While I must uphold Army regulation, I am not always present. And," he paused. His voice lowered as he continued. "I also know the staff is often overwhelmed with the numerous wounded. Do the best you can to aid them, but be aware of the eyes that watch you."

She wanted to faint. He told her to help? She gulped. "Yes, sir. Thank you, Major."

"Make no mention of it." He gave her a half smile that

quickly vanished. "With that knowledge, I must also inform you that you and the nurses, with the rest of the medical staff, must pack quickly and head to the main house, located a half of mile from here. One we have…acquired, as it were, for a better medical facility."

Ada's eyes widened. The battle had started and already, command knew it would be bad. With a quick nod, she bid him farewell and raced to find the staff. As she'd witnessed before, things would go downhill fast, so she pushed all thoughts of her distant love aside and braced herself for the bloodbath to come.

"...the North is determined to preserve this Union. They are not a fiery, impulsive people as you are, for they live in colder climates. But when they begin to move in a given direction...they move with the steady momentum and perseverance of a mighty avalanche."

—Sam Houston, Governor of Texas, 1861

Chapter 4

WHAT HE HAD READ IN the papers on the horrors of battle didn't even begin to touch the picture of the real moment. Francois had reacted, as the rest of the Tigers, on the Union assault, firing his gun, reloading and firing again toward a sea of blue that did not seem to stop. Smoke filled the air and Morris had sworn reinforcements must surely be on the way, but the rise behind them cut the Tigers off from the rest of Lee's forces. It was as if they were alone, fighting Goliath but without the rock and sling to bring him down.

The fighting became intense. Francois followed his compatriots and attached his bayonet to the end of the weapon, swinging it like a club at the oncoming Yankees. One soldier pressed closer, too close it seemed for him to twist the gun to hit the man so he plunged forward, sinking the triangular blade into the enemy's gut right before he received the same attack. The soldier's eyes widened in fear as he gurgled blood that rose into his mouth and spat it at Francois, who tried to duck but couldn't total escape the red stream. With a yank, he pulled his gun free and his opponent fell, never to move again.

Francois stood, feet frozen to the ground, unable to move, his ears ringing. His weapon gleamed in red blood that dripped off the bayonet and gunstock. The angle he had to use to disengage had turned the rifle into a funnel and the blood had oozed down, covering his hands. Well, he assumed it was the fallen man's blood, though with all the carnage around him, it could be from any of them, maybe even him.

"Come on!"

The push against his shoulder, the violent shove by Morris, snapped Francois back to the present. He blinked but nodded as he grabbed his rifle. "To where? Got them all around us."

"Hays be there," Morris pointed.

Their commander was still on his horse, but surrounded by Yankees swarming in. His sword was in the air and it took Francois a moment to realize the man's panicked look spoke a million words. He was going to surrender due to numbers but with the soldiers so close, he couldn't sheath his sword without damaging his animal or worse. Almost in response to the tension the equine could sense, he bolted with Hays still onboard, clinging to the leather as the horse raced to the bridge.

"Now!" Morris yelled, stabbing the Yankee in front of him with the bayonet before he took off to the river.

More blood. Francois could barely comprehend the scene when the need to survive kicked in as another set of soldiers appeared. He raced down the slope with Morris, toward the river. He could see Hays's frantic ride across, driven by a steed running with fear, but the Yankees firing at him clogged the opening to the bridge.

"We gotta take the river!"

Francois looked down at the water, the urge to argue against it dissipated as bullets whizzed through them, barely missing him. This was war. What he'd been able to avoid and now raced into...

"Come on!" Morris raised his rifle above his shoulders to keep it from the water and jumped.

Francois moved toward the edge, hesitating still. Most of these men had been hardened by the years of fighting but he'd managed to remain home, running the plantation since his father was a senator for the new government and the number of slaves they had kept Francois at home to manage them. It wasn't that he was afraid, he thought, but...

A roar from behind and the rustling of leaves as Yankees came closer drove him to jump.

He plunged into a river, not realizing its depth and he sank to be covered by an icy temperature that felt like a hundred knives stabbing his entire being. Disoriented, he quickly sought to get out when the water around him pinged, as if rocks were being thrown in. Bullets. Those Yanks were firing at them in the river!

He fought his way to the surface and found Morris was still pushing ahead. Fighting against the cold, Francois drudged through the water, dodging bullets, praying to the Lord above to make it, when he bumped into a log just under the water. His knee stirred it to surface and he swallowed hard. It wasn't a log but a body of another Confederate—one the Yankee shots had found. Still keeping his rifle as best he could out of the water, he worked his way around it but was slow, fighting the water and the revulsion.

"You comin' or you plannin' on joinin' him?" Morris

yelled.

Francois looked up and found his friend on the bank. He grimaced and took another step when the icy water pain was replaced by a shear of red-hot pain ripped his upper left arm. Those bastards shot him! Instantly, he dropped the flaming shoulder into the water, begging the cold water to deaden the agony. Somehow he kept the rifle from falling into the water. Anger raced through him and he wanted to turn and fire but the pain ripped through him, almost made him drop the rifle. Thankfully, his grip was still tight and Morris's urging him kept him going.

The whiz of bullets echoed in his ears and the sound of a cannon in the distance roared but he made the bank and Morris, with two other soldiers, pulled him up. It was great to be out of the ice but now, in the evening air, he shivered. Still furious over his wound, he spun.

"Those damn bluebellies shot me!" He glared at Morris as he pulled the rifle into position, aiming at the Union soldiers facing them on the other bank. His shoulder pinched with the move but his furious mind ignored it until Morris nudged the barrel down.

"Yes, I see that. They done us some damage tonight that's for sure. All them still over there be prisoners and you saw those already meetin' Jesus. Can't lose you as well. Come on!"

Inhaling sharply, trying to control his temper, Francois snarled as he turned to follow Morris. Granted, the Yanks won their spot along the other side of the river but he'd refused to let them win again. With each step, his arm throbbed and the pain riveted down his spine to his legs, making his steps slow. The torn shirt was dirty and soaked with blood. As it dripped onto his pants, he looked as if he'd been run over by a battle. The days of riding across lush fields and playing were long over, to be replaced by pain, fury and the drive for vengeance— for an issue he had no one to blame but himself…

It had been a long day. Ada rubbed her brow and inhaled deeply, trying to ignore the horrific stench of sweaty, dirty and wounded men. Steeling her shoulders and backbone, she lifted her chin as she stepped toward the bed, the re-filled water basin in her grasp.

"They're coming so fast," Maybelle whispered.

Placing the bowl on the table and wringing out the washcloth, Ada didn't have to look at her fellow nurse to know Maybelle was white as a sheet and shaking. The freshly arrived wounded usually looked grotesque, their battlefield wounds ragged and sharp with blood and vomit competing for attention.

"Maybelle, why don't you make sure the buckets are filled and the soap and washcloths are ready." She turned toward the newly arrived soldier and bit her own tongue to keep from gasping when she saw the raw flesh, red and oozing, dangling a foot by a mere strand of muscle.

Maybelle nodded but stuttered, "How can you act as if none of this affects you?"

How did she explain it? "Oh, back home, where there wasn't much around, I was the best practitioner anyone could find." She ripped the fabric at his trouser leg and grimaced. "After my daddy died, while being the only doc around, I picked up the slack. Mostly ladies and children," she added. She wanted to scoff. That's all they'd found 'suitable' for her to attend. "But I've seen my share of awful. It does affect me, but all I want do is help, so I do. You, my dear, look like you've seen a ghost, so helping us on the wash water would be most grand."

Maybelle nodded and excused herself so fast, she nearly ran into the bed behind her. Ada shook her head and returned to the boy on the bed.

"I ain't gonna die, am I?"

Her patient's question surprised her, because she'd thought he was unconscious. There was a glazed look there, like the steward had already poured spirits down him in an attempt to subdue him before surgery. "No, I don't think so." Her voice nearly graveled when she added, "You hold your own, son. The doctor will be coming shortly."

He tried to grasp her hand. The pressure was weak so she met his grip partway but her eyes started to blur. So many emotions swirled inside her. Despair, because his chance of survival was grim from the looks of the wound. Amputation would be the call and rightly so, for the leg had a tourniquet on to stop the blood from pouring out and killing him, but even she could tell the signs it had been on for too long. Anger for this boy losing a foot and more for a rebellion that should've been stopped before it happened filled her. Anger for tears bottling up, as she was forced to do, to take care of these patients and the frustration because she could do nothing, unless it was only Will. And a constant wonder as to why she was here…

"Nurse Lorrance, if you will, please."

The bustle behind her crowded her and she released the boy's hand to step aside. The surgeon's team was here to collect him.

"They'll help you, son," she stated boldly, and hoped she sounded sincere.

He gave her a weak smile that slid from his face after a moment, when they hauled him up to carry him to surgery.

She bit her bottom lip in a way to stop from blurting out what needed to be done, though the surgeons would know. Clenching her fists, she shuddered as the tightness inside her struggled to say nothing.

"Nurse Ada."

She looked up to find Maybelle giving her an odd stare. Absently she wiped the tear that wanted to run down her cheek and pushed the memory of the boy from her mind. Swallowing deep, she straightened herself.

"Yes, Nurse Maybelle?"

The young woman pointed her nose a little higher, trying to be subtle but Ada noticed. The New Englander seemed a bit too high strung, she decided. She and most of the nurses, schooled with her in a large walled tent for sleep, were hardly warm, Ada recalled, and most blamed that on their cold climate and Puritan upbringing. Though studious and helpful, Miss Maybelle never approached her except formally.

"Well, I do not wish to be quite so frank, but," she paused. "You and Dr. Will seem to be overly close. Now, I know it ain't my business, so to speak, but the other nurses are talking."

Ada bit back a laugh. Nosy little girl, she thought. She rolled back on her heels. "Miss Maybelle, I assure you, Dr. Will and I do know each other. We grew up in the same street, as it were." A thought raced through her mind and she wondered. "You don't, perhaps, wish to set your cap for him?" The idea made her want to chuckle.

The girl blushed but she managed not to change her expression. "I'm sorry if I said something out of line. I just wished to bring it to your attention that tongues are wagging. As to my preferences, I believe I'll keep them to myself. Now, my deed is done. If you'll excuse me." She spun on her heel to leave.

Ada bit her bottom lip, shocked at the nurse's behavior. The air was thick, Ada believed, mostly coming from that nurse's rudeness.

"Pardon me, Nurse Maybelle, but we do need to see that all the rags and bandages are cleaned, the bowls ready and the sponges close by for the surgeons. Please see to that after you've bathed the patients in the front parlor.

Maybelle didn't turn but stopped and now, nodded her head. "Of course, ma'am."

As Ada heard her walk away, she clutched her strand of buttons in her pocket, her fingers rubbing the large Union eagle one. Part of her wanted to laugh, for the nurses figured she and Will were flirting and perhaps, Will was, though she doubted it. He knew her heart was hurting for the man whose button she held tightly, in remembrance of him and prayed he'd return to her…

The firing of a cannon in the distance answered her wayward thoughts. He wouldn't be as long as the North and South tried to kill each other. Inhaling sharply, trying to stop the blur from taking her vision, she stood and grabbed the basin. It was her hope that none of her patients died on her tonight.

"There are but two parties now; traitors and patriots."
—Ulysses S. Grant, prior to the Civil War

Chapter 5

"THERE YOU GO, SUR, RIGHT as rain."

Francois flinched as the hospital steward pulled the last stitch through the wound on his upper arm, the raw flesh still throbbed even with the skin sewed shut. The splash of whiskey, hardly enough to even swallow, was the only painkiller used, and it burned fiercely. A final tug and a snip ended the torture and Francois relaxed as best he could until the man had the nerve to wrap a bandage around his arm.

"It might seep a little and that's to be expected. Good towards healing and such. Be thankful that bullet only grazed you, sur. You'd have lost your arm otherwise." The steward schooled his supplies into the leathered box beside him and left.

Francois snarled, trying to ease his arm into the tattered shirt he had worn. The gaping hole had bloodstains on it but it was the only shirt he had and he refused to leave it, knowing his jacket, made of wool, would hardly be better to wear against bare skin. Buttoning his cuffs was trying, for even moving the fingers of the damaged arm made a thread of stinging stabs course through him. Damn the Yankee who'd shot him!

Standing up, he snagged his jacket and shoved his arms into the sleeves, ignoring the pain but he couldn't help but glance at the sleeve of his wounded arm. The rip by the bullet held little trace of the blood…though the dirt on the jacket probably hid most of it. Another ripple of disgust washed through him. This jacket was the only uniform one he had, as retrieving uniform pieces appeared to harder from what he and Morris discovered on their journey east.

The bound arm ached and it limited his movement. He muttered a swear word, only to quickly cross himself as he got closer to the camp. Small fires pitted the site, amongst the hastily arranged shelters across the wooded land. The sounds of leaves shuffled by his bootheels grew softer as the soft tones of a violin and chimes rang with the sound of clanking wooden spoons in the Creole songs of back home. Instantly, he relaxed, the tensions of the day ebbing, though the throb of his wound didn't as he rounded the corner into the campsite.

"Francois! Over here!"

He found Morris with a few other men, sitting on fallen timbers, holding metal plates in their hands. The smell of burnt pork fat and cornmeal wafted around him and his stomach growled. He needed food, badly enough he'd take a hard cracker if they had one. The closer he got, the sounds of the music increased and the expression on the soldiers' faces were not so hard.

He stopped and snorted. "Nothing like hunger makin' even burnt bad food smell appetizing."

Morris laughed, scooping a ladle from the bottom of the stew pot and dumping the remains on a plate. "Here, then, join us in this repast."

The hunk of black, smoldering food looked anything but appealing. "Merci. And your chef this evening?"

"Moi!" Morris bowed.

Francois raised his brows as he steadied the dish level with one hand, trying to avoid jostling the wounded one, and sat on the stump next to his friend.

"We heard Hayes was hurt worse than you," Morris told him. "They'll like reassign us to another commander."

"It ain't right," muttered one of the other men.

"We're Hayes' men!" the Creole sitting on the ground added.

The one off to the left eyed Francois with a narrow gaze. It was the one Francois recalled from earlier, Wiggins.

Finishing the mess on the plate, a grueling task only a starving man could do, Francois put the tin ware down. His temper flared, no doubt added to with the sharp pain in his wound. "Is there something you want to say to me?"

"I'm just trying to figure out why a rich planter, like you, would care to throw down managing a homestead, free, apparently, from service, to ride halfway across this nation to fight Yankees?"

"Ronnie, that's not a viable question to—" Morris started.

"That's a fairly reasonable question," Francois interrupted. "One, I believe I shall answer. You are correct. I could avoid the bloodshed, the shower of bullets and so forth. Under the law, my family owns over the required limit of twenty slaves that would keep me safe at home, but circumstances beyond my control, pushed me to enter the army."

"Whatever could drive a man into this madness?" a young lad, Francois guessed no older than twenty, piped in. Peter Perlotti, he recalled, was one of the few Italian dock-workers who signed on to the military. Better pay than the docks of a now occupied New Orleans, Francois decided.

Francois sat for a moment, chewing the inside of his lip, teetering on how to put this. He could lie but the truth, for once, seemed the correct choice. "A lady."

The men all grumbled, nodding their heads.

"She push you to enlist for the favor of her company?" one asked.

"Or she tell you, you'd have her love if you fought?" another questioned.

Francois snorted, swallowing hard. "She married my brother."

"What?" Wiggins jumped up. "What a snake!"

"Wait," Perlotti said. "Ain't he Jack Fontaine? A Yankee officer that took over after Beast Butler and his like left?"

Francois warmed. General Benjamin Butler was commanding general during the beginning of the occupation of New Orleans and his presence wasn't welcomed, particularly by the rebellious ladies of the town, who dumped their chamber pots, among many signs of protest, on his troops. When he issued the order to have anyone participating in such acts arrested as if they were *a lady of the night*, the citizens referred to him as Beast Butler. Francois heard that Lajoyce had been one of those ladies, which made him chuckle, since she was one of those types of damsels.

"Yes, he did, though Jack is hardly a beast." No, he was the man Emma loved, and he felt her slipping away the moment his brother arrived. The look in her eyes tore his own heart to pieces. Fighting him barehanded would never win her back…he shook his head to make the memory vanish.

"But that land be yours and your pappy's, the senator for the South!"

"Yes, it is, though at the moment, it sits under Jack's control. I could not stay under such circumstances, as you might imagine."

The group nodded.

"Ain't right to lose a southern belle to a Yankee," one of them muttered. "You done the right thing. Us Tigers will help Marse Robert win, then you can win her heart back."

That statement they all agreed on and with that issue resolved, they turned back to the war in their talk. Somehow, confessing his reason with that story got him over the hurdle of being accepted. As to winning Emma back, he knew that was a lost cause.

Ada had a wave of exhaustion sweep over her with a rush that made her balance teeter. She blinked furiously as she steadied herself, grabbing the top rail of the wooden strait-back chair next to her. Suddenly, a strong male arm encircled her, the man giving her support as he slowly turned her so she could sit.

"Ada, are you all right?" Will. She should've known he'd be there. He always was when she needed him the most.

Swallowing the lump that lodged in her throat, one made of dust and dirt that left a sour taste in her mouth, she nodded. "I'm fine. Just a bit tired."

"You've been pushing yourself too hard." He shoved a cup of tepid water to her. "When was the last time you ate?"

She tried to think, but found her thoughts fuzzy. A blur of Will reached for the basket on the table and yanked a slice of bread out, lacing the top of it was honey from a pot he suddenly had.

"Here, eat this."

His command surprised her. "This bread is for the

wounded, too."

"Which, at this moment, includes you. Eat."

Scowling at him, she took a bite. The guilt at partaking of some of the food for the patients evaporated when her stomach growled and the piece she tore off tasted like heaven dripped in honey.

"I feel like a thief," she complained right before she took another bite.

Will gave her half a snort as he shook his head. "I know they hardly pay you a pittance for what you lady nurses do. And I'm also aware you often times don't eat, saving more for the wounded, as well as work a heavy load. Makes me wonder whatever drove Madame Dix to push to get you involved."

Ada swallowed and savored the honey coating it left in her mouth. "She is not a madame, Will."

He cocked his head, brow raised. "Isn't she? I heard she requires ladies to be elderly, plain looking and dull."

She shot him a look. *He thought she was old?*

He caught it. "Oh, don't get your feathers ruffled. You are well below her elderly rate of thirty...She must be getting desperate. Or, knowing you, you pushed her."

How could she tell him she'd tried to get on as a surgeon, or even a hospital steward, only to have the Secretary of War direct her down to Miss Dix's room for recruiting women nurses? She knew she was eight years shy of the thirty mark, but her determination and her medical training persuaded the woman to relent and let her go. Of course, there were several younger ladies allowed to go as well. Will was correct. After close to three years of bloodshed, the need for nurses grew.

"I persuaded her that my skills were slightly more involved than simple household ailments." She shrugged, gobbling down the last bite. "Where did you get the honey? The medical stores held none for consumption."

Will's lips thinned when he rolled them in and glanced away. "It is possible that I, too, may have a few tricks up my sleeve."

She frowned but he said no more. Eventually, she'd find out, because he always shared with her. Her mind scrambled with ideas. He had a sweet tooth but honey also held a good potential to ward off infections if the wound was laced with it. Every housewife would use it. Question she had was, there was war all around them. Had he hidden this all along? She opened her mouth to ask when he promptly shut her down.

"So, let me take a gander here, and please, correct me if I'm mistaken, but," he started. "You diving into work makes one wonder if you received a note from home, or," he paused. "That vermin in the west."

Revived and now irritated, she stood, straightening her skirts. "Will, not now."

He snarled, "I knew it! Ada, what is it going to take for you to realize he's an outrageous liar and no good?"

Anger flared inside her, her blood in flames. "How dare you! You have no reason to give us half a thought."

"I beg your pardon," he shot back, the words dripping in sarcasm. "Why are you here, Ada? This isn't a place for a lady, nor for one love-struck on a jack—"

"Doctor, I would stop, here, and now, while we're are still on speaking terms," she seethed back. She inhaled deeply, trying to control her breathing and saw he, too, panted, his face red with anger. "What would you have me do, Will? Go home?"

He calmed. She saw the rigid stance relax. "Yes. There is nothing more than blood and war here. Not a place for a proper lady."

Ada shook her head. She'd heard that for years. Particularly in medical school. "We both know I'm needed here."

With a step toward her, Will took her hands, his face contorted. "So do the women and children at home. Did you think they would fair well without medical aid? People are sick at home, too."

The familiar argument. Women doctors resigned to only seeing women and children. She thought Will saw the bigger portrait of this conflict. Now, she knew better.

"Will, I am here to help. Those soldiers, those men, need help in ways that surpass all you and the other surgeons can handle. Dorothea Dix saw that, and for that, she has helped the army medical staff beyond their recognition." She bit her lower lip, the next few words a sting she had to endure. "Perhaps Richard is part of the reason I joined, but frankly, I can also put that blame on you, too. They need help, and in the worst way. I'll stay, until it is done." Or I perish, she thought abysmally. Nurses received low wages, were provided no provisions and pushed to give part of their earnings to care for the sick. But she was determined to survive.

It was that moment, when their heated argument cooled, that another officer entered.

"Excuse me, Surgeon Leonard, Nurse Lorrance."

Instantly, Will released her hands and she quickly pulled them back. It was Major Surgeon Jonathan Letterman. Ada gulped.

Letterman gave them a stern look. "I understand we've had a heated discussion, or so I was told. As to the truth or not, I cannot have that between my nurses and surgeons. We are all under pressure to care for these wounded souls, so tempers can be short. Among my surgeons, I expect protocol of an officer. Among my nurses," he eyed her. "I expect gentility, fortitude and duty. Are we clear on that understanding?"

She bit her tongue from arguing she was more than qualified to aid beyond bedpans, wound cleansing and fever reduction and nodded. Will murmured, "Yes, sir."

Letterman walked past them, toward the back of the walled hospital tent. "We are moving our facilities back, toward another farmstead. The main house is sufficient for better surgical conditions and the upper floors, along with the outlying buildings should suit our operations well." He spun on his heel. "General Meade is pushing another assault on the morrow, so we need to move supplies and as many patients as we can, as our position is precarious here."

"Yes, Major," they both answered.

"And keep your 'discussions' to a minimum. The last thing I need right now is to remove either of you as the Union needs your assistance in the worst way." He gave them a curt nod. Ada could see the smile he fought to hide. As if they were children in the pantry and he caught them with the cookies in hand. "Get to work. Dawn will arrive shortly."

After Letterman left, Will gave her a glance. His own gaze softened, but he took off toward his corner of the hospital to pack. Ada wanted to giggle. She should return to Philadelphia to help the people she was ordained to help, when there were plenty of doctors who avoided the army at all costs and gladly took on the patients? Obviously, no.

"Miss James, Maybelle," she called, knowing the nurse was no doubt around the corner, eavesdropping. "Call the other nurses. We need to pack!"

She heard the muttered 'aye' and smiled. Going over to the medical chest, she began to re-pack it for the new location. Purpose. She was here for a purpose. And it was a way to keep herself going during the loneliness and the heartache that ran deep. Now if she could just bury the frustration of being reduced to a nurse when she knew she could help so much more…

"During the night of the fifth, two men came back to the Lacey House, both slightly wounded. One was a Rebel...the other one of our men. They had got together, both had lost their muskets, and as the brush was getting afire they made the best of their way out of it together, taking their chances as to which of the two lines they might fall."

—Union Soldier, Grand Army of the PotomacBattle of the Wilderness, May, 1864

Chapter 6

November 20th

"HERE."

Francois looked up just in time as Morris shoved a tin cup his way. The waft of acorns and whiskey rose from the contents. "Thanks, I think." He sniffed again, not sure if he was to drink from it or what.

Morris laughed. "You knew that stash of coffee wouldn't last long. Not with this group."

"Acorns?" He had a hard time seeing how the tree nut could be used as a drink.

"Yessir," Wiggins joined, walking up and plopping himself down on the tree stump nearby. "We Southerners find a way to get by." He gave them a lopsided grin. "'til we see the next supply train, or house."

Still frowning, Francois brought the cup to his lips. The

cold had seeped into his bones by now and the slow rain that started to fall made it worse. He wanted coffee but at this point, anything warm would do. He took a sip. The fiery drink virtually burned his lips and tongue as the liquid lit a flame of warmth as it went down his throat. The whiskey that was in it, very mild but there, smoothed the edge of this brisk day.

It took him a moment to realize both men were watching him. "May I help you?"

"Just wondering what you thought," Morris answered. "Recipe is my own."

"And the whiskey?"

"End of the line for now," Wiggins sighed. "Takes the edge off the cold."

It definitely took the sting off the tree-scent. Francois took another sip. The liquor eased the stiffness from the inside out and he relaxed just a bit, taking in all he'd witnessed and done. The wool on the uniform was stiff and if he moved right, the cotton lining on the jacket didn't stop the roughness. It scratched through his cotton undergarments. The army only issued uniforms, the undergarments were lacking so he had to rely on his own and the shirts Morris told him to bring. Since it rained, the roughshod brogans, which were not well made to start with, were soaked. The stiff shoes were sucked into the mud and many times, he really just wanted to leave them there, but knew that wasn't ideal. Out here, when might he get another pair? Probably off a dead man and that he refused to think about, though this pair might have come from that very source since he suspected this wasn't a new outfit. War….

"So, I figured where I've seen you."

Francois turned. It was a private he'd run into on the battlefield first, then seen in camp the last few days. Joshua

McFadden, from New Orleans, an Irish lad with a freckled face on a bronzed complexion and red hair dirtied by camping with the army.

"Where might that be?" He didn't recall ever seeing this boy before, but if it were in town, he rarely took note of the laborers. His business was always with shippers, lawyers or LaJoyce.

"I've done see you in that whore house, down on Carondelet. Bonne Jeux. That colored corner, all fancy looking with the pretty girls." McFadden nodded. "Yes, that was it. You were talking to that fancy madam who runs it. Miss LaJoyce. She's a luscious sweet darky."

There was something about the gleam in the Irish lad's eyes that made a flare of rage tick off inside him. His jaw tightened and lips clenched as his shoulders steeled. "Really?"

Wiggins stared at him, as did the soldiers trying to warm themselves over their fire. Morris jumped.

"Of course you did," Morris stated. "Those lovely beauties come from the Fontaine plantation."

Francois's had a pang of some emotion he couldn't name strike at his gut. Most of the girls in LaJoyce's house did come from Bellefountaine. LaJoyce did not come from there, but she knew how they managed to accrue such exotic creatures.

"Oh, I've seen those tarts," Wiggins added. "Way out of my pocket, that's for sure! But they're a beauty to be enjoyed with a glance. Mulattos often are, though as I seem to recall, don't they have different colored eyes? Like blue or green? Don't often see those in the coloreds."

The men around them nodded, murmuring some had seen them and what beauties they were. Francois knew exactly why they had unusual hues, but he didn't offer it.

For some odd reason, another emotion raced through him, one of feeling guilty and that irked him.

Another one of the men, one whose name escaped Francois, spoke. "That be right. Right tasty, too. But those colors do grab ya, that's for sure. The talent makes them even better."

The hair on the back of his neck bristled and his irritation inched upward, he couldn't decide if that was because of a guilt he'd never felt before, or because to earn a living his girls had been used by these men and that last thought really unnerved him. Wasn't that why he turned them over to LaJoyce? He knew she'd protect them—well, as best as any madam could do, under those circumstances…

"Yes, I see it now," Sylvester McComb said, sitting down on the boulder nearby. "Since you got your face, I see a semblance." The Irish boy tilted his head. "Even now, sitting like you is, I see a reflection of those ladies, like you in dark, like them, with blue eyes."

The men around him turned, each studying his face. Francois tempered his breathing, working hard to manage the flaming anger inside him. One thing, it warmed him despite the chill around them. Even though it was November, the ride here and the days in the field with the army had exposed him to the elements unlike he'd ever been in his life.

"That, my boy, is one roasting by the sun!" Morris chuckled, midway through their ride east. They had stopped to water their horses in northeastern Alabama when Francois took his hat off to splash his hot face in the water.

"Oui," he replied, trying to move his lips more to one side of his cheek as he dabbed the other with a damp handkerchief. "I do feel the pinch. Don't believe I've ever felt this hot." His skin prickled to the touch and the water cooled then sizzled, it seemed.

Morris jammed his own hat down. "Just need to get you a better hat. That fancy one you got doesn't have a brim worth a damn against this sun."

Francois stared at the hat. It was one of the latest, from England, one he received while New Orleans was still in Confederate hands. "But it makes me look handsome, I believe Miss Rollins declared." He smiled for a moment. Clara Rollins had made that remark, at a picnic held at Eastertime. Before Emma arrived...his smile vanished. And his exposure to the sun continued, making his pale skin red...

His buddy laughed now, before this quieted group.

"See? I declare you owe me a silver dollar!" Morris chuckled, slapping Francois's shoulder. "That burnt face is almost as dark as the rest of these heathens. You'll be fine."

The others broke their stare and mumbled. One of the first things Francois had noticed was how all the soldiers had bronzed faces, tanned from months in the field. He was definitely an initiate, all pale with a bright red burn but as time passed, and the burn peeled, only to repeat and repeat on their journey, that by now, his complexion was darker with a tan.

McComb still glared at him. "Fontaine, yes, now all coming back. Remember the slave auction, where that name was mentioned. Bell'fontaine, if I recall right. You don't need to buy any slaves or so I've heard."

Francois remained silent, letting a small smile twitch at his lips. No, they hadn't purchased any in a long time. Sold, though, was another matter. McComb looked frustrated, as if he wanted to say more but was either lost at the words, or more likely, not as dumb as he appeared, because if he defiled the Fontaine family...

"Attention! Company!" Roared an officer who rode into camp, with his staff behind him.

The soldiers around them rushed to collect themselves and fall into line. It took another minute before Francois or McComb moved. McComb was breathing hard, his face flush, thinking he'd nabbed the rich planter's son at some sin. Francois didn't answer. He teetered between wanting to agree some of his slaves were attractive, and wanting to strangle the man, because his innuendo was plain. The desire to tell him the real story tugged at his conscience. But in the end, he stood and shoved his hat on his head, falling into line with the rest of his comrades.

"Shoulder arms!"

The corps, in unison, brought their rifles up, muzzle resting on their right shoulder as their palms scooped it to stay. Francois followed suit and couldn't help but be amused. The eldest Fontaine, destined to inherit a legacy of the family, stood now with normal people, who had thrown their lot in with their new country, the Confederate States of America. He never would have thought he'd be here, but that charming feminine laughter that plagued him still echoed in his ears. Even now, he could see her and he instantly brought his free hand to rub against the hidden pocket over his heart, where the miniature portrait of her rested. *Oh, my Emma…* Her name rang in his ears as they started their walk to the battle stations and for once, he hoped those Yankees would end his torment for loving a woman he could never have…

The sound of a trumpet rang through the air, soft through the trees and tents but noticeable. It woke Ada with a start, making her sit up right from the slumped position she'd taken over the top of the table before her. Papers rustled beneath her as her hands steadied herself, then braced her when the soreness of falling asleep while writing a letter hit. In fact, ink from the pen bled on her hand, making her forefingers dark. After all these months, hadn't she gotten used to the revelry being called every dawn? Staring down at the crumpled paper, she gathered not.

Slowly she rose, feeling the ache from her crouched position. Outside, she heard the men across the compound, scurrying about camp, shoving on hats and coats to run to the call. She inhaled deeply and pulled herself together, adding another petticoat under her skirt and a sontag to wrap over her bodice, as a cloak was too much to wear in the hospital tent. The dark navy wool dress was warm but the chill in the air still made her shiver. She hadn't thought the South would turn so cold, or she'd have brought more wool dresses and another quilted petticoat or two to wear. That made her stop. No, she would not have, because she had condensed her clothes to two carpetbags, not the trunk needed for all those clothes.

Her 'room' was a corner room, no wider than a cot and small table shoved in, with a curtained doorway, since the actual door had been removed for a surgical table. The closet area next to hers was not much bigger, though enough to fit the other three nurses snugly, also curtained shut. Neither area could sport a fireplace and the single-paned window in her area offered no real wall to block the late fall cold. She shivered. Just like the makeshift storage area, this space was tight, yet it was the only way for them to have any privacy from the patients and staff. The tacked up sheets over the doorframes offered little buffer to the groans and moans and other noises spouting from the patients. But the women gladly took the faint privacy from the men, a chance to close their eyes and try not to dwell on the sounds that echoed through the adjoining room.

Steeling her back and shoulders to help her face the day and the patients it would bring, she stepped out into the ward. The room itself had a dozen makeshift beds, filled with the wounded. A chill swept through it because two of the windows were propped open, fighting with the fire that attempted to keep it warm. Drowning a growl in her throat, she went to the first window and removed the nail that kept it open and lowered the sash.

"Thank you," the patient lying nearby whispered. "It turned a might chilly."

She went to him and touched his forehead. It was warm, though his jaw trembled, lips sealed to keep the chattering teeth quiet. Quickly, she went to the trunk near the wall and yanked a moth-eaten wool blanket out.

"Here, this will help you thaw," she greeted as positively as she could and hoped she'd masked the worry of his condition from showing on her face. She tucked the blanket around him. "How is your stomach fairing today?"

To her eyes, he still looked a bit squeamish but how could he not? He'd come to the surgeon with another flux of diarrhea and the doctor issued blue mass to stop it, but when that medicine stopped everything, protocol demanded opium be administered. It had opened his system back up, but the blue tinge from the first treatment still remained on his lips, which Ada found disconcerting.

"Thinkin' better, Miss. Thank you. Might thirsty, though."

She gave him a smile and water then darted away. It wasn't the method she liked to use but who would listen to her? She was only a nurse in their eyes, setting off another furious flame through her. When she jammed the poker into the dying fire and the vibration of hitting the brick fireplace flooring reverberated up her hands, she jolted.

Sparks flickered off the prodding, making her step back to miss them. Last thing she needed was her cotton apron to get singed.

"Nurse Lorrance?"

She put the poker down and rubbed her hands against her apron. "Yes, Corporal?"

The soldier, who had been commandeered by Letterman when he discovered the man had been a doctor's son with a desire to become one himself, stood before her with a worried look on his face. "The laundresses. They've done nothing in cleaning the bandages since yesterday's move here. Word has it the General is planning an attack this morning. We won't have what we'll need when the wounded arrive."

Ada tried to keep her voice quiet but she wanted to laugh. "Corporal Stokes, did you inform them we are in dire need?"

"I did, ma'am, but they just be piddlin' out there."

"And you believe this battle will happen?"

"Yes ma'am. Troops be strapping on their trappings and forming lines for a march, that is, if the fog lifts."

Ada glanced out the window. The cold temperature, after all the rain of late with the end of fall warmth, produced a haze this morning. Outside, she now noticed the fog that held in the distance. Another fight with the Army of Northern Virginia, men used to the climate and grounds here, would definitely mean blood.

"Thank you, Corporal." She spun and headed out to the building toward the tents out back.

Outside, the air was soupy yet crisp. She determined the fog was worse than earlier and with the damp air, would not help the laundry any. Ahead of her, stood three black women and one white. The three coloreds were runaways and since many slaves ran to the bluecoats when the Union army was near, the army commanders universally chagrined at the incoming mouths to feed but ready help they needed. In this case, the women were put to work at the laundry and the head of that contingent was a sour looking woman who stood at a pot, her arms crossed and a scowl on her face the closer Ada got.

"Nurse Ada, what bestows us the honor of your visit?" The woman spat tobacco juice at the ground, never breaking her gaze on Ada. It was a disgusting habit and so unladylike, Ada wanted to roar, but Mrs. Kirkpatrick would only smile at that. The old Irish woman was set in her ways and answering to a woman nurse wasn't on that list, Ada discovered.

Drawing up her backbone and straightening her already squared shoulders, Ada did her best to paste a grin on her lips. "Good morning, Mrs. Kirkpatrick. Ladies." She nodded to the coloreds. "I've come to inquire on the status of the wash."

"It'd be gettin' done."

Ada raised her brows. Eying the stack of filthy rags behind them, lying on the wet muddy ground, she grinded her teeth to keep from snapping. "Yes, well," she started, rounding the women to the pile. The top bundle was still blood-splattered and a mangle mess, glued to the one beneath. The fact that they sat on the mud only infuriated her. If she were home, she'd burn the stack and start new. But here, in Virginia, out in the fields, that was not an option.

"Madam, are you aware these will never make it through the day, clean nor not, left in such a disheveled place?"

Kirkpatrick stirred the pot with a long stick and snorted. "You done give me these vagrants, who won't lift a finger."

Ada frowned as she turned toward the ex-slaves. "Ladies, as I understand it, you came to the Union line for freedom, am I not right?"

The smallest of the three, and the lighter hued than the other two, raised her chin just a hair but her eyes locked onto Ada's. "Yes, we did, missy. We've come to get free."

The other two nodded at her triumphant tone.

"What is your name, if you please." Ada's gaze swept over them, trying to get a hold on how to approach help that was unwilling to work.

"Lily. And these two are Liza and Bethany." The girl cocked her head, a defiant look in her eye. Ada couldn't fathom who she was fighting.

"Yes, well I'm Nurse Ada, and in this camp, no one is simply waiting for food and doing nothing in return..."

"We've done worked our whole lives for vermin, only to get little to eat and beaten—or worse—cause we be property, chattel to be so spit on. We hear the Lincolnites are to make us free, so we're here. Free." She stood rigid, as if begging to be knocked down so she could fight. Ada mildly thought this woman would be better on the firing lines and quickly quelled that thought.

Ada truly didn't have time for this. "Lily, Bethany and Liza, glad you are here, yet no one just sits. If these 'Lincolnites' don't win this battle, chances of your freedom dwindle. But you could help us in the cause, as it were. Mrs. Kirkpatrick has a nasty job to try to accomplish on her own. I'm not sure what your chores were under your master, but here, if you don't know this, Mrs. Kirkpatrick will teach you—"

"You can't make me do washin' no more," the determined girl hissed.

Ada rolled her lower lip in, realizing her arguments to

practice medicine no doubt sounded just as strong as this girl's will to not do a chore again. For her, she compromised and turned to nursing. She had to strike the chord with these three.

"Miss Lily, there are men fighting out there for your freedom and to end the sin of slavery. Even some of your own kind are out on the lines, risking all for freedom. But the fight," she paused, trying to form the words. "Sometimes, the best way to help these soldiers is to be their support. If they get wounded, they need help as soon as possible. Many of the wounds are terrible." She blinked and stared at the three. "No doubt similar to the same horrible wounds you witnessed on your owner's land, though these are done by bullets and cannon fire and the mess is horrendous. We need bandages for them and these need to be cleaned. General Meade is planning an attack today, and we expect casualties, so I need your help."

None of the three moved or even flinched.

"You may be free, but there is a cost to freedom. Are you willing to justify their loss?"

Lily fumed. Ada heard Mrs. Kirkpatrick spit again—she was going to have to have a word with that woman. After an eternity, though, Liza spoke.

"We be glad we're free. What would ya have us be doing?"

Ada sighed in relief.

"They must have anticipated immense slaughter, as no less than a hundred of their ambulances were plainly visible."

—Confederate cannoneer observing the Federal activities from across the river at Rappahannock Station, VA, November 7, 1863

Chapter 7

Rapidan River Valley, Virginia
November 26

FRANCOIS SQUINTED, TRYING TO SEE through the dense fog that shrouded the Rapidan River. Perched on a fallen tree limb, he hugged his jacket tighter without dropping his guard, ready to swing his rifle into action. He was miserable, the cold seeping through his wool uniform, damp from the rains. At least he was off the ground, where the mud caked his brogans and he could swear it fought to ooze through the rough stitching. *War was hell...*

"You'd think they'd be moving," Wiggins grumbled.

"They probably are," Francois replied. "Just can't see them through this soup."

"Yes, Corporal, you are correct," a stern yet gentle voice added. Francois glanced for a second and found General Lee sitting on his horse, just back a bit. "Those people will move. The question I cannot ascertain is where to? This unbroken forest gives them a breaking point to either head to Richmond or move up the Rapidan, upon our right flank, neither of which can we allow to happen."

"General, the fog has to lift. We will know by then."

"And that, sir, will be our undoing. No, we must move forward and now." Lee pulled his reins to the right and rode off, leaving his watchers.

"He'll have us attack." Wiggins scratched his stubble chin. "I'd rather do that than just sit like ducks."

Francois nodded, though his thoughts whirled. War was a strange beast. Perhaps, he should have listened to his brother better, but his prime motivation was to run from that house and the woman he could not have, so rational conversations with the man who'd won her heart was futile, as his own heart broke.

"Seems futile to attack a foe we do not see," he finally added in a desperate attempt to distract his attention from visions of his love that continually threatened to invade his every thought. Absently, he rubbed the locket-sized portrait in his breast pocket.

Wiggins's brows furrowed. "Marse Robert says we move, we go." He paused. "You're a strange fellow. You fight but the fire only burns in the heat of it. Otherwise, you ain't here."

Francois snorted. The Cajun had figured him out. "I'm chased by ghosts, Private Wiggins. Ghosts that I can't run fast enough from, but," he leaned forward, giving the man a half smile. "She disappears in the smoke of battle. Then, I am free."

Wiggins pulled back, a puzzled look, mixed with disgust in his gaze. "You be lookin' to die on these grounds? That'll cost more than you, I reckon."

"No, no," he argued. "I don't wish to die but I will not turn down the reaper if he appears. I will not go down without a fight." He prayed that dispelled the cast he had just set over his fellow soldier.

Wiggins gave him a half grin and the twinkle sparked his eyes. "Good. Let's go kill us some Yankees!"

Francois followed him as the drums rolled, calling them to formation. He'd wipe the thought that his brother was one of the Yankee-type and was thankful he wasn't here. Whatever the hold 'Marse' Robert, or General Lee, had over these men now pulled Francois in. One thing was for sure. Lee had beaten and pushed off the Northern invaders time and time again. Despite the fog, the muddy ground and chill that wanted to stab him, fire ignited and he hoped, it'd burn the hole in his heart, making him forget her.

The day turned into chaos. Ada had found herself with the misfortune of witnessing this before and every time, her heart sunk as the wounded poured in. Scores of soldiers with ghastly rips in their flesh, buried bullets that brought dirt, material and skin with it. Men moaned and cried, some shrieking from the pain. Yet the doctors and nurses with any experience, worked the best they could with the limited time and supplies they had. That had always irked her. The Federal army had the means to supply them well yet their medicines and supplies bulked up an advancing force, too much so to make it practical to take them yet they were sorely needed when the two sides clashed. So they worked in a climate not to their choosing nor liking, often with poor lights, inefficient supply of water, not enough fires to clean what they had and instruments that never seemed to be enough for the call needed.

"Nurse, nurse!"

Ada spun, trying to find its source, but it was repeated and by many. The closest to her was the hospital steward, across the former dining room, trying to restrain a patient who struggled to get off the bedding.

"You ain't gonna touch me, damn Yankee!" The rebel sputtered those words. She'd not guess his side since they'd managed to have him somewhat covered and his jacket was missing, along with half his shirt, she noted.

"Nurse Ada," the steward started. "If you'd give a hand, please."

She raced to the patient's other side and took his shoulders with her bare hands. The soldier flinched as she pressed him down and despite her cooing to calm his nerves, when his shoulders hit the mattress, he roared in pain. She looked at him a bit more carefully and discovered her own hand, on the one side, was covered in red blood.

"His wound is cleared of lead," the steward reported. "Clean shot, straight through." He glanced at the patient. "Sir, you'll do in a couple of days."

Her patient, though, was passed out by the time the steward finished bandaging the wound and moved on. Gently, she laid the sheet over his wound.

"He'll need it sweet watered."

She glanced around to find Will rubbing his hands. They were blood stained, just as she found hers. Wiping her palms on her apron, she nodded. "I'll have Maybelle attend to that."

Will frowned. "She may not be the best suited for that kind."

"What? The wounded, or the fact he is a rebel?" To her, a patient was a patient.

"You know what I mean."

"No, I do not." She stood, facing him, fully aware the men around them needed care, not to be neglected by them. "These men in here are wounded. Sides do not matter."

"Ada, please. We must attend our own first."

She tightened her jawline. "Dr. Leonard, medicine knows of only one side, and that is those needing help."

"And orders stand—" he started when a crash rang through the air.

Without another word, she followed Will as he bolted to the back room from whence the noise came. She wasn't ready for what she found. In the center of the room, Maybelle stood, her one arm clutching around her middle, the hand of the other over her mouth as tears streamed down her face. Around her feet stood a puddle of spilled, dirty water, a wet rag and the broken bottle of some liquid, its brown concoction swirling down the waxed wooden floor.

"Good, Nurse Lorrance, glad you arrived," muttered Surgeon Waxler. "One of your staff has loss her wits. Please replace her at once."

Ada took Maybelle's bent arm, tugging her to follow her. Poor Maybelle was pale and she could feel the girl tremble.

"Maybelle, surgery is the last place for you to be," she said softly. "I left you to see to the lads in the front, those with the least wounds."

"I did as you said," the girl replied, sniffling. "But Dr. Waxler required aid and no one was available, so he took me." She shuddered. "I want to help, but I wasn't ready..." she whimpered.

Ada guided her out of the building to the front porch. Wounded were on the floorboards, most had tourniquets on, or their hands resting on packed bandages over wounds the surgeons had yet to see. Out here, the surgeons regulated the minor injuries, the type that could wait while they tackled the harder cases first. Still, she noted, many were pale and their moans were building as their pains increased.

She took Maybelle back to the bucket off the side, where a lonely chair sat, and another bowl with dry rags nearby. "Rest. We will need you, but this time, stay out here or head to the laundresses and see how they fare on those bandages. I fear we will need the rest shortly."

Maybelle nodded as she took a drink of water. Ada noticed her color was returning to her cheeks. Why Waxler would take this nurse, a young woman with no medical knowledge outside the basic, just confused Ada, but then again, Waxler despised women nurses. He'd thrown up argument after argument for Ada and her kind to leave but Letterman held his ground. They needed help, after all.

With her mindset and a reprimand for Waxler forming on her lips, Ada stormed back into the hospital only to run into chaos unfolding. The patients appeared to have multiplied while she had stepped out and the escalade of moans, with a painful yip periodically, grew. She could barely move through the remains of the front parlor thanks to the influx of men. The setting sun outside, or the faint remains of it, darkened the hell just that much further. Fearing she'd step on some of the wounded, now many lying on the floorboards since all the beds and settees were occupied. Some of the men tried to catch her attention, pulling at her sodden skirts and she found her resolution to make it across, to the supply table, was being tested.

"Miss, miss, please," one man pleaded, his pitch high enough it did stop her.

She made the mistake of looking down. What she found

made her heart weep. A young soldier, his sandy-colored hair matted with blood and caked with mud, had a gapping gash on the side of his face framed by black soot from black powder. One hand had a tight grip on her skirt hem but the other had was missing half its fingers from the looks of the blood-soaked wrappings, and his clothing, half ripped open as many soldiers did when hit, searching for the wound, exposed an oozing hole on his side. Swallowing the bile that crept up her throat, she bent and unwrapped his fingers from her skirts.

"Soldier?"

"Private Matthews, ma'am," he replied, his lips curling in a smile. The shock of pain in his eyes beat on her soul. "Am I gonna die?"

"Yes," she wanted to tell him. The stomach wound deemed his death. How he'd made it inside versus being left out near a tree, one they always found to rest these poor souls under, she'd never know. To her, he'd risked his life in the debacle, he deserved the truth. But his youth and the need in his voice made her shake her head. "You hold on, Private Matthews. Help will be here in just a few."

He closed his eyes and nodded.

Feeling her heart clench, she tore away, upset and angry that all the lives here meant little, just to gain a goal against the enemy. Her hands fisted at her side as she fought the anger. More needed help, not her opinion. She headed back to the supply room, a break sorely needed, when she ran right into Will. Surprised, she stepped back.

"Apologies, I did not see you."

He gave her an odd stare, as if he hadn't seen her at all. A curl of his dark hair fell across his forehead and she saw the lines that formed from concentrating too hard, a distant look in his eyes.

"Will, are you all right?" She didn't like his appearance, as if he wasn't here mentally, but all the blood on his white surgeon's coat and the stain of it on his hands told her he definitely was. When he didn't answer, she pushed again, "Dr. Leonard?"

He shook his head, as if to shake off a moment and gave her a terse grin. "Ada, this is too much. I am exhausted and just at wits end."

She went to the warming stove and pulled the coffee pot off, careful how she maneuvered as the tin ware was hot, and poured him a cup. "Here," she stated, shoving the heated cup into his hands. "Surely the incoming will stop soon."

Will snorted. "Heard Meade has declared a success but is pulling back. Typical." He drank. "They've also brought us more secesh. All shoved to the side, deeming our men first." He shook his head. "I'll have no strength left by then." He gave her a sorrowful glance. "This is a time we need all the help. They shouldn't keep you back here, as nothing more than a nurse."

"I'm helping as I can," she retorted, relishing a moment of no patients. "I am a nurse. I'm doing the best I can."

Will started to speak, but a roar from the Confederate room exploded. Without another thought, they both took off toward the racket and entered into another room of hurt.

Ada saw the man. He appeared tall, taking the entire length of the makeshift bed, his dark hair slick with sweat and rain. But it was his piercing blue eyes that drew her. They were brilliant blue, like sapphires, and glowing with anger at the men around him on the dining table where he was laid. His uniform was dirty but definitely a rebel uniform. It was torn but she found no blood until she glanced down at his legs. His left pant leg was ripped and soaked in blood. Dr. Waxler held his left foot in his hand, raising it slightly, looking for the injury. The soldier squirmed under the pain, requiring another soldier to hold him down.

As Waxler twisted the foot, trying to pull the socking off, the man's scream rippled loud and clear. Blood dripped onto the table. Waxler snorted.

"Foot's injured. We'll need to amputate."

She witnessed the soldier's eyes widen at the surgeon's pronouncement and he let loose a blood-curdling scream.

"Emma!" Then he collapsed, passed out.

Ada couldn't take her eyes off him, his outburst too hard to ignore. Made her vaguely wonder who this Emma was, a wife probably, so dear to him, he'd call for her now in dire need. Waxler put the foot down, shaking his head.

"We've got our boys to deal with first. This damn rebel will have to wait." He turned to leave, the attendant at the man's head, followed suit.

"So you'll leave him to die, perhaps, because he is the enemy?" she sputtered, her total surprise at this surgeon's abrupt departure.

Waxler tensed. "As I recall missy, you claim to be a doctor yourself. Men like him don't worry if you are or not, just that the pain will go, so I'll leave his care to you. I, and Dr. Leonard here, have more pressing cases to attend." He started to walk and added over his shoulder, "Dr. Leonard, if you please."

Will blinked, stunned as Ada at the man's statement, and mouthed apologies, leaving her.

It took her a moment to realize she'd finally gotten what she wanted. A chance to prove her training, but heavens, staring at her patient, she couldn't move. He was the enemy. If he died, no one would care, but if she succeeded, perhaps she'd be able to truly help more. Steeling herself, she gulped. *God help me!*

"The hoarse and indistinguishable orders...,the screaming and bursting of shells, canister and shrapnel as they tore through the struggling masses of humanity, the death screams of wounded animals, the groans of their human companions, wounded and dying and trampled underfoot by hurrying batteries, riderless horses and moving lines of battle...a perfect hell on earth..."

—Massachusetts's private recalling years after the 2nd day of Gettysburg, 1863

FRANCOIS LET THE DARKNESS PULL him deep into its embrace, letting his mind drift. Scenes returned, but not of that Southern belle who had his heart, but of gunfire and smoke. Soldiers hollered, some from pain, others bellowing orders. Bullets whizzed through the air, nearly missing his ear, and his eyes strained to see through the grey field of gun smoke. Yankees poured over the ridge and for every one he witnessed hit and fall, ten more appeared to take a stance. It was one of the few times Francois felt alive...and living on the edge. Fear and bravery pushed him toward his command and beckoned to their orders. When the man next to him got shot in the head, blood splattered, rising up like a fountain and a portion of it fell onto him, smearing his cheeks and neck.

It was then his memories heated like a furnace. Fighting

against the ooze of the blood and stumbling forward, what he hoped was sweat falling into his eyes, he realized he'd have to jump off the ledge to follow his troops. It was an easy jump, so similar to the type he made back on Bellefountaine, near the river. Without a second thought, he jumped and at that moment, his world crumbled. The edge of the ridge buckled from too many soldiers doing what he was attempting. Add his distorted vision to the mix and he floundered off the hill. The moment his feet hit the ground, he realized he'd slipped and landed hard on the rock below. Pain shot up from his heel, like a hot poker shoved up his leg. He stumbled, realizing he couldn't stand as a bolt of lightening hit his ankle hard, crippling him. Another hit of fire raced across the same leg's calf and he fell, striking his head on a stone. Then all memory stopped, till now.

He woke to bright lights, with fleeting figures and a drone of voices that ranged from low mumbles to a few words. His head throbbed and the chattering in the air with the light only made it worse. It took a moment to realize there were men around him dressed in white, not the black he envisioned hell would wear. But the blood-red streaks on their white coats made him reconsider that thought. He tried to gain where he was, all came to a screeching halt when the creature at the foot of the bed he was on, pulled on his brogan, yanking the poor torn leather off. Pain engulfed him, like a river of fire, erupting from his heel. He roared, wanting to yank his foot from the man's grasp but realized he couldn't. Amidst the sea of pain, he heard the man speak, the words chilling to his heart.

"Reed! Bring me that bag," the man called. "Need to amputate this..."

Amputate? Francois rolled, the scene around him blurred. *They'd take his foot?*

"Emma!!!" His world blurred but he refused to fall into the dark that wanted to consume him for fear if he did, they'd cut the injured limb off and that he'd refuse at all costs! He started to try and break free from this demon's hold on him, despite the fear he was swimming in a river with his movements slow and sluggish. Each attempt seeped his energy but his will to stop the bone saw was huge.

"Shush, now," a cool feminine voice whispered to him. "Relax. I won't let him take it." She cooed softly, lulling his body to stop contorting against a now vacant ghost.

He tried to open his eyes, blinking to clear the fog that filmed his gaze. It was a woman that he knew from her voice but the lady before him was in a navy blue prim dress with nothing adorning it other than the white collar and the white pinner apron. Only hints of her tawny golden hair danced outside her white cap.

"Emma?"

"No. Sorry," she replied softly.

He couldn't see her face as she was bent over, examining his foot. So far, she hadn't grabbed it like that man had, when he twisted it and sent the jolts of pain riveting through his body. No, she gently held it on the sheet it rested on.

"Are you an angel or the devil in disguise?"

She gave him a slight chuckle, one barely audible, but he did hear it.

"I'm a doctor," she replied, her gaze still fixated on his leg. Finally, she glanced up. "My apologies. I'm Nurse Lorrance, sir."

He frowned. "Doctor or nurse? Or a ghost?" It had registered in his thinking that other men he'd seen were like her, dressed in navy, the Union's color. A casual glance beyond her, into the other room, showed a Federal flag on the wall.

He hadn't remembered being caught but then, he didn't recall anything after that fall.

"That, my dear sir, is a good question. For now, let us stay with nurse. It is easier on your palate, I've no doubt."

He caught that hesitation in her tongue, as if she'd spent a lifetime justifying her worth. He was familiar with that to a certain extent. He watched her intently as she worked. Her touch was soft, like Jenny's back at home. That elderly matron slave had been a mammy to them when they had minor aches and pains and she, too, had chuckled when he squealed as a boy when she poked at an injury. This Miss, or Nurse Lorrance did the same, though he kept his complaints quiet. Flinching was another matter.

She cocked her chin, her eyes narrowing at the limb. Still lifting his heel slightly, she looked about and found in reach a butternut coat that she wadded up under his calf when she lowered the foot. The wool of the material scratched his skin but the pain kept him from moving.

"Stay there, sir," she mumbled as if that command was an afterthought. "I'll return shortly." She turned to leave when he bent and grabbed her arm.

"You're not going to let them take my leg!"

Her lips pursed as she peeled his fingers off her. "I will do my best, Private…" she raised a brow, expecting him to tell her.

"Corporal." He dropped his hand to the cot he was on. "Corporal Francois Fontaine."

"Corporal Fontaine," she repeated. Her eyes mesmerized him, playing a myriad of colors at once—amber blue with a silver glint. Realizing he was staring at her, he blinked and when he looked again, she was gone.

His leg throbbed and when he'd reached for her, he'd set off a sting in his arm from the previous wound. Parched but too weak to do anything about it, he rolled his head and closed his eyes, praying the girl wasn't a ghost but an angel, though God knew he didn't deserve one...

Ada raced into the linen closet where they had stored some of the medical supplies. Biting her bottom lip, she couldn't shake the scared but determined look on that man's face out of her mind. She knew Waxler and the other surgeons would diagnosis the foot unsalvageable and amputate it, but she didn't think, from her view of the wound, that it was that severe. She needed to clean it to see it better.

"How is that soldier?"

She gasped and dropped the cotton bandages to the floor. Stooping to retrieve them, she glanced over her shoulder.

"Will, you should have announced you were there."

He shook his head wearily. "If you'd looked, you would've seen me." He sighed. "I had to step away. It's a mess out there."

His hands were scarlet stained from blood and his hospital coat splattered crimson.

"There's coffee in the kitchen. I'll have Maybelle bring you some—"

"While you do what?"

She squirmed under his narrow gaze. "I'll need hot water and one of the medical kits."

Will laughed. "They are all in use, Ada. No one will let a nurse have one, especially not for use for the enemy."

Anger struck her with those words. Wadding the cotton into ball under her arm, she swung around and hit him square in the chest with the palm of her free hand.

"Enemy? He's a wounded man, Dr. Leonard. One bleeding and needing attention. In fact, there's a whole ward of them back there. They deserve to be seen just as the men in there!"

"Ah, my abolitionist lady has turned soft on the slave-owners?"

Her blood boiled more. "Get out of my way, Will!" She stormed past him and into the former dining room, where hell greeted. Surgeons at work over the ghastly wounds of the Union men, many moaning, one screamed from the work being done. She hadn't been this close to the pit of Hades, as Lettermann kept the nurses only in at the periphery.

"See why you were refrained from this?" Will stated. "This isn't the worst, either."

Still angry at him, she went to the empty table, no doubt where he stationed himself, and snagged his kit. "You don't appear to be in need right now."

"Ada!" he called after her.

She blazed back to the Confederate. He was insensible once more. She was thankful for that. Now, she needed that water.

"Here."

Will stood next to the bucket of hot water. "Let's see what he's got."

She dipped the cotton strip into the water and cleaned the wound. "Appears the bullet entered here," she took the wand with the pearled ends. She gingerly put the probe into the wound and searched. After a moment, she pulled it. The pearl tip was still white, though dripped in blood. She went around to the other side of the leg and found a smaller hole.

"The exit, I believe." She probed the area and again, the tip remained white, not great in size but enough to indicate exit wound.

Will sighed. "So we've irritated the Major over a simple gunshot wound. Ada..."

She took the foot by the ankle and turned it slightly, feeling an unusual bend in the ankle that made her groan. "Easy wound, one that should heal, but I strongly suspect there is a break in the bone."

Will stared, only to sigh again, running his hand through his hair. "So, he's lame. He'll limp at best, if it heals. Though if Waxler finds it, he'll amputate regardless."

"Will, we can't let him!"

She realized she sounded frantic and he knew it, too. He frowned, his gaze burning.

"Ada, what are you doing? This man is the enemy, for God's sake! A Southerner, the type who supports the one thing you've been ranting against at those rallies, falling in with all the other abolitionists. He's a slaver, probably owns a share. So why, in all that is holy, do you want to waste your time on him?"

His words stabbed at her soul. She knew he was no doubt right and even she couldn't understand the need to save him, other than as a physician, that was what was right, even if it did rub her strangely.

"Will," she started softly. "We were trained to heal, not ignore those who are sick or injured just because of what they say or believe. You know they will not let me help like I'm trained to do and when you and the rest of the corps are overwhelmed, I'm regulated to the nurses."

"You shouldn't be shamed by that, Ada," he murmured, taking her hand. "Nursing is a good position. Besides, you know better what is needed and I know I've never been without what I need."

"Will, please. Let me take care of this ward. Or at least

him. Major Waxler will let these men suffer due to their uniforms and that isn't right. You know that," she argued.

She could see him wavering. He was a good doctor so she hoped he'd see her position.

"All right, Ada. I'll do the best I can in keeping Waxler unaware of your absence. But don't waste too much time back here, you hear me?"

She couldn't help the grin that formed. "Yes! Thank you!"

Will shook his head and turned to leave, but not without motioning to the hospital steward who had come to the doorway, to help her.

Lifting her chin in triumph, she called to the steward. "Corporal Jakes, I need your help."

"Our bleeding, bankrupt, almost dying country...longs for peace...shudders at the prospect of...further wholesale devastations, of new rivers of human blood."

—Horace Greely told Lincoln, 1864.

Chapter 9

IT WAS THE DREAM THAT stabbed Francois the hardest. It was spring, with the lilacs in bloom and the soft whisper of birds and bees milling about him. The blossoming of the countryside, the rebirth after a winter that never seemed overly harsh in southern Louisiana, was a welcoming sight. A period he relished. More so that spring of last, when Emma had arrived. Since the war had started, Francois had run Bellefountaine in the absence of his father, Pierre Fontaine, who sat in Richmond as a Confederate senator. Running the estate was a challenge he found fulfilling despite the lack of his usual haunts. When she arrived, though, everything changed.

Emma consumed his attention and his heart. He couldn't help but smile at the memories that portrayed themselves to him at this moment. But then, a sudden stab jolted through him, as he walked across the greens toward her. It was a crippling pain, in his right ankle. The smile he had crumbled as he faltered. It intensified and he couldn't help the agonized yelp that bordered on a scream, enough that the whole world he saw before him shattered, to be filled with a room in a house that stank of male sweat, urine and a myriad of other stenches he didn't want to think of.

His eyes shot open and found a man with a stern look, brown hair and mustache above him.

"Nurse Lorrance," the man called.

Francois tried to bolster himself upright and curl his leg away from the white coat figure near the foot of his bed but the man above him pinned him down.

"Let me go! Ouch!!" Another pain ripped through him.

"Just as I thought," came the very feminine voice, just past his jailor. "Corporal Jakes, hold him for another minute."

Francois's eyes widened. He was trapped in a house of horror. Again, his foot was manipulated and he squashed the roar that begged to come. No point in giving them any satisfaction their torture was working. Then he realized his foot was being bandaged. He was lightheaded and woozy, confusing him further.

"There, I believe I have finished. Thank you, Corporal."

"Yes, ma'am." Jakes released him, grabbed the rag off Francois's chest and turned to walk away. The scent of the rag wafted to Francois nose and it hinted at sleep—a temptation he so wanted to take as the trace of chloroform swirled in the air. His lids grew heavy and he felt distant from what was happening, the last thing he swore he saw was that woman in white…

For once, Ada's exhaustion had a certain mark of gratification to it. She stood in the supply 'room' as the corner was referred to, and let herself sink into the over-stuffed chair, every inch of her five feet, six inches screaming for her to halt.

"Ma'am."

She looked up and found the young man who had assisted her, Private Kelleher, holding a porcelain cup full of steaming coffee. The scent of the java pulled her lulled thinking out of its daydream and she accepted it with gratitude.

"You did well today, private." She sipped the dark brew, savoring the rich taste as it awakened her exhausted body back to work. "Have you helped a doctor before?" The boy had been there, anticipating her next request with an accuracy that unnerved her a bit, perhaps because it had reminded her of herself when she followed her father on his calls to patients.

He shuffled, looking at his feet for a moment. "A time or two. Was hoping to be one one day, before this war."

She smiled. "You'll be good."

He opened his mouth to say something when Letterman and Waxler appeared, the latter one's face contorted in anger.

"Nurse Lorrance," Letterman greeted. "Might I have a word."

Kelleher disappeared but Waxler loomed large.

"How dare you go against my command on that rebel!"

Ada's blood raced and it took every ounce of her restraint to keep her tone low. "Doctor Waxler, you left a wounded man to be cared for at some distant time because of his uniform. He was bleeding profusely. He needed aid."

"He is the damn enemy!" Waxler snapped. "Our own men needed aid as much as the damn enemy, therefore, by rules of war, ours get treated first!"

She bit her tongue. Arguing with him would be pointless. What was done was done.

Letterman eyed her but she couldn't tell what he was thinking. Commanding the medical corps had to be strenuous enough, without two of his underlings arguing over who to treat first. Finally, he spoke.

"What was the man's prognosis?"

"He had a—"

"Doctor Waxler, if you please, I asked her."

Waxler fumed, making Ada swallow a knot that formed in her throat. Letterman put her in an awkward position, but then, she no doubt put him in one too, with her being a doctor herself.

"A bullet had penetrated his lower leg, near the ankle. By all appearances, it had scored his leg, but the damage it left would easier lead to death, if left on its own."

Letterman's lips waggled as he listened. Waxler's face turned red.

"He is the enemy!"

Letterman didn't register Waxler's outage but asked her, "And you were able to stop the bleeding?"

"Yes, sir." She squared her shoulders. "I also believe he has a fracture in his heel, sir. The bone wasn't stable and he reacted to the movement when I cleaned the wound."

"It needed to be amputated! And we have no time to deal with the rebels when our own need help," Waxler continued to argue.

Ada glared at him. The man was an excellent physician, from his education and his practice she had witnessed here, but his attitude needed adjusting. She so wanted to blurt out at him but grinded her teeth not to.

"So the wound did not lean toward amputation?"

She blinked, realizing Letterman was asking her. "No sir. Though he may have a long recovery, if it is indeed broken."

"It'll hinder him, if it is in the ankle." The major inhaled. "One less rebel to fight us, I'd say. Good job, doctor. I'll leave those handful of secesh in your care."

Her breath left her. He'd called her doctor for once and left her a ward to care for. Stunned, she vaguely heard herself saying thank you and as he left, heard the strangled Waxler gain his voice, uttering arguments against it to their retreating commander.

"Congratulations, Ada."

She turned to find Will at the doorway to the hall, grinning. Instantly, a wave of excitement race through her. She'd won recognition for her skills. It was a victory she hoped she'd earned well and prayed the major would never regret it. Gathering her strength, she thanked him and took her cup and headed toward her patients with renewed spirit.

Francois woke, groggy and swore his mouth was full of cotton. He licked his parched lips, trying to gain his senses, but too weak to push up off the thin pallet he was on. He stretched in an attempt to shake off the layer of lethargy that encompassed him, but his right leg rebelled. To move it sent shards of pain streaking up and he moaned, angry and hurt. Vague memories of falling, of waking up and finding himself in agony, but pinned as the devils worked on him haunted his thoughts.

Where the hell was he?

The sound of pouring water made him turn his head, gauging the distance to that mouthwatering liquid. There was a woman, tipping a pitcher of it into a basin and his parched mouth begged for the whole bowl. He opened his mouth to speak but the cotton that lined it and down his throat gave no volume to his voice.

The woman turned. When her gaze found him, he recognized her. She was the one he'd begged to stop the others from taking his foot, the word amputate still ringing in his ears. Instantly, he shot a look down at his right foot, fearing he'd find the source of his pain coming from a severed limb but when he saw the bandaged form, he collapsed in relief.

"Good morning." She was at his side, lifting his head with her arm, a cup of water in her hand, pressing it against his lips. "I wondered when you'd wake."

The water tasted like manna from the heavens and he craved more but she murmured.

"*Tsk, tsk, tsk.*" She pulled the rim back slightly. "You've had chloroform and been out for some time. If you take too much, you may choke."

He wanted to snarl, but even that made the water in his throat skip and he fought against the cough.

"See." She took the cup back and laid him down. "There will be more. Relax."

He stared at her. She was the angel, or was it the devil he recalled, burning his feet earlier. Even now, she was moving toward the end of the pallet and he immediately tried to escape her touch.

"Do not touch me!" he growled.

She gave him a raised brow, yet continued, lifting his calf and shoved a wad of blanket under it. "Have no worries, soldier. You'll keep your foot. But you were shot and though it went through, it didn't go deep. You'll recover, though it might have nicked a bone. We'll wait and see."

Slowly the colors in the room blared and he saw the navy uniform on the medical staff and what appeared to be a Union flag in the corner hanging.

"I'm in a Union hospital? I can't stay here," he retorted.

"I need to get back to my men."

"There'll be no leaving anytime soon," she continued her exam, ignoring his reference to being captured.

"Let me go!"

She took a step back, shooting him a questioning but stern look. Biting her lower lip, she crossed her arms. "I can't stop you. While I'd advise against it, that is, if you want to walk again, go ahead. Leave."

Francois heard the smugness in her tone and that irritated him. Some Yankee witch thought she could prevent a good Southern soldier from doing his duty? At the moment, she was the only one here. In his peripheral vision, he noticed four other patients, none of who appeared awake or moving. Assessing the odds, he sat up and went to swing his legs off the pallet when a sharp, jabbing pain exploded in his injured leg. The minor lift of it sent a cascade of lightning shards burning through him, his ears began to ring and he felt lightheaded. He fell back on the bedding, furious to be held back.

Instantly, she was back at his side, shifting his bandaged leg back over the padded blanket. "You should've listened to me. Hopefully, you haven't damaged yourself further."

Settled back into his bed, Francois grimaced. "Charming. Didn't realize the North be sendin' women to fight us."

The woman smiled as she pressed the cup of water to his lips. It was a grin that made his insides melt, as if she was simply a lady and he, a true gentleman, meeting her at a soiree or dinner.

"No, sir. I, myself, and the other ladies here are to help men like you, hurt in this ghastly affair. The color of your uniform does not matter. Our job is to tend the wounded."

The trickle of water this time, was easier to swallow. He nodded his head as thanks, his energy evaporating quickly as the pain subsided. But the notion of him being a captive echoed in the back of his mind, and he wondered if he'd ever wake again when his world turned black.

There were bugs here. Their buzzing had been soft but now grew and Francois turned his head in a vain attempt to shoo the noise away. It was a wasted effort. He swatted at them and found nothing there. Slowly, he opened his eyes, expecting to find a swarm around him and found no insects. Nothing but the room he'd seen earlier. The bothersome noise, though, took on a new facet and that he discovered by peering down the bed he was on to find another set of doctors, or so he assumed, considering they were in white jackets and looked a bit more studious than the lady with her hair pulled back and garbed in black with a white apron, carrying a cup in her hands.

One of the doctors rubbed his chin as he stared at Francois's leg. He threw back the sheet and without even taking note that his patient was awake, he twisted the foot, moving the bandage aside. Francois growled, dying to move his leg but the pain stalled him.

"That was her prognosis?" the doctor muttered, never even registering Francois's pained expression. Instead, he frowned and continued. "The wound looks plausibly good, though I see no pus at this point."

"She's very good, sir," the other doctor replied.

"You say you studied with her?"

"Yes, sir. At Pennsylvania, sir. She," he coughed, his tongue thick as he went on. "She was enrolled in the medical school. To be a physician."

"Heard about that damn school allowing women in. Disgrace to us all." He turned the foot again, sending another jolt of pain through Francois. "He'll still loose the use of that foot. Should've had it amputated, would've been the wiser move. While it now appears relatively well, though without a clear pus, I doubt it'll be of any good."

Instantly, Francois remembered this physician. "I'd appreciate it if you'd leave my foot alone," Francois jumped in, as he saw the surgeon's hand reaching again toward his limb. "Sir," he corrected his manner.

The doctor looked startled. "Oh, didn't see you awake, Reb." He pulled the sheet over the leg. "Dr. Leonard, do tell her I approve."

"Yes, Dr. Waxler."

Reb? He just called him Reb and then ignored him? *Damn Yankee had no manners!* Francois opened his mouth but Waxler spun on his heel, and stalked away, his hands clasped behind his back with the other know-nothing doctor in his path.

Slamming his jaw shut, he tore his gaze off the retreating physicians and finally took a look down at his injured leg. An achy throb increased from it being manipulated but outside that, all Francois saw was bandage. The foot, including his ankle, was wrapped in linen, a stained fabric, though he could see where part of the pinkish tone was red, right over the part of him that hurt the most. He forced himself upright, into an almost sitting position, slinging the good leg to the side as he tried to move the other. In his heel, ice-hot pain seared him and it took ever energy he had not to yell. Yet, he could move some, for he saw his toes wiggle a tad. Every ounce of him wanted to scream every expletive he could drum up, but for what?

"Surprised to see you up."

Francois spun his head, gripping the side of the pallet

to stabilize himself when the scenery around him began to waver. He found one of his Tigers laying on a pallet, his arm bandaged, as well as his chest.

"Wiggins, you shot?"

Wiggins snorted. "Not bad, so they say. At least, I wasn't threatened to lose a limb."

Francois guffaw. "Not if you had that woman waiting on you. Asked her to not let that beast take my foot and guess it worked. It's still here." He gestured toward the wounded foot.

"Yes, well, I been seeing her about here. Appears she got some pull, or bad luck, depending." Wiggins chuckled. "But she's been most attentive to you. Thinkin' she's got her hat perched for ya."

Francois sighed. "I don't need a meddling nurse, pretty or not."

"Ah, so you did see her. Boy, we've been gone for so long, anything in a dress is worth the look! And she ain't sore on the eyes at all!" Wiggins grin widened. "Think from all the fussing she's been doing, she's taken care of the most of us rebs. That doc with all the bars not likin' it none, either, but he don't wanna handle us, either. Ole school teachings of saw off the damaged limb. Done took Charlie Webb's arm off." His face turned somber. "Gruesome hit. All tore to shreds. Didn't live nigh on a day after that saw-bones did his work."

Francois saw the empty pallet next to Wiggins, guessing that's where the young soldier from New Orleans had been. He recalled Webb. Good soldier but might a young, Francois thought, with his rifle almost taller than he was. But bullets didn't choose who they hit, just whoever crossed their path. Francois couldn't help but shudder, knowing he'd be in the same lot if that officer had had his way.

"How long I been out?"

"Day and a measure, I reckon. Thinkin' its start of December."

December 1? The battle was four days ago? "Did we win?"

"Don't matter much. We're here. Prisoners to Yankees." Wiggins spit on the floor.

"No doubt, they'll be seeking exchanges," he muttered only to be shorted by Wiggins, who laughed loudly.

"Non, monsieur. That Yankee general put a stop to them a while back. Prison, most likely. Prisoner of war camp." Wiggins shuddered and that made Francois's stomach knot.

They'd have to escape—even if it killed them.

"I have fought against the people of the North because I believed they were seeking to wrest from the South its dearest rights. But I have never cherished toward them bitter or vindictive feelings, and I have never seen the day when I did not pray for them."

—General Robert E. Lee

Chapter 10

EGOS. *THIS WAR WAS TRULY a battle of egos.*

Ada blew a steady stream of air to get the loose strand of hair out of her eyes and blinked hard. She needed to concentrate and it simply wasn't possible with the raging officers storming around, barking orders as if the enemy was charging on them here in the hospital. *Egos…*

Waxler busied himself, examining one of the soldiers in Ada's wing. The lanky lad who had an impish smile when she brought him water, squirmed under the ranking surgeon's perusal. Waxler had left the initial care to her but now stood like a hawk, inspecting her work and expecting failure by her hand. He picked up the man's arm and peered at it.

"Soldier, how does it feel?" His question was more of a command than a question. Even Ada felt the floor tremble.

"Fairly well, sir," the Creole snapped back, tampered with trepidation. He was in enemy territory, after all.

Waxler ignored the man's tone, still looking at the

wrapped upper arm. "Dr. Leonard, well done indeed. Amputation would have been a better course, of course."

Will opened his mouth to speak but Ada jumped in.

"Yes, sir, but it wasn't needed." She tipped her chin up in defiance before she added, "Sir."

Waxler snarled. "Nurse Ada, I did not include you in our conversation."

She inhaled, her hackles rising at the insult but she squashed the emotion as she glided to them.

"Yes, Dr. Waxler. I just wanted to add to Dr. Leonard's great assessment, considering the situation, sir."

The commanding surgeon cocked his head, his gaze narrowed. "Your work seems to be beneficial, though your role here is supportive. Men are to be treated by the proper physicians, Nurse Lorrance."

He was trying to provoke her and it was working. Will stood to the side of Waxler and he gave her a stern headshake. She bit the inside of her lip to keep a stoic face.

"Yes, sir, but with the lack of supplies back here, we had to make do. The wait for one would deem the wound ill-suited to repair." She so hated having to correct the man's horrible mood of women physicians. He always made it sound as if she'd be better kneading bread instead of saving lives.

Waxler's brows inched upward as he glared at her. "Correct." He glanced down at the rebel soldier. "You are in good hands, soldier. She's one of the best nurses here." He spun on his heel and went to the next patient to finish his rounds.

It took everything she had not to throw her tin cup at him.

"You did an excellent job, doctor." Will's quiet praise cut through her anger.

"I question myself, though," she countered, her vision starting to blur. "That one private, if only I had gotten to him quicker." One of her patients had died yesterday, despite her desperate attempts to save him.

"Ada, stop. Internal wounds are not easy to find and the bleeding can do them in before we even locate the source. You did the best you could."

She blinked hard, trying to swallow the tears that wanted to form. He was the first casualty she'd had in the ward under her care. He wasn't the first to die while she was serving the wounded in war, but he took the place of her first failure as a doctor and that hurt her deeply.

Will took her by the shoulder and escorted her across the room, filling her cup with water, shaking her remorse off with the distraction.

"Ada, I gave you the care of these men. I can't continue to cover for you. Waxler's teetering on rejecting all of the Dragon's nurses except it would cut his staff short." Will snorted. "As much as he'd hate to say it, your abilities and skill on organizing the staff have enabled us to manage the lot. But do remember, he's not the type who welcomes women in the army, especially ones who are physicians. Just be careful, Ada."

She put her hand on his sleeve and squeezed. "Thank you. I will."

"Apparently, the fight is done here, from what we've heard. Be ready to pack up and move." He tipped his head as a farewell and left.

Inhaling deeply, Ada realized her heart was racing. Will had more or less turned the ward, with its five Confederates, over to her. Four, she corrected herself. It was four. Steeling her backbone, she put a mask of sorts on, so the rebels wouldn't see her worries and went to the man with the ankle wound.

The patient was half-propped up, his sapphire blue gaze piercing into her soul, as if he wanted to know the hell she found herself in, thanks to officers like Waxler and the bulk of the staff. Yet, she couldn't help but wonder if that look was desiring something…

"Good morning, soldier," she started, moving the sheet off his injured foot. She yanked out the linen wrap in her apron , putting it on the bed before she began to unbandage his wound.

He snorted. "Yes, it appears early in the day. Your commander starts his demands early, I see."

Ada couldn't stifle the laugh. "Yes, Dr. Waxler is up with the birds."

"If there are any left to be found," the man concluded. "I appreciate the care for my injury, though as much as you all want to view it, perhaps leaving it uncovered would be more beneficial."

She stopped and frowned. The mischief in his eyes danced to a tune she didn't hear but it made her give him a smile. "Perhaps, though covered it should fare better. I want to inspect it and see." She pulled the used linen off.

"See what, whoa!" He managed to move the limb out of her reach. "Just what are you doing?"

Her grin widened. With a twinkle of her own, she exposed the feather she'd scratched across the ball of his foot, pleased he felt it enough to withdraw it. "Excellent. You felt that?"

"Of course," he snapped, trying to move it again. "It tickled. I wasn't aware you Yankees were made to repair us only to torture us in return."

"Hardly. You are too quick to assume," she stated, now peering at the stitched incision at his ankle. "It held and

I see little swelling. You can move it, so all appears good."

"It stings."

"Yes, well bullet wounds do that, I hear." She dipped her sponge into the basin of water near the foot of the bed and wiped the area gently. "What is your name, sir?"

"Does it matter?"

"To me, it does. Makes our conversation a little more comfortable."

He snorted. "Corporal Francois Fontaine, 9th Louisiana Company."

The man to his right muttered something she couldn't hear. It slightly irritated her but now wasn't the time to teach these Southerners etiquette. "Your friend found that amusing."

"Oh, Wiggins finds many things humorous." As she tucked the end of the bandage into the wrapping, Francois leaned forward. "I will walk again, right?"

Ada swallowed. "Yes, given time. Rest. We will try moving you later, to see how you fare." She quickly tried to hide the fear in her voice as she re-wrapped it. The surgery was correct, she was sure at the time. She'd cleaned it, stitched the rivet in his skin shut and carefully set the ankle and foot in line, as nature would have it, so if it was fractured, it'd mend. Only time and rest would tell. Problem was, he was the enemy, now a prisoner and maimed. She could only pray he'd heal.

"Get some rest, Corporal. I'll check on you later." And she whirled out of the room, the demons of failure chasing her.

Francois watched her run from him and instantly became agitated. This nurse, a woman way too pretty to be stuck in a building of sick and wounded men, ran from him. He'd never had a darling dash away like that. He growled.

Wiggins started to laugh.

"I fail to see what is so damn funny." Francois twisted to see his fellow Tiger but the move jostled his leg, sending a myriad of pain from his ankle.

"You." Wiggins maneuvered himself to a seating position, despite the useless arm, still slung around his neck. "I saw you eying that nurse. Not sure which is worse. You or her gawking over the other."

"I do not 'gawk' at ladies," Francois snarled. Though the woman in question could provoke that, even in her dark brown dress, her hair pulled back with no adornments of any type on her person. She was attempting to look severe and plain, and was doing a damn good job at it too, if it weren't for her smile.

"If'n you ain't, I still declare she got her bonnet, as it were, set for ye."

Francois took a look at himself in the mirror that was across the room. He frowned. A mirror here was an odd article to be found but a quick survey of the room, with its papered walls of Greek monuments and the white wainscoting, with the windows pristine but lacking drapery, he'd guess this was the dining room. The window dressings, he now noticed, were all over the room in different areas, like the set he saw folded under his injured leg. He doubted the Union had olive green silk blankets for their men. His neck bristled at the looting of the house and the damage that would remain, like the stains he saw on the wooden floor planks, darkened with blood.

He returned to his image in the mounted looking glass. His cheek was bruised, with another one on his exposed left shoulder and his hair was tousled in the most unbecoming way, as if he'd had a busy night with LaJoyce... The bandaged foot looked large and it made him wonder if it was just swollen or over-wrapped. He raised himself further, to bend over and check but the move made the leg flare again and he groaned in frustration.

"Damn! We're here, imprisoned as it were, and I don't even remember how this came to be."

Wiggins sighed. "The Yanks made a massive move forward, more than we anticipated on our part. Marse Lee dun thought they'd be over yonder. If they did there as well, I've no idea, but we tried to hold our own." He shrugged. "It wasn't pretty. At one point in the retreat, we jumped over that ridge to make it out from their rifles, but, if I recall right, the rocks slipped from all the rain that'd come through. I barely made it but got hit, and by the time I managed to get up, done have a whole regiment of Yanks pointing their guns at me." He exhaled. "You slipped on them rocks and I heard you hit the ground as they started firing. When you saw them upon us, you reached for your gun but that Yank done hit you with the butt of his and that was all for you."

Francois's faulty memory of that battle flittered through his mind. Now, at least, he knew where the bruise on his face was from and the throb in his temple. "We're not in a good position." He glanced at the other two soldiers. Both were asleep, one with his leg wrapped and the other with his head and chest.

"Yessum," Wiggins agreed. "Hard to tell with them two. O'Reilly hasn't been up but once and then, he retched everywhere. Tourant's got a fever, been saying odd things without being awake. Not looking great for them, either."

Francois exhaled. He tried moving his foot again and bit back the pain. He swung the better leg over the side of the bed and slowly brought the other up. The stinging was painful but not enough to stop him. He grinned at Wiggins. His friend's eyes narrowed. He ignored it and sat upright, leaning over till his feet touched the floor. His good foot steadied him but when the other touched the boards and he put his weight on it, a lightning bolt exploded, and crippled, he fell to the floor, his last thought was of Emma and how he had to get out of here. Then it all went black.

"[I]f Meade ever did a noble act in his life, it was when he concluded not to fight Lee in his strong hold upon the banks of Mine Run at a temperature of the weather, far, far below freezing. Newspapers blame him and call him a coward for not doing so, but let their editors…have seen and felt what I saw and felt up that occasion and instead of taunts and ridicules, they would bestow words of commendation."

—Union surgeon, Daniel Holt, December 1863

Chapter 11

December 2, 1863

PREVAILING WINDS INCHED UP ANOTHER notch, their freezing path decimating anything that was exposed. Even in her bedchamber, Ada curled, still clothed in her woolen dress with her wrap on and the drapery the laundress shoved into her hands, a long lengthy piece of silk, now folded in four, covered her. Sleep that night was next to impossible, for even if she got her teeth to stop chattering, Maybelle and the other two in the curtain space next to hers, continued. *Who ever thought that Virginia could get this cold?*

Slam!

The window in her closet had one of its shutters break loose of its hooks and it banged into the windowsill only to fly back open onto the house. She nearly jumped at the sound but, when she recognized the source, she got up, tossing her covers aside and pushed the window open and relatched the errant piece. The blistering cold air rushed into her room and managed to seep through her garments to brush her skin, making it prickle in the cold. A shiver raced through her, but she didn't step back from the window until she witnessed the soldiers far out scurrying in the dawn air, collecting their supplies. She also saw the first of what would be many ambulances pull up the drive where it halted. They were moving.

Her mind raced. There were many patients and not enough help, if all was left to them to accomplish this. Straightening her skirts, re-pinning her pinner apron on and dampening her hair so it laid flat in its tight bun, she raced out of her room to wake the other nurses.

"Ladies, wake up! We are needed right now!"

Many mornings, it seemed to take an act of the Almighty to get these three moving but today, they burst through the blanket flap door, ready to move.

"We could hear them not too long ago, stirring the pot," Maybelle answered Ada's quiet question. "I could see the men getting ready, so we've been getting ready."

"I'm pleased to see that. It's a might chilly, so fortify yourselves with some coffee." As they headed towards the kitchens, she turned and ran right into Will. He chuckled and gave her his cup.

"Looks like you'll need this. We've got a lot to do today."

She took a sip of the black drink and relished the heat that spread down her throat. "I wasn't aware we were leaving so fast."

"Meade has ordained the Confederate numbers are too big here for him to squash Lee after all. We took this place, he claims, but the bigger plan would be thwarted." He shrugged. "Or so I hear."

"Your diagnosis is McClellan-disorder?" She couldn't resist. General McClellan had held off fighting the rebels for half a year, claiming the other side outnumbered his, though she'd read too many newspapers claiming otherwise. After all, the population of the South was less than the North.

Will opened his mouth but another voice boomed across the room. Waxler.

"Dr. Leonard, Nurse Lorrance, we have a hospital full of patients we must ready to leave. Start with the less wounded, sir, and we'll get them out first."

"Sir, what of the Confederates?" She knew the moment the words spilled out, she'd cause a stink and watched it become a reality as the officer's face turned a shade of red.

"They can stay here and freeze, for all I care," he snapped. "Our men go first. Doctor!" He eyed Will and with a nod, took off toward the main rooms, where the Union patients were.

"Ada, don't push the man," Will warned. "We won't let them freeze."

As he turned, she grabbed his arm, flooded with concern. "Where are we headed?"

"Back north, winter's quarters, I've heard." He stalked off.

Downing her coffee, she noticed Maybelle watching her. "Yes, Nurse?"

The girl had a knowing look in her eye and it made Ada wonder what set her off, but then her fellow nurse lapsed into a dreamy-eyed stare.

"He's quite dapper, is he not?" Her voice sounded dreamy.

Ada shook her head, her brows knitting together. "Dapper? Dr. Leonard?" Will was nice enough young man, though dapper in this setting didn't fit well.

Maybelle laughed. "Oh, heavens, not him. Dr. Waxler."

Ada's heart skipped a beat and she blinked. "Maybelle, you are aware that Nurse Dix does not approved of nurses who sign on to find romance. It is inappropriate, to say the least." It even made her blood curl, but then again, if her own heart's desire was here, could she hold true to that one requirement?

The nurse tilted her head, a knowing look in her eye. "Nurse Lorrance, I'm only going by the precedence I've seen you set, setting your affections for a surgeon."

Ada closed her eyes. There was no time, and as if on cue, a loud crash of metal clashed in the other room. "Now is not the time, or place. Come, we must devote ourselves to our wounded." And she'd pray to God not to allow her alone with the girl again. Romance had no place in the medical ward.

The sound of the wind whipping past the house, its trail singing a song with the windows and shaky shutters only seemed to reinforce the chill that had grabbed hold of him, worse than any he could recall ever. Francois wanted to curl up under the thin wool blanket but the throbbing in his ankle kept him grounded, even though his toes were ice.

How he slept amazed him. Perhaps it was the medicine they gave him. Laudanum. The bitter concoction of whiskey and opium had been watered down but the taste never could be hidden. It set his mind to swirl, thoughts blending of home and the war and Emma, childhood and LaJoyce, to even his father. It made him sluggish and as much as it deadened the pain, he'd give anything just to think straight.

The long night seemed to toll but when the first ray of sunlight peaked through the clouds, he breathed a sigh. He'd lived through the night. Not that he should be worried, he thought. Anytime he thought he'd died, all he had to do was nudge that injured leg just a tad and the buckshot of pain reminded him he was still condemned among the living.

"Fran, you hear all that?" Wiggins whispered. "Sounds like either there's been another fight or they're leavin'!"

He struggled to hear what his buddy was saying and it seeped though the walls that there was a lot of motion, with an occasional clash of furniture and dishes. "Oui, it does sound as if they're breaking camp."

Wiggins wiggled out of his bed and crept to the window, his bare feet making no noise. Glancing out the window, he laughed. "We must be on the backside of the house, because all I be seein' are some slave shanties and the cookhouse. Ain't nobody back there doin' nothin'."

Francois smiled. Wiggins was joking, because even he could see the movement outside. Not that he could focus, that damn laudanum still seeping through his system.

The door burst open and four Union soldiers came in, armed and looking dismayed they'd been sent in to see to the rebels.

"Time to get you boys rollin'!" the one with the most stripes ordered.

"I do beg your pardon?" Francois noticed only he and Wiggins were awake and none of them were dressed.

The man's response was to throw a set of Confederate clothes to him. Francois recognized his uniform quickly. Still thickheaded, he stared at them, toying with the shirt. It was still stained with mud and filth.

"Ain't got all day, boy!" the soldier near his bed snapped. "Gotta get you all on the road."

The other two wounded were rousted and Francois could see their confusion. None of them were exactly well enough to dress.

"Dressed or not, you're going. It's colder than Hades out there, so if you be wanting to stay warm, I'd figure out how to get that secesh-shit back on."

Perhaps he had said something, Francois mused. Getting the shirt on wasn't hard, neither was his shell jacket. It was the trousers that proved difficult. One leg in was relatively easy. The other? It wouldn't bend so he laid back and breathed deep. The others were forced up, but they weren't struggling with a wound like he had. Wiggling out of the one pant leg he got on was easy but to get the other, he'd have to try it first.

"Come on!"

Anger mixed with the laudanum set Francois off. When his legs swung over and he tested his injured foot, Francois saw the Yankee shooting him a look. Inhaling deeply, he put the good foot down, but his hesitancy to move fast enough triggered the bluecoat to snap. The man grabbed Francois's shirt and yanked him up.

"I done told you to move!"

Without even considering the consequences, no doubt due to the pain that ripped up his leg when the injured foot had been forced into use, Francois's curled fist stuck the Yankee squarely in the jaw. The man yelped, curses flowing out of his mouth like a faucet, yet his grip on Francois broke. Francois fell to the floor. A ping rang and he looked. His miniature painting of Emma fell to the floor. He would not leave that behind.

"Get up! Ain't got time for this, Gardner!" The other soldier pushed his buddy out of the way right, but as he rose, he kicked at Francois's outreached hand before he reached his possession. Pain roared from the kick and he doubled, falling to the floor when Wiggins got to Francois's side.

"Here," he said, putting his arm around him to help him up.

Staggering, they limped down the hallway to a wagon in the back. The pain subsided as he hopped along with Wiggins' aid. He bit his tongue from wanting to put that white trash soldier down a notch or two but when he opened his mouth, Wiggins nudged him and gave a short head jerk 'no'.

"We ain't the only ones leavin'," Wiggins remarked low.

Francois took a look about. Everything was moving in a mass wave of boxes being packed, staff scurrying about and other patients being geared to leave. He wondered about that woman, that nurse, oddly finding his search futile.

"Wonder where they're taking us."

"I can tell ya where you traitors are headin'," the guard spat to the floor, the planks stained by the tobacco he chewed.

Francois scowled at the impertinence of the man. Yankees here apparently had no manners, but he restrained the reprimand that formed on his tongue seeing no point in trying to correct this miscreant.

The soldier never noticed the disgust on Francois face. Instead, he cheerfully said, "Sending you to prison, where you can waste away. How's that for 'state's rights', huh?"

The guards snickered but none of his group even peeped a word. Men like this, Francois thought, will have their own time in hell. Of that, he was sure.

Another jostle, made as the guard pushed Wiggins forward and his support faltered, making Francois land on the ball of the injured foot. He bit back the swear word that came and found his comrade's support again as he limped out of the ruined mansion-hospital to the buckboard that awaited them. It'd be a harsh ride to bear, heading straight to jail. He inhaled deeply. He had wanted to escape the hell of living in the presence of a woman he loved but could never have and he'd succeeded. But that damnation just changed its perimeters to four walls. Emma would never know what happened to him.

But he couldn't silence the small voice that echoed would that nurse here wonder? *To hell with war!*

Ada worked furiously all day long. Packing a hospital, particularly one set up temporarily, was difficult. Every time, she wondered how things had been so strewn all over the place, only to discover once she thought she had everything, another drawer was opened, or box turned. What had been so organized, that she had known where to go for what, evaporated the moment the command came to pack up.

To make matters worse, she had to get the laundresses motivated and the cooks to continue their meals yet pack at the same time. Not to mention her own tasks with the patients, which reminded her of her ward in the back. The Confederates. She'd yet to see them all day and had sent Maybelle back but had yet to hear a report. Every time she'd thought she'd run in to check on them, Waxler summoned her with new orders.

"Damn Meade wants us out now!" the surgeon had groaned. "Letterman is nowhere to be found. And Meade's convinced the Rebels will come if we don't skedaddle." He shook his head, then stormed off.

"Here, drink this."

She glanced up and found Will. He held a cup for her and she frowned. "Poison or wine?"

Will snorted. "Neither. Just water. Sides, can't have you dying on me, I mean us. You hear the news. Waxler's fit to be tied over it all."

She downed the liquid and realized she was thirsty. And hungry, but there was no time to break. Wiping her lips with the back of her hand, she peered at her friend and pushed. "How are my patients?"

"Fine, I reckon."

"Fine?" her brows shot up. "I thought you went to see them."

"Did. This morning. All fit as can be, considering. But you know they've been escorted out."

"Out?" Shocked, she grilled him with her gaze. "None of them were in a condition to be moved abruptly."

"Well, not sure how abruptly is was, but they were moved. Been sent to prison, I hear."

"Prison??? Will, you know as well as I do, they'll not survive that!"

When she started to turn to try to find Waxler, determined to find out where he'd sent them, Will caught her by her arm.

"I wouldn't do that. Not now."

"They're in danger!" she argued. "That one may never walk again if he isn't cared for properly."

Will snorted but refused to budge out of her way. "We'll find out later. You know, we've got to go!"

She hated when he was right. Biting her bottom lip, holding back, she turned and continued her mission. But she was determined to find that rebel again.

"Always mystify, mislead, and surprise the enemy, if possible; and when you strike and overcome him, never let up in the pursuit so long as your men have strength to follow, for an army routed, if hotly pursued, becomes panic-stricken and can then be destroyed by half their number."

—General Stonewall Jackson, CSA

Chapter 12

Washington D.C., December 1863

WILL LEONARD SMILED. TO DO so actually hurt, he decided, as his lips curled upward and his skin pulled with muscle ache. What had seemed a millennium since he'd truly smiled was probably no more than six months, he'd guess. But then again, most of that time had been out with the army, during a war he quickly learned to despise, yet the call to aid the wounded kept him grounded to it.

"Here, here!" he joined in with the rest of the men at his table and raised his glass of wine.

"I'd gather this is better than anything you've had recently."

Will snorted. "Oh, I can't say field rations can be held up next to roast goose, no. And true bread certainly holds its own against hardtack."

"Truly, you were rationed hardtack? I am amazed." Dr.

McKendrick took a bite of his roast beef and grinned. "I thought, as an officer and a surgeon, you fared better."

Will looked down at his plate, taking a view of the chinaware, the true set of silver utensils, the crystal stemware and the meat, real vegetables in a wine sauce, the bread with authentic butter and inwardly he groaned. Those men on the field, who sacrificed it all for the Union, lived off raw beef, poorly self-cooked, with hardtack, desiccated vegetables and water, of which over half of the rations were ill-prepared and kept in a manner that would send them later to him for treatment for stomach and digestive problems.

"We did, to a certain extent, but overall, rations were hard to get at times. Particularly if the rebels cut off our supply lines." He took another swig of wine.

"Does this mean, being with us tonight at Albert's, you're out of the war?" the petite brown-eyed minx next to him queried. She'd placed her fingers on his sleeve to capture his eye, and she was lovely enough to make him want to give her more attention, but he was not falling for that. Too many men in this conflict had died, forcing him to write the letters of condolence to wives. That awful task made him shy away from the idea of love at this time.

"No, Mrs. Featherstone, no. We are at winter's quarters. While the army is training, I am left to care for the sick and wounded, though in a much more comfortable setting." He grinned.

"No doubt, being here in Washington is far more attractive than some tent in a field. Here, here!" Mr. Featherstone stated. The older, grey-haired politician was double his wife's age, Will decided. No wonder she'd turned to him.

"I dare say, if you don't mind, I'd like to have a word with you," his colleague, Dr. Theodore Sattler, on his other side called.

"Teddy, any time." Will grinned. "It's been a long time, old friend."

Sattler leaned closer. "You know I'm working at Fort Delaware."

Will frowned. "The prisoner of war site?"

"Yes. Look, I have some of your sick and wounded. Not yours, really, but from the recent fight in Virginia. One in particular is a trying case." Sattler's face was too concerned for the night of celebration they were having, drawing Will's attention. From what he'd faced in the last month, he shouldn't be surprised, but the doctor inside him nudged him to find out more.

"It must be bad to bring it up here."

"Yes, I believe it is. Will you come with me on the morrow to look?"

The trip to Fort Delaware wasn't one Will wanted to make. His assignment over the winter was an easy one. Most of the severe cases were released and homeward bound, since they'd be unable to muster again, or dead. He was left with the sick mostly. But the walls surrounding the Fort, high and foreboding, on an island of sorts, brought the war slamming back to him and he sighed.

"Dr. Sattler, Dr. Sattler!"

As they disembarked the ferry, a young man was scurrying out to see them on the quick.

"What is wrong, Adam?"

"It's that secesh. He's burning high. Won't take to lying still or taking any drink. Got the others all worked up."

As they hurried toward the building the orderly raced back to, Will turned to his friend. "Adam, what is ailing the man?"

"He's some damn Frenchie, probably one of those Tigers, all pent up with anger and all that. He came in with a foot wound. Didn't look like it was bad. Pus was clear and some minor swelling, to be expected and in fact, less than most cases. But didn't last. Turned wicked. Feared we'd have to go back in and amputate, but that's when he turned violent. Kept yelling 'she tole me I'd keep it' and nonsense like that. Don't know who he's speaking of, but once the fever raised, figured it was his girl back home. I don't have the equipment here to do this." He shrugged. "They don't give a prison much in medical supplies. Perhaps you might recall him, since he came back just nigh on a fortnight or so."

Will's brain was working, trying to recall. They'd had enough of the Louisiana Tigers to deal with and plenty of leg wounds. But the moment they turned the corner and the lock tumbled, opening the door, it only took one glimpse to see the man Ada had worked so valiantly on. Visions of that morning, when they were ordered to retreat, General Meade convinced Lee's numbers would do his army in, despite their winning the battle, all the wounded were readied for the journey and the hospital packed. The Union patients were the top priority, and Ada had been forced to now see 'her ward' as she referred to the prisoner area, ready to move. When twilight fell and they loaded the end of the Federal soldiers, she had raced to the wing with the Confederates to find it vacant, those men already shipped to prisoner of war camps, though they didn't say which one. She had stormed and demanded to know, erupting like a volcano. She argued fervently that they needed medical care and he recalled how Waxler stood solid, a gleam of satisfaction in his eye as Letterman tried to talk her off the edge of insanity. She was furious, and rightly so, Will thought, but he said nothing as well. She'd pay for her outburst, that he did know and he'd tried to block her at first but it was a losing battle.

He shook his head now, trying to re-focus on the matter before him, shoving that memory back. It didn't change the matter that the one patient she'd fought diligently to save, this man, who in Virginia looked like he'd recover to his fullest, was now pale, glistening with fever and a gaunt look, his eyes encircled in black. His heart sank.

The secesh's eyes locked on his. It was that moment that Will realized he didn't even know the man's name. He was a rebel, that was where the knowledge stopped, except for his injuries.

Will glanced down at the man's ankle. It was swollen and red.

"You. Yank! Don't you let them take it!" The man snapped when the orderly moved the pillow it was resting on. The motion showed in the sunlight a yellowed linen cloth and Will took that as the wound was no long spewing clear puss but yellowed.

"See what I've been talking about?" Adam rhetorically asked, as he pulled the bandage back. The threads stuck to the wound reluctantly gave, making the patient wince.

Will bent to take a closer look. A brief scent of it didn't hold the morbid ribbon of decay but it did look ugly.

"Its fine," the patient spat.

Will looked up at him. The man's gaze was fevered. There was heat radiating from the wound. "Can you bend it? Flex?"

The man swallowed hard but obeyed quietly. The pain etched across his face but the determination controlled it, as he got the foot to move.

"Painful?"

He nodded harshly.

Will took a step back and Adam jumped right in.

"Your prognosis?"

Will shivered, and he didn't think it started because of the temperature. "Damn, it's cold in here!"

"It's a prison. I'm not in charge of housekeeping," his buddy muttered. "Just its patients."

"Who is this rebel?"

"I'm Corporal Francois Fontaine, sir, at your service."

Will spun and they both looked in shock. The patient had managed to prop himself upright, looking anything other than comfortable. Fever did strange things to patients, Will recalled from some medical lecture what must have been ages ago. Something about the name, though, prodded Will to ask, "So Corporal Fontaine, where do you hence?

"St. Charles Parish, Louisiana, sir. As does my father and brother."

Will snorted. Memories started to come full color as the accident and name registered. "And, pray tell, your family planters?"

"Oui. Sugar, mostly. Plus other measures."

He ran his fingers through his hair as Adam glared.

"Why you conversing with him? Wanna take up the slave issue with him, too? This man is a traitor. The enemy! Will, I didn't bring you here to discuss politics, but for opinions."

The patient, despite his feverish appearance, glared at Adam. Will, watching this scene before him about to explode, nodded at the man.

"We'll do what we can, soldier. Dr. Sattler, if you please." He nodded to Adam and motioned for them to leave.

Out of the room, Will paced. "First, it's too damn cold in there for their well-being."

"Will, they get what they deserve."

"I can't believe you said that. They are men." He shook his head. He'd thought off the battlefield, the world was normal. Apparently, he was wrong, at least, in a military prison. "How can you work in that?" With a shiver, he now took in how his fellow doctor wore his entire uniform and the medical coat, layered for the temperature.

"I do the best I can."

"You need to try harder," he sneered.

"Then you call the Colonel about it," Adam shot back.

He looked around his fellow-surgeon's office. It didn't look any warmer than his medical tent on the field. Astounding. "You really don't have much."

"No, I told you that. And I definitely do not have what I need, considering the number of men here. Not only do I have Confederates, but also political prisoners and Union disturbers. My hands are tied." Adam gave him a narrow gaze and added, "Who is that prisoner to you? I saw your eyes. You know him, more than just passing through your field hospital."

Will snorted. "Yes, I do. And it's because of a debt owed his family, I need to get him out of here and be properly cared for, since you yourself admit to lack of equipment here to do so, considering."

Adam jumped upright off the chair he'd taken. "You're not going to free him!"

"No, no. I'm not, but I'm not going to let him lose that leg when I think I know someone who has worked with wounds like this, and better than I, nor let him die of gangrene here because he's a prisoner and not deserving common care." Will slumped into the other straight-back chair. "My father and this soldier's family are well acquainted. His father saved mine from a debacle that would've ruined my family. I owe him."

"And who do you know who can get him out?"

Will wondered that, too. "I'll figure it out. Give a moment."

Adam yanked a piece of stationary and started scribbling. "Here, take this. I've written the man's release for better care, stating he is dying. I know we're considered one of the better 'hotels' for the condemned, but the commander here is striving to show he'll have no deaths, outside of age, on his watch. Perhaps, written by his physician, that'll help."

Will nodded. "Thank you."

All he had to do was find Ada and pray she would talk to him and the patient he returned with. In more ways than one, he needed her to fix him or he'd have hell to pay.

"Hello, Massa…bottom rail on top dis time."

—Freedman soldier to his former owner, now a prison of war.

Chapter 13

Armory Square Hospital, Washington DC

AFTER A WHILE, ADA BELIEVED she no longer heard the moans of the patients in the wards. The noise had turned to a low buzz to her ears. But today, their sound grew louder. With a bowl in hand and a rag over her shoulder, she stopped and looked down the row of patients and inwardly groaned. Christmas was but a week away, yet there was nothing cheerful in this building, despite the bows of evergreen that were draped from the rafters. The doctors had balked at the greenery, but she and "Dragon" Dix had argued the pine scent chased out the smell of rotting flesh and infested wounds, though the combination that she inhaled was ghastly, a present of pain encased in holiday cheer. *Perhaps the surgeons had been right…*

On cue, one of the patients sneezed. And sneezed again. Apparently, Lt. Fitzgibbons was not enjoying the seasonal scent. She went to his bedside first, pulling out one of the handful of handkerchiefs she shoved in her dress pocket for him.

"Here, Lieutenant."

"I'm so sorry," the ruddy-faced young man muttered before he blew his nose into the proffered linen. "Guessing that pine making me sneeze."

She touched his forehead. The man had lost his foot during battle, an amputation that wasn't done right. He'd come into the hospital with a high fever and a swollen stump, red with infection and crowned with the jagged point of bone jetting out of the closure. Another surgery was required and that reopening of the wound to round off the bone and make the closure right had a higher mortality rate. Thankfully, he had lived.

"Well, perhaps your reaction to the decoration is good," she decided, daubing his face with a damp cloth. "You're healing enough to notice it."

He peered at her and a hint of a smile came. "So I'll make it, you say?"

She bit her inner lip, swallowing the doctor inside her. Allowing that had been her ruining three weeks ago, thanks to Major Waxler. "That is what the surgeon says. Your fever is less and you're not red or swollen. All good signs." She grinned at him before she gave him a sip from his cup after she'd dropped a bit of laudanum in it for the pain.

The drug worked quickly, as she registered the placid gaze shade his eyes and his shoulders slump against the lumpy pillows. The tenseness evaporated from her as he fell asleep, not a natural one, but one vacant of pain. Slowly standing up from the edge of the bed, she picked up her rag and bowl and turned when a young boy ran up to her. He skidded to a halt, panting hard.

"Whoa, boy, what has you scurrying so?" Only reason anyone would come barreling into a hospital was a pandemic or the Confederates attacked—but this was the capital, it was too quiet for a barrage.

"I came lookin' for Nurse Lorrance," he gulped, then quickly added, "Ma'am."

She bit back a smile at his manner correction. "And you are?"

"Matthew Caruthers, ma'am."

She rolled back on her heel. "This is she, sir."

The panicked look in his eyes returned. "I needs you to come with me. Tole to tell ya, it be an emergency."

"Where to, may I ask? Ladies don't just leave with suitable young men without prior knowledge," she stated, the grin escape her stronghold.

He inhaled, bringing his shoulders up and straight at her compliment. She'd guess he wasn't much past twelve…

"Mrs. Turner be needin' your help, ma'am."

Ada inwardly groaned. Beatrice Turner, the woman who owned the boarding house she roomed at, had turned very gleeful, knowing she had a woman doctor in the house. More so after Ada helped the woman's daughter, Miss Ellen, when the girl had fallen ill and needed a doctor. Their regular physician was unavailable but she offered her services. Since then, the woman constantly delivered Ada patients, mostly women, for feminine needs. And according to Society as a whole, that was the only type of patients she *should* see.

"Thank you, Matthew. Let her know I'll be there right directly."

As the boy scampered off, she put her supplies down, looked down her ward to find her work done. She grabbed her wool cloak and darted of out the building. Within minutes, she pounced up the front staircase to the brownstone, both annoyed and curious what the latest crisis was. What she discovered on opening the door to the boarding house, wasn't what she expected.

"Dr. Leonard, what a surprise to see you," she greeted, skills of etiquette not entirely washed away by the war. He was stationed at one of the other hospitals and rarely came here.

He stepped closer. "Ada, please, I brought you something of note from New York."

That caught her attention. "Truly? Why, whatever would you find among all that mess?"

A smile full of mischief played across his face. "Shall we see?"

She frowned. "Will, this isn't the time or place for this. Mrs. Turner has ears everywhere."

"I hear your nursing has been excellent." But when she shot him a dagger look, he straightened and dropped his voice. "Actually, I do have a favor for me and a challenge for you. One I hope you are willing to tackle, as it were. You recall that rebel with the ankle wound?"

The one with the striking blue eyes? How could she ever forget him? "Yes, I do. And he is one of the reasons I had a warning from Miss Dix, to refrain from doctoring."

"Ah, yes, I figured Waxler had made good his threat to report you. But you and I both know you are more than qualified in the surgical area. And I'd wager a month's pay, you saved not only his foot, but the respect of several other surgeons." He paused. "Now, remember, he was sent, as a prisoner of war, to one of the confinement areas."

Her heart kicked into beating harder as the anger roiled in her blood. "Yes, I remember clearly my patients being yanked from me so. What are you getting to?"

The mischievous cheerfulness evaporated. "I found him, at Fort Delaware. He's not doing well."

"Whatever do you mean?" She badly wanted to forget

him.

"The wound is faring poorly. Infected."

She shook off the concern. "Surely the surgeons there will attend to it. Why come to tell me, other than verify Dr. Waxler's statement I'm not a doctor of means."

"Ada, you know you are!" His face was red and it was obvious he was mad. "I was called to the Fort by the surgeon there. They hardly supply them and the wound was apparently mangled by the Federal troops who hauled the prisoners away in Virginia. You know, our boys can be rather harsh with the secesh. From what I could tell, the leg is swollen with a stench of infection. It looks off center. They'd amputate but haven't the right staff or supplies to be able to do it."

Ada started to pace. She shouldn't care. Didn't want to. "Last I saw of him, he was doing well, well, as best as I could tell in twenty-four hours after surgery." Then she stopped and turned to face him. "Why are you telling me this?"

"I managed to..." He cleared his throat. "Bring him back with me."

Her throat dried. "You what? How? Why? Surely that isn't possible."

He looked away and the tenseness thickened. "I, well my family, owe his family for a deed of years back. Once I learned his name, I couldn't leave him there."

"Oh dear, Will, what have you done? What could they owe you to jeopardize your position?" Shock rattled through her. To move a prisoner, just because of an injury, wasn't something allowed, or so she believed.

He got closer and took her hand. "Ada, please. It is your work. Besides, they won't be watching you. I know you've been practicing outside the army hospital—"

"Will," she started but he cut her off.

"Please, Ada. I've already risked everything, asking for favors to cover this, but it is very important. What they've done, long before the war I will say, saved my family, and for that, I'm indebted to him and his. As you can see, I cannot care for him here. He's not to be here. Rebel or not, this is important. But while I'm tied by rank, you could."

Of course, he couldn't take the man under his care, ruining his career, but she could. Anger flared at the mere thought that she could sacrifice but not him.

She'd been furious her patients were taken from her so easily that day, Waxler demonstrating how her place was not in practicing medicine. He'd gone further on that once they'd returned to Washington, complaining to the right set of men who'd reduced her position back to nursing, despite all her education and proven abilities. The only slight redeeming factor was the patients she helped through Mrs. Turner's recommendation, women who were in need of medical care since the majority of physicians were dealing with the Union soldiers. Granted, this case might heal that wound Waxler had started…

"All right. I'll try. Where is he?"

Francois swung between confusion and unstableness to vaguely cognizant of where he was, or so he thought. Pain was the one constant, ebbing from stabbing deep and sharp to mildly annoying nuisance. What he wouldn't give to not have it at all!

The last few days, maybe they were weeks, a small voice in his head echoed, teetered in his mind. He'd seen the darkness and the hell that rose from its depths, to bright light and warmth. That had made him wonder if he was dead, waiting for judgment while sitting in purgatory, except he didn't think that room had everyone else come and go, as he seemed to see people then they were gone, and if his recollection was in place, he didn't think they were dead.

Memories of the battle danced in his head. The sound of the artillery, the squeals of maimed horses and the moans of wounded men, the whizzing in the air like insects but these bites tore human flesh with a voracity that could kill. Cold and dampness never left, or so he thought. The battlefield was freezing and the prison no improvement. Even now, in purgatory, he shivered, yet the blazing hell ate at him at times before another blanket of ice settled.

He'd seen the house he was taken to, controlled by the Yankees but after that, the scenes blurred. There was a march of sorts, one he stumbled through before collapsing and being thrown like a bale of cotton onto a wagon, to end up in a barrack with no heat, fed sparingly of greasy food and murky water. Vague memories of his fellow soldiers danced in his head, as did the changeling angel, who looked like Emma or his mother or this woman at the Federal house who'd prodded at his injury like he was a piglet. Damn, he was thirsty but had no strength to see if there was any water or perhaps fearful there was, because the dark cell's only drink was actually grimy to swallow, as if it carried sand or poison or both, leaving an odd taste in his mouth. The thought made him pale…

Suddenly, a brisk of air flew into the room as the door opened. After the hours of silence, the commotion was startling and Francois nerves tingled at the coolness, interrupting his warm nest on the bed. A bed, he realized, that was like those at home—soft and cozy. A true bed. God, it'd been long time since he'd been in one of these.

But his sudden realization and longing to snuggle further came to a screeching halt as his movement jostled his injured ankle, sending jabs of pain racing up his leg. He bit his inner lip, refusing to let these visitors see him agonized. Besides, he had no idea who they were, perhaps angels… or demons…

"Oh, my dear Francois, what have you done?"

His mother loomed over him, concern etched across her face. He tried to focus. Marie Fontaine was a force to be reckon with, so these white face ghosts that hovered behind her were in for a rude awakening. That thought almost made him laugh. What was his mother doing here? Wherever here was? But there was something about her being nearby, to see her loving face and the golden glow of her hair making her look angelic warmed him.

Marie gave a quick examination to his ankle and *tsked* angrily. *"I knew I should have forbade you from your self-conceived doubt. War is no place for my boys."* She shook her head and it sent a pang that reached inside him, wrapping around his spine and making him shudder.

Then she made a light, casual touch of his foot and the result ripped through him like a cannon shot. He nearly leaped off the bed, wanting to beg her to stop, as her hand still maneuvered the ankle and foot. It wasn't a harsh, abrupt exam, but it was enough to make him groan. He squeezed his lids tight, working hard to control the pain and bite back the roar that threatened to escape.

"Shhh," Marie whispered, her tone soothing and touching his soul. She rubbed his cheek softly. *"Don't move. Tell me what happened."*

He opened his mouth to answer but she tipped a cup to his parched lips, and with it being his mother, he couldn't refuse. The liquid wasn't tea, as he suspected, but it had an odd taste, one he swore he knew. Whatever it was, a wave of calm spread through him and his thoughts blurred, and the pain ebbed. For once, in a long time it seemed, he was comfortable, warm and felt the wave of love coming from his mother. He wanted to sigh with relief.

But the relief never came. Instead, the cozy feeling shattered as hell returned. He shot halfway upright automatically as she moved his foot, the lightning hurt raced through him.

"What the hell!" He roared, his eyes wide open when he saw her. That nurse from the Union hospital. Confusion mixed with the torment and he collapsed without hearing her answer. He fell back to the bed, angered, mad and scared.

Now what?

The moment he hit the mattress, the pain overwhelmed him and the darkness won.

"We are not enemies, but friends. We must not be enemies. Though passion may have strained, it must not break our bonds of affection."

—Abraham Lincoln's Inaugural Address

March 4, 1861

ADA FOUND HERSELF LOST. AT a standstill, she blew the wisp of hair that had freed itself from her coiled braid pinned at the nape of her neck and fell into her eyes. Staring blankly at the wall of supplies, she could not recall what she'd come in here for. With a deep breath, she steeled her shoulders, straightened and forced herself to concentrate. She'd spent too many hours at the hospital and way too long caring for that man that the lack of sleep was catching up to her. She bit back the growl that threatened to escape her lips and yanked the bottle off the shelf and turned to return to the ward when she ran right into Dr. Waxler.

"Nurse Lorrance."

She jerked back, juggling the bottle with fingers that seemed very loose. "Dr. Waxler, I beg your pardon." He actually ran into her, she was convinced, but waiting for him to apologize would take a month of Sundays, so she darted to the right.

"My dear, you look a bit pale. Are you all right?"

His words brought her to a stop. Her mind raced. Last thing she needed was a prying doctor. "I'm fine, sir. Just a bit in a hurry. If you'll excuse—"

"Yes, you have done your duties here quite well, considering."

That remark made the hairs on the back of her neck bristle. "I do what is required of me," she snapped then bit her tongue. How dare he provoke her so? "I'll do whatever is necessary to help our men to recover. You know that." She paused for a moment. "Sir."

She saw his mouth wiggle, as if he was fighting to hold back the smile of satisfaction. He made her skin crawl, because he knew perfectly well she could be aiding the patients so much more but it was an argument she had no time for. The end of her shift was coming and she had her own patient to see to. Again, she spun and this time, escaped any further words.

Grabbing the washbasin and her rag, she gave the young man in the bed a cooling wipe of his brow and prayed the fever was finally gone. But as she gave him a pasted smile, she soon found her mind wandering to her own patient as she continued to wipe his brow.

"Nurse Ada?"

She stopped and looked down at him. His face betrayed his youth, no more than sixteen she'd discovered. And after the race to 'join up' with his friends, he now found himself without an arm from battle. Her heart clenched.

"Yes, Private Sparks?"

"I think I'm pretty good, Miss Ada."

It hit her that she'd doused the poor boy's face with too much water from the rag and even his sad pillow was sopping. "Oh, dear, let me see to that." She went to rise but he grabbed her hand.

"It's fine. But you look lost, Miss. Maybe takin' care of us is hard to keep doin' day after day. We all be a sorry lot."

Tears wanted to form but she bit her tongue to stop it. Instead, she gave him a sympathetic grin. "No, you fine young men risked your lives for the Union. It is I and the country that owe you a thanks. Tending you is a pleasure," she reassured him.

He snorted as he squeezed her hand. "Hope you sleep well tonight, Nurse Ada. We don't want ya gettin' sick and not able to be here for us."

A lump formed in her throat. With a nod, she took her supplies and virtually ran from the room.

Will had left that man in the room adjacent to hers at the boarding house. It wasn't an ideal setting, but Will had quite the knack to sway anyone to his way when he set his mind to it. She wasn't sure what he'd told Mrs. Turner but the woman had been very quiet when Ada tended to a man in a room next to hers.

Her patient's fever had lessened to barely there. That first night, though, had been rough. The rebel soldier nearly catapulted off the bed when she touched his injured limb, but then he passed out. Placing the back of her hand against his forehead had verified her fear that he was burning with fever. The ankle and foot were swollen and the incision she had made now looked puffy yet hard with puss that had leaked.

"Will, hand me that pillow," she pleaded. Will handed her the cushion and she placed it under the bruised foot. "We've got to get the swelling down. Whatever happened to him?"

In a broken voice, the patient answered. "Damn Yankees made me walk!"

Ada's eyes widened in surprised, a sickening curl in her stomach when she knew if that happened, the wound was damaged then, for it wasn't ready for the pressure. "Will, I need morphine, ether and a surgeon's kit."

"Ada, I can't do that and you know it! I've risked enough as it is."

She spun to face him. "Let me put this to you as it stands. If what he said is true, it would tie in with this infection. You say your family owes his for some past indiscretion you wish to not tell me. Fine, but I'll lose him if I can't open this back up and reset it, if I can, or it will have to be amputated, and that I'll do my best to refrain from. My only hope is to clean it out and pray, do you hear me?"

Will had stared at her and she couldn't tell if he was on the verge of having her locked up as insane to demand this, or if she'd touched a chord inside him to help. His response, though, spoke volumes. He growled and left in the flurry but in quick time, he returned with her request.

As long as the man remained unconscious, she didn't dare use the ether but wanted it in case he woke, and she'd bet he would. Tipping his foot at an angle to see the former incision, she saw the clotted blood and crusty layer. The mess would block it healing right and he'd need it amputated!

"We've got to clean it." She looked at Will, who gave her a nod but remained silent. Irritated, she glanced about for a cleaning agent. Nothing was in reach.

"Will, hand me your flask."

"My what?" he mumbled in a mocked surprise.

She shot him an angry look and promptly reached across, her hand slipped under the flap of his coat and found what she knew was there, inside the pocket. Pulling out the silver flask, she opened the lid.

"Ada..."

"Will, please. Now hold him." She barely waited for him to brace the unconscious man before she poured a smidgen of the

whiskey on the wound. As the alcohol burned through the dried glaze and blood, the rebel's eyes shot open and he screamed at such a pitch, made her wonder if that was what the 'Rebel Yell' was since it sent a jolt of ice down her spine. Will fought to keep the man down but the patient's roar was short and he fell back into the mattress.

"You've got no choice but to give him some ether," Will grumbled, straightening himself after he released the man. And he yanked his flask from her grasp.

Francois suddenly found he couldn't breathe. The pressure against his chest was heavy, like a wool overcoat, wadded into a lump that occupied the space over his heart. And it vibrated. Struggling to get air, he shifted in an attempt to thwart the weight. Whatever it was, it responded by moving. The motion woke him and as he struggled to focus, his eyes too dry to see at first until he blinked several times, only to discover the object on his back was a mound of black fur. A being that turned and zeroed its golden eyes on him. Startled, he realized it was a cat and he wanted to snort but the animal was laying on top of him. Where the hell did a cat come from? One thing was certain—the feline had to move! Lifting his right hip, he managed to push the cat off him, though it remained at his side. Falling back down, he could finally inhale.

His foggy brain, juggled images of a dark, dank room, filled with filthy, ragged men, the stench of confinement filling the air but what he saw now was the opposite. The room was airy, the heat from the fireplace, one that was vacant in the memory, heated the room. He was on a mattress. His fingertips pushed against the pad beneath and verified it was a read bed and not ticking thrown on the ground, imitating one. The air was clean in comparison, the fragrance of wood burning the main feature. He frowned. *Where the hell was he?*

Then he saw her. The angel in his dreams, though at times, he was convinced she was the devil when she touched his injured foot. That made him glance down quickly, to make sure the limb was still there and found it wrapped in linen, propped up on a pillow. With a sigh of relief, he fell back. He peered at her again since she hadn't said a word and found her slouched in the rocking chair, near the bed, a book on her lap but her head bobbed down, asleep.

Did angels sleep? Somehow, that amused him, because he couldn't imagine those celestial beings needing slumber. Francois couldn't take his eyes off his angel.

Her blondish mane was pulled back and knotted, he'd bet, at the nape of her neck except tendrils had escaped the pins and the glow from the fireplace made her appear haloed. Her skin was pale and she had an adorable nose, which struck him hard that he'd fine it attractive, but it wasn't large, bulbous or red, like so many of his fellow Tigers, no doubt from the cold. Her hands were small and delicate. The dress was a dark navy, almost black in appearance, with a white pinner apron and a narrow white collar. From what he could tell, she wore no jewelry, not even earbobs, which was interesting, because most ladies adored baubles.

He could hear her softly breathing and a small gasp snuck in, as if she was dreaming. That small noise made him smile. She was so pretty, he couldn't wait to see what color her eyes were. He should know it, for he'd seen her before, but his memory failed him. Frankly, his throat was parched, like he'd swallowed a mouthful of cotton, and he wanted a drink of water yet refrained from waking her. Instead, he caught a glimpse of a china cup on the table near him and if he could just reach it, he'd bet the pitcher near it held water. He yanked his arm from under the blankets and went to grab it, but the motion nudged the cat, which meowed as it pulled itself upright and then jumped in the direction he was reaching for. Again, he wasn't expecting that and, right as he bent to reach out for the cup, the cat leaped in the same direction. The cat's agility put him ahead of Francois, so it hit the table first, his paws danced to avoid Francois's fingers and ended up tipping the china cup over. It fell to the hardwood floor, breaking in two.

The commotion startled the girl and her eyes shot open wide as the jumbled skirts and hands knocked her book to the floor with a sudden thud. Upright and at his bedside, she instantly put her palm to his cheek and forehead.

"Are you all right?" She scanned his form, pausing at his injury.

He bit back snapping at the cat. "Considering, I've felt better. Just thirsty." He gulped on dry air. "Feels like I swallowed a bag of cotton."

She bent to collect the broken teacup, shooting a glare at the cat. "Gwendolyn, I do declare…"

The cat sat on the fireplace mantle, licking her paw fastidiously. Precocious animal, Francois swore.

"Please pardon her. She thinks she's in charge," the woman stated as she continued to search for another cup. "As to your thirst, that I've no doubt you are," she answered, pressing the cup to his dry lips. "You've been asleep for three days since you got here."

The water was like gold, and its richness filled his parched soul. He wanted to gulp it but she stopped him, pulling it back a bit.

"Slowly. Hate for you to be wearing your innards, even if there isn't much there."

Retching sounded appalling to him as well, so he forced himself to sip. "Where is here?"

"You're in the capital."

"Washington?" Even though his thinking was muddled, he couldn't recall anything after that soldier forced him to march and some of the jail, but he knew that wasn't here. "How did I get here?"

Her cheeks flamed, giving her a splash of color on a truly ivory-colored face. She was adorable, he decided.

"Apparently, your wound turned rancid. You were teetering on death's door, according to Dr. Leonard, who was visiting a friend on the prison staff. So you were sent here to truly recover." She gave him a smile. "At Amory Square Hospital."

Now the frown set hard. Glancing around the room, taking in the curtains at the multi-paned window, the carved posts at the bed, the damask covered armchair and settee off to the right and the fancy six-drawer dresser with looking glass, he somehow doubted her. "Are Union hospitals this luxurious?" He glanced at the feline still perched on the mantle. "Hospital cat included?"

She licked her upper lip nervously. He was enthralled, his own gaze locked on her.

"No, no you are not at the hospital. In all truth, you shouldn't be here." And with that, she turned to fill the dressing stand bowl with water and grabbed a linen rag. She gave the impression she was like one of his parent's slave children, who'd snatch a biscuit before the cook could stop them. As he remembered, cook swore at them to stay out but chuckled every time. But was this a chuckling moment or not?

"Then, where am I?"

She glared at him before she moved the sheet aside, exposing his wrapped foot. "You are a prisoner of war. Confederates up here normally are under lock and key, not lounging in a bed in a boarding house."

He noticed her tone changed in that last sentence. "Understandable. It is a war. I am injured and, I might add, pardon the words, hurt like hell. An injured man by all accounts, so why are you scolding me so? If I'm so horrible, why did you free me?"

Her mouth tightened but instead of replying, she lifted his leg to release the tuck of the linen strip. He tightened, expecting it to hurt but it was numb and that confused him. Memories of extreme pain echoed through his memories, not numbness.

As she unwound it, she replied, "I did not. Dr. Leonard, apparently, has some sort of obligation to fulfill." She shrugged. "You can't be taken to the hospital. It would throw his career down the river, bringing a rebel in when the prison should have you." She stopped for a second, taking the rest of the strip off. "He brought you to me as, it seems, we have a much in common so to speak."

Francois took a look at his foot and was amazed. It was bruised but not twisted, for which he thanked the Lord. Then, her words caught him. "You're a rebel, too, in disguise perhaps?"

She giggled with a smile. It lightened up her face and all the hardness that had defined it softened. His angel was quite lovely, he thought. *As all celestial beings would be…*

"Yes, I would say so." She dipped the rag. "Though mine is not as a fighter for your absurd belief in that peculiar institution. No, I am a doctor, as trained as the men here are, but…" her voice trailed to silence.

"But you cannot treat men. Yes, I know women who are as qualified as the physicians are, back home, even some of the slaves, but they aren't allowed to advocate a practice except on women, children and slaves." He paused. "So, what are you doing here? And, if I may be so bold, what is your name?"

The last question brought a splash of color to her pale cheeks. "I'm Miss Ada Lorrance, Dr. Lorrance, though to be able to help in the army hospital, I had to sign on as a nurse." She instantly turned back to his injury, as if mentioning her position was bad.

A memory tugged at his thoughts. "Wait. I remember. There was that surgeon that said to amputate it and I recall objecting. You saved me." Those images were clear in his head now, as was the next one that pushed itself through. "You did the mending of my ankle?"

"I attempted to fix it," she corrected. "Dr. Waxler would've taken it off, but he felt his first priority was to the men in blue, thus leaving you and your comrades to suffer till much later. I simply could not let that happen. You were the worst, and you might've died before they got to you."

That halted his thinking. Blinking hard, he realized she truly was an angel. "Thank you."

She stopped when he said those words. Gratitude, softly spoken, but she could see on his face it was genuine. His sapphire blue gaze was mesmerizing and she found herself unable to break free. This man, a rebel and an enemy to her country, a member of that awful slaveholding society, laid wounded and needing her skills. If it weren't for her desire to help others, she could turn him back in and leave his wound to fester. Yet, at the moment, she questioned herself as to who held whom. With those eyes and dark brown, almost black hair, high cheekbones, narrow nose, he had an aristocratic look, one that attracted her. He was surely the devil in disguise, and that was undoubtedly how he lured people to do what he wanted.

She shook her head to vanish that thought and re-concentrated on his wound.

"You appear to be mending, sir. The swelling has dropped considerably and it no longer is hot or weepy."

He frowned. "Weepy?"

"Often wounds will seep as they heal. Many surgeons believe that is good, though I've come to dismiss that as such, because that accompanies fever and inflammation, thus failing in the 'cleaning' as once believed." She put her hand on the ball of his foot. "How does that feel?"

He gave her a sly grin. "Do you really want to know?"

The question was seductive and she bit her tongue, moving her hand to stretch against the sole of his foot and pressed. "And this?"

That made his smile disappear. "I feel it. It tingles some."

She released and stepped back, dropping the sheet back over him. "We'll let it rest a bit more and perhaps, try to stand tomorrow. I'll try to get you something to eat in the meantime." Anything to escape, she thought, her heartbeat quickening as she raced out the door and away from temptation, for he was all that and more. *What was she doing?*

"We had a run for it. Staff officers yelling and calling on the men to rally and support the artillery and the men throwing away their guns and running like mad men and them Rebs a yelling as they came up on the charge with that peculiar yell they have. It sounds like a lot of school boys let loose. I thought Hell had broke loose."

—Samuel Bradbury, Union Army Engineer in a letter home following the Battle of the Wilderness, 1863

INHALING DEEPLY, FRANCOIS CONCENTRATED AGAIN. He rocked in the seat, determined to win against the pain yet decided his problem wasn't his wound, but more so his prison. It was a multi-faceted cell. Far better than that prisoner of war camp he was locked in, but a cell nonetheless. It was very nice, some ways too nice. Lush stuffed chairs, Persian-style rugs and a bed that cushioned every move reminded him of home in Louisiana, not army life in Virginia, nor the Yankee prison up north, yet it locked him in, with no freedom to leave because he wasn't mobile. An injury received while fighting for the Southern demand of freedom from the repressive and control-driven Northern government. For a man who, in the deep South of Louisiana, with little exposure to the war, thanks to a traitorous brother, now found his core yearning for states' rights and the Confederate cause—a cause that now filled his whole being, along with the frustration of his situation right now.

Basically, as long as he remained immobile, the longer he'd be under the heel of the Yankees. Even if that heel did belong to a very delicious nurse, no, doctor, who apparently had risked a lot to help him. He frowned, for that alone was another mystery. Why would a Northern lady, medically inclined or not, take care of a rebel like him?

That thought set off a flame of anger, and passion, from deep inside him. He'd walk again, dammit! Placing both feet on the floor, the injured one a bit more gingerly set, he grabbed the bedpost and pulled himself up. The torn flesh at first refused to let him put his heel to the ground, so he stood, that foot balanced on the ball of it. With a grimace and force, he pushed that heel down and released the grip on the frame. At first, it felt all right. His fierce expression relaxed, as he allowed himself to pat himself on the back for this achievement.

Then, the heel rebelled. All the nerves set on fire and Francois crumpled to the floor. *Damn it all to hell!* He panted, trying to control his anger and the flash of agony that raced up his leg. Steeling his shoulders, he demanded his body to achieve what he desired. It took every ounce of energy and strength he possessed, plus more, but he pulled himself back up to the mattress, ignoring the next surge of pain. Collapsing on the bed, he struggled to stay still and collected himself.

This was one battle he refused to lose!

Ada inhaled deeply, collecting her scattered thoughts. It had been a long day at the hospital. One of the men had died today, despite her best hopes and prayers. He was an amputee from the Virginia campaign, an artillery barrage had shattered his one leg, one arm and pitted his torso with shrapnel. The arm had been removed, the leg a week later. His morale sank, his stumps inflamed and pussed madly as he sank into a fever that stole his soul. He was a sergeant in a New York unit, the number she'd forgotten, but his name was etched into her soul at the moment. Robert Wright. A young twenty-year old law clerk with a new wife he'd left behind for the glory of the Union. Writing the condolence letter to the widow nearly undid her. Those duties were not for her, but since she'd nursed him and couldn't stop the feeling that she'd failed him, forced her hand. Tears flowed and it took longer to write as she worked hard not to weep across the letter, smearing the ink.

The whole ordeal made her nearly forget the morphine and cane she'd procured for her own patient. Thankfully, she'd placed them near her cloak and bonnet. Wiping her eyes one last time, she collected her goods and left for the day.

At the boarding house, as she drudged to her patient's room, her mind still tied up with Wright's death, all precautions to keep her activity quiet from the landlady fled her mind as she gave a slight rap to the rebel's door and opened it. What she saw before her made her gasp and the cane hit the floor.

Sitting on his bed, the traitor was laughing with the young housemaid who'd brought him a pitcher of water. Ada glared. The girl was giggling.

"I say, I like your accent, *monsieur*." More giggling. Ada wanted to slap her.

"Merci, ma petite," he replied, taking her glass from her. Over her shoulder, he caught Ada's optical daggers, so he straightened and gave the maid a wink. "Now, Mary, if you'll let me rest, I'll see you later, ma *chère*."

Mary glanced over her shoulder and caught Ada. "Oh, yes Mr. Francis, I mean, monsieur." She bobbed before him, then spun and nearly fled from the room, blushing.

Ada frowned. "Truly?"

Francois tilted his head, looking surprised. "I was thirsty. She came to bring me more water. Is that wrong?"

She wanted to throttle him, but just like Mary, his accent and the Southern drawl worked wonders and unraveled her anger. Perhaps it was exhaustion of dealing with him and the hospital…or the loss of young men like Robert that always took a toll on her. His sweet face looked so clear when he passed told her how peace looked. Then she returns to this patient and her blood boiled.

"The thought was to keep quiet and not alert our housekeeper a rebel was here."

The man chuckled. "I doubt that'll be her first thought. A Frenchman yes, but prisoner

no."

That raised her brows skeptically as she chewed that thought. "A Frenchman? Yes, well, I heard you speak and you did very well, but your Southern drawl embraces every syllable." She sighed and pulled her nursing cap off as one of the pins had been stabbing her neck for the last two hours. "Besides, she's too young to notice, since you put on a vile manner to hopefully seduce her, despite your injury."

"Seduce her? My, daresay it was a long day for you?"

He wasn't going to distract her that easily. "I've stayed here for nigh longer than you, and have never seen her outside the kitchen below. How did you get her up here?"

He blinked in surprise, then shrugged. "Perhaps my fall made a slight noise."

She bit back the snarl in her throat but couldn't erase the fear he hurt himself more than he appeared at the moment. "Let us take a look at how we're are progressing." And she threw the cover back, exposing his damaged leg. As she reached for the linen wrap, his limb trembled. With a frown, she looked up at him.

"It appears slightly red and a touch swollen." Moving the foot slightly, she noticed he clenched his fingers in the sheets. "How did you fall?" He had to have moved it, tried standing or something.

"I tried to stand."

That made her jerk upright. "You did what?"

"You heard me. It wasn't throbbing and I grow tired of just laying here with nothing to do, so I thought I'd stand up, test it out."

Ada hadn't realized how her jaw had dropped open, but it had and now, she slammed it shut. She wanted to roar until another notion came to her. "Tell me, dear sir, just how did that go?"

With a disgusted snort, he sank back to the pillows. "Not well."

She nodded then went to her satchel and withdrew the vial of laudanum. In an empty cup, she poured three droplets and filled it with tea from the pot near the fireplace.

"Here, drink this."

"I really do not like that brew."

That made her laugh. "The tea itself, or the laudanum?"

Her laughter lightened the mood because he gave her a lopsided smile. "The latter. It gives a rather sour taste to the tea."

"Well, in this case, I want you to try something." She pressed the cup rim to his lips, just like she'd done to hundreds of wounded men recently, her mind argued, as if this was everyday chore. "But I think a little pain killer may aid us, since you obviously did not achieve flight."

His brows furrowed as he swallowed the poison. His blue gaze did not falter, holding her attention fully. She sighed. No wonder the house servant gave into his whims. A small voice in the back of her head mockingly taunted her, would she do the same? Stomping that noise out, she yanked the cup back.

"Let us not down the entire cup, sir. It is only to take in small measures."

He scowled. "Do make up your mind, doctor."

The title rolled off his tongue and sent a shiver down her spine, one that was warm and enticing. Finally, a patient who accepted what she was....unless it was in jest. Another stab she shoved aside while putting the cup on the table. She pushed the bed sheet to the side.

"Please put your legs over the side of the bed."

Dutifully, he did. He bare feet slightly brushed the carpet next to the bed. Ada went back to the doorway and picked up the walking cane.

"Here." She handed one to him. "Put it next to the wounded foot and stand, weight on the good one, please."

He grappled with the cane, trying to put his hand on it so it was stable. His good foot hit the carpet and with one hand on the mattress, the other on the walking stick, he rocked to stand. But he couldn't raise himself.

"Let me help." She bullied her way under his right arm, wrapping her arm around his waist and urged him up. He was heavier, she discovered, than she'd imagined. Or perhaps, her long hours at the hospital and worrying here had drained her more than she knew, but as he leaned on her, she bit her bottom lip, determined to help.

"Put some of your weight on that cane, if you don't

mind."

He grunted, pulling himself all the way up. His body trembled as he adjusted his stance. Looking down, she saw the injured appendage still remained off the floor. "Look, soldier, I need you to put some weight on that foot."

"It's Corporal."

She snorted. "Corporal, however, regardless of title or name, please put that foot to the floor."

Gingerly, he put it down but the heel was still in the air.

"How does it feel?"

"Not bad, nor is it great, either."

"Yes, of course." She tried twisting to catch a better view, noticing the chair across the room could have held her spot right now. Disgusted she missed that, she went back to trying to view him, fearing if she let him down to grab it, he'd refuse or couldn't get up again.

"Can we try putting the heel down?"

He glared at her. She couldn't help it. Her lips curved in a smile, because despite his determined look with a touch of anger, he was still handsome. His dark hair had a few strands that strayed into his eyes, his angler cheekbones with those sapphire blue eyes just plain held her attention. She shuddered, realizing she needed to watch his movements, not fantasize about a man who stood a traitor to her country, enslaving people for no other reason than back breaking labor he could order them to do. It was then a cold wave washed over her, drenching the attraction, almost on cue for he stepped down then.

"Argh!" He hopped the damaged foot back up. "I can't!"

"Shhhh," she whispered. "Stay right here."

"What?" He teetered between the good foot and the cane.

She dragged the chair over for him to grip. Sure he was

steady, she bent down, thankful crinolines were not allowed in the hospital. Reaching under the sole of his foot, she got to his heel.

"Slowly, lower."

"No."

She glanced up at him. "Please. I need to see—"

"That was how I fell," he bit back. With his heel raised slightly, he added, "This feels better."

Ada shook her head, remembering he had had a major infection and the wound was severe. Maybe she was pushing too much…

"All right. For tonight, why don't we eat, let you rest and try again tomorrow?"

He grumbled about hunger. She nodded, anything to get him fed and rested. The truth was, the longer he was here, the bigger the trouble this would be. She needed him standing and walking. Taking a glance at him, seeing how again, he looked so handsome. Again, she shook her head, thinking his recovery had to be soon, before she strangled herself!

"... I am heartily tired of hearing about what Lee is going to do. Some of you seem to think he is suddenly going to turn a double somersault, and land in our rear and on both of our flanks at the same time. Go...and try to think about what we are going to do ourselves, instead of what Lee is going to do."

—General US Grant snapped at his officers for worrying over what Confederate General Lee would do to them.

The Battle of the Wilderness, May 5-6, 1864

Chapter 16

SURGEON WILL LEONARD WALKED DOWN the hallway of the hospital, papers in hand, his mind calculating how many patients remained and, of that, which were the mostly likely to be leaving. The holidays were coming and he knew it would be a dismal time for those who remained here, since many of the staff were given furloughs, the ones with sufficient time to make it home for the holidays. Even now, the dreariness crept through the windowpanes as the sun set earlier and the cold breeze of winter descended.

It was then he saw her. Ada stood from a sitting position next to a cot, her expression strained as she pulled the blankets up and over the head of the patient. Will sighed. Another one dead from a war that never seemed to end.

But what concerned him more was Ada. She looked

drained and not herself, her step appeared to falter and he feared she'd fall so he raced in. Scooping his arm around her waist, he pulled her upright.

"Are you all right?" He steered her to an empty chair near the table to the side, sitting her down.

"Thank you," she whispered. "I don't know what got over me."

He frowned, pouring her a cup of lukewarm coffee from the top of the warming stove in the center of the room. "It's not hot," he said, shoving the cup into her hand. "Those damn stoves weren't made to warm wards this big."

She sipped and gave him a smile. "It will do the trick."

The color returned to her cheeks, only demonstrating how pale she'd been. The dark circles under her eyes worried him.

"You look exhausted."

She snorted. "Why, good afternoon to you as well."

"How is our patient?" His tone was barely above a whisper. No one else needed to hear but her.

She inhaled. "I'm quickly coming to the conclusion that pussing isn't good, despite what Waxler and all you think. Fevers seem to spike during that and there is a smell one can't escape."

Will tightened. Again, she was questioning established logic. How many times had they squabbled over facts? This time, he'd let it pass. "I meant the one you are attending, privately," he added softly.

Her lips tightened. "He's slowly recovering. Even stood yesterday."

"That is marvelous!"

She grabbed his hand, pulling him down to her level. "And fell, nearly letting the cat out of the bag, as it were. The house maid came up to see."

"I told them he was your brother."

Her eyes shot wide open and she shook her head. "I understand that, but when he speaks, that slavery-drawl ekes out."

Her abhorrence of the man's way of life, put this way, made him laugh. "Southern, my dear."

"Yes, well, what is the next step? The inflammation was nearly gone, and will be soon. I've done all I can do to rid the infection. He'll never walk right again, running will be out of the question, so doubtful he'll return to the fight. But I can't keep him forever."

Will stood, running his fingers through his hair, scanning the ward. The half dozen remaining patients were asleep, or so it appeared, so he kept his voice low.

"I'm not sure yet."

"What?" She now stood. "Will, please!" She paused then a shocked look passed over her eyes. "You can't return him to the war. He's a prisoner!"

"Shhh," he reminded her. "I can't keep him with you, either. Dr. Waxler reported your worn out appearance to Dragon Dix."

"That old biddy can just calm her horses," she snarled. "I am fine."

"Just a warning. Go home and we'll talk in the morning."

She gave him a nod, her quick acquiescence to his order unnerved him more. She was sinking in a pool of mire with that man and running herself ragged here. One day, she'd raise hell on him for this and that could end his career…

It was another gruesome day. Ada blew the strand of hair that had managed to come loose from her tight bun sometime during the day and strongly considered cutting it all off, since hats, combs and any other 'adornment' was prohibited by Dorothea Dix, but then, she'd be cold with no hair. She was tired, disgusted and constantly feeling like she was beating her head against a brick wall. Oh, she smiled when she talked to someone, especially the patients, often swallowing the bile that threatened when she looked at the wound that simply refused to heal. Despite Will's, and every other doctor's opinions, she was sure the puss that formed from that poor private's stump was an infection and, sure enough, it killed him.

Another death for a race to beat those slave-owners and cure that infection!

She inhaled deeply. The cold air on her walk home chilled her and brought her own fervor down to sociably acceptable levels. She needed to conquer what she'd endured to get through tonight. And what if that man had the housemaid in his room again? That made her stomach twist. If Mrs. Turner was still up and at the front parlor, Ada couldn't walk in like a warrior, ready to tackle anyone in her wake. Working to control her features, she drudged up the stairs to the front door and entered.

It was the laughter to the right of the hall that caught her attention first. She stopped and turned to find Mrs. Turner seated near the fireplace and across from her was that man, Monsieur Louisiana. The snake in her stomach coiled. What mischief was he up to *this* time?

"Good evening, Mrs. Turner," she greeted her hostess, her gaze still locked on the soldier sitting across from her. Her quick assessment surprised her. He was upright, dressed remarkably well, in black pants and white shirt with a maroon waistcoat. She swallowed the saliva in her throat, unaware she'd held it, and her breath, overwhelmed by his transformation. His hair was combed and pomaded back, his face shaved and those sapphire blue eyes shone with glee. He was enjoying her unease.

"Ma *chère*, so pleased you have returned." The mischievous smile that hinted at his lips nearly undid her.

"How did you...." She realized her thoughts jumped ahead of her. "I'm pleased you've recuperated enough to manage to make it here. Surprised, as you can imagine, but pleased." At the odd look from her hostess, she added, "My dear." Hopefully that affectionate phrase worked with his. Will had told her he'd informed Mrs. Turner they were siblings. While she doubted the old woman would think that way, as they looked anything but related, she played the game.

"Mrs. Turner here was so kind as to bring me a cane, seeing as Miss Turner informed her how I had fallen."

She saw the stick leaning against the chair, the silver knob on top barely noticeable with the fire in the pit burning. It was much fancier than the one she'd brought him. Then she noticed his shoes. One brogan peeked out from under the pant hemline. That made her frown. His foot had been swollen last night...

"I just couldn't fathom a grown man pleased to be confined to bed," Mrs. Turner gushed. "Mr. Turner was barely able to sit and yet, refused to be bedridden, God rest his soul. So, I found his cane and offered it to your husband." She grinned.

It took every ounce of energy she could muster not to let her jaw drop open. *Husband?* Another swallow.

"How very kind of you to do so, Mrs. Turner. I'm sure it was well appreciated." She glanced at her patient. "I didn't think you were up to moving yet. That wound was severe."

"Yes, I was telling her how that horseshoe nail had been

difficult to see when I was loading our trunks." He turned toward Mrs. Turner. "I'm sure she'd been so busy, helping the boys in blue at the hospital, she neglected to say much. She's such a dedicated soul."

Ada nearly exploded. *A horseshoe nail?*

"Another hard day, my love?"

Spoken in English, the affectionate term was too much. Her heart was taken by another man. A more worthy one, she might add. Her skin crawled that this southern rebel might think he could compete with him!

"Just a lot of patients," she stated as casually as she could. Re-pasting the smile that had fled back on her face, she added, "Many are improving."

"Good," Mrs. Turner replied.

"Yes, indeed." Her patient grabbed the cane and using it as a lift, managed to raise himself upright. "Mrs. Turner, thank you for the cane and the splendid company. The tea was enjoyable."

"Oh, you are welcome, Mr. Fontaine." She smiled, red cheeked and squinting. It made Ada want to retch, seeing how her landlady was swooning over him.

He was grinning ear to ear. That sparked an angry thread inside her. The desire to slap his cheek and snap him out of this sent tingles down her arms.

He hobbled over to her, gently slipping his hand under Ada's arm while over his shoulder he said, "Now, if you'll excuse us, I believe my wife needs to relax. If it is possible, could we get bath water?"

"This isn't a Southern farm," Ada sneered in a hush tone, incensed he'd ask for this, as if there were slaves available here for such a luxury.

He smiled. A smile that grew larger when Mrs. Turner replied.

"I'll see if I can't send some up directly. Good night, Mr. and Mrs. Fontaine."

Ada could barely contain herself. *Mrs. Fontaine?* As he halfway directed her toward the stairs, using his other hand to manage the cane, she realized he was walking. It was slow and deliberate but it was a walk, not a jump or slide of the foot. Her anger kept her lips shut, for fear she'd blurt something vile at what he'd done, but her inner self had a dozen questions to ask him. That is, if she didn't kill him first.

Like how had he gone from prostrate in bed, his foot swollen and ugly, to walking?

Francois felt the robe of intense anger wrapped around his physician as he guided her to the stairs. If she wasn't a doctor, he'd wager she'd push him down that staircase in a second, but how else was he to explain his presence? Brother was highly doubtful. They looked nothing alike, and he came from a family where it was obvious who was related to whom, so his dark hair, high cheekbones and blue eyes held no counterpart to a slim, petite lady with dirty blonde hair, hazel eyes and a temper that blazed easily.

Besides, Mrs. Turner was somewhat suspicious of Ada, which was fairly obvious. She'd told him how she thought the world of Ada, for helping tend those 'poor, wounded soldiers,' though that was far from a ladylike course of action. Her tone, changing from praise to pettiness, had forced him to do the only thing he could to protect her and him, and that was claiming they were married. Now, he'd have some explaining to do. Wonder if he could do it without her throwing him out, or worse.

Thankfully, their room was at the top of the stairs, second to the right. As he pushed the door open, a task that was a little harder than he imagined, since he cradled that foot, balancing with the cane. But it swung open to the small sitting area that was adjacent to the bedroom. The discovery that she'd spent her nights curled on that small settee while he took the bed had angered him. Ladies should never have to give up comfort for men like him, he'd argued with himself. Yet, he knew he had no choice.

"All right now," Ada exclaimed, stepping away from him to close the door and shed her cloak and gloves to the chair. "Let us get you into bed—"

"My, I don't believe I've ever had a lady order me to bed," he chortled, hobbling toward the mattress. The stairs had been grueling. His ankle and heel were sore.

"I'm not ordering you for any nefarious reasons," she shot back. "I can tell you're hurting. Probably pushed yourself too hard, to stand and walk."

Wheeling slightly with the cane in aid, he climbed on the mattress, his feet swinging off the side of the bed. It'd taken the last of his reserved strength to get up here. He never understood why it had to be so high off the ground.

"I could no longer take being held hostage, as it were."

"Hostage?" she asked in a painful voice. As if she held him there by gunpoint.

Perhaps that phrase was a bit harsh. Yet, that was how he felt. Stuck in the land of *those people*. He snorted softly. *Those people* was General Lee's expression for the Yankees, something Wiggins had told him that made him laugh. Of all the times for that to pop into his head...

She didn't even flinch at his laugh. Instead, she appeared entirely fixated on his injury as she lifted his foot up to the mattress. Her brows furrowed as she stared at his boot.

"I had wondered..." she murmured, inspecting his work.

Francois steeled his shoulders as she lifted the trouser leg to see the boot he'd managed to shove on hours earlier. Then, she turned his limb, causing a shot of pain to face up his leg. Contorting his face to prevent himself from yelling, he countered her move with, "That is still sore."

She glanced up, a look of shock on her face, as if she'd forgotten he was awake. "I'm sorry. But we need to get this off."

He swallowed hard. This was going to hurt.

She pulled the linen strip he had tied around his calf. "I'm amazed you did this. Where did you find the knife?"

How was he to tell her? He'd tried to stand and the only plausible way was to not have his heel hit the floor. So how was he to walk? Scanning the room for answers, he'd found his worn out boots. He now regretting not having the brogans most of the soldiers wore, but supplies were slim and when his pair fell apart, he switched to the boots, happy to have another set of footwear to wear.

"I had to borrow yours, because I'd never get that leg part around my foot."

She gave him a narrow glance. "My knife? You rummaged through my medical bag for this?"

"Yes, ma'am."

Horror hit her as she stared at the raw leather. "That is not a knife for common use. It is a surgical instrument." She closed her eyes. Cutting through the boot no doubt dulled a tool that lives could depend on. In fact, operations like she'd done for his leg...She bit her bottom lip in pure frustration.

"I'll replace it, if it's that important. But I needed to get my foot into my boot, to test my theory, and I couldn't even fathom attempting to do so with all that constriction."

She peered at him and wanted to snort. "You'll get me a replacement? I was unaware the Confederate army paid so well. No wonder you all won't stop fighting." She paused. The damage was done. She'd worry about it tomorrow. "Let's get it off you and see how you look."

It took a bit of finagling to get the leather shoe off, with him spouting off in French—she'd bet two to one it was a swear word. The bare limb was exposed and with care, she moved it slightly, quickly examining it.

"I am surprised, sir. It's a little warm to the touch and only slightly swollen. Tender, still?"

With a rigid jawline, her patient nodded. It was more than tender, she decided, since he was silent verbally. She grabbed the pillow off the bed and put it under his foot to elevate it.

"Whatever made you do this, again?"

He settled down a bit. "I noticed it didn't hurt if I put more on the ball of my foot, so figured if my heel was off the ground, I might be able to move."

Pretty good assessment, she nodded. She pulled a long strip of linen out of her medical bag and doused it in the water in the basin, soaking it thoroughly, then put it close to the window, which she propped open. The cold air whipped in, and she shivered. Stepping back, she stoked the fire in the fireplace, thankful it had been lit and used its heat to warm up.

Ada was also aware he was watching her.

"I'm sorry I ruined your medical equipment. I didn't do so with malice in mind."

On that, she laughed lightly. "No, on that, I believe you."

She walked back to grab the now ice cold linen and went to him, wrapping his ankle in it.

He flinched at the first touch, even moving the injured foot, which caused a deeper groan. "Ouch! I said I was sorry!"

"Apology accepted, but I'm still wrapping your ankle." She drew the linen around and continued. "I want to bring the swelling down. There, see, it's not that bad."

"Then bind your own!" he snapped back.

She ignored him. "You may have a point, that is, on using that small heel on your boot. Though, you've destroyed the shoe overall."

"I'll replace it."

"That'd mean returning you to your side. Last I recall, you are a prisoner in Yankeeland." She giggled at her twist on the word Yankee.

"You goin' shoot me if I leave?"

Now she *harrumphed* and rolled back on her heels, crossing her arms. "Go ahead. You wouldn't make it out the door."

He grimaced with a snarl.

Knock, knock.

Ada jumped. Gathering her wits, she went to the door, slightly opening it. "Yes?"

Mrs. Turner laughed. "Had the boys bring up a tub and water. Looked like your husband was right, missy. You look plum tired. Nothing like a hot bath to make ya new again." She glanced past Ada and winked at Francois. "Evenin', Mr. Fontaine. Brought it up, just liked you asked."

"Merci, Mademoiselle Turner. Greatly appreciated."

Ada watched the older woman blush. "You be needin' anything else, you let Mary know, now."

The 'boys' were strapping young lads, one carrying a tin

tub, the other two buckets of hot water. After they set their goods down near the fireplace, they darted out for three more buckets, dumping each in the tub.

"Thank you, Mrs. Turner. We thank you. Now, good night." She shushed the landlady out the doorway and shut it fast. The steam of the hot water was inviting, she did have to admit that. The desire to crawl in it elevated, until her patient spoke.

"See now, perhaps to make up for the knife?"

Mesmerized by the tub and the longing to take advantage of it, she almost didn't hear him. But when it registered in her mind, all thoughts of a bath fled.

"Not likely," she said, walking around the room, picking up her cloak and gloves to put away.

"You need to take a bath."

"I beg your pardon?"

"Doc, you look close to death. You're pale as a ghost, which is whiter than most consider acceptable. Far from porcelain," he argued. "Your eyes have dark pockets, you're skinnier than a whippet and look close to falling down. You work all day at that hospital, only to come here and nurse me. No, you need to take a bath."

She ran her fingertips across the top of the water. It was warm and so inviting…then it hit her, not only was he right, but the other issue was him. He was here. In the bed in the room where the tub was. Despite her longing to climb in, there was no way to block him from watching her. He was too attractive, even injured, even as the enemy, even as a slaveholder. The last made up her mind.

"Perhaps, but you are here and that forgoes the bath."

"Stubborn woman!"

That made her smile. "My father said the same thing when I told him I wanted to be a doctor."

"I promise not to look."

She shot him a shocked glance. He held a straight face, except for the twinkle in his eyes. Her will was being torn between wanting to soak to wanting to thrown a book at him. She toyed with the idea of taking the partition that stood to the side and putting it between him and the bath but...

"Oh, for all the saints!" He leapt off the bed, scooped her up and dropped her in the tub.

Probably not the wisest of moves on his part, Francois admitted immediately. First, his doctor screamed in surprise, the water splashing up everywhere, soaking her and his front. Second, the impulsiveness wasn't the best, as he put weight on the healing foot and nearly caused him to collapse. But he couldn't take her whimpering glance at the tub any longer. Things had gotten way too out of hand when the war touched immediate moments like this, over desiring to bath or not. He'd pay the price for this, in more ways than one, as he inched back to the bed, looking downward in a feint attempt to keep his word and not look.

"What have you done?" She stood in the tub, drenched like a soaked rat.

"I helped you make up your mind."

She growled.

Maneuvering his foot back up took more guts than he had at the moment. Easing it back up, he sank into the mattress. It was then he was hit by her bodice. The half damp wool garment slammed into the side of his head before it fell to the floor.

He peaked at her. All the splashing he'd heard as he lifted

his leg up had been her disrobing. Now, she sat in the tub in her chemise, her head resting on the back rim. The coiled hair, bound so neatly in the knot at the nape of her neck, unraveled, halfway draping over the tub, the other in the water. She looked like a nymph, seductive in her undergarments while in the water and elusive in that she refused to look his way.

Part of him stirred in ways he hoped it wouldn't. Had he been that long without a woman's touch? Apparently…

Suddenly, she laughed. It caught him off guard and frowned.

"Now what's so funny?"

"That you found it a necessity to throw me, your doctor, into the water, probably setting your recovery back further, and just lay there, in pain, eyes shut to keep your promise." She giggled again. "It all seems rather inappropriate, since you instigated this with Mrs. Turner."

Now he looked at her. "You're wrong on one thing. I did look, after you threw your dress at me. Uncalled for, I might add."

"Uncalled for? You're the one who made it soaking. It'll take days to dry."

He cringed at that. She was right. "That may be, but you need a good soaking. Cleanses the soul."

The smile that came to her lips radiated heat all over the room. Well, at least on him. Enough, she eased the ache in his heel.

"I have my doubts on that, soldier." She stretched her arms at the water's surface, making her chemise billow in the water. "I thought most of you refined Southerners were officers."

Despite the throb in his ankle, he couldn't tear his gaze off her neckline and the white in the water. "I joined late, as it were."

"A poor decision, I'd say."

"No, it was the right one." As much as it pained him, he stood, hobbling to one side and grabbed the long linen cloth off the end of the bed. "Thinkin' it be time for you to get out. That water is chillin' and I don't want my physician to come down with consumption or such."

She shivered almost on command. That unnerved him. So did her acquiescence to his request. She grabbed the edge of the tub and slowly stood. It was like a siren, luring him to his death, for as she stood, the cotton chemise clung to her body, detailing every line, every curve. It plastered to her chest, allowing him to see the tight nipples of her full bosom. She leaned back to squeeze the water out of her hair, the motion thrust those beauties towards him and without a thought, he bent forward and suckled one through the cloth. His teeth skimmed the nub before he pulled it into his mouth. It was heaven!

Ada caught her breath. Her first reaction should be to soundly beat him, but the tingles in her breast screamed *please!*

She'd never bathed in the presence of a man. So his reaction wasn't what she was thinking. In her mind, she was covered, she just hadn't considered the water-soaked material would glue to her form. She had no one to yell at but herself for being so displayed, though she had to admit, his tugging at her nipple set off fires in her belly. A low flame that churned, begging for more.

Then, he pulled back, catching her totally off guard.

"Mon Dieu, I apologize." He quickly wrapped her in the

towel and stepped back, collapsing again on the mattress.

Ada pulled the sheet tighter around her, trying to cope with the excitement that quickly stopped when he let her go. She was cold, now that she was out of the water, but her insides were still inflamed and taking longer to chill. One thing was for certain—her undergarments were too cold and she'd catch a chill shortly. That man was a menace, of that she was sure!

She yanked her gown and wrapper and stepped behind the partition to change. Peering through the gathered cotton that filled the openings of the tri-fold piece, she saw him on the bed, foot again on the pillow and his eyes shut.

And then, he snored.

"General Grant is not going to retreat. He will move his army to Spotsylvania. I am so sure of his next move that I have already made arrangements...so that we may meet him there."

—General Robert E Lee to his staff, May 1864

Chapter 17

DR. WILLIAM LEONARD SHOOK HIS head at the hospital steward, who quickly pulled his box of supplies back. Will reached down and closed the young soldier's dulled eyes. The boy was too young to fight and it irritated him more and more that the recruiters took whoever came in. The only smart ones he knew of were the substitutes, who took the money for signing up to fight for a richer man and then vanished to start it all over again. Those men avoided the Grim Reaper, at least for a while.

But then there were the young ones, like this poor soul, who signed on for a cause and a chance to make money, to be clothed and fed. According to the record, he was seventeen. And it would be another dismal letter for Will to add to the list to do, so the boy's parents would know.

"Mail call!"

Will turned and found a former patient, a private, who still served, but now as a courier after losing three fingers on his right hand at Gettysburg, making him unable to fire a rifle. At least as a mail carrier, he could bring better news, to those who got parcels…

"Dr. Leonard!"

He grabbed his envelope and saw the one in the boy's hand for Ada. "I can take Nurse Ada her letter as well."

The boy nodded and went on his way. Will looked at the envelope and secretly prayed that malcontent who held Ada's heart was not the writer. Part of him wanted to burn it, just in case it was, but he didn't. He went in search of her and found her, sitting at a bed, her eyes drooping as she attempted to write a letter for the boy on the cot. Of course, the boy was gone and she had probably taken his last words. He prayed she had before she'd drifted off.

"Ada," he whispered in her ear.

She jumped, knocking her pencil stub and paper to the floor. "I'm sorry," she shook her head. "Will, why are you scaring me so?"

"Ada, your patient is gone."

"I know. Poor soul. Pneumonia stole his life away, and at such a sweet young age," she mourned. "I had just jotted his last words down, for his mother, when he passed." She wiped her eyes.

He reached to pick up the letter. At least one he didn't have to do, he thought absently, then mentally chided himself for the thought. He motioned to the orderly to come and take care of the boy.

"You have a letter."

Instantly, her face lit up. "Oh, how nice!"

"And Dr. Waxler has called for you."

Her shoulders steeled, as if she was a warrior ready for battle. "Of course, he did."

"Ada, be careful. I still hope he hasn't heard of our *friend*," he added in a low tone.

On that, she snorted. "I've no fear all is good. What I

reckoned he heard was of my newly acquired husband."

Will snapped upright. "Husband?"

"My landlady has been led to believe that creature is my spouse."

"I told her—"

"I know what you said." She stood, flattening her navy wool skirt. "But he introduced himself to her, in his very Southern ways, swaying her off with sweet little nothings, and told her outright we were husband and wife." After making sure her apron was straight, she glared at him.

"You owe me, Will. Never forget that."

"I think you are being a touch out of line, Dr. Waxler."

Waxler grinned. He'd waited a long time for this meeting. The fact that Dorothea Dix was there would not take the enjoyment out of this.

"We are in shortage of nurses. There is no rule to rid us of one that is perfectly suited for the position."

"She claims to be a physician. She's practiced under my command, without any clearance from me. I will not tolerate this further. Perhaps you should lower your demands and recruit from a broader base."

Dix sat prim and proper on the chair in the office, her hair pulled back and tied tightly in a bun. Her own face worn and tired from working the last three years for the war effort, but surely she had to know when she'd gone too far, Waxler thought.

"I have worked diligently, sir, to aid you and the Medical Corp during this trying and distressful war, worry for better care of the wounded my top priority. I have the President's approval and my own experience that surely outranks your narrow-minded thoughts over a nurse who is overly qualified for the position. And, perhaps, you might learn a thing or two, from a woman like her."

Waxler bit back the grumble desperate to escape his lips. No point making this one mad as well. While Ada might be missed at first, Dix's departure would not go well, so he constrained his contempt and tried to formulate an approach that could bring the Old Dragon around to his way of thinking.

Willard Bliss, surgeon with the Third Michigan Infantry, appointed superintendent at Washington D.C's Armory Square Hospital, was present, at Waxler's request. The surgeon sat off to the side, rummaging through reports and keeping to himself. Waxler hoped the superintendent would keep his mouth shut and let him do all the talking. Alas, only time would tell.

A scratching at the door prompted Miss Dix to answer. Waxler straightened his back, a flare of victory coursing through his veins. *Upright woman, thinking she was his equal! Ha!*

Ada entered. Waxler had to admit, she presented herself well. She adhered to the rules Dix had for the nurses—she had on a plain, unadorned navy wool dress with a corded petticoat underneath and not the crinoline as that was outlawed by Dix. She wore no jewelry and her hair was pulled back into a pinned coiled braid. Her apron was only slightly marred from use, not a surprise this late in the day. Her manners were excellent, except when he needed her to keep her place. Like when the wounded arrived...

"Nurse Ada, please come, take a seat," Dix suggested, her tone not warm but not cold either.

Even without a crinoline, Ada seemed to float to the chair and sat gently. "I understand you needed to speak to me?"

"Yes, well, let us cut to the chase, shall we?" Waxler started, the need to mix niceties seemed a bit much at this time. "You have broken the rules of nursing. You have acted as a practicing physician, upset the wards, acted as surgeon and refused to accept your position."

The color drained from her face. "I do beg your pardon, Dr. Waxler, but I am a physician and have the credentials to prove it."

"A degree from some utopian school and a list of female patients do not qualify you to operate on our men! Nor is it approved by the Federal government." He started to pace. "You have usurped my rules, operated against orders and acted as if you are better than any other surgeon here!" The last words sank into his thinking and he quickly turned toward Bliss. "Except for you, sir."

Bliss looked up, running his fingers through his hair. He didn't make a remark, didn't even show much of an expression. The bland overture only infuriated Waxler more. He needed support from this buffoon from Michigan, not indifference!

"What do you have to say, Miss Lorrance?" Dix queried.

Ada's blood boiled. This overgrown child was trying to get her fired! It took every ounce of energy—which was in short supply after the mischief her house-patient had caused last night. She'd hardly slept! But, she pulled from reserves she didn't know she had and did her best to hide her anger.

"Dr. Waxler is a good physician, and has risen to the mark every time after a battle," she started. It wouldn't hurt to ply the man's ego. "Even managing a team of doctors and nurses during the chaos of numerous wounded arriving is commendable. But he failed to utilize every asset he had, and that includes another doctor, one as trained as the rest, but who is not a man. Because I carry a womb, I, somehow, cannot operate under stress, according to Dr. Waxler. So he'd let men suffer due to that affliction he claims I have.

"Only once did he allow me to help, and that was after the battle fought in Virginia. Mine's Creek. And even that was only in aid of the wounded rebels, as he tended not to care if they lived or died—"

"I object!" Waxler's face was red with anger. "How dare you."

She returned his stare. "I have no worries telling the truth. Do you?" She stood, strength pumping her blood now. "You let me in because one of your own wasn't as keen on the injuries, and you claimed he was needed for the men in blue, when I consider all who suffer are to be taken care of."

The notice of another surgeon lacking skills caught Bliss's attention. "Who was this other surgeon?"

"He's of little note," Waxler stated. "He's a good doctor. Truth was, I needed him to work on our men over theirs."

Dix's eyes were as inflamed as Bliss's were.

"Plus, Miss High and Mighty here," Waxler continued. "Has recently been slacking in her duties, even falling asleep on the job."

Ada gasped. Dix's gaze on her narrowed and even Bliss shot a glance her way.

"Are you all right, Miss Lorrance?" Bliss's gaze glanced up and down her.

"I am myself, sir. Just a bit tired. Tenants at my boarding house were a touch in the drink, I reckon. Kept me up half the night."

Dix settled back down. "The plague of war, my dear."

"When was the last time you were granted furlough, Miss Lorrance?"

Ada started at Bliss's question. "It's been a while, sir."

"Well, then, let us agree to you taking one," he started, turning toward Waxler. "You are granted holidays at once. Miss Lorrance, you get yours now too."

"But sir—" Waxler started at same time as Ada.

"Your patients will be fine. We do have a full hospital here," Bliss stated as he sat back down. "Full of doctors, since the armies have gone into winter camp. Two on leave will cause no worries. You are granted two weeks. Now," he looked up at them, over the rim of his glasses. "Go."

"Grant is a butcher and not fit to be at the head of an army. He loses two men to the enemy's one. He has no management, no regard for life…I could fight an army as well myself."

—Mary Todd Lincoln's remark after Grant lost fifty thousand men in The Wilderness Campaign, 1864

ADA BLINKED, HER MIND RACING. Two week's furlough. Two weeks with no pay. Two weeks with no work. What was she to do? She had a patient, the enemy, perched in her room, telling all he was her husband. No, he'd only told their housekeeper, but no doubt the word had spread. Now, she couldn't take him anywhere like home, and he wasn't well enough to send back to prison or wherever he was to go. At this point, she didn't care, other than she was stuck and wanted to scream.

Then again, she could turn him in. While a certain amount of satisfaction would arise, so would the problems. Problems like her getting the blame for have an escaped prisoner. For Will having aided in that endeavor. And all his recovery would no doubt be in jeopardy as he was thrown back into the prison or killed. She sighed, frustrated and angry.

Thankfully, she could enter the house without seeing anyone, especially Mrs. Turner. It appeared her Confederate roommate was not downstairs either. Part of her wanted to know how his foot was, if he had walked more and if it was swollen from it—a thought that made her step falter, aggravated this man was trying to work his way under her skin. *Damn slaveholder!* Gathering her wits, she turned to head to the room, when there was a knock at the door behind her. Startled, she looked and discovered it was Will.

"Will, what are you doing here?" she said softly, allowing him in the door.

He looked nervous, even skittish. "I heard of your upcoming departure." He leaned a little closer, dropping his tone. "Waxler is inflamed, of course, but you, you deserve some time to rest. My concern, though, is our patient."

She bit her bottom lip and started to shift her weight, trying to keep her own pent up anger quiet so as not to raise the attention of Mrs. Turner or anyone else.

"That is a good question. I, too, was not expecting to take a holiday leave. I can hardly take him with me, as you know. Therefore, I must leave him in your hands."

"Oh, by heaven above, you can't!" Now Will started to pace, a frantic look on his face. "You are not the only one leaving. I requested leave. I must return home for a family affair. I can't drag an injured prisoner with me!"

Quickly, she motioned with her hands for him to lower his voice. Yet his denial of his responsibility lit her ire. "You can't leave him with me. First off, you know this isn't right. He is a prisoner, one that *you* freed for some unknown reason. You know it wasn't legal, despite whatever you claim, therefore he is your responsibility, not mine!"

"Ada, please," he begged.

"I told you, he's claimed to Mrs. Turner that he is my husband." She walked a few steps and pivoted back. "I wasn't in a position to call him a liar, as he sat down here, having tea with her while I was at the hospital!"

Will's brows rose with surprise. "He's recovered enough to walk. You are an angel, I do declare."

"Stop crowing. Yes, he's managed, in a shamble of his boot, to hobble his way with a cane. But that is beside the point. The main fact is," She stopped and glared at him. "I can't take him back to Pennsylvania with me. What if Richard is there?"

Will snapped his head around to face her. "Richard? That man is a scoundrel, Ada. Why do you continue to pine away for a vermin that is not worthy of your attention?"

She sighed.

"Because we love each other, Will."

"Poppy-cock! That man has no morals, I can assure you."

Her anger flared. "The rebel is your problem! One that you foisted on me and now, you think you can just leave him in my hands? I'll turn him in tomorrow, if needs be! He's the enemy, for Christ's sake! And a slave-owner!" That final title made her want to retch.

"Ada, please. I know you. You would not abandon a patient."

She growled. "He's not my patient." It came out as a snarl.

Will shook his head. "I know you too well. His wound was a challenge for you. Plus, you'd never leave a man to fester. That's not our job, to decide who lives and who dies."

"Dying wasn't his problem." She clenched her teeth.

"Ada..."

"No, he's your concern. You need to take him."

"And have my career ruined and be imprisoned for helping him escape?" He moved closer, his tone dropping. "Would you do that to me?"

Ada glared at him. Will had stood by her when every

other man wanted to throw her out of medical school. He was her supporter in the medical corps. But now, he was infuriating her. Obviously, he was taking advantage…. though, she knew his skills were not ready to handle this. Damn, he was so correct. She couldn't leave. "I still can't take him with me."

Will took her hands in his. "Please, take care of him till I can sort this out. It is very important to me to repay his family for what his did for mine. Take him to New York. To Sweet Briar. No one will be there, so it will be safe. I'll do my best to have a solution by the end of your leave."

Her insides twisted. Will's plead ate at her desire to rid herself of the man. Plus, Richard had not stated he was on any leave, so her probability of seeing him wasn't high.

"Sweet Briar is your retreat. How is it I can suddenly arrive and just assume your servants will heed my word that you said I could stay there?"

On that, Will withdrew an envelope from his coat pocket. "I had it written, in high hopes you'd accept. This will explain it to them."

Very slowly, she took the letter, never taking her gaze from him. "Your debt to me is growing large."

"Thank you." He kissed her forehead.

That undid the last of her civility. Like so much of his life, Will found himself in over his head, like medical school, and relied on her to save him. But his time, the complications outdid the good. Anger flared and she snapped. "Get out of here, before I scream."

His eyes widened in surprise, but she saw the thread in them that told her he knew what he'd done to her. Jamming his hat back on his head, he slid past her out the door.

With her head pounding, her heart thudded as the fire inside her escalated. It was the last that made her slam the door shut behind him, which she instantly regretted. So much for quiet, she thought. She shoved the letter into her reticule and stormed up the stairs. The next two weeks would be anything but restive, she knew. Instead, it'd be hell.

Francois smiled, relishing the moment as he stroked her hair. "You are beautiful."

La Joyce snorted, but her eyes sparkled. "And you, monsieur, have quite the mouth."

He winked at her. "And, as I recall, you enjoy that."

She laughed and rolled out of his arms, getting off the bed. As she padded across the room to the washstand, he watched, admiring her body. She was lithe with large hips, small waist and breasts that begged for his attention. He drank in her curves, accentuated by her ebony skin that glistened in the oil light. The slight bounce to her bosom and the hint of the apex of her thighs as she splashed her face, nearly drove him mad with desire. He always imagined her as his and his alone, which she wasn't, but....

Suddenly, the heat of her gaze drew his attention upward, to where he could see her staring at him through the burnished looking glass poised above the washstand. Her almond colored eyes, one of the most mesmerizing pair of orbs he'd ever seen, grabbed his attention.

"Darlin'," she cooed, grabbing her wrap off the chair and shrugging it on, hiding herself from his view. "As much as I enjoy your company, you need to be finding a woman for yourself."

"You, my dear La Joyce, are all I need." He pulled up and swung his feet over the edge of the bed. The moment he moved his right one over, pain streaked up his leg, starting in his heel.

La Joyce spun, a concerned frown etched across her brow. "Massa, whatever did you do?"

Fighting through the burning stab of his ankle, he managed to reply, "La Joyce, you don't have a master." He adjusted, trying to find the way to stop the rip in his inner foot, not sure what caused it.

She laughed deliciously. "Of course, mostly due to you ain't being one, but maybe you need to be, to be taken care of. Or maybe you need a wife to watch over you."

That comment struck a nerve inside him, one that irritated him, as if it was something he was avoiding. "Now, see here, missy."

He tried to rise, all intention to take her in his arms…

His eyes popped open at the sound of the door slam. It was dark in the room, the glow of the embers in the fireplace barely visible. Blinking hard, trying to focus, he sat up when a pain sliced into his foot. Grimacing, he berated himself for forgetting his injury. That almost made him laugh. As if he'd forgotten. His thinking was muddled.

The door propped open slowly and he discerned a cloaked form sliding in. Ada. She went straight to the pegs on the wall and hung her bonnet and cloak. She hadn't noticed him, so he took the time to drink her in, focusing on her and not his throbbing injury. She yanked a hairpin out of the coiled bun at the nape of her neck and a cascade of bronze locks fell down her back. In the minor glow from the embers, the strands shimmered.

Hunger slammed into him hard, snaking down to his manhood, which twitched at the mere thought. When she poured herself a glass of wine from the decanter on the bureau, his gaze was glued to her every movement. Her downing it, all at once, like a man would do, she dipped her head back making her mane loosen and it was so inviting.

The vision of her leaning back, the motion of her swallowing, made his mouth go dry. In fact, it distracted him so, he didn't catch himself from knocking over the cane that he had propped next to the bed. It crashed to the floor.

He leapt to try to catch it right as he saw her snap her head around in his direction. It stopped him in his tracks, halfway off the bed.

"Good evening," he drawled, trying to give her a half a grin.

She stood perfectly still, the glare she shot him was hot. Unsure what he'd done this time, he determined she was never going to like him. She saw him as the enemy, and from the snarl she gave him over slavery, she most likely fell into that abolitionist trap. Even now, he could see how her shoulders were locked, and the twitch in her jawline. She was ready to fight and this time, he had no clue as to why.

"Evening."

The reply to his salutation was cut short on purpose. Whatever had riled her didn't dissipate. She grabbed a carpetbag and started throwing clothes into it.

"Are we going somewhere?" The moment the question came out, he expected her to throw something at him and he braced.

Ada stopped her mad packing, her hand frozen over the bag's opening with a rolled pair of stockings clutched in her fingers. Inside her head, she still debated her line of action. Will had left her without much choice, unless she chose to dig herself out of this mess.

In that second, she decided. She would turn this bastard in to the authorities. The mere thought settled part of her nerves yet she couldn't look at him. If he wasn't so handsome, it'd be so much easier, she thought.

"*We* aren't going anywhere." She went back to packing.

Out of the corner of her eye, she saw him slowly slide off the mattress—a comfort she'd given to her 'husband', leaving her with the settee. Another wave of anger rolled through her. Slowly he stood, but she chose to ignore him.

Crash!

She spun around. The man was on the floor, spitting out curse words as he rolled in pain.

"What did you just do to yourself?" she asked, racing to his side.

"What the hell do you care? Damn!"

Ada bit her bottom lip, ignoring his cursing. She went to the table, got her medical bag, and placed it on the bedside table. Offering her hand, she said, "Come on. Let's get you off that floor."

He took her hand and she felt a tug, as if he wanted her to fall as well, but the pressure stopped immediately. She looked at him, a frown on her brow when she tried to pull him up, only to have him suddenly weigh like a horse she couldn't budge.

"Here," she handed him the cane that had fallen.

It took a minute for him to adjust his weight to the cane for her to help get him upright and back on the bed. She noticed he favored the wounded foot.

"Would you care to tell me what happened?"

This time, he only stared. *Rude Southerner!*

"I might, if you explain why you're planning on leaving me."

That caught her off guard. Refusing to show him her surprise, she went on with her exam as if he hadn't spoken. She pushed the drawer legging up. The injured ankle and heel were swollen, red and hot to the touch.

"Thought I told you to rest today, not go drilling." She gave him an attempted smile, prodding his military background, drowning her concern in her tone. If the wound was inflamed due to infection, she feared he might lose it. Amputation was never good in the first place, let alone this long after the initial shock. She cringed inwardly, knowing survival, especially at this point, dropped dramatically from the seventy percent chance of recovery if they'd done it right away. No, she was determined to give him a chance to keep the appendage, even if that meant keeping him with her longer than she'd hoped for.

His reply didn't return the favor. "I tried that, but it's dull to boring here. So I tested out walking on it again, though this time, without the boot. Found out that the whole foot is stiff, so when I tried to bend it, it burned."

Taking a linen cloth, she soaked it in the washbasin with water and draped it over a bottle near the window. "Hmmm. You may be trying a bit too much too soon." Grabbing the now cold linen strip, she returned to his ankle and wrapped it. The cold made him jump.

"Ouch! You trying to kill me?"

She laughed. "Now, we've done this before. It'll get the swelling down." She put the injured foot on a folded blanket to elevate it. "We'll try to slowly unstiffen it and keep it on the heel for a bit more."

"Hard to see how it'll 'unstiffen' when you freeze it," he growled.

That made her smile. "One thing at a time." She leaned back, her medical background working a mile a minute when the reality hit her in the gut. Will knew her too well. He was correct. This injury was a challenge and her with her undying need to help others, the one that drove her through medical school when women were barely permitted to breathe, the same drive that pushed her to help the Union army medical corps, despite their refusal to accept her as anything other than a nurse, now compelled her to see this patient recover. Again, her analytical mind went over the chain of events. He seemed so close. If her surgery on him worked, he'd shown her he'd possibly walk again.

Fury pounced again up her spine. Damn Will and damn his knowing her so well! Crossing her arms as she now started to pace, she realized she couldn't turn him in. Oh, how she wanted to scream and squash the inner thoughts that plotted out a course of action to get this soldier moving again.

It was the warmth of his gaze as he watched her traipse back and forth across the room that finally grabbed her attention. Inhaling deeply, she realized what she must do.

"As to the packing," she started. "We're leaving here. I'm on furlough for a fortnight. We will work on your rehabilitation, but not here."

His shoulders straightened and he sat upright more sternly. "I take it you mean to send me back to prison."

She frowned. "Where did you get that idea from? In reality, no, we are heading north, to New York."

There. She said it. It was done. She was doomed.

"Get hold of all the food you can...Cut haversacks from dead men. Steal them from infantrymen if you can. Let your aim be to secure food and food and still more food, and keep yours eyes open for tobacco...Fill your canteen at every stream we cross and wherever you get a chance elsewhere."

—Advice given to new Union privates during Grant's maneuvers against Lee, May 3, 1864.

Chapter 19

Next day

FRANCOIS HOBBLED AWKWARDLY ALONG THE train car. He'd be damned if he'd be stuck lying down any longer. A man had to prove he was in charge of his own being, but his heel claimed otherwise. It'd taken all night, with it elevated and wrapped tightly, for the swelling to decrease and for it to stop burning like a torch. Of course, he'd spent most of the night berating himself for pushing it so hard, but dammit, he was tired of being unable to fend for himself. Plus, his nurse, or doctor, whatever she was, had tired of him. Perhaps claiming she was his wife had been the straw that broke her gentility, but he had no choice. He understood women like Mrs. Turner. A lady living with a man who was not a relation, condemned her to being a whore, regardless of what she claimed.

Another step forward, him leaning on the brass handle of the cane supporting him, he stumbled into the seat with a heavy sigh.

"So how does it feel?"

He glanced across at his keeper. Ada took the seat catty-cornered from him. For this journey north, she'd donned different attire than what he normally saw her in. Since he'd known her, she'd worn dark dresses, no crinoline and no adornments, her mane pulled back and tight. But today, she wore a rose calico dress with the wide pagoda sleeves, sheer white under sleeves with her cage crinoline on. While her dark blond hair was pulled back, curled tendrils fought to remain free, framing her face in a golden hue. The straw bonnet, all decorated in rose ribbon and cream flowers screamed lady, as did the drop pearls that adorned her ears. Even her dark grey coat added to her aura. She was beautiful and it took his breath away.

She raised one of her brows at his lack of response. The elegance of that expression took him by surprise. This woman, who fought to help the wounded, often fighting against the wave of men trying to put her 'back in her place' like the home front, had a solid, determined look. This one across from him now was virtually a complete opposite in that she not only looked like a lady, her movements refined and sophisticated. It took him a moment to grasp they were the same woman.

"Better. Sore but manageable," he finally squeaked out.

"Good." She settled back in her seat, withdrew her fan from her reticule and stared out the window as she started to fan herself.

It was that moment he saw his reflection in the window and it wasn't good. His hair was long, that he'd realized, but not seeing himself in a looking glass, he didn't realize just how unruly it had become. A shadow from his whiskers darkened his face. He ran his fingers over his jawbone, feeling the stubble and inwardly snarled. He looked as if she'd woken him up and dragged him here, which, in some respects, was true, but the reality was, he was a patient who had fought infection and pain with no regard for his appearance. That almost made him laugh, because if nothing else, Francois Fontaine had always made himself look as immaculate as possible. And now? He shook his head.

"I need a razor," he announced, still eyeing his appearance.

Ada whipped her attention back to him. "I beg your pardon?"

"I look like white trash. No wonder you despise me," he drawled softly.

Her jawline twitched. "I don't despise you. I just disagree with your lifestyle."

"So for that, you let me look like a vagabond."

"How dare you! I, I," she stammered. "I don't have those tools in my reserve."

"You have a straight razor. I saw it. When we get there, I will have use of it."

Her lips contorted. "It's not made for your whiskers."

That made him laugh. "By God, woman, yes, it is. Granted, Southern whiskers might be stronger than any Yankee—"

"Hush." She glanced around. "We don't need you to start a battle here, on the train." She settled back, a smile hinting at her lips. "You are on a Yankee train, after all."

It was her smile that took his breath away, making her words more of a whisper. But it did sink in and he returned her grin, though his was a bit more chagrinned, and he sat back, dropping the hat she'd given him over his eyes.

He'd sleep. It was the only way to beat this battle with her. Though he hadn't lost. He'd have that razor and soon.

It was the longest train ride of her life. Ada had to keep from clenching her armrest as the miles slowly rolled by. First off, she'd hadn't dressed up in years, or so it seemed. She'd spent the last two years, barging her way into the army hospitals, adhering to their rules, which included mundane dresses. She wasn't sure she'd fit into her traveling clothes and was pleasantly pleased when she could cinch herself up fine. In fact, the waist on this dress was a tad too big.

The next obstacle had been to get him up and dressed and out the door successfully. His ankle swelling had dissipated, and she had to note how frigid wrappings were beneficial. Granted, most of the time, the army had no ice or cold water with Southern temperatures heating it too fast, but it was worth recording. With the three-inch straight piece of wood she'd pulled from the fireplace, she managed to get his injured foot into the boot, stabilize it with the wood and with ties, make a make-shift support with which, along with the use of the cane, he'd done very well.

Yet his remarks on his looks did strike home with her. He did look a mite ill-kempt. His analogy of white trash was perhaps a bit overdone, though she believed she could understand. Her straight razor was for medical aid, though she doubted his whiskers would ruin it, plus he could sharpen it on her leather strap for that, easier than she could. The hair, though, she mulled over. Perhaps a visit to the barber would be in order. It could be the best treatment as she was well aware that patients often improved if they felt better about themselves.

Her insides tightened. She recalled his looks when he'd arrived last month. He was handsome, even with the dirt from fighting all over him, mixed with the black streak across his jawline from the black powder. She'd seen that too many times, along with the blacked gums too. Add to that the weeks of tending to him, seeing him minus clothes. As a doctor, she'd trained herself to focus, but the memory of his trim, muscular figure now revisited her. For a planter, he was very much solid, his abdomen lined, along with his shoulders, arms and legs, with muscles, the type that formed from days of riding and maneuvering in the saddle. The recollection made her heart skip a beat and a fire burn inside her. She fanned herself harder, trying to push those thoughts away. She was spoken for, she reminded herself. But even memories of Richard were faint next to the image of Francois in her head.

Irritated, she wanted to be far away from him, only to find herself more like his private physician. A personal doctor to a slave-owner. Anger boiled deep, making her hands fist even though she stared out the window at the passing scenery. This needed to change. Two weeks. She'd have him walking and independent by then, or she'd turn him back over to the Federal authorities, her own reputation shredded.

It was that focus that drove her once they made it to New York City. She managed to get him up from slumber and moving, her inner self-arguing that sleep helped in his recovery and her rude awakening was uncalled for, but then, they had to exit, so she shushed the inner voice up. Hailing the first carriage, she directed it to Sweet Briar and prayed.

Francois had not been to New York in years, but it hadn't changed. Way too crowded, too many horses, too much smoke from the factories, the type that made breathing hard and seeing more difficult. When they'd made it off the train, the congestion made him gag and he'd almost suggested they get back on and ride it further north, to Albany or Rochester, but his lady-doctor walked ahead of him, hailing a carriage. That rubbed his dignity, for he was the gentleman and it was his duty to call do so, but then again, considering the circumstances, he couldn't complain. The sight of policemen along the busy street easily reminded him that he was a runaway rebel, one whose capture would easily propel a policeman's career forward.

He found if he kept a steady pace, slow but even, using the cane in stride with the injured foot, he could manage well. Not fast, but moving. She had a carriage waiting by the time he'd caught up. The driver didn't move off his box to assist him climbing into the vehicle, so Francois swallowed the cussword on his tongue, threw the cane into the carriage and used both hands to haul himself up. Ada leaned forward off the seat, a concerned frown on her face.

"Can I help?"

He looked up at her and bit back a chuckle. Could she help him? In her current mode of dress that would be difficult, though even in a nurse outfit, she'd never really been able to pull his weight up. Without the use of that leg, he didn't doubt he weighed twice his weight.

"No, I'm fine," he mumbled, hauling his body upward.

He sat across from her, and noticed as the carriage rolled, she wouldn't look at him. That annoyed him. The growing feeling that he was a nuisance to her stirred in his gut. Made the driving urge to get mobile again surge through him. He knew New York, he had means to get out of here and, as they passed more and more storefronts with glaring signs of enlisting for the Union and Federal flags, a coldness gripped him, the like he hadn't felt before. He'd gone to war to forget Emma. The cause was irrelevant to him. His broken heart drove him. But now, the alienation of these northerners was seeping into him and for the first time, he needed to get out of here and return to the sunny South.

The carriage continued, the lull of the steady pace making him sleepy. He snapped his eyes back open. Being in this state, in this condition, was not one that he should fall asleep in. Heaven only knew what she'd do then. Perhaps drop him at a local sheriff's office, as a prisoner of war? He glared out the windows, trying to ignore gazing in her direction. It was obvious to him she hadn't taken her eyes off the scenery, so he'd do the same. Besides, to watch her was making his skin itch. She was too pretty to be so immersed in a war that was bloody and full of sights no woman should ever be subjected to. Half of him wanted to save her from the torment, but a voice deep inside countered she wanted to be there, to help the wounded. He shifted in his seat, the odd feeling that he was one of those types she wanted to help, yet he knew his side disgusted her, putting him in a precarious spot.

Yes, he needed to find a way to maneuver better and leave her, to return to his people.

That wayward thought, of *his people*, made him chuckle. And as much as he tried to contain it, the merriment was audible, enough it caught her attention with a questionable glare. That made him laugh again.

"Do you ever laugh, my dear?"

Her lips pursed and she returned to looking out the window.

"Of course, I laugh."

"You do realize, in all the time I've know you, I've only seen you smile once. It's a very pretty smile. You should practice it more often."

This time, her brows inched high. "I'm a doctor. What I see most of the time is nothing to be jovial about."

"Oh, that, I don't deny, even from my own perspective. But, perhaps, it might lighten your heavy load and make us poor souls, so damaged, feel better."

She growled.

"Like now. We are here, in New York, and it is the holidays. Granted, I'm still mending, but maybe, a little lightheartedness might be the medicine to help a poor soul like me." When she didn't turn, he added, "Think about it."

The twitch in her jawline made him smile. He'd hit home. Good.

The carriage wheels slowed to a halt. With that, she jumped, adjusting her hat and coat.

"We are here."

He glanced out the window on her side. Here was a rather large brick mansion with a white-pillared front of a three-storied residence. Sweet Briar, as she called it, was anything but warm. The design and surroundings pointed toward money. This was where they were to be, to help him recover on her leave? Baffled, he grabbed his cane and hissed as the pain streaked up his leg.

How the hell was he ever to get out of here?

"I can't spare this man. He fights."
—Abraham Lincoln stated in reference to Grant.

Chapter 20

JAMES STOOD STOIC, HIS GAZE on the couple who'd just arrived at Sweet Briar. The girl he recognized, and it was helpful that he'd received the letter indicating her arrival. She appeared in good form, dressed in a neat travel gown, even if it was a bit dated—a notice only a man like himself, with managing a large wealthy estate, would notice. There were lines and shadows on her face that indicated a long, tiresome trip.

A limping man who followed her. He looked more like one of those useless men the butler found in the market square. Soldiers from the war sent home with injuries incapacitating them, mixed with the pickpockets and drunks that loitered the area. It took every ounce of years of service to his employer to keep his expression bland and unreadable when inside, James wanted to roll his eyes.

"Miss Lorrance, welcome to Sweet Briar." James motioned to the doorman to take her cloak and the man's coat.

She gave him a smile. "Thank you, James. How nice of you to remember me."

"Master Leonard notified me you'd be arriving, so we are prepared."

"Is Will here?"

"No, madam. He told me to let you know he'll arrive before the end of your stay."

She looked momentarily perturbed but inhaled, steeling her shoulders. James inwardly grinned. He'd always liked Miss Lorrance. He'd always felt she'd be a good match for Master Will…With a deep inner sigh, he threw that wayward thought aside.

"Did he tell you I'd be bringing a…" she paused. "A guest?"

James's gaze narrowed. Before he spoke, the man jumped right in.

"Perhaps in our hasty departure, he didn't include it." He gave the butler a look. "Francois Fontaine, a distant cousin, twice removed."

James bit back the snort. The slight southern drawl with a French curl would indeed make this individual distant to anyone the butler knew.

"Of course, sir," he acknowledged, then turned his attention back onto the girl. "Maid Katie will be at your disposal, Miss Lorrance. I'll have one of the footmen assigned to your *cousin*. Your rooms are on the second floor. They are ready for you and I'll have baths drawn. Supper will be in an hour, if that is convenient enough for you. I've no doubt your travels during this busy time have been tiresome. If you'd like me to send trays up, I'll be more than happy to do so."

"No, no thank you. I appreciate the gesture. We'll refresh and be in the dining room at the appointed time."

"Yes, madam." He motioned for the maid who stood at the stairs to take them up. And as they moved that way, James mentally washed his hands of them. Cousin indeed. Trouble was more like it. It wouldn't surprise him if the man wasn't really a Confederate…

Francois hobbled down the hall, behind Ada and the maid. He knew Ada was exhausted but, as was her character he decided, she'd want a formal dinner. Probably the first real meal they'd had in a long time, though he beat her on long time. The boarding house in Washington had meals but he was mostly confined to the room. Here, he'd have to manage the stairs as he was more determined than before to regain his ability to walk.

The first door they stopped before, the maid motioned to him.

"This is your room, sir."

Ada eyed him as he ambled past her. "You take your time. If you are not able to attend, I'll have a tray sent up."

He snorted. "And I'll do the same if you fail to arrive."

"Rather bold coming from you." Her tone was low but very sharp. She stopped herself, he'd bet, from saying 'secesh' at the end, which made him want to chuckle.

"Look, we're both beyond patience. Let's freshen up and I'll see you down there." He blew her a kiss and heard her hiss as he slipped into the room, taking a silent glee at her reaction. He knew he shouldn't bait her, after all she had helped him keep his foot from those butchers who'd cut it off, but something deep inside him couldn't help it.

The room was definitely a masculine room. Paneled walls, large four-poster bed with pineapples on the top, a decoration that made him smile, reminding him of home. The fire was burning and a metal tub sat in front of it. The servant who stood near came right up to him.

"My name is Bradley, sir. I'm here to assist you. Where,"

he looked past him. "I'm sure your baggage will be here shortly."

Francois laughed. "I believe there's a carpetbag. Nothing to worry yourself over."

"I beg your pardon, sir. I'll need to prepare your clothes for your stay."

Francois frowned. He knew he had another set of drawers and shirtsleeves with a pair of stockings. Ada had scrounged for another set of trousers for him and a shirt but he had only the waistcoat he'd worn for duty and his frock coat was replaced with some drab black piece she'd found in the hospital. It was ill-fitting but he wore it.

"Bradley," he started as he slowly climbed into the tub, using the servant's arm to steady himself. "I'll tell you what I do need, once I'm dressed for dinner."

"Yes, sir?"

"I need paper and a writing instrument." He sank into the hot water, letting the heat loosen the muscles that were stiff. The warm water felt miraculous on his injured foot. He sat, relishing in the concept of a true bath and then, when Bradley poured a bucketful of hot water to reheat what was here, it made him want to purr. It'd been months since he'd had a good soaking bath.

The bath also revealed one thing he knew for sure. While he wasn't ready to travel on his own yet, he could get better clothes. And that thought alone lifted his spirit immensely.

Ada sat at the table, running her fingertips on the table-top, her anger simmering. She'd refreshed herself and come to the dining room after hearing the doorway to her patient's room shut. He was next door to her. Will had probably arranged that, keeping patient close to doctor. Katie was a good maid and only slightly raised her brow when it hit her where she was taking Ada. The room had a door that adjoined the rooms. It was closed and locked, the key on Ada's side, but it was noticeable. Especially since the man on the other side now proclaimed they were cousins.

She'd been to this house many times as a child. When they pulled up the drive, it'd taken her breath away because she'd forgotten how huge it was and so ornate. Will's father was rich, making his fortune off lumber. As a child, she'd never paid much attention to the grandness, but now, it made her squirm. Her family was well-to-do, but never this wealthy. Of course, her father was a doctor, and not much money was made by physicians, a fact she'd learned all too well when she started her practice. The Union Army paid less for a nurse. She'd spent so long, living among the soldiers and spending any available funds for their care, she was poorer now.

Reaching for her wine glass, she saw the worn fray of her cuff and bit her bottom lip. The dress and its accessories were over two years old. She swallowed hard. Two weeks she had to survive through and it appeared she'd have to see about her wardrobe with funds she would be reluctant to spend.

"Apologies for my tardiness."

She glanced up and found her patient in the doorway. He stood, leaning heavily on the dark wooden cane, but looking cleaner and more debonair than earlier. The whiskers of earlier were gone, as well as the plaid shirt and dirty brown pants. Now, he'd donned a white shirt and cravat, his dark blue waistcoat and cleaner, more pristine black trousers. He came to supper in his shirtsleeves, but she'd not fault him for it. The fact that he made it down the staircase in his condition spoke volumes.

"Apologies accepted. You made it down here with ease, it appears. How do you feel?"

He snorted as he ambled to the table. "Outside of exhausted, my hunger drove me. As to the appendage." He collapsed in the chair. "It is a touch sore, but better than I expected, though the snail-pace I keep is rather discouraging."

She laughed. "The fact that you make it at all at this point is amazing."

A servant appeared, pouring Francois some wine and then setting their plates down. The silence between them during this drove her a bit mad, but there seemed no point in alerting the staff any more than necessary that one of their guests was a Southerner.

When the servant left, Ada leaned forward and whispered, "I appreciate you holding your accent, considering."

He frowned. "I wasn't aware I was doing so, though my ability to not be confined will probably help me keep it at bay as much as I can."

The southern drawl was light but the roll of his *r*'s, like the French, did catch her attention.

"Well," she started, her voice back to her normal level. "We are guests here, so please act accordingly."

He chewed on a bite, gazing at the walls, before he asked, "I assume you and the residents here are good friends? Or are you, by chance, engaged to this 'Master' Leonard?"

She nearly choked. "Engaged? Heavens no. I've known Will all his life, or a very long time. We went to medical school together."

"Ah, the doctor in the field. I saw you two cavorting." He sipped the wine. "That man is quite smitten with you."

"Smitten? No. We are just good friends. Now, he may

favor me, as I did help him through school. Some of the subjects were a bit dense in the text and such."

"Hmmmm."

"You should be pleased I know him. He argued for my skills to help you and your comrades, as Dr. Waxler holds little value of the captured men. Will convinced him to let me tend to you."

"I shall make it part of my agenda to thank him."

"No! I mean," she squirmed. She'd said too much. Searching to veer him off the topic, she did her best to switch topics. "As we are here and I have no other duties, we shall commence with a plan to get you more mobile."

He stared at her. "Exactly what I'd hoped for."

She grinned. Thrilled to get him off Will, Ada continued dinner, formulating in her mind their time at Sweet Briar. They had so little time, and Will had promised to find a solution to this man's future, she felt the least she could do was to make it so he could stand at his execution for being a secesh and owning slaves…

The rest of dinner ran smoothly, Francois decided. He'd gotten her to smile, which was a big accomplishment. The woman spent most of her time buried in patients, including him, and the concentration mixed with frustration made her so severe, he feared she'd develop wrinkles before she turned gray. Not that he knew her age, but he'd guess in her early twenties. So once the conversation switched from that other doctor, one she seemed most determined to protect, which escaped him, he made the subjects a little more light hearted, like where she was from. When she answered Pennsylvania, he was lost. When he came north, it was New

York. Rest of the North was uninteresting to him.

As they slowly ambled back to the stairs after dinner, he hated to admit it even to himself, but his damn foot hurt. It was an inner vice that tightened every time he tried to put his heel down. At this rate, he'd never walk the same again.

"Your ankle hurts?"

He stopped and gave her a look. "Yes, I believe I've pushed it too hard today."

Her lips tightened as she tapped her chin with a finger, deep in thought.

"We shall wrap it for sleep and tomorrow, try to find easier exercise for it. If you want to walk, again, that is."

He snorted. "Yes ma'am, I sure enough do."

She let out a disgusted sigh and that irked him, for any-time he talked and his southern accent drawled significantly, she tightened up. And that irritated him, for he knew she was dwelling on his status of being a Southern slave-owner. If there was one thing that he'd break her from it would be condemning him for his way of life.

"Well, come along." She started again and headed right for his room.

That, plus the sway of her hips, got his mind off the pain. One thing he did know was he didn't need a working ankle to make love…

She opened the door and went right to the washstand. She propped the window up, wedging a book to keep it open, making him cringe. He hated the cold wraps, despite they worked well on swelling.

"Sit here, please," she patted the mattress.

Every nerve inside him came alive. Fire ignited in his lower stomach, making his member twitch. It took every ounce of energy he had to refocus. It was quite clear she was in her medical persona and any hope of a good toss was not on her agenda. Putting the cane aside, he sat.

She frowned. "Really, Private, let's get those fancy clothes off you before you wrinkle them beyond repair."

"It's Corporal," he corrected. "And I like your bold tongue."

Her chin snapped back. "I beg your pardon?"

He sighed with a tone of disgust. "Never mind." He began to unbutton the trousers, but the mere suggestion had made him slightly hard. It wasn't easy getting out of them, unable to stand on one foot steady, and it grew more cumbersome since every moment his manhood begged to be at attention. The worst part was when she went to help, taking off his mangled boot and pulled at the cuff downward. Her actions were more methodical, like a male doctor would be, and that he found irksome. He'd never been blatantly ignored, no, actually treated indifferently, as if he was a piece of furniture, which ran a spike into his gut, killing his erection instantly.

Still bent before him, her head tilted downward, concentrating on his ankle, she lifted the foot and examined the limb.

"Interesting. It's not hot, nor is it very swollen. Does it hurt if I do this?" She turned the ball of his foot to one side.

A streak of pain shot up his ankle, mixed with his burning desire and anger, he bit out, "Yes."

"And this?" She twisted it the other way.

He bit his inner lip. To be so thrown aside still hurt somewhere deep, perhaps close to his heart, or his groin, the emotion refusing to settle. It made him realize that his foot wasn't throbbing that way. "Not as bad," he gritted out.

She hummed as she reached for the chilled cloth and placed it on his ankle.

"Ouch! That's cold!"

"Of course, it is. It's cold outside. Now, be a good boy and let it work its magic."

"I have other magic I'd rather see happen," he snapped, as the biting cold seared his skin, before he realized what he'd said. "Magic like all this be gone, and I'm home with a good leg."

On that, Ada laughed, her grin lighting up her face. *Damn, she's beautiful! That is, when she wasn't torturing him so.*

"You and every other soldier I've treated have had the same dream. It's my goal to see you able to do so." She pulled the now warming linen off his ankle and stood, returning it to the washstand.

"I suggest you sleep and tomorrow, we'll start seeing if we can't get you walking straight yet." She turned to walk toward the door.

Francois stood, a move driven by the power of her smile, he almost forgot his injury, until his heel lowered to the floor. He grinded his teeth, trying to drown the squelch in his throat before it escaped but it didn't matter. She whipped around.

"Whatever are you doing? I said good night."

Fisting his hands at his sides in an attempt to gain his strength, he muttered, "Go to sleep isn't a good night." He hobbled over to her, looking like a rogue—or more like a shambles in his drawers—as he took her arm. "The least I could do is walk you to the door."

She giggled again. "Now turning gallant on me? Please, I do not want you putting your progress back by such foolery."

"I'm fine," he promised.

They were at his door.

"Perhaps it would be wiser to let me out without my guardian in his drawers. I'd hate to have the maids tattle, or worse."

He'd like her to be the 'worse' but he nodded. Leaning on the doorknob, he opened it.

"Good night, my lady."

She gave him an odd look. Was it his Southern French drawl by chance? He couldn't guess as she paused before him. She was so close to him, and her smile had coaxed his body to harden again, so the feral need seemed to consume him when it came to her, an emotion he wasn't sure what to do with. Yet, it told his soul what to do and in response, he bent to give her a kiss.

She must've seen it coming, for she quickly turned her head so his lips touched her cheek.

"We are not acting husband and wife here," she reminded him.

"No, we are cousins," he replied.

She didn't bite. "We don't kiss, as cousins."

They hadn't really kissed anyway, he thought. "Awe, but we might be kissin' cousins." He gave her a wink and attempted to woo her with a smile.

He caught the twitch in her jaw and the widening of her eyes—both subtle moves but he saw them. But they were not how he hoped.

"Here in the North," she shot back sharply. "We are not. Good night, sir."

"Thank God! We have a country at last, to live for, to pray for, and if need be, to die for!"

—Former US Congressman Lucius Quintus Lamar of Mississippi, on the formation of the Confederate States of America, 1861

Chapter 21

FRANCOIS COULDN'T DECIDE IF SHE was a miracle worker or just a smiling torturer.

"Don't stop. You need to actually use it all the way or you'll soon be unable to walk."

He counted his breath, clamping his jaws shut. This was the start of the third day of this treatment and the agony building in every step, though he feared her prediction and that was what drove him.

After that attempt to get her to kiss him, he wasn't sure why he wanted her lips near his. She had set up a new torture here in the library. She'd looked so pleased, he recalled, putting two stuffed quilts on the floor, over the Oriental rug. Having him sit in the chair, she had him remove the now shoddy boots he'd been wearing and then she rubbed the injured foot, slowly loosening the tension that had built as he hobbled. A stress-point reached up into his calf and thigh the longer he walked, even with the cane.

She smiled at him as she massaged the sole of his foot. "We need to work this foot in an attempt to get it working again."

The kneading started to untangle his stiffness. "I could just sit here all day with you doing that."

She glanced up at him. There was ice in those eyes at his remark. "Yes, well, you might have had a chance with one of the slaves you held, but not with me." Abruptly, she stopped her hands and slowly stood. "Actually, what I need you to do is stand up and follow."

Her tone had returned to doctor on that last statement. Inwardly, he sighed. She'd be a tough one to handle if things were different but he'd never jumped to her conclusion when he thought he was complimenting her on her ministrations. He swore he'd never understand women.

Grabbing his cane, he hobbled behind her, still favoring the injured foot, but stopped at the edge of the flooring.

"I'm to walk on this soft blanket? With a cane?"

She laughed. It was an honest laugh and it sounded like a siren's call to him, luring his full attention. The sparkle in her eyes, the flush of her cheeks made her look so alive and no longer the bleak nurse he'd met in Virginia.

"No, no," she murmured, trying to regain a straight face, an attempt he hoped she'd fail at. "My thoughts were, you put your damaged foot on the cushions but keep the other on the hard floor. Start with the cane on the hard floor, so your whole weight isn't on the other, not until you get the feel of this."

He raised his brow.

And so, it began. Now, he could stand and manage without the cane. But two days of working the stiff foot on the cushion had been hard. Painful. It had exhausted him.

"So, I think you've made great progress," she decided from the sideline. "Today, let's try it without the blankets."

"With that surface, perhaps you'd like to be my support," he prompted. The arch of his foot and ankle remained sore and that was with him leaning on the cane.

Her gaze narrowed. "You need to bend that foot as you walk. Heel to toe. The cushion gave you a leeway from that.

Now, you need to do it. Look, I'll give you my hand at first, but the exercise is to make that foot work, otherwise, you'll be lame all your life."

He growled but took her hand. Setting his heel down on the hardwood, the muscles in his foot stretched and he clenched his teeth. Her suggesting he'd be no better than a lame horse—and he knew the future there wasn't good—drove him to push harder. As he took a step forward, he clenched his teeth when the foot bent. The muscles screamed it was too much, but he forced himself to ignore it. He'd be damned if he was shot dead due to lameness!

After five steps, she slipped her hand out of his grasp, leaving him freestanding. The freedom was uplifting, and he rejoiced, though it was still with trepidation that he took another step. Again, his foot was in agony. He gritted his teeth.

"How are we doing?"

Francois closed his eyes, French cusswords streaming through his mind, but he answered, "Good, I think. It still hard."

"And it will for a bit, I'd imagine. That wound was damaging and their abuse of you added more to it." She stepped closer, almost within grabbing distance, he thought. "That initially hit five or so weeks ago. The body takes time to heal."

He nodded, his tongue lost for fear he'd issue an epitaph of swear words at her. Five steps later, he was at the end of the rug and struggled to turn around, losing his balance and in a frantic motion to try to stop his falling, he reached for her right as she came closer to help. Yet despite his desperate attempt to not fall, he stumbled, dragging her down with him in a thud on the floor.

Ada should have seen this coming. All hope that her experiment on retraining his injured foot came to a crashing halt, literally, as he turned to retrace his steps but lost his balance and tumbled forward, with her in his path. In a desperate attempt to stop his fall, and hers as well, she grabbed his arms but his hands grasped hers instead. She lost her footing as he tilted her backward and then tumbled to the floor, with him halfway across her, crumbling her crinoline dress. The contact with the floor with this man on top of her took her breath away and she gulped, blinking furiously.

From that awkward position, they looked into each other's eyes. In that split second of time, she didn't see a patient, or a prisoner of war, but a man. Handsome, alluring and dangerous, the type that made her blood race through her veins, a tingle that she couldn't control. She should scream or struggle to push him away but a voice inside begged for him to hold her closer.

"Oh, ma chère, I'm so sorry," he mumbled, releasing her hands and trying to steady himself.

The entire situation was a fiasco, and Ada couldn't help but laugh. The doctor was pinned to the floor by the type of man she couldn't stand, but considering everything, it wasn't a surprise. She had pushed him to extend himself too fast, making her realize her plan to get him back in shape so she could rid herself of him had backfired marvelously.

He stopped halfway up, surprised. "I rather expected you'd demand I get off you immediately."

She snorted, inhaling now with a good breath. "No, I think I've pushed you too hard."

The door to the parlor swung wide open and James the butler stood, with another male servant with him. They raced into the room.

"Master Fontaine, Miss Lorrance, are you all right?" James asked as he and the other servant lifted Francois upright before he offered her his hand.

"Truly, we are fine, James. Thank you, though, for coming so quickly." He was there in a flash, making her wonder if the servant hadn't been watching through the doorway lock. She gave Francois a look, scanning him from head to toe for injuries.

"Are you hurt?"

The Frenchman smiled. "You, dear lady, are a saint. I'm no worse for wear, but you, are you all right?"

She stood, stretched her fingers and shifted on her feet, testing herself. "Thank you, I feel fine. Perhaps a little shaken, but overall, fine."

"What a relief, ma'am. A man his size could easily have hurt you," James inserted, handing her the shawl that had fallen off her shoulders. "I'll have Mrs. Mooney prepare tea to revive you."

Tea. She wanted to laugh. Only polite society would think of tea and, no doubt, biscuits, to 'revive' someone. Hardly medicine, she thought, though perhaps, as she found her throat now dry, not a bad idea. "That would be lovely, James."

As the butler left to get the tea, she turned toward Francois and found him grinning. "What has you so amused?"

"In my part of the country, ladies would be swooning, with their mothers demanding smelling salts and a priest for nuptials for having so 'invaded' their daughters. You? You appear to brush off such conformities and worry how I am."

"I am a doctor, and you are my patient. My goal is to have you recover, not reprimand you for falling during therapy to restore your abilities to walk." She wrapped the shawl around her tightly, the flush that spread all over her from his warm smile made her uncomfortable in a way she couldn't explain.

With a heavy sigh, he bent to pick up his worn-out boots and hobbled to the chair to sit. She watched him put the shoes back on and inwardly grimaced. Since they'd been hacked down to accommodate the injured foot, they barely worked as a shoe. And frankly, she determined, he'd need better support, especially when she saw the seam ripping apart on the sole.

James reappeared, followed by a maid carrying a tea tray. In the butler's hands was a pair of brogans.

"Miss Ada, perhaps Master Leonard's shoes might aide you at this time."

The man was a good servant.

"Thank you, James. What an excellent suggestion." She took the shoes to Francois. "Perhaps this will help. They are not falling apart."

Francois frowned. He hadn't noticed the commotion of the servants. If nothing else, he'd been fumbling at putting on his own shoes and not doing well at it, as his blood raced hot from the contact with her on the floor. A myriad of emotions swirled in his head, ranging from angry at his inability to walk to feeling like a clumsy oaf to a man wanting to kiss her. So now, he stared dumbly at the pair of shoes she handed to him, trying to rationalize his thinking and failing.

"Yes, perhaps." He reached for them but she'd already

dropped to her knees, the skirt pooling around her on the floor as she gently removed the torn pair from his feet.

"It doesn't appear to be swollen from the fall, which is good." She guided the foot in and loosely tied the lacing. "I think that is all of the training we shall do today."

"Good. It doesn't feel too bad, just tired." He offered his hand to help her back up as she struggled to gather her skirts to find her footing.

"Thank you." She straightened her skirts once upright.

Francois smiled. But she didn't return one to him. If nothing else, she appeared agitated or worse. Her tension was something he couldn't pinpoint. He was recovering but not near perfect. Perhaps it was her trying to hide him that drove her mad. Or was it something else?

She said nothing during their lunch. He was too worn out to push the conversation. Besides, what would they talk about? With her attitude and her strong dislike of his southern heritage, that left little on which they could converse. Or maybe, he didn't care at the moment. He ignored the throb in his foot. These shoes were better for his coordination, so he hoped his recovery might be smoother.

Yet it was definitely the entire issue of him recovering that stuck in the mud in his head. He had a private physician as it were, one that wanted him well for her own agenda, but the tension between them was drawing tight. The lines were drawn between attraction, for he knew she felt it too, as well as the sectionalism that had caused this war. She could turn him in to the authorities in a heartbeat, or help him walk again. How could he bridge that gap?

Watching her over the wineglass at lunch, he decided to make an attempt, even if it'd cost him in the long run.

"Miss Ada, perhaps fresh air would do us good."

She stared at him hard. "Fresh air? You mean, outside?

You do realize it's winter and cold, right?"

He laughed. "Yes, I can tell the chill in the air."

"And we're in New York, a truly Yankee state? Not the area for your type."

Her tone turned condescending on that and it irked him. He wanted to see her smile, not snarl at him. "I'm well aware where we are. It might surprise you, but I've been to New York on several occasions. Granted, not generally during the winter, but still." He crooked his lips upward, in an attempt to lighten the atmosphere. "I just was thinking it might be nice to step out in the breeze, as it were, and with a longer space, stretch my legs some. Being confined makes exercising it sore."

That made her giggle. "You realize, that makes no sense."

He shrugged. "Ole Doc Williams used to urge us young'uns to go out and stretch our limbs, when the growing pains hit. Mama encouraged it. I think it helped, in its own way."

Shaking her head in disbelief, she gave him a glowing smile that was like a gold Spanish coin. "All right. Let's get our coats and do so."

With more gusto then he thought he had, Francois took her hand, devouring her feminine charms like a dying man. Only vaguely did the ghost of a Southern belle seem to whisper to him…

"From this time on till the end of the war, a soldier was simply a machine, a conscript...All our pride and valor had gone, and we were sick of war and cursed the Southern Confederacy."

—Sam Watkins, Maury Grays, 1st Tennessee Regiment, CSA, on extended enlistments, requiring all 'able-bodied white men, 18-25 years old, to serve for 3 years', summer 1862

Chapter 22

THE MAN PUZZLED HER.

Ada braced as another blast of cold rushed over her as they ambled down the sidewalk in New York. Her woolen cloak was heavy, the mink muff warm, almost toasty with her leather gloves on, but her silk lined bonnet and cotton day dress were no match for winter. Thankfully, she had her woolen undergarments on, or she'd be an icicle. How had she been convinced to take a stroll?

Out of the corner of her eye, her reason walked next to her. Francois had made the suggestion, and since he'd seemed so adamant about it, she didn't want to discourage him. Her own medical practice had taught her that patients who pushed themselves often made a faster recovery than those who succumbed to their handicaps and embraced a life of inertia.

Frankly, she was surprised how well he was doing. His

cheeks, though gaunt from lack of food thanks to the war and imprisonment, were flush and gave him a glow. Will's wool overcoat engulfed him, yet he sported it well. He stood tall, shoulders straight, even though he used a cane, rather fashionably, too, to walk. It was as if he had adapted to the walking stick as if it were an accessory. Even now, on the wooden sidewalk, he guided her with his free hand on her elbow with only his body between her and the street.

"I insist that you walk on my left," he'd stated when they exited the carriage.

She frowned. "This is just a short jaunt outside for fresh air. Not a societal affair."

He laughed. "While that may be correct, it is nigh mid-afternoon. You are well aware, that eyes will be on those walking the fashionable district at this time. Tongues will wag if I was not the gentleman and stood as the brace between you and the wild beasts and their wheeled-contraptions kicking up mud and whatever else."

She giggled. "Beasts, you say? All right. I will not insult your gentlemanly task." She moved inside his left, but whispered in his ear, "If you over do this, please let me know. I will not have you hurt yourself over some farce of worrying about 'wagging tongues.'"

"Of course, my lady." He tipped his felt hat in her direction.

That had been virtually an hour ago. The cold was burrowing in, past the layers she wore and she'd bet he was miserable, too, for it wasn't just his face that was thin. That lack of food had slimmed him and while they'd had two days of good food at Sweet Briar, it'd take more to fill him out. She gave him a glance as they walked and saw not only determination etched in his face but also amusement. He was enjoying this. To a Southerner, a man not accustomed to the cold of the north, this was bitter cold. Then, the skies began spitting snow at them.

Francois looked upward, his brows furrowing, his lids squinting as the flakes struck his face. He stuck his tongue out, as if licking them from the sky and that made her laugh.

He grinned at her. It was a contagious grin, and one that caught her full attention. His dark hair, even combed under the borrowed hat, gleamed. His blue eyes sparkled and the shade of whiskers that he'd missed shaving gave him a dandy appearance. The mischief that lurked behind his sapphire gaze should make her watchful, but instead, it drew her closer. This man was dangerous yet she couldn't pull herself away.

"What is so funny?"

"You can't catch snowflakes."

"I wasn't trying to catch them but to taste them. They're a rare occurrence where I come from."

That intrigued her more than she liked. "It snows in the South?"

"It can, during a hard freeze, which I only recall less than a handful of times." He shrugged. "They never stick and what little we have melts fast."

"They're plenty where I hail from. Pennsylvania can be covered for weeks with the stuff."

He hummed. The noise held her too close, she decided, and turned to look in the storefronts near them.

"Christmas is almost here." She eyed the ribbon bows on the dress hanging in the dressmaker's shop. Christmas. Balls and soirees galore sprung up from what she could see in the morning post and the stack of invitations that filled Will's front table in the foyer. She bit back a sigh of envy.

"Yes. Do you hear the carolers?"

She turned back to see him but said nothing, straining her ears for holiday music. The sounds echoed softly and she found the handful of singers just down the street, near the train station.

"Ah, yes. Very nice."

Francois nodded. It was then she caught the shiver he tried to hide except his grip on her arm tightened along with the tremble she saw in his jawline.

"Perhaps we've been out too long," she decided, determined to turn them around but he stopped her.

"Let's walk in here and warm up." He nodded toward the dressmaker's shop.

Reluctantly, she agreed. They'd warm up and then head back. She didn't want him to come down sick. He needed to recover and Will had to retrieve him, though she buried the wayward thought that it was nice to be so escorted…

Yes, it was cold. Francois swore to himself that the Yankees could have it, for he'd stay in his warm winter state any day. The chill had managed to work its way through the heavy winter overcoat he wore, and despite the work it took to walk and keep balanced while escorting a lady, he was freezing.

He was thrilled to escape the confines of the house. Ever since his capture, he'd discovered being bound in a hospital or prison made him feel way too confined with no escape. Hospital from his injury and prison, well, it was confinement. As to his nurse, or doctor as it were, he grew more and more aware of her chomping at the bit to break free herself. What she wanted in the long run, he couldn't guess, except a husband, her own home and children, like most ladies. Then again, most ladies he knew had no formal medical training like her, so his assumption of throwing her into the lot with the rest was probably wrong.

As he eyed the stores they passed, he noticed several things. Mostly that Ada was a beautiful lady, but kept her beauty locked up in that tight bun, stark color dresses and no jewelry. Here, where she wasn't under a military rule, she dressed more like a lady and he found that appealing, even though it wasn't easy for her. The dress she wore, and it was the one she wore two days ago, looked like dresses he'd seen before the war and it showed mending. Apparently, she only had two dresses. Her hair was still pulled back, though now the bun was a mess of braids wound up in the back. She wore no earbobs, though he swore he could see holes in her lobes for them. All in all, she looked presentable, but he'd love to see her truly attired in the current styles, so the dressmaker's shop caught his attention.

The bell above the door rang when they entered. The shop was large, with bolts of material on one side of the room, stacked on tables, with the other half filled with chairs, dressing screens and small tables where pastries sat and tea cups waited. But mostly important—the building was warm, heated with a warming stove placed near the center.

He went to warm his hands and noticed Ada, rubbing hers together, had floated over to the rack of silks. Given any other time, he'd order her a dress or two to have made. A time before the war, when he had thrown all away, simply to escape his heart.

"Good afternoon."

He glanced up and found the proprietress standing nearby, a grin on her face. She wasn't a young woman, years of experience etched into her face. But her eyes were warm and welcoming, a sight he hadn't experienced much since joining the fight.

"Bonjour, madam." He smiled. "Pardon our interruption of your day, but the cold drove us to seek any warm haven."

The woman nodded. "Entirely understandable. Welcome to Madame Florissant's Boutique. Your accent, 'tis francais, n'est pas?"

He snorted. "Oui, merci beaucoup."

"We have little of that here, now that the war is continued." She sighed. Searching the table of accessories, she pulled a gray and navy plaid wool scarf and looped it over his head. "For the cold, monsieur."

"Ah, merci, but I fail to have anything to pay you with." The army prison had taken anything he had, failing to return it on his departure, though, that was an unplanned journey. Yet, it still irritated him.

"It is of little concern. I'd like to give it to you, for the cold, of course."

He nodded. The North wasn't so cold in nature, he decided. His gaze returned to Ada. She milled through the leather gloves, her fingertips skimming across the tops of them. Again, he noticed the outfit she wore, along with the lines on her face. He wondered what she was thinking, for her jawline was rigid, probably from gritting her teeth, he decided. All around her were silks and laces and ribbons.

"Madame Florissant, may I have a word with you?"

Ada's nerves were on edge. Shops like this only reminded her of what her decision, to be a doctor and to help the Union Army, had made her give up. The Army needed any trained doctors it could find. The fact she was a woman, though, kept her away from actually doctoring the soldiers, except…

She shook her head. No point on dwelling on what was done.

The gloves displayed on the table were lovely, but not useful in a hospital, nor on the warfront. However, the stack of men's leather gloves sitting to the right, grabbed her attention. Her patient had bundled for the weather, thanks to Leonard's butler who'd equipped the man in his employer's spare coat. It made Ada want to giggle, that Leonard had clothed the Southerner, but she stifled the noise edging up her throat. The wool coat was sorely needed, as was the hat stuck on his head. However, he lacked gloves. His hands looked rather chaffed when she gazed at them, and nothing could make one colder than to lack a hat and gloves. So, while he conversed with the owner, she sneaked a pair of gloves, eying them on size, guessing they'd fit, and nodded to the young attendant that stood in the shadows. Slipping her the money for them, she pushed her purchase into her coat pocket and smiled.

It was then she noticed he was looking straight at her. She flattened her skirt, a nervous habit she'd picked up somewhere. The need to escape the finery made her miss Francois, who stood in her exit route. She ran right into him.

"I take it, my lady, you are warmed enough to continue?"

She nodded, her tongue in her throat. Why did this man, the enemy, make her heart skip a beat?

As they walked out of the shop, a loud commotion across the street flared up. Ada narrowed her gaze to find the source and there it was, plain as day. A marching group of freemen, beating a makeshift drum and chanting to set the slaves free. The scene excited her, for she longed for abolition, until the man politely escorting her, the one who held her elbow, tensed.

"This happen often?" he queried.

She cleared her throat. "A little more, since the war started, I'd gather."

He growled. "Well, ain't a sight I'd see down home."

That made her snort. "No, I'd bet not."

"You do realize, slavery is a necessary evil, right?"

"No, I don't. We get along just fine up here, with no men in chains and whips in our belts," she argued.

His eyes swept over her, as he shook his head. "I'd like to see that, you with a whip and all." He sighed deeply. "We know it's not any better than holding an alligator by the tail, and if you all in the North had a more practical solution, we'd be thrilled to hear it. But invading our states, our land, isn't the method to use."

Silence filled the air for another block as she toyed with an idea.

"Would you like to attend a lecture on the suggestions you call for?"

He frowned. "You want me to go to one of the abolitionist affairs? I might be roasted alive there."

"We'd sit in the back, where it's less crowded and quiet."

He didn't reply and she walked, hope filling her. No answer gave the possibility he might say yes, eventually. If she could bring him into the abolition gathering, she'd won half the battle of converting him to the abolition camp. She held her breath when he finally answered.

"While overall, I have no burning desire to see my homeland accused of dastardly affairs, I also realize I do owe you for my life, for my leg still working and for that reason alone, I will accompany you."

A thrill raced down her spine and she wanted to jump, but doing so walking downtown on a busy street in New York was not advised. Instead, she smiled broadly and squeezed his frigid hand. The icy skin reminded her of her purchase and slowly, she pulled the gloves out of her pocket.

"Here, try these." She pushed them into his hand.

He stared at them, as if confused, but he slowly unclenched his hands and slid them on, every inch slow and the pain screamed across his face until they were ensconced in the leather.

"Thank you," he murmured, his cheeks flushing.

"You needed a pair." She gave him a grin but saw how he leaned on the cane much more. "Come, we need to get you back and rested."

"Yes, ma'am."

As they returned to the house, her heart was aflutter and she buried her wayward thoughts, ones that pushed Richard aside as a new face began to form. *Francois.*

America will never be destroyed from the outside. If we falter and lose our freedoms, it will be because we destroyed ourselves.

—Abraham Lincoln

Chapter 23

THE MERE SUGGESTION OF ACCOMPANYING her anywhere intrigued Francois. It kindled a warmth that seeped into him when he was in her presence. Almost enough to bury his heart's pain, and it thrilled him as well as made him leery. Of course, the mere thought of going to an abolitionist rally chilled that warmth, though curiosity probably would win.

The gift of the gloves surprised him. Like a sly fox, her consideration of him truly amazed him. She was a woman of many facets. It was now making him realize she might have more secrets about her and that got his attention.

But at the moment, his body screamed 'stop' and he managed to get to a chair before he collapsed on the floor, despite the cane's help.

Her lyrical laughter filled the air. "Well done. I was about to suggest we stop for tea."

He frowned with his gaze silted as he drank in her glow. As a doctor, she radiated. How had the Union Army resigned her to drudgery, he wondered? Though, now, he'd give anything just to sit and not move.

"I'd hoped for more than tea, Doctor," he argued, her title taking on a French flare as his native tongue slipped out.

"Alas, I fear not."

The door to the study opened, and James followed the maid who brought the tea tray.

"Miss Lorrance." The butler handed her a tray of envelopes and with a schooled look of surprise at the stack, Ada took them, pulling one out immediately.

"You were not expecting love letters here?"

She stared at the first letter until his words sank in. "Hardly." But she stopped, not moving, as if the letter was poisonous.

"Bad news?"

She glanced up, her emotions disappearing under the mask he'd seen her wear in the hospital. Her jaw tightened, anger fighting to surface, because he thought he had a moment to see Ada as a woman, a lady, not just a doctor with a jovial bedside manner.

The professional eyes bore into his as she countered. "How is your ankle doing? We've put it through quite a test today."

Before he could answer, she moved closer, bending down to the floor near the injured foot, raising the trouser hemline for a quick inspection.

"It's throbbing a bit, though not as badly as it has before."

"Mmmmm," she hummed, her focus on his foot. He bit back the pain as she moved it to the side, yet the reality was it didn't hurt too much after the initial adjustment, which amazed him.

"I don't see much swelling. But you're sure you're all right?"

"Tired. Not bad too much."

She smiled. "Perhaps it's healing well."

"You sound surprised."

She shrugged. "It was a small, almost hidden break, in an area that we constantly use. It was a surgery that they don't teach us."

Francois looked at her, taking in a new view of her. This woman had broken the common societal guidelines and chose helping others instead of marriage, children and running a house. And with that desire, she had saved him.

"Thank you."

Quickly she looked up, a puzzled look on her face. "For what?"

"For saving my foot. If you'll recall, that doctor wanted my foot amputated." He shuddered at the memory.

She frowned. "Yes, well, as I have said, he wouldn't have anything done, with you being the enemy. Wasn't right to have you and your men left untreated."

He grinned. "Merci beaucoup."

Her lips pursed as if annoyed, but quickly that dissolved into a small smile. "Thank you."

She stood and went to her seat, but not before he caught a glimpse at the mail. He couldn't decipher most of it, but he didn't see anything other than the corner of one that was stamped official by the manner it was written on the return. The one she reacted to was left open, with sparse words, though he thought he could see it signed by some officer. And the third piece she hadn't opened but he recognized the name on it. From a Miss Reginald Prescott – *Amelia.* The memories flooded back to him. Amelia Prescott had been the young northern lady both he and Jack had favored, even fought for her attention, summers long ago. It made a warmth race through him.

And now? Was she married? Or a spinster? His mind

spun at the mere suggestion lovely Amelia remained unattached. Glancing back, he estimated by the size of the letter, he'd bet the contents.

"So, will you remain true to your word, and come witness an abolitionist rally?"

Francois snorted. "To submit to such enlightenment, I barter a trade. I will go with you to your event if you will attend the Prescott Christmas Ball with me."

Ada gasped.

She sat, her mouth agape, which she quickly realized was most unladylike—she could hear her mother's admonishment—so she shut her mouth, her thoughts still replaying what he'd just said. A ball. What would a lady doctor do at a ball?

"Miss Lorrance, you have a visitor," James announced, right as he was pushed aside by an entourage of women.

Ada remained speechless as the modiste, Madame Florissant, with two of her young helpers, barged into the room. The dressmaker, with a flair, acted as if she was the queen. In the girls' arms were sewing supplies and material.

"Yes, oui, mam'selle and monsieur. I have the outfit commissioned near completion and require final fitting for any adjustments, though," she paused with a smile. "My work never requires any."

Ada frowned. "What commission were you awarded?" She hadn't requested one, neither had Will from afar she was sure, so what was she talking about?

"It is of no matter. Please stand up."

With a frown, Ada stood. The two girls leaped, gathering around her and working to get the dress on her for fitting. Vaguely, she noticed the room had cleared of all but the modiste and her underlings. Francois had slipped out. It stunned her he had done so.

The silk dress was stunning, she had to admit. The fabric had stripes of brown, ivory, and gross-grained gold with a shadow of dark gray. The skirt rustled as she was turned and the sound mesmerized her. In no time, she was fitted in two bodices and the skirt, with pins flashing and the modiste furiously remarking and writing as they toiled. Ada couldn't help but compare herself to a rag doll with the little girl who owned her changing her clothes. That almost made her giggle and one did escape.

"Apologies." She swallowed. "But who, Madame Florissant, ordered this?"

The French woman snorted. "Your husband, of course." Then she continued in a trail of words Ada couldn't understand as reality kicked her in the gut. That prisoner posed as her husband to get this made? Who did he think he was? And now she'd have to pay for this?

Oh, she'd make him pay for this! In more ways than just money...

Grandview Hall

The crowd was more than Francois could imagine. As they filed through the double doors, into the main auditorium, he managed his way best he could with the cane and his lopsided walk. Ada was at his side, guiding him through to the side stairs so they could view the event from above, which he was grateful for, because his skin crawled as more people poured in, all to hear about the evils of the peculiar institution, the polite phrase for slavery.

Constantly, he asked himself why he'd agreed to this. The

only answer he had was a flimsy one at that. To get out of that prison of a house and breathe, plus to be at her side. It was the last excuse that now made him almost trip on the stairs, because she was one of these people and therefore viewed him as evil, being Southern and a slave-owner. He shook his head.

"Are you all right?"

"Yes, just misjudged the step." He'd have to watch himself more closely. An accident here might be more deadly for him than a battlefield.

"We are just a few feet away. I think this will give us a better view."

He wanted to laugh. As if he wanted to see this. He glanced at her and noticed she wasn't wearing the new dress.

"You did not like Madame's creation?"

He caught her swallowing hard.

"No, it isn't that." She struggled. He could see it in her eyes. "But I didn't consider this the place to wear such a fine piece."

He nodded. "Entirely understandable." His own attire, pieced together by the butler from the owner's wardrobe, was somewhat underrated, but to him, fit an abolitionist yelling match quite well.

They took their seats near the front balcony. She smiled warmly, as if she'd caught the cat who drank from the pitcher of milk, and though perhaps she had in luring him here, he drank in her grin as if it was dessert for a starving man.

A banging on the podium below brought the roar of the audience to a lull and attention on the man behind the stand. He was a tall white man, dressed in his finest. His face had the look of a politician, to Francois's opinion. As he addressed the crowd, Francois watched the people sitting behind him on the stage. There was a stern-faced woman in a fancy dress, two other white men looking so severe and a black man, with graying hair that was a bit out of control, looking out of place to Francois as he was dressed in fine clothes. Now Francois wasn't naïve to freedmen, but for one to be dressed so well, outside of New Orleans, surprised him.

"Ladies and gentlemen, I welcome you here tonight, to listen to a profound orator, a true witness to the evil 'peculiar institution' running rampant in the South..." the leader of the event started.

Francois narrowed his gaze. The slanderous tone of this man, condemning all in the South for slavery, rubbed him wrong. He worked hard to conceal the anger that started to burn in his gut, for he'd bet his last Confederate dollar, Miss Ada had brought him here to irritate him. Or, perhaps, to see the 'error' in his ways, but considering how this was turning, he doubted it.

The lecturer came to the podium as the audience clapped, including Ada. Francois moved his cane to the front of him, letting the sound of the tip on the wooden floor be his only contribution.

"To my fellow enthusiasts, I humbly rise, to give witness to my ordeal while residing in Alabama not too long ago..." His cadence was good, the words well spoken. Yet to Francois, the irritation grew stronger. *No slave spoke that profoundly! Except for LaJoyce and Uncle Jonathan and*...he cut the thought immediately. He refused to believe this charlatan.

The crowd, though, adored him. He recalled being cussed at, dragged by chain to the fields, under watchful eyes while working with an armed overseer, being beaten for insolence, for running away and returning, being marked as a thief for having run and that stain was the 'x' on his right cheek, and how he and his fellow slaves were starved. As the accusations grew, Francois tightened. The runaway told them everything this audience wanted to hear and with every second counting, as a Southerner, his safety was declining rapidly. He gripped the cane handle tightly, considering it might become his only weapon against a mob if they knew who he was.

Ada cheered with the rest, which dug at his nerves, except her tone lightened as the lecture continued. Perhaps she'd discovered he wasn't joining her, or maybe she worried that being with him, she too could be pummeled because of who he was.

Finally, the crowd gasped and applauded, standing as the orator bowed. Francois's gaze narrowed, deciding the man was partially what he claimed to be, though the rest was theatrics. And it was that magic these people devoured. This magic sent them invading his homeland. Finally, the atrocities brought by this made his anger roar in contempt.

"Now," she started her tone low. "See how bad it is?"

He inhaled, trying to calm frayed nerves. She could turn him in and they'd hang him right away. What was he to say?

Ada watched. The rally had been moving, to her at least, but the heat of tension radiated off him like a fire. His knuckles were white from where he gripped the cane. As the rest of the hall exploded with excitement, she realized she'd maybe gone too far bringing him here. He was her patient and his health should be her main concern, but she let her hatred of slaveholders rule the day. How could she gracefully get them out of there?

He turned to face her, a grin on his face and those sparkling blue eyes alive with fire.

"It appears his life has been horrific. Some households are run poorly." He shrugged. "Like some of the factories up here and the Irish."

That comparison stabbed her. "The Irish? They are papists!"

"I'm Catholic," he replied. "Do you think I'm a papist too?"

"You know what I mean. That religion is ruled by a priest in another country."

He laughed. "And just like this runaway's tale, you'll sweep all slave-owners to being like this?"

Again, he twisted the argument. "You know as well as I that owning another, because of his skin color, is wrong!"

His brows rose as he gave her a contemplative look. "Miss Lorrance. Doctor. There are lousy slave owners. As to their skin color and being a slave, I'll leave that to the scholars and clergy to argue. But," he leaned forward. "No bondsman is so badly treated at my family's home. Slaves are an investment and too expensive to damage."

"You can't convince me of that!" Of course, he'd say that, she decided. But how could he prove that?

He raised his chin as he offered her his arm. "I have attended your event, listened to the lecturer and now understand your position. I believe you now owe me in return."

He was just going to throw this off, as if it meant nothing? She fumed. "We are fighting to gain their freedom! How can you just move forward and expect me to do the same?"

"Because, if we don't and we continue this discussion,

others might realize that I am a Southerner and you are harboring a runaway Confederate. And that, my darling Ada, would do neither of us any good. Now, take my arm and let us leave, peacefully."

Stunned at his apt appraisal and the sudden pit in her stomach when she knew he was right, she grabbed her shawl.

"Well, thank you for coming with me," she murmured, attempting to make amends since they were residing in the same house.

"It was an interesting show, one I will contemplate more on. There is still so much more you do not understand. Because my type do exist, the North makes money off our peculiar institution. It funds this country. Cotton is the largest export, prior to hostilities. My family grows sugar, another good selling commodity. If we free the slaves, who will work those fields? You? Hardly. The Irish? Doubtfully. Then who? Because the money made is notable. Consider that in your judgment."

Totally breathless, she took his arm. If what he said was true, what would this country do?

Thankfully, he guided her out as quickly as he could with his halting walk, without being stopped. Her hope to make him see his wrongs now made her wonder how they could solve this issue and free the coloreds. Otherwise, this war would go on forever.

"No wonder we cannot find or see a reb until we get right upon them. Swampy, hilly, bushes thick as dog hair, grape vines, rotten logs and fallen trees, make up this pretty picture. A fine place to fight in surely: a perfect quagmire."

—Dr. David Holt, 121st New York
Battle of the Wilderness

Chapter 24

THE CARRIAGE RIDE BACK TO the house was deathly quiet. Ada sat still, her back perfectly straight, her cloak pulled tight and her vision focused on the city streets they rode down. Out of the corner of her eye, she saw Francois adjusting his seat, moving the injured leg slightly, as if trying to find a better position. She should worry about the discomfort he might have incurred in their hasty exit, yet it was their departure out of the rally that still got her irritated, deadening her concerns.

What really irritated her was how he'd managed to throw back at her as quick as her arguing against his old life in the slave owning South. Frankly, she hadn't cared about their absence of workers when the slaves were emancipated. It hadn't mattered, but since he brought the subject up, she was at a loss to say anything. The obvious, which she could clearly see now, was to hire the newly freed slaves, for the freemen would need jobs, but already, she could hear the rebuttal from men like their speaker, who'd have nothing to do with the South ever again.

The argument was at a standstill. She inhaled deeply. No wonder there was war. And at this rate, who would budge? Or would they be forever killing one another?

Her inner thoughts came to a screeching halt as the carriage slowed to a stop outside the house. The doorman instantly appeared and she waited, to see what her patient would do. Again, the man surprised her. He managed to move rather nimbly out the door, a one-foot hop to the ground and then he turned, holding onto the carriage.

"My lady." He offered his other hand with a sparkle in his eye.

Trying to figure him out exhausted her. Slowly, she put her hand in his and stepped outside the carriage.

"Thank you, monsieur."

"Always a pleasure to help a lady." He grabbed his cane from the doorman and offered her his arm. "Shall we?"

At his gentlemanly spirit, which was the opposite of what she thought he'd be, she gave him a quick nod. Once inside, though, things turned quite cold, as he released her arm and murmured goodnight before turning toward the stairs.

"Would you like a glass of wine before retiring?" The chill in the front hallway surprised her, more so since it came from him.

"I think tonight I shall pass. Our…event…has taken all my energy. Good night."

As he continued toward the staircase, Ada's eyes widened, ice skittering down her spine. Her exposing him to the abolitionists had hit the desired effect she'd wanted. Only now, she wished it hadn't. How would she get that spirited Southerner back or had she driven him away?

Her stomach felt like she'd dropped a hot rock into it,

and with each of his slow steps, she realized she regretted it.

Francois sank into his chair, slowly raising his injured foot onto the pillowed footstool the servant had put before him.

"Thank you, Billy." He shook off the boy's help to undress but took the offered glass of wine as the servant slipped out the door. Alone at last, Francois closed his eyes as he sipped.

The evening hadn't turned out like he thought, while at the same time, it did. It wasn't his first time hearing those crazed reformers rant on about the horrors of slavery. To him, from what he'd seen in the northern factories, it wasn't any different, though here they were just workers and not called slaves. Nevertheless, Francois could count the number of landowners who treated their property like that speaker claimed. He always thought they were one of the stupidest type of people, because slaves were worth a fortune in investment alone. Hell, he'd once considered buying one man's set from the looks of how they fared, except he knew the owner would simply go out and buy more.

He downed the wine, realizing it was a losing battle. The price to own them had skyrocketed to make it too expensive an endeavor to maintain. Even he knew that. He hadn't really meant to pounce on Ada that way, but the saintly halo she put on, as if he was the devil himself, made him angry. Now, he wanted to laugh. That creature in the White House had freed the South's slaves, according to the papers, so what was there to argue about? Except that slavery itself wasn't abolished.

Finishing the wine, he looked down at his foot. It wasn't hurting much as long as he didn't race. And it wasn't swollen from escorting her rather quickly out of that lecture hall, which now made him wonder. There was the ball she now owed him…

On that notion, he stood, grabbing the cane and headed out the door in his shirtsleeves. Slinking down the stairs as quietly as he could, which was probably in the end worthless with the cane and a limp, but he tried. At the foot of the steps, he found the back parlor had a glow and he heard the fire crackle. Ada had to be in there, so he headed in that direction.

Rather pleased that he'd made it this far without a fall or a sudden move to alert his presence, though he was sure the house mice heard him, he made it to the room and peered through the slit in the slightly closed door. His prey sat at the desk, furiously scribbling on a sheath of paper, a glass of wine at her right. She stopped her writing, still staring at the page and he caught her lips curving slightly, as if smiling to the person she was writing to. That thought made his anger flare. He didn't know who she was writing to, but if she gave him that sly a smile, he'd warm instantly, though if it was another man, the mere idea of her with another irritated him. Yet why, he pondered. She was his doctor and she did save his foot, thus basically his life, yet she despised him…How had he come to earn for a woman who didn't like him, strictly because of where he came from?

The only answer he could fathom came from deep. Like a coiled snake, the hiss and rattle at the mere thought suggesting she was interested in another man could not be denied. He bet the man was the other doctor, the one who saw him in that prison, because that was the only one he'd seen her with—suddenly, he tilted, his mad thoughts making him misstep and he lost hold of the cane. It crashed to the hardwood floor with a loud bang.

Ada's head shot up her eyes wide with surprise.

"Francois, what a surprise." She stood quickly and raced around the desk, coming to his side. "Are you all right?"

No, he felt like a fool…damn it, he missed the rut in the floorboard.

"No, truly, I am fine." He took the cane back, fighting the heat that started to crawl to his cheeks as embarrassment flooded him.

But she didn't seem to see his stupidity and looked concerned. "The rally was a lot to take on. You did so well, despite the verbal mauling it did to your way of life. I'm sorry it affected you so harshly."

She was utterly amazing, to now make such a statement. He snorted. "My dear, you knew that would happen, and if I recall correctly, it was exactly what you wanted."

She opened her mouth but he put his fingers over her pretty parted lips, the touch of the soft petal skin branding him like fire. "It is fine. Merci, ma chère, I will live." He paused, the grin he thought he should hide burst through. "And now, you owe me a dance."

The pressure of his fingers against her lips had surprised her, the tingle that raced through her made her thoughts swirl, but she did catch the end of it. She stepped back, out of his reach, her brows furrowing.

"A dance? You must have a fever."

His devilish smile only broadened. "No."

She inhaled deep. *What was he up to?* She had walked back to the edge of the desk, turned and leaned back on the top edge and gave him a questioning stare.

"We barely made it out of there without you stumbling. And you had your cane. Perhaps you might tell me how you'll dance? Because leaning on a lady is not considered polite."

"Well, I thought, perhaps we can practice."

"Practice? When? Here? *Now?*"

Still using the cane, he stepped closer. "That's a lot of questions, doctor. I do think here and now. What else are you doing that would prevent you from helping your patient?"

He was so close, she couldn't breathe. What was it with this man, this Southerner, the enemy in more ways than one, that could make nerves jump? What was she doing? She wanted to shout she was writing to the love in her life, but even now, Will's jabs at her about Rich's intentions jabbered in her mind. The man before her interrupted her thoughts, made her heart flutter and almost forget about what she was doing.

Swallowing hard, she answered, "Nothing that cannot be accomplished later."

His gaze sparkled and he offered her his free hand, a look of victory on his face. As she slipped her hand into his grasp, she couldn't help but snort.

"We have no music."

He managed to spin her in front of him. "Are you sure? I can hear a tune in my head."

That made her openly giggle. "Really? Then you'll have to lead me the way."

He tossed the cane onto the settee and put his left hand on her waist, the other remained holding her tight as he took a step to the left. The dance was a slow waltz, and on the carpeted area near the settee, she was shocked that he could lead her without making them tumble. His sapphire blue gaze never left hers, the grin though faded as the steps continued. He turned her once, and at the end of it, his fingers tightened on her, making her worried he'd fall but he didn't.

"You do well for a man who needs a cane." She prayed he'd take the compliment warmly.

"It's a project I have a drive to achieve," he replied, turning her again, though a bit more slowly. This time, he double stepped, fighting to stay upright. She tensed, wrapping her fingers around his hand to hopefully help him.

By the end of the noiseless dance, he stopped, bowing to her curtsy, breathing hard.

"Are you all right? You didn't hurt yourself?"

He looked up and gave her a wink. "Better I've done this time than without a partner."

"Perhaps you should sit and let me take a look—"

"No! I mean," he shouted, before correcting his tone. He inhaled deeply and gave her another debonair smile. "Shall we go again?"

"Francois, please. I don't want you to be worn out."

"I am fine, ma chère. Please."

She had to agree that he had pulled the dance off. Slowly, but completely, he had waltzed with her. Did she have the patience to do it again without fretting the whole time he'd make himself entirely lame? But her body betrayed her as she put her hand back in his grasp. *Heaven help them both!*

Francois stood somewhat precariously. His ankle throbbed, though he discovered if he shifted his weight off it and centered more on the ball of his foot, to the side, he could manage relatively fine. Enough to sway to a slow dance. He liked the waltz, as it always let him be closer to the lady but he had to manage not getting too close, or he'd have a mother to answer to. Inwardly, he chuckled. *There was no mother here to interfere.*

Ada was light on her feet, which was a pleasant surprise. This woman confused him. She was a doctor, and from his own experience, with excellent skills. She was intelligent yet naïve, in thinking freeing all the slaves would eliminate slavery's hook on the land. Or that it was reasonable for owners, like his family, to simply let them all free, even give them a starting dowry, as it were, on marriage to a new life as a freedman. And what would the South do for workers? Had the abolitionists thought that far? Or were they simply guiled by runaways with horror stories? Francois had heard the arguments before, rather loudly, too, on the last summer he'd spent at the family's New York estate. He'd had a rather interesting discussion with their neighbor, a true believer of the movement, and he hadn't answered that question either. It was as if the South was to figure that out, to hire who they could at the spare funds they'd have after letting their investments walk off the land, and when the country paid by the lower profits coming in from trade, it might be too late to reverse.

As he spun her back in front of him, he grinned. Ada was also a beautiful woman, one who could catch any man's eye, if she allowed it. So lovely, she could turn his world upside down and have him signing emancipation papers for all the slaves at home, if he didn't watch it. The prim dress of a Union nurse did not dim her glow, but the wear and tear of the war wore on the edges. If nothing else, he hoped dancing would lighten her mood.

"Stop staring at the floor," he warned her.

With a shock, she shot him a look. "I wasn't staring at the floor."

Still swaying her in time, he gave her a questioning look.

"I was just making sure you were okay," she argued.

"I'll let you know when I've had enough," he replied softly.

He couldn't handle the pitying look she gave him. As if he was an invalid and of no value, which rubbed him wrong, so he spun her to the right and back three steps. The move caught her by surprise and she laughed, her smile catching his attention so strongly that he mentally silenced the throb that blossomed in his foot. He was mesmerized by her enjoyment, warming him deep inside, making part of him sizzle with the mere thought of touching her. He wanted more.

So he raised his right brow, trying to hold the grin at bay, particularly when she tilted her head, wondering what he was thinking. This time, he swung them back to the original spot, careful not to step that hard on his bad foot, and then pulled her closer. Without any warning even to himself, he reached up and traced the contour of her cheek to jawline with a gentle touch. Her skin was soft and heated with the blush that now pinkened her cheeks.

"You are so beautiful when you're not fighting."

That made her raise her chin. "Fighting? I believe you are mistaken. You are the soldier."

"That wasn't what I meant." He continued his stroking, his fingers slowly tracing back through the dropped curls that hung so precariously off her hairstyle, to the back of her neck. "The demands of medicine and fighting against the likes of me."

He saw her swallow, as if trying to find her breath, like

he was attempting to do. The heated snake in his groin snapped and he hardened.

"Yes, well, I'm trying to save you."

He snorted. "From what? Death? The Union Army?" He cocked his head.

"From the war and eternal damnation."

That statement made him lose his step.

The moment the words came out of her mouth, she nearly kicked him as he came to a sudden, and very close, halt. In that instant, her doctor-self rose through the blushes and social statutes and she stopped, making him stop.

"Are you all right?" She looked down again at his foot and tried to disengage herself from his arms with no luck. Inside, a soft voice scolded her for being too bold, and she agreed, for she had enjoyed his touch but doing this had made it stop.

"It is good."

She shook her head, still staring down. She shouldn't be this close to him, should not let him caress her so. She was in love with Richard, not this sinner. He was not worthy of her! Yet how could she stop her heart from racing when she was around him? Now that he was mobile and no longer a bedbound patient, she'd started to notice how debonair he was, even with the stubble on his chin, the fading sunny glow he had from marching through the countryside and the limp that would be with him forever. His dark hair and sapphire eyes, the icing to a man who walked with the gait of the rich, getting everything he desired gentleman, a steady pace with an attitude of authority, Francois Fontaine was as attractive and as dangerous as a chocolate cake with chocolate icing was to her waistline. The whole affair made her growl.

Trying to fortify herself against her body's longing for his touch, she stiffened when he broke through her defenses, pulled her close and kissed her. The impact of his lips sealing hers caused her to whimper and that surrender gave him access to her mouth. But he didn't advance boldly. No, this warrior was stealthy, using a very seductive lick into her mouth, his tongue slowly enticing hers to dance. He had the taste of rich wine and bold masculinity. She could feel the advance of his army, as his arms embraced her, his hands moving to caress her up her backside, with one balancing the base of her head in its palm, giving her support as he slightly tipped her back. His seduction of her mouth now twisted slightly as he cocked her head with his hand, allowing him to deepen his kiss.

Her stomach burned and a pool began to form internally, just near the apex of her thighs. It was a desire for more, a longing for something she'd only experienced years ago, when the call to arms tore her love away. But even now, the memories faded under this Southerner's seduction, though the heat it awakened scared and excited her. She should stop him and, as much as she tried to wrench herself free of his arms, she discovered the only part of her attempting to halt him was a voice in her mind, a voice that grew fainter and fainter the deeper his kiss became.

When his arm around her waist tightened, and he tipped her upper body slightly back, all fight left her. The trembling inside her, starting from the hotspot that was growing wetter by the moment, now took control and she slinked her arms around his neck, locking to hold him close and kissed him back with a fury she had no idea she had. It was a war and she gave in to the glory he tempted her with. She was lost…

"[L]ying on the ground with his cocked rifle by his side and his ramrod in his hand, and his eyes set on the front. I know he meant to kill himself in case of fire—knew it as surely as though I could read his thoughts."

—Union artillerist commenting on a soldier with two broken legs. Battle of the Wilderness 1864

Chapter 25

FRANCOIS HADN'T MEANT TO KISS her. No, that was a lie. He had, but the rest came over him the moment his lips touched hers, the soft petals so enticing. The taste of her own sweetness was so delicious, he feared he'd devour her all at once, with no regard to reason. All he wanted was her.

She responded to him, returning his passion with her own, and that only fed the wolf that'd been caged for too long deep inside him. His insides tightened and the fire in his loins ignited to a blaze. But they were here, in the library, with only the small settee. The floor was out of the question, the rug was hardly plush enough for her delicate form. Not a place made for a proper ravishing. So the only place left was upstairs in the bedroom. As he swept her up in his arms, delving deeper into her luscious mouth, the faint but persistent throb in his foot kept him still in the present. Could he get her up the stairs or would he literally fall in the attempt?

Determination, though, won. Breaking free of her lips

with his inner core yelling not to, he lowered her to her feet and he took her hand, scooped up his cane and said, "Come with me."

They headed out of the library without a sound except for the cane. He noted how strange it was for her to be so complacent but he wasn't about to ruin it. Slowly, he led her up the stairs and headed towards his room. But as they turned at the top of the landing, his toe caught in the fringe on the carpet and he tensed in an attempt to not fall, making his hold on her delicate hand tighten hard. She didn't squeal as he fought to stay upright, and for that he was thankful.

Once in his room, he released her hand and went to stoke the fire that burned low in the fireplace into a better flame.

"Now, the general always told us to be diligent on the march, that those Yanks could be around the next rock or up in the tree to prey on us. We remained quiet as a mouse and watchful." He replaced the stoker and stood upright. "I just haven't decided if you're a Yankee sharpshooter or you want to be here."

She widened her gaze as her hands smoothed down the skirt that wasn't needing it. "I came because you took my hand and," she swallowed hard. "And because I wanted to."

A flutter raced down his spine while his heart skipped a beat. Unsure still, he poured her a glass of whiskey out of the bottle he'd requested be kept in his room, handing her the glass before pouring one for himself. Picking the drink up, he raised it high.

"To the lovely Miss Ada. I owe you my life." He drank, watching her reaction.

She rolled her lower lip into her mouth, as if thinking. "That is my job, sir. I am a doctor and it's my duty to save lives."

He nodded but nudged the drink in her hand to her lips. "Then let us celebrate."

The whiskey burned down her throat, making her want to spit it out but she downed it, a shudder washing over her afterward. She'd never had a sip of hard liquor before, mostly sticking to wine and punch, but she didn't want to insult him after he'd praised her skills as a doctor.

But what of her skills as a woman? That one daunted her. She'd focused for so long on her medical career, intimacy eluded her. A fire burned in the pit of her belly and a longing from that area that craved his touch. She must be mad.

As he poured them another drink, she muttered, "I shouldn't be here."

He gave her a wicked smile, a dangerously alluring one. "As a doctor? Or a lady? Perhaps I think you should be here."

She took another drink, the burn this time was not as painful. "No, this isn't appropriate."

He laughed. The humor lit his face. He snorted. "Appropriate? My lady, from what I've seen, I'm not sure you have ever adhered to appropriate. Proper ladies do not go to medical school, treat the wounds you've dealt with, nor get involved with the scullery types that make up the abolitionists." He put his glass down and took her free hand.

His touch scorched her, sending fire through her veins and fed the burning spot deep inside her, the one that begged for her to ignore politeness. As she stepped closer with the pull on her hand, she found she was starving and the handsome, rugged man with the southern accent and its French flair, was the dessert she desired. Despite all her upbringing and the manners she was taught, the moment their lips touched, she threw her arms around his neck and succumbed to his embrace.

The kiss was deep, like everything wild and abandoned. She couldn't help but feed off the allure of his touch. His fingers moved over her back and to her front, without breaking the kiss. The path of his hands blazed a fire, as he started to undo the hooks on her bodice. Before she knew it, he had undone her bodice and peeled it off her shoulders and freed her arms, exposing her corseted torso. A cool breeze danced off her neckline until he embraced her again, slowly distracting her by leaving a trail of kisses down her neck. With practiced hands, he undid her skirt and crinoline, sending both the dress, over petticoat and hoops crashing to the floor.

Heat flooded her cheeks and cascaded down her neckline as she stood in her undergarments before him.

"You are so beautiful," he murmured, shaking off his waistcoat, trousers and shirt to the heap on the floor.

He stood shirtless and in his drawers. Not that she hadn't already seen him so attired, but this time, it was entirely different. Before, he was a bedbound patient and in pain. Now? He stood, handsome and desirable, with her hungry beyond measure. Since when had she turned into a harlot? The word made her shudder and she pushed it aside, focusing more on him.

He pulled on the ribbons of her corset, loosening them to free her of the contraption. With a swift toss, it too was added to the pile on the floor. Next to follow was her chemise and now she stood naked except for her drawers and stockings. A shiver passed through her, tightening her nipples.

His hand scooped up her breast and he swooped in, planting his lips around her nipple and suckling on the exposed tit. Ada moaned as the tingles branched out of her pearled tip, echoing the pleasure in the other one as well, and fueling the fire at the apex of her thighs. The split pantalets moistened as her lower lips swelled. Blood racing, she felt her temperature spike when Francois picked her up and laid her on his bed. Her legs were slightly parted, opening at the leggings and she swore he drooled when he caught a glimpse of her petaled core. He bent over and kissed her lower abdomen, on the cotton material, nearly sending her off the mattress. In a moment of sheer madness, her hips did raise her enough, he undid her waistline closure and as he pulled up, grinning no less, he shimmed the pantalets and stockings off her, leaving her entirely naked.

Engulfed in animalistic heat, she panted, her mouth dry, her body begging as she watched him through a slitted gaze. He gave her a wicked smile as he lowered to suckle her pearled nipple, his lips the only flesh touching her. It sent her into a wild frenzy, her back arched and legs parted a bit more, trying to get closer to him. He answered with a trail down her body with his fingertips lightly skimming down her until they reached the curls just above her core. She actually trembled, her nipples screaming for more when he lowered the hand and a finger slid inside her slick core.

She moaned at his invasion. As his finger slid in and out, she heard the sound of her juices at the movement and she turned hotter. Another finger entered. But it wasn't enough. She wanted more.

When he pulled his hand away, she groaned in frustration.

Francois' entire body was tense. His cock was so hard, it drove him to push her a bit farther, and she appeared to welcome it. Wearing nothing but what she was born in, Ada was breathtaking. Her scent drove him to madness. Exploring her with his fingers made his hand a sopping mess. She was wet, willing and begging with his body crying to answer her.

Faster than he imagined, he shed the rest of his clothes. Later, he'd realize his ankle had not ached, mainly because his manhood demanded attention. Climbing onto the mattress, he gave her a glance. Her hair was wild, the hairpins long since gone, her cheeks flushed and she bit her bottom lip, letting the petal flesh slowly loose after being scraped by her teeth. It was one of the most erotic motions he'd ever witnessed. Unlike what he thought was his style, of slowing and enjoying the moment longer, he now poised himself between her legs, the tip of his erection at her core. At the touch, she pushed down with her hips and he met her, driving inside her.

The mating was intense. United, they paused. His heart was racing and from her short breaths, he'd bet hers did, too. With a jovial snort, he plunged deep. She met his invasion by pushing down on him, encompassing all inside her. Their hips rocked to the dance of the ages, each push just a bit faster, the breathing harder and the gaze on each other burning.

She wasn't like anyone else he'd had before. It was like she knew what to do and craved it as much as he did. The bed squeaked beneath them as the bed boards held them. Her slick sheath clutched him, squeezing tighter, sending off excited tingles through his body and he repeated the gesture as often as he could. Doing so made them both pant louder, a slight sheen breaking out on her face, even in the depths of New York winter. Her core got slicker and tighter and he fought to stay in when his world shattered and he filled her with him.

Stars still danced in her eyes when he collapsed on her, waking her up to what had happened. As her senses smoldered off the high heat, Ada felt exhausted and yet happy. Mentally, it took her a moment to realize what had really happened. This handsome man, rugged, yet sophisticated Frenchman, a Southerner, a prisoner and a patient, had just made mad passionate love to her and her body ate up every second of it. She had been starved for affection, or so she cringed at her body's need, and he fed her. Could she learn to live with this feeling, though, of doing something wrong?

He was the enemy.

But he was a man who made her body sing.

Inhaling deeply, she pushed the growing concern back down. Lying with him naked in bed was not the time to berate herself for going against everything she believed in...

"Are you all right?"

She couldn't help but smile. The heat of the moment had made him whisper into her ear accented in southern-toned French. And she realized he worried he'd hurt her?

"No, monsieur, tres bien." That was the limit of the French she could recall from schooling years back.

"Merci, beaucoup." He leaned up. Not off her all the way but moved a little to the side, propping himself up on the mattress to look down at her. He pushed a wayward curl off her cheek, making her laugh. "You are beautiful."

She giggled. "You, sir, are a rebel in more ways than one."

"Why? Because I showed you a tiger could still prowl, even injured?" The smile on his face took her breath away.

"A tiger?"

"Louisiana Tiger, mademoiselle." He nodded his head in a mock bow.

"Ah, yes, the newsprint paints your compatriots as murderers, thieves and pick-pockets."

His eyebrow rose as he pursed his lips for a moment before he answered. "Perhaps we are, though I don't think I picked your pocket. I, perhaps, filled it instead."

Her cheeks suddenly turned very warm. Trying to escape his embrace, embarrassed by his innuendo, she added, "I need to go to my room. Would not do well to be caught by the servants like this."

He grabbed her wrist before she got free. "No, I guess it wouldn't."

She could read the hunger still in his eyes and it matched her own. As he tugged her back to him to kiss her, she realized she was his.... except for a small, distant voice struggling to be heard in the back of her head.

Richard, please forgive me....

"A ghastly sight indeed! Arms and legs lay outside the operating tents, and each table had a bleeding man on it, insensible from either and with the surgeons at work on him."

—Theodore Lyman, Union General Meade's aide
Battle of the Wilderness 1864

Chapter 26

THE NEXT MORNING, THE SUN poured into the room, sneaking through the drapes, which didn't quite close, and the brightness of the winter's glow woke Francois up. Squinting at the light, he threw a pillow on his head and moaned. He was exhausted and struggled to shrug off sleep. Then, memories of last night flooded his mind and he reopened his eyes, searching next to him, where he found.... nothing. Just an indent in the mattress. Another groan escaped him.

Why would he think Ada would still be by his side? Their lovemaking had been fabulous. Watching her leave had been a mix of frustration and arousal by the view of her swaying hips as she left without a stitch on. Rubbing his eyes, he realized the truth. She feared the servants seeing them together. He had never worried on such matters, but there was something about her that still held her back. Was it men in general, or just him? He quickly answered himself that it was just him—a rebel, who was also a slave-owner, a sin she could never forgive him for.

Sitting upright, he shook his head, discouraged. His ankle was sore, though it wasn't as bad as he feared it could be, with all that dancing. He hoped tonight, at the ball, it would continue to function, for he wanted to show her just how wrong she was about him.

A scratching sounded at the door. His heart skipped a beat that it was Ada, being discreet, but it was the wrong door. As the hallway door cracked, Francois's heart sank just a little.

"Good morning, Mr. Fontaine."

"Good day, James."

The man went to straighten Francois's clothes that still laid in a heap on the floor. His face remained the perfect blank expression of a trained servant, making Francois want to laugh. At least, back home, the house slave that tended him was young and with just enough sass to liven Francois's day, but here? Made him almost wonder why Ada cared if the servants saw them last night or not.

"Miss Ada has requested your presence for breakfast, sir."

He blinked. She'd called for him? A shot of heat raced down his spine, making his heartbeat quicken. "Good, good."

The servant still didn't break his stride and put the only other decent set of clothes out for him to wear. "I'll have the dress clothes ready by this evening, sir."

"That'll be fine, though I do expect another package will arrive today with another set. If you'd get those ready, all will be grand."

James's brows did rise, though it was up and down so fast, Francois virtually missed it.

"Yes, sir."

Standing still while the man finished putting the waistcoat on him, Francois snorted. They'd never asked about the package that arrived yesterday, nor the whereabouts of this one and how a houseguest during war, with a southern accent like his, could get so much when he'd arrived looking poor and destitute, like the secesh prisoner he was. It totally amused him.

The question was—what would Ada think?

It took him a bit longer to make it down the stairs, even with the cane. At the bottom, he managed to get into the dining room, driven more by hunger now. Apparently last night had worn him out more than he expected, especially when adding in the last two months of infantry's meager fare and hospital bland.

His appetite deepened when he saw her at the table. She looked beautiful. Memories of her lying beneath him, that succulent mouth slightly parted as she mewled when he plunged into her…he had stop those thoughts, because part of him was responding to those delightful ideas.

"Good morning, ma chère."

She gave him a quizzical glance. "How are you today?"

He smiled, ignoring the doctoral tone of the question. "I'm feeling grand!"

One eyebrow raised, she stared at him, though her cheeks flushed red and that thrilled him to his core. He took the seat across from her, working feverishly not to collapse into it.

"And you, Doctor, how is your morning?" He took the cup of fresh coffee and inhaled the aroma, relishing in it, remembering how, when he was with the Tigers, they'd bartered the enemy in late night banter for a bag of it. Sure beat crushed acorns steeped in water…

"I fare well." She put her fork down. "I believe, though, we should reconsider the ball."

Swallowing a mouthful of toast, he frowned. "Why?"

"Well, to begin with, it is dangerous for your injury."

"Poppycock. It'll be great to actually be out, like a healed man."

"But you're not," she countered.

"Well enough to be seen."

"Plus, we are in New York. If word were to spread you are with the rebel—"

This time, he laughed. "Wouldn't that send a thread of excitement in the air? To think a secesh was in their midst."

"You laugh off what could lead to bigger problems."

He hummed as he took another sip. She looked totally perplexed. "I think you're more worried about what to wear."

"I beg your pardon?" She looked astonished. "If that were the case, I might add you to that problem."

"Why did you reject Madame Florissant's confection? It was for you." It had floored him when the modiste had ranted on and on about Ada's refusal to accept the gown, which had totally surprised him. He'd yet to see a woman ever turn down a new gown. What the hell was the issue?

Ada had spent the better part of the pre-dawn hours arguing with herself for falling under his spell. After the euphoria evaporated, she realize she needed to get out of his room to save whatever was left of her integrity. All night she never truly slept, worrying about what she'd done. She was a doctor and her heart yearned for another man, so what drove her to throw all aside for this rebel? The harder she fought the memories, the angrier she got, and in an attempt to bathe the night away, no amount of scrubbing cleared the stain.

Now he asked about a dress she'd never ordered. As if he had ordered it for her. Eying him again still showed a soldier who might know how to dance, but Confederate bills, if he had any, held no worth here.

"I did not order the dress, nor did I have the funds to cover such an expensive piece. Miss Dix would reject such an outfit, no matter how pretty, to be worn in the hospital." There. That was enough, or so she thought.

"It wasn't to wear in the hospital," his tone sounded tense. "It was to adorn you, here, while on vacation from the war. A gift."

"A gift? From whom? You? Last I saw, you had nothing outside a rather torn uniform. And Confederate money isn't accepted here."

"I have means."

Those words were spoken in a very New York way, not a Southerner dialect. Now, she was getting confused. What was he talking about?

"Perhaps I had a golden coin on me…"

She shot him an accusatory look. "You stole off another? One of your own, as he lay wounded, or dead? Or did you lift that from a guard?"

His face mottled. "I was thrown into isolation, very ill with fever. Even that accusation is ill-founded."

She'd raised his temper. He did have a weapon, of sorts, in that cane. Memories of his touch reminded her he wasn't evil, but could she believe it?

"I mean," she started, biting her lower lip. "Confederate currency is of no use here."

The anger on his face vanished as he laughed. "No, none of that. I have access to funds for the dress. When she returns today, please accept. As my gratitude to the doctor who saved my life."

He was hitting the right spot as a man who understood her value as a surgeon. The squeal inside her banged to be heard but she bit her tongue, offering him a small smile and a slight nod. "For that, I thank you. But as to the dance…"

"We will go. If you recall, that was the deal. I put up with being blamed for all the badness you Yankees heap on us, your Southern brothers, so I expect payback in full." Then he smiled big, a devilish grin that made her nerves tingle with anticipation as the words struck home. Even her lower abdomen grew warm.

"No, we can't," her voice faded. Swallowing hard the lump in her throat, she added, "What we did was very inappropriate. You know that as well as I."

"I would not think it inappropriate. You enjoyed it as much as I," he argued. Leaning in slightly, he added, "Unless you hold feelings for another, perhaps one that writes you those letters."

She nearly dropped her fork, aghast. Had he seen her pull that letter from Richard? She didn't think he paid any mind to things like that.

"I do have feelings for another man, yes." She took the handle on her teacup.

He was staring at her. It was a questioning gaze, not a snarl. "A soldier? Fighting for your abolitionist wing?"

She didn't answer at first. "He is a doctor for the Union as well."

"Out in the field? Or here?" He snorted. "Men miles from their woman's touch will often turn to others to fill that need."

"How dare you!"

"Not all, but many."

"And do you have a lady at home that you thought of when we were…?"

He shuffled the utensils at his plate, not looking at her right away. "No. The woman I love cannot be mine."

His tone startled her. He'd lost someone. The air in the room chilled. She cleared her throat. "All right. I'll accept your gift out of courtesy and since we had an agreement, to which you held your end admirably, considering. But hear me well. The moment the slightest ache hits, we will depart. Am I understood, sir?"

He surprised her with a wink.

Why did she feel like she'd just made a deal with a serpent?

It took him hours to finally calm down. So she did have another man she cared for. A doctor, of course, he sneered to himself. Well, perhaps he should give himself a few marks, as he had her moaning to him last night, not some other Yankee off to heaven knows where. He'd be pacing, to work off his anger but with his foot so injured, and him wanting to dance tonight, he contained himself to a few strides.

He passed the hallway looking glass. A glance at himself brought him to a complete halt. He was too thin, walking crooked with the cane, hair way too long and a shadow on his face from the whiskers. Hardly ballroom material. He snarled.

"James!"

"This will, in all probability, compel him to try and throw himself between us and Richmond, and in such a movement, I hope to be able to attack him in a more open country, and outside of his breastworks."

—General US Grant in regard to General Lee

Battle of the Wilderness, May 7, 1865

Chapter 27

ADA TRIED TO KEEP FROM shifting on her feet, but her blood raced and she needed to do something other than just stand. The rustling of her new silk dress drowned her hearing, or so she chose to believe, instead of the racing of her heart.

"You look beautiful," Francois whispered in her ear.

She tried to grin, but the pressure on her was building. Trying to wiggle inside the corset, which was impossible to do as laced as it was for this outfit, she replied, "Thank you."

He chuckled softly. "It's a lovely gown, not a prison. Relax, let the beauty just flow through you."

She raised a brow. The man next to her was very dapper. His long dark hair looked so neat, pomaded back for the dressy event. He was clean-shaven, wearing a white shirt, dark blue silk waistcoat that matched his sapphire eyes, with black woolen frock coat and trousers. How stunning he looked, all cleaned up and dressed well. She'd witnessed him the reverse, with blood stains and a starved look in his eyes. To see him now nearly knocked her off her heels. Of course, where he got the outfit she was afraid to ask. Will dressed nice when needed, but none of these pieces matched any she'd seen on him.

Flattening her skirt, she returned his smile. "Thank you. Again. For the compliment and the dress."

"A lady as talented and pretty as you are, deserves a little pampering." He winked.

She rolled her bottom lip inward—another nervous response of hers—trying not to give another look at the devil in disguise next to her. "So you have your wish and we are here. Now, may we depart?"

He laughed. "My lady, the ball has barely begun. Unless you are unwell, we have no excuse to politely excuse ourselves. I think you need to relax, feel the music the quartet is playing, and dance. Time will fly faster that way."

He was right. She rarely swore, but right now, the cuss-word dangled perilously close to being heard. Pasting a smile on her face, she forcibly unclenched the hand that clutched her fan as if it was a life raft.

"You are correct. We shall stay." She bit back a chuckle. "You did survive the crowd last night. I can do the same here."

He gave her a beaming smile. "I take it you've been amiss of social affairs lately."

"Yes, well, I have had duties at the front."

"For the whole war?"

She looked away from him, counting back to the night before Richard left and the impact it had had on her, one that found her at Dragon Dix's office the next day…

"Nurses don't have time for frivolities and such."

He frowned for a second but when the string quartet stuck up the music, he held out his hand. "Shall we dance?"

She gave him her hand and he dragged her out onto the dance floor. He spun her in front of him and it was then she saw he'd left the cane near the chair.

"No cane?"

He shook his head, just in time for her to curtsey before him and him to bow in return. Offering his hand, he held her tightly as he turned them to stand behind the next couple. The opening dance was a parade of sorts, couples that would swirl in lines around the room, weaving through everyone so everyone could see who was there and what they wore. It was a gossiper's dream and a lady's nightmare, worrying what if her hair was amiss, her dress lacking style or her escort failing? She had none of these issues, except for her feeling overwhelmed. Thankfully, the rebel seemed to know the protocol more than her, and took charge, for which she'd have to remember to thank him later.

She had to admit, the scene before her was breathtaking. All the bright colored silks, ranging from gold to pink to blue and white, decorated in ruffles, ribbons and silk flowers, mixed with the laughter of the ladies wearing the concoctions, with their gloved hands resting on their partner's hand. Men wore black, blue, greens and browns with colorful waistcoats, well-cut frock coats and hair slicked back. The candlelight from the sconces and candelabra danced off them all and the scent of the lilacs and lilies with the evergreens made it all wonderful.

"Doctor, perhaps you might close those pretty little lips," her partner whispered in her ear.

Instantly, she realized her jaw had dropped open so she quickly shut her lips, her cheeks heated. "I apologize. It has been a spell since I've seen such, such…"

"Elegance? Yes, compared to what we've both seen, it is quite a contrast." He squeezed her fingers that draped over the edge of his palm. "More the reason for us to stay."

All she could do was nod. "You must think me ill-couth for making such a scene."

Now, he chuckled as they bent the corner as the line snaked through the ballroom. "Not hardly. I believe you've been so driven to prove your worth in a profession that refuses to release its control by the male gender, that you might have forgotten what a lady can do."

She spun her head to take a glance at him. Had he figured her out? That scared her. He, though, concentrated on the dance and they never missed a step. But right as she opened her mouth to make a comment, the music ascended to a halt, ending the procession and now the line broke, the gentlemen leading the ladies to the side.

He escorted her to the pillar at the side and looked about the room. "It's time to fill ladies' dance cards."

"And will you peruse getting yours filled?"

Francois leaned against the pillar, his cane back in his grip. "If you recall, my dear, my injury will keep me sidelined for most of the night."

Ada nodded, confused as to why they were here, if he could not dance. But she didn't have long to worry. A few gentlemen came forward and asked for a dance. Her card didn't fill every line, but at least she wouldn't be condemned as a wallflower.

The musicians ran a few notes, indicating the first dance would start soon. The young George Stillman offered her his hand. She instantly compared him to Francois and found the twenty-year-old was lacking in stance and looks but she could not refuse him. Hopefully, he'd not step on her feet. Nodding to Francois a short farewell, she followed her partner to the dance floor, virtually regretting it in the first few steps of the dance. He was far from Francois in every respect. What was happening to her to think that?

Francois gladly took the glass of champagne from the servant and sipped slowly, letting the bubbles tickle his nose as he tipped the glass, enjoying hearing them pop as it slid down his throat. A drink he'd had plenty of times, but now those days were an eternity ago. Fetid water, brackish and slimy to the taste, had been the common drink of the soldier. Sometimes, they'd get lucky and make an awful concoction of fermenting meat and turpentine with a few other additives to forget the war. So this was heaven…

"What a surprise to find you here, Mr. Fontaine."

He glanced up and found a young lady standing before him. Her dark hair was piled up on her head with curls fighting to be free but pinned by pearl hairpins. Her ivory skin with those warm brown eyes that danced in the candlelight made her angelic, though her dress teased every part of him to throw aside civility for the wild.

"Why, Miss Prescott, how could I even consider not coming?" He stood, using the cane to lift him up. Amelia was the one reason he'd come.

"My, are you okay?" The shock on her face as she stared at his cane made him grimace. "What happened?"

"The war."

Her eyes widened as she lowered her voice. "You were injured in the war? You're not like Jack. Saw him not long back, lookin' mighty fine in that Union uniform. But you?"

"Signed on with the Louisiana Tigers." He gave her a lopsided grin.

She laughed. "You two boys could never agree, could you?"

"Outside us both falling over you, I suppose not. But in this war, who does?" Once the words fell from his mouth, he realized the truth in that all too well and it surprised him.

"Quite a profound statement from my carefree Francois." Her frown tilted up in her smile. "But we are not here tonight to commiserate the war, but to celebrate the holidays. Come, let us dance?"

"Always the leader, my darling Amelia." He stood with her and put his cane aside, praying his foot would not make him crumple in pain.

"Well," she took his escort to the floor. "Waitin' on you does me no good." Once in place on the floor for a cavalier dance, they went through the opening bows and curtsies and then took their places for the six partnered dance.

"The lady you came with just continues to show what a rebel you are," she whispered during a spin.

He raised his eyebrows, surprised she'd know Ada. "You know of Dr. Lorrance?"

"Doctor? Oh, yes, I do recall that she took to doctoring. But I mostly know her for her part in the abolitionist movement."

Francois said nothing as he spun her, restricting his steps to protect his foot. He needed to distract Amelia, or he'd hear nothing but the freemen cause. So on the next encounter, he said, "Did you know Cerisa was in New York for a bit this last year? Ran away, so to speak, from the family curse."

That caught his partner in surprise. "Cerisa here? In New York? Is she still?"

"No, no. She's back home, with a husband in tow."

Amelia laughed as they broke in tune to the dance, faced each other and bowed.

"Cerisa wasn't to be held back any more than you two boys. Good for her. And thank you for the dance."

He nodded. "My pleasure."

Amelia disappeared, off to greet other guests, so he scanned the crowd to find Ada. He caught the whirl of her blue gown in the distance. Relieved, he headed back to a chair to sit when he heard another familiar tone.

"Well, my oh my, look what the cat dragged in."

Pleasure raced through him at the sound of her tongue and he turned. "Jaquita?"

Ada laughed at what her dance partner said without really hearing him. A business owner of something she didn't pay attention to, he had asked her to dance and she had no viable reason to refuse. They were at a ball, and protocol insisted that one accepted unless the man was vermin, at which he was escorted out. So they danced, and now he escorted her back to the place she'd been prior to his invitation.

"Thank you again, Miss Lorrance." He gave her a slight bow and she did her best not to flinch at the angular way he bent, nor the way he had combed his hair over the bald spot on the back of his head. It was obvious his back was hurting and he was older than he looked, but she said nothing. Years of experience taught her men in particular did not want any medical advice from a lady. So she bit her bottom inner lip.

"The pleasure was mine, Mr. Wright." She gave him a weak smile because it was hard to do more when she was gritting her teeth. He offered to stay at her side until her 'party' returned, but she fanned him off, telling him she was fine.

Once he was gone, she uttered a sigh of relief.

"Was he that bad a dancer?"

Ada turned and found Will by her side. "Will! Where did you come from?"

"I just arrived. A tad late, but Amelia was understanding. Being a surgeon from the front carries some weight."

She punched him in the arm. "And bearing insults as well."

"You know that's not how I meant it," he replied, rubbing the mock pain in his arm from her swing.

Will Leonard stood before her, in his dress uniform, looking rather dashing, she thought. Too bad she just couldn't think of him in any romantic way. The problem of being friends, she decided, made any idea of intimacy out of the question.

"It is good to see you." She smiled. "Granted a leave as well?"

"Yes. Ten day's leave. Never long enough." He scanned the room. "So how is our patient faring?"

"Remarkably better."

"Good. Word has it you had an escort."

"Yes. Mr. Fontaine insisted on being my escort." She flipped her fan open and started fanning herself, knowing the moment those words left her mouth, Will's curiosity rose. And in fact, his eyebrows inched higher as he stared at her.

"Truly? Why a ball?" He frowned. "You brought a Confederate to a social event here? In New York?"

"Yes. He apparently knows the hostess and insisted on this as a recompense for me taking him to the rally the other evening."

"Rally?" Will looked shocked. "You dragged a wounded

secesh to an abolitionist stomping event? Ada..."

"He needed to see the error of his ways," she insisted, fanning faster. Who was he to judge her?

Will laughed, shaking his head. "I think being in battle and wounded, maybe to never walk freely again, is a lesson well taught."

She shot him a hard look.

"Ada, please give the man peace. He's got nothing, according to the proclamation Lincoln issued. You've won."

That comment blew the wind out of her sails. She let out the breath she didn't know she was holding. Will was right. Acknowledging that mentally, she could feel her body relax as the tension evaporated. She folded the fan back up and smiled.

"Thank you." She took the champagne glass he handed her from the servant wandering through the crowd. After a sip, as the bubbles tickled her nose, she added, "I'm surprised to see you here. Didn't think balls were your favorite event."

He snorted. "I rather enjoy them. All the lovelies here..." He gazed over the crowd.

She rolled her bottom lip inward, thinking since he was here.... "Have you found a solution to getting him back to jail?"

Will downed his glass all at once. The silence was deafening but she'd wait, until he finally replied, "I see your escort is doing rather well on the dance floor. Bravo, doctor! Say, who is he dancing with?"

She quickly turned to find her patient. It didn't take her too long to find him and his partner. Squinting with disbelieving shock, Ada saw the woman in his arms was a slim freedwoman, pirouetting with the grace of a swan to his every move. She was beautiful and it made the hairs on the back of Ada's neck bristle. A flush of jealousy rocked through her core, which was another unexpected feeling for this rebel. The woman looked vaguely familiar, but she couldn't pinpoint as anger clouded her vision. All she could think was, how could he? His moves on the dance floor, spinning her in time to the music and the smiles on their faces enraged her.

They were the perfect vision of a slave owner forcing his slave to his commands. That thought consumed her as she gave Will her glass, grabbed her skirts and headed to the dance floor.

"Ada!" Her ears pounded as her blood raced, so much so that Will's call fell on deaf ears. *Who the hell was she?*

"It was amusing to see him—the Commander-in-Chief—whittling away with his knife upon the bark of a tree, pausing now and then to throw in a word or sentence in the conversation of those grouped about, and then going to work again with renewed vigor upon the incision of the pine."

—Observer in Union General US Grant's camp
Battle of the Wilderness 1864

Chapter 28

FRANCOIS LOOKED UP IN SURPRISE. "Jaquita? Oh, mon dieu! Tres grand!"

He wrapped her in his arms and spun on his good heel with her giggling.

"Now, Francois, put me down!"

He set her down, letting his hands skim down her arms till they reached her hands. "It is so good to see you! I had no idea you were still here."

"I live here, you fool." She straightened her skirt.

He couldn't contain how happy he was to see her. Eying her over, he stood back a step so he could take in all. She was just a few inches shorter than him. Her black hair was pulled back, braided and curled with pearl drops hanging from her earlobes. The yellow gown that draped her slim body was decorated with ecru lace and red roses. Her lovely blue-brown gaze sparkled with the same excitement he felt and her lips curled upward.

"So, do I pass inspection?"

"Yes, my dear, as always, you are pretty."

"Hah! You tell Cerisa the same, no doubt." She pouted.

That made him laugh. "What can I say? Shall we dance?"

He did his best to sway her on the dance floor. Subtly, he was aware of the stares, but he decided it was because of her beauty and not because a white man was dancing with an ebony lady.

There was a minor flurry near them. A vision of blue came into view right as he slowly turned Jaquita on a turn and had to stop because of it. Thankfully, they were near the edge of the dance floor, because the look on Ada's face wasn't happiness. The man behind her, that other surgeon, Dr. Leonard, if he recalled correctly, appeared slightly amused before he saw Francois shoot him a glare.

"Miss Lorrance, you constantly amaze me this evening," he said since she was breathing too hard to speak right away about interrupting them. "What boldness for even a doctor at a social event from a lady who didn't want to attend."

"May I ask who is she?" Ada blurted out.

Francois's eyes widened. She was jealous?

"This is Miss Jaquita Fontaine—"

"McHenry, my dear. Mrs. McHenry."

"Oh, yes, indeed. You had not informed me, darling," he replied back.

"I hadn't had the chance…'

"Fontaine?" Ada narrowed her eyes. "A former slave?"

"Oh, dear, you didn't tell her, I see," Jaquita said softly. "I am his sister."

Francois saw the color drain from the doctor's face. "Ada?" He and Leonard both reached for her before she collapsed.

Sister? That black girl? Well, she wasn't really all that black...

Ada's thoughts whirled so fast in her head, she feared she'd faint. They escorted her to the side, to a small sitting area, away from the bulk of the crowd. Many of the southern slave-owners raped their slaves, Ada'd heard it from the runaways. But this lady, looking so elegant and graceful, with the most stunning bluish eyes, looked anything but a runaway or one fearing being sent back to the South enslaved. No, she held an air of importance, which Ada understood.

"Ada, here."

Will handed her a glass, but she didn't think champagne was needed. "No, I am fine." She looked at the other two. "Would you care to explain?"

The woman laughed while Francois sighed. "Jaquita is my sister of the same father. She chose to move north."

"Understandably," she argued back. "You two look somewhat alike."

Jaquita openly laughed. "Yes, Momma Fontaine didn't take a likin' to that too much, right Francois?"

He shook his head. "Not particularly. Look, our father made sure Jaquita has no worries—"

"I am familiar with who she is," Ada snarled back. "She's a major organizer for the Albany Abolitionists Society."

Francois gave his sister a glance. She shrugged.

"Darling, are you all right?" Another man suddenly appeared. Instantly Ada recognized him too.

"Yes, my dear. Just discussing family business," Jaquita murmured, looping her hand on the man's coat sleeve. "Francois, may I introduce my husband, Senator Thomas McHenry III."

"Tom," McHenry corrected, extending his hand to Francois. "I have heard all about the Fontaines. Good to meet you. Surprised to see you up North, unless you're like your brother Jack."

Francois snorted. Jaquita's husband was a politician as well as a big boned man, with Grecian-defined facial features, the sort that could take control easily and all would follow.

"No, I'm a good Louisiana boy, born and raised down there. Fighting to keep the Yanks from imposing their will on us." And on that, he winked.

Ada's heart was in her throat. Now was not the time for political debate! She cleared her throat. "I apologize for interrupting your dance. Just worried that Francois's foot might be needing him to take a rest."

The senator nodded, and she took that as he agreed with her on turning them away from a possible sectional discussion. "Yes, this is holiday time. Rather rude to discuss the situation when we're here *not to* do so. Jaquita, darling, we should retire."

With a slight hesitation, as if wanting not to leave, she gave her hand to his, but she did lean toward Francois. "Papa wrote. I hear Cerisa was here?"

"Yes, for a while apparently. With Abraham, too."

"Wish she had contacted me."

"Mrs. McHenry? We had no word of your marriage," he nudged her with a brotherly familiarity that Ada was surprised over. "Plus she didn't bother to inform us, either, of where she was."

"Considering the circumstances Jack told me of, it's not a surprise."

"When did you talk to Jack?"

"Francois, I hear from him periodically." She stood,

pulled toward her husband. "All right," she gave and turned to leave, adding over her shoulder, "We should talk later. Good night!"

He nodded toward her. As he watched her walk away, he realized how much he had missed her. Out of all the staff at his family's estate, Jaquita had been part of the family. Her presence wasn't a surprise throughout the South, he thought. Many mulattos, fathered by the white owners, were raised with the white family's children, but his father acknowledged Jaquita as his, despite Francois's mother's dismay. Educated together, they all knew each other, so when Jaquita wanted to stay in New York that one summer, prior to the current unpleasantness, Pierre Fontaine did not deny her. So that'd make it six years and apparently, she'd done quite well, he decided.

It was then he heard the faint tapping next to him. Ada. He closed his eyes briefly, inhaling deeply. He wasn't ready to disclose his family's secret to her, of all people. Slowly, he opened his eyes and gave her his attention. He wasn't ready for the glare of the devil. *Oh, bloody hell!*

Ada stood, confused, angry and speechless. His sister was a mulatto? Jaquita McHenry? What else was he hiding?

"Ada, please, your mood will attract unwanted attention." Will warned her. Nothing new on that, as he always seemed to be trying to protect her. It was annoyingly unattractive. She stopped tapping the floor.

"So Mrs. McHenry is your sister?" It still made her insides twist. The irony was overwhelming.

"Yes," he muttered, leaning on the cane as he stood. "You can't tell me you don't see the resemblance."

So did half the room, she reckoned. "That is beside the point. Do you know what she does?"

"She's a wife to a politician," he shrugged. "I do not know him. Heavens above, I wasn't aware she married!"

This was not a laughing matter. "She's one of the main supporters for New York's abolitionist movement."

He raised his eyebrows and smiled broadly. "Yes, you did state that. No doubt she would be. Always was ready for the fight." And he laughed again.

Ada fumed. He was making light on a serious matter! "How—"

"My, oh my," Will interjected with a yawn. "I think it's been one top rate night! I'm exhausted. Aren't you?"

Francois didn't break eye contact with her but replied, "Yes. As always, my injury reminds me it is here."

"Good then. Let us bid our adieus and leave." Will turned toward Ada. "Am I not right, doctor?"

She snarled. Whenever he used her title, it was useless to argue with him. "No, of course. Our patient needs his rest."

But as they made their way to the hostess, Ada quelled the insane desire to slap them both.

The carriage ride home was a wall of silence. Francois shifted in the seat across from Ada, finding her anger gave her an intense look as she worked to appear indifferent, staring out the window into the darkness. But she still breathed heavily, the valley hinted at between the mounds at her chest, still heaved, stirring his passion in the most vexing way. She was mad, which floored him, that his half-sister was such an influential person. What were her grounds? He had no control over who his father sired. Was he to remain white trash in her eyes? Or given any credit to his background? And what had happened to that other surgeon? Dr. Leonard had disappeared after they bid farewell to Amelia, apologizing for having to leave.

It was obvious he was going to have to do something to appease this woman, or she could turn him over to the authorities as a rebel and a prisoner of war.

As the carriage pulled up to the house, she lit out of it as quickly as the coachman opened the door and offered her his hand to disembark. Even in her long gown, she was quicker than Francois could even attempt to be, in his debilitated state. As he hobbled up the stairs, cursing in his head at the pain riveting up his calf, he made it to the door and inside, scanning for where she was.

"She went to her room, sir."

"Thank you, James." This crafty servant seemed to not only appear without warning, he also read minds—a skill equal to Fanny back home, a trick he appreciated and despised at the same time. Gripping the railing, Francois nodded at the servant and stumbled up the stairs.

The door to Ada's room appeared closed but when he went to tap on it, the door wasn't latched and swung open for him. Inside, he found her sitting at the dressing table, Katie the maid, unraveling the pinned-up curls of her hair. Her gaze seemed locked on the looking glass in front of her, not even flinching when the door opened. Katie didn't stop her work, though she did glance his way for a second.

"Ada," he called softly, but at the sound of his voice, her shoulders tightened.

"It appears, sir, that protocol is lost on you. The door was shut and I seek no conversation with you."

She was still mad, which confused him. How had their closeness evaporated that quickly? All due to his half sister

Jaquita? That made no sense. He nodded to Katie, prodding her to leave. Without a word to her mistress, the maid put down the brush and scurried out of the room.

With half her mane falling down her shoulders and two locks remaining pinned high, Francois ambled up to finish the maid's job.

"I can do that," she stated flatly.

"I am well aware of that," he replied, pulling one of the last pearled cap pins out. "But why not let me, since I am here?" He pulled the other curl loose.

She stiffened. "I'd prefer it if you did not."

"*Hmmmm...*" He ran his fingers through her dark blonde locks, working the tangled curls free of the bonds in which they'd been held, twisted up for the cascading styling she'd worn. The strands felt like silk to his touch and he relished it in. Then, as he pulled it all back to drape down her back, he bent and kissed her bare neckline.

He felt her tremble. Pleased at that, he also knew a bolt of lightning shot through his veins, igniting a fire below that had been burning embers since their night together.

"Please stop."

He ran the tip of his tongue down her neckline, to her shoulders and then back, taking a nip at her neck. "No."

She melted at his touch, or so he chose to believe as the tenseness vacated those tight shoulders. He'd swore if he looked up, her eyes would be closed. Satisfied, he kissed back up her neck and when he reached her earlobe, he pulled back a tad and let his fingers free her ears of the dangling pearl earbobs. Again, she shuddered.

"I think you've done this before," she mumbled.

"Hmmmm, what?" He untied the fiche lace bow in the back before he started on the bodice lacings.

"How to undress a lady."

That made him smile. "I might know a thing or two."

She leaned back, as if melding to his body. As he pushed the now unlaced bodice forward, to peel it from her body, she straightened, locking her arms in a way that stopped him.

"No, I can't let you do this."

Puzzled, he tried again. "Do what? Make love to you?"

"No." She wrangled out of his reach, turning to face him while clutching the bodice to her form. "You made quite a scene tonight. And we left way too early. Tongues will wag."

He inhaled, trying to keep control of his passion, which had started to spiral out of control. Even now every part of him turned uncomfortable as his member throbbed, hard and pulsing.

"I danced. You danced. All rules were followed. You coming out onto the dance floor to accuse me of some infraction can easily be interpreted otherwise, since you tell me Jaquita is so well known in the abolitionist world. You, no doubt, were dying to meet her." He winked, hoping that'd curtail her withdrawal from him. "Plus, Dr. Leonard left with us. So, we are not the only ones."

Her gaze flickered, her lips tightened and her breathing deepened. "I just don't know, Francois."

She'd called him by his name. That hit a chord in him, telling him she was slowly responding to him.

"You truly can't be that mad at me," he murmured, leaning closer, his lips feathering hers, then plunging down her neckline to her chest while his hands sneaked behind her back, taking the open flaps back into his hands and gently bringing them forward. "She's my sister, after all, not another woman who'd take me from you."

She moaned as the bodice fell from her body, exposing herself a little more, down to her corset and chemise. He'd won! But apparently, that was only for a moment.

"I can't do this." She cleared her throat, though he saw how she left her bodice off. "My affections go to another man."

"Dr. Leonard?"

"Oh, heavens, no! No!" She smiled, a blush to her cheeks as she turned, pacing. "Another doctor, though. One in the field."

"A husband?" Shocked she didn't say something before.

"Oh, no, well, not yet."

He paced, feeling slightly thwarted. But her tone suggested she wasn't happy about this, so perhaps this man had jilted her in a way. Taking the initiative, he took her hand and squeezed it tight.

"He may not be here and may never be. The war could take him, or he may not be true to you. The warfront changes a man." He paused. "I know I've changed. He could too. So be with me, here and now. We may not have tomorrow."

And on that note, he pulled her to him and kissed her hard.

All the thoughts in her head jumbled when he kissed her. It was his touch that unnerved her so. She wanted him and despised him, all in the same breath. He was the enemy, fought for a life of sin, destroying people. He was a southerner, true in every way to their rebel ways, but when he touched her, when he murmured sweet nothings into her ear, she melted. She wanted his kiss, wanted to dance with him and curl up in his arms. *Oh, how she had turned so wicked!*

On that thought, she gave in. When he wrapped his arms

around her, she snaked hers around his neck, molding her body against his. Despite the metal stays of the corset, she adhered to him, relishing in the warmth of his body, the hardness of his chest, the rock-feeling of his torso and knew the bulge that pushed against her skirts was his desire for her. The excitement made her mewl in his mouth, despite their tongues dancing madly.

He growled, low and hungry sounding. Before she knew it, he had untied the corset strings and the skirt hooks. It took a tight squeeze around her waist to pop the busk on the corset, opening it all the way as the skirt and petticoats shimmied to the floor in a puddle around her feet. A cool breeze at being so exposed, despite the chemise, pantalets and stockings, her body was peeled of the shell she'd been covered in. Immediately, it fed her desires and she hunted for the buttons on his waistcoat and shirt beneath, after she'd pushed the frock coat off him, trying to never take her lips off his.

The frantic race to undress him matched him unclothing her. Thankfully, her bed wasn't far from the dressing table and before she knew it, he'd pulled her down to the mattress, yanking the last of her undergarments off her. She thrilled as he shed the rest of his but he was suddenly stopped when she wrapped her hand around his hardened member. With a smile, she slowly stroked his manhood, watching his eyes turn dark blue to black with the need for her. And she knew the moment he touched her, she was soaking, her core begging for him.

No more words were said. They slowed down as he pushed her back to the mattress and placed himself between her thighs. He gave her a lopsided grin as he bent over and slid right into her. She swallowed hard, tipping her hips up to take him fully inside her, rocking to his every thrust.

All thoughts of anyone else fled her mind when her world shattered.

"Negro property is the most unmanageable property and has been our ruin."

—A Southerner master whose slaves ran to Union lines for freedom.

Chapter 29

Next morning

WILL LEONARD ARRIVED AT SWEET Briar in time for breakfast. He was energized, still working on how to accomplish what he needed to do, before this entire event backfired. It'd taken every tactic he had to arrange this furlough, but it might not be long enough to complete everything.

He walked into the house and found the houseguests were in the dining room, He headed there, needing to check in with Ada but wasn't exactly sure what he'd gotten into when he breezed through the open doors.

"Good morning!" He greeted only to come to a complete stop. At the table before him, he found Ada and the Confederate across the table from each other, eyes glued on each other instead of the breakfast before them. She was dressed in her usual style dress, a simple calico day dress with prim collar and cuffs, her hair pulled back to a braided bun and simple earbobs. Fontaine was dressed, though only in shirtsleeves and waistcoat and trousers, with his dark hair smoothed back and a half cock grin on his lips. They looked like a married couple. Will shook his head, not sure what he'd interrupted, but this appeared way more personal than a doctor and patient.

Ada broke the locked gaze and turned toward Will with a smile. "Good morning, Dr. Leonard. How nice of you to join us."

The flash across the rebel's face was hardly warm. Will ignored it.

"Of course, you know I couldn't stay away." He walked up and kissed the back of her hand. He gave the Confederate a nod. "Good morning, sir. Trust you have no dire pains from last night's escapade."

"None are noticeable, doctor." The man watched him warily. He couldn't blame him. Being in Yankeeland and with a Union surgeon here, the ex-prisoner knew his luck could change. Will appreciated that.

"Will, will you have a bite?" Ada asked as the servant handed him a cup of coffee.

Will inhaled the caffeinated drink. "You never know just how much you miss a good cup of this stuff until you're stuck at the front." He grinned and took a sip. Over the edge of the cup, he could see a slight impatience in her, which intrigued him. Particularly when he saw a similar, though colder, reflection on the rebel. *What was going on here?* As to the invitation to join them, he finally responded, "As to partaking of this fine repast with you, I must decline. I've had breakfast and still have errands to attend. I just needed a few things."

"Are you leaving?" She sounded a bit panicked.

"My leave wasn't granted for the length of yours. Waxler is a tyrant, one that doesn't rejoice in the holidays, even directing us from his own enforced leave." He snorted as he put the empty cup down. "But I am curious if you'll be at the Amherst soiree tonight. My last hurrah, so to speak, before returning to the drudgery of ill and grumpy patients."

"Amherst's? No, I hadn't thought so—"

"Reginald Amherst? The shipping king?" the Confederate piped in.

Will frowned at him. "You know who he is?"

The southerner gave him a lazy smile. "Old family acquaintance."

"Yes, well, you are correct. They have a holiday soiree tonight. Light dancing, games and festivities." He turned to Ada and pleaded, "Please tell me you'll come."

She chewed her bottom lip, a reaction that always held his attention, because he wanted to soothe it from the scraping her teeth gave it.... the mere reaction made him mentally shake. Despite all the years he'd known her, he could never grab her attention the way he desired. No, instead she wasted her time on that lowlife scoundrel, Peregoy.

"I had not sent a reply. It may be considered too late," she finally answered.

Will beat back the disappointment that threatened. He needed her to attend. "I'm sure a simply failure of the post to deliver would be understandable, considering the current state of affairs. Besides, it's a rather large event."

"If it would not be considered rude, yes, I'll go." She gave him a smile. "What time will I expect you to pick me up?"

"I think we all will go about seven."

"All?" Her eyes widened and he caught the rebel's eyebrows inch higher.

"Of course. You can't leave your prisoner alone," he smirked. He reached for a pastry off the buffet, adding, "Until tonight, adieu!" And he left the room with a chuckle, for mimicking the rebel's French accent and for getting what he wanted.

He'd told her in the beginning he'd find a way to erase the Confederate's escape and he had discovered one. Their attending tonight was a win for him and his plan and that made him wash away the silent glances on their faces. Affection could not be happening, he reassured himself, because Fontaine stood for everything she despised about the South. She could never be falling for him…

Ada sat in the library, reading the mail Will had brought for her, but she couldn't concentrate. Instead, her mind kept returning to last night.

She lay on the mattress, inhaling deeply, still heated from their lovemaking. Never in her life had she thought she'd be in a bed, panting like an animal, hot and glistening from mating. Nothing had prepared her for this.

A male chuckle rose and the mattress crumbled as he turned toward her, propping his head up on his arm. "You are beautiful."

The compliment was simple and one he'd already uttered to her at the ball. But now, she wasn't in an elegant gown, all powdered and coiffured for a night of dancing. Now she wore nothing but her stockings and a layer of him.

"You are very free with that compliment, sir."

"Ah, but it is true." He bent forward and suckled on her exposed, still hardened nipple. His teeth scathed the tender skin, washed in his saliva. The motion set off a flurry of pulses through her body, branching from her breast down to her core.

"We should get up," she murmured, suddenly feeling very self-conscious of being naked next to him. She braced her palms down to push up when his arm snaked around her middle and

scooping her closer to him.

"Maybe." He nipped at her neck, upping her heat level again.

"You're not tired?" she asked, when his now hardened cock nudged against her hip. "Is your ankle sore?"

"Mais, non," he whispered into her ear, nuzzling against her skin.

"Your French accent is more pronounced now."

"Perhaps you bring out the animal in me."

"Animals talk in French?"

He laughed. "You talk too much." And he flipped her onto her back. He separated her thighs with his knee and wedged himself between them, lifting her hips with his hands and slid right into her inviting core. She couldn't help the mewl that escaped her lips when he filled her.

Neither said another word but panted and moaned as they reached higher and higher. She swore he touched her womb and she exploded like a volcano erupting, stars bursting inside her head as he gave that final thrust with a groan, his seed filling her core.

She'd fallen asleep in his arms, still silent like him. But when the sun had barely peeked above the horizon, he'd awakened her with tiny kisses, waking every nerve inside her. Tipping her on her back, he'd raised her hips with a pillow. She'd opened her eyes to find a handsome Creole above her, his dark hair sleepily messed and his eyes dark with passion. His chest, covered in dark hairs, raised up and down as he breathed deeply.

Then, still quiet, he lowered his head between her legs and licked the slit to her core. The sensation nearly took her breath away. A tremor started inside her, the wetness gushing out as his tongue teased her. Her hips began to roll and she felt the pressure inside that overwhelmed the embarrassment of him doing this to her rumpled self. He was bringing her again to that point of explosion when he stopped and gave her a grin.

Her body was so busy begging for his return that it stole her voice. She could only groan, reaching for him when he stretched and fell across her, his erect manhood sliding right inside her. Again, they danced the ancient dance and, amidst moans and gasps, her world turned upside down as he unloaded his seed, his tightened rod vibrating deep inside her.

They remained that way, locked in an embrace until they cooled some. He pulled up, giving her a Cheshire cat grin and he rolled out of the bed. Scooping up his littered clothes, he gave her a nod and slipped out of the room as quietly as he could.

She realized when he left her, the loneliness she'd hidden most of her life, now filled her enough to make her want to cry. He was everything she despised. Why was she longing for him now?

Mad at herself, she got up, went straight to the washstand and with the linen rag, scrubbed every inch of her she could, particularly her breasts and the apex of her thighs. She then picked up her clothes, laying them across the straight back chair, straightening the room as if nothing had happened, and crawled back into bed.

By morning, she met him for breakfast and all that anger that filled her last night dissipated when he gave her that seductive glance. She was hooked, until Will arrived…

She groaned in anger. Pushing the memories of last night to the back of her mind, making sure any of the pleasant parts laid buried. Mad at herself, she wondered what was wrong with her to sleep with him? Could Will tell of her transgression? Would Richard know? Oh, how she had betrayed the man who loved her. She wanted to scream.

"No, no, mix 'em up. I'm tired of States' Rights."

—General George Henry Thomas at a Union cemetery at Orchard Knob when chaplain as if burials should be by state like other cemeteries.

Chapter 30

Amherst Mansion, New York City

AGAIN, THEY WERE AT A social gala that made Ada's skin itch. Laughter filled the air along with the scent of evergreens and lilies. Greenery swung from every rafter, ribbons of red and gold woven in that danced off the candlelight. Men in Union blue, officers from what she could tell with insignia and designations, drank with New York's wealthy and the ladies attending vied for every man of standing who might be single. The laughter is what ate at her soul, for she knew of the hundreds who'd never see another holiday, dance another dance or attend a soiree ever again, thanks to this awful war. The thousands who now lay in the hospital beds, recovering—or dying—or sick with illnesses most here would never see. What would these people think if they knew of those soldiers? Would they stop? Would they help? Outside of donations to the Sanitary or Christian Commissions, no, and even that was doubtful.

"Here, drink this before you go make a scene."

Ada snapped out of her inner conflict to find Francois shoving a champagne glass into her hand. She eyed him with a narrow gaze. "Was I that obvious?"

"Yes, ma'am." He gave her his lopsided grin, knowing it'd get her to smile. It always did and succeeded now.

The man was too dapper in his black frock coat, gray waistcoat and black trousers. Those sapphire eyes sparkled in the candlelight, amusement hinting at his lips. He could take her to ecstasy and destroy her with one southern lilt. Whenever he touched her, she melted. But then left to her own devices, reminding herself of who he was, turned her blood to ice. He was tearing her apart.

"You realize Christmas is in four days."

She took a sip of the bubbly drink to swallow the lump that formed in her throat. "Yes, I seem to recall that."

He twisted his lips, deep in thought. "And your furlough is over when?"

"Six days after. Travel will be needed then to arrive back in the capital by the second." She smiled. Work. There was a certain amount of comfort and clarity in that.

"Would you like to dance?"

That caught her off guard. "Are you sure you want to? After last night's gala, it might pressure you too much, slow your recovery."

He shrugged. "I'd rather risk that over standing here, seeing Federal blue and trying to be polite. Keeping me on the dance floor will distract me."

"As long as we dance," she replied. "And nothing more."

"You slay me," he moaned, clutching his hand over his heart in a dramatic fashion and it made her laugh. He snorted with a smile and put their glasses down.

He escorted her to the dance floor and swung her in front of him right as the string quartet strummed the first chords. "As always, my beautiful angel graces me with a waltz."

She tightened. Waltz? Shaking off the tension that threatened, she put her hand on his shoulder and the other in his palm, quickly reminding him, "It is a dance. Remember your space."

"Oh, darlin', but I like to be in your space." He leaned in. "And inside you."

Her mouth went dry right as the music started. He gracefully led her around the dance floor, in a space that he confined to one area but his moves led her to believe it was all over. The steps were smooth, and she watched his face, looking to see if he was in pain but he masked it well. Eventually, she relaxed and let him lead her, content to have a moment of no pressure. Since Will had picked them up, the atmosphere in the carriage and the first few moments after they'd arrived were edgy. Francois was his usual silent self, or his old self. It took her a few minutes to reconcile that since he'd taken her, his quietness had evaporated into conversation, one that always hinted at seduction. But up to that one comment, he'd remained quiet and that had thrown her off.

"See? Music is the key to our souls."

She giggled. "Dancing seems to be."

"Except for that fella over there," he nodded to the left.

She glanced over. The couple dancing to the right were having a difficult time. The man was stumbling through the steps and she looked like she wanted to kill him. It made her laugh.

"Thankfully, that isn't us."

He gave her a quizzical glance. "How so?"

"Your injury, my dear sir, could have been much worse."

"Amen! God deemed you fit to fix this old soul and I

thank you," he said as they came to a stop, the last strum of the strings indicating it was over. He pulled her hand up to his lips. As he kissed the back of her hand, he winked at her.

Her cheeks flooded with heat. Charming, he got her blushing and she mulled the response she wanted to give. But before she had a chance to say a word, he took her arm and escorted her back to the spot he gotten her from.

"I am parched!" He tugged at his collar. "May I get you a drink as well?"

The room did seem rather warm. "Yes, that would be delightful."

He gave her a half bow and told her he'd be right back. She watched him walk away. Despite the dance last night and this spin on the floor, he was managing his pace rather smoothly. She was rather pleased, because despite her attempt to fix the break, that part of his foot made it hard to tell if she was successful on the operating table, and afterwards. Once this dance was over, and they returned home, she'd insist he rest.

That thought made her scan the room for Will. He'd hinted he had a plan…

"Well, hello darling."

She jerked her head to the right, the smile on her face growing by the moment.

"Richard!"

Francois made it across the room, stifling the pain that screamed inside him. The waltz should've been a slow dance, and it was, except his foot ached and if given a choice, his body would've refused him the dance, but the opportunity to have her in his arms drove him onward. If what Dr. Leonard suggested was true, their time together was almost at its end and he needed to drink every memory with her in.

Once at the refreshment table, as the servant poured the drinks, Francois looked up and found the host, Reginald Amherst. Francois wanted to chuckle. He'd met the man years ago, at a lawn party here in New York. Amherst Shipping specialized in sugar and cotton transport, a commodity in short supply, he thought. But the man still had boats and one way to return South was by water. His ticket home stood at the end of the table, retrieving a glass of champagne. He wondered if the shipper would remember him. Taking a gulp as he lifted the glasses served him, and straightening his back, he took a step toward him.

"Mr. Amherst, I wanted to extend my thank you for a grand evening." When the elder man narrowed his gaze, his brows furrowing, Francois added, "Francois Fontaine, sir."

"Ah, yes, Pierre Fontaine's son? Louisiana, correct?"

Francois grinned. "Oui, I wondered if you remembered my family."

The older man chuckled. "Throwing that French at me, just like the ole times. When things flowed so much better, hey? Cheers!"

Francois raised his glass. "Cheers."

Reginald Amherst was a few pounds heavier than Francois recalled. The large sideburns and mustache also an addition. The shipping magnate was dressed in the best wool frock coat and waistcoat, in jewel tones, with black trousers and white gloves looped over his frock coat pockets. Obviously, the war had not hit his pocketbooks. Francois inwardly grumbled.

"What brought a good Southern boy like you up here?"

Francois snorted, looking down at his injured foot. "Unexpected business." He straightened, pushing his shoulders back. "As you might recall, the Fontaines own a house near here."

"Ha, like the rest of you rich planters. Come north to beat the summer heat. I had forgotten." He downed another gulp.

Francois waggled his lips, his mind racing. Amherst ran one of the top shipping lines in the north. He knew his father had done business with several, but Amherst Shipping was always one of the major lines Pierre Fontaine utilized for the sugar they harvested. That got his mind turning.

"How has business run for you now? Not much cotton or sugar to haul, I'd reckon."

Amherst shook his head. "Sadly, the usual consignments have been terminated with the blockade. It has made me going to haunts like the West Indies for sugar. Feisty set down there, those Europeans. They're making a killing on the War, of course." He gave Francois a narrow gaze. "Periodically, we send boats to the Carolinas and Florida, when we can, that is."

That caught Francois's attention. "You don't say? Very interesting." He casually looked around, finding that most others near them were really far enough away from earshot, plus locked into their own conversations. Considering the circumstances, and the ill-fated return to Yankee imprisonment, Francois leaned closer. "So, have you taken passengers on these unexpected chances to land in the South?"

Amherst's chin tilted up. "Passengers, no. But I have crew that land. Why?" He gave him a tight grin. "Yankee cold making you long for home? Or you and the missus on the out and out?"

"Missus?" He cocked his head, confused until he heard a giggle that sounded like Ada's, though she shouldn't be so close. To be honest, he wasn't sure the shipper would consider the trip if he knew the true meaning of transporting a runaway Confederate." I might have need to return home and it'd be dangerous to take her, considering."

"Indeed, indeed. I'm sure something can be attempted," Amherst answered.

"Great!" Then his thoughts stopped. How could he arrange this, since he stayed with her? He remembered Dr. Leonard had whispered opportunities, making him wonder if this was what he was referring to. Another giggle distracted him. This time, he turned and found Ada in another man's arms as they danced, swinging in and out with the other couples on the dance floor. He shouldn't care, but a flair of jealousy snaked down his spine with anger in hot pursuit. She looked like she was having way too much fun with this varmint, with a dreamy look in her eyes that he could see from here.

"If you'll excuse me. I need to return back to my Ada. I will be in touch soon." And on that note, he took off across the room, vaguely hearing his host warning him to not be too long. But seeing her dance partner's hand swept a bit lower than acceptable, Francois's temper exploded. *Who the hell was this man? And why did she look at him like that?*

His shoulders locked, his spine steeled and any pain in his foot vanished as he stormed forward, determined, the demand forming for this interloper to go to hell!

Ada's thoughts whirled, just like her heart and her reasoning. During the next spin, her love was holding her hands, his infectious smile and warm brown eyes melted her heart, pulling her closer to the man who had left her to help in the War. He'd arrived, swooped her off her feet as it were with the surprise visit and whispered how happy he was to see her.

And she, thrilled to death to see him, hugged him in return before she playfully snapped back, "Why didn't you let me know you were coming?"

His reply, as they separated, was a wink. At times, he was so irritating but she could never be mad at him. He was here, with her now, and she'd take every second she could. The lead couple took hands and walked down the line between them, with the split lines of ladies and gentlemen following suit. After ducking under the couple's raised arm-bridge, they all separated just as the music faded and they bowed on queue.

Ada was thrilled, especially as he offered her his arm and she gladly accepted it when she got a glimpse of a slim, dark-headed bull storming her way. *Now what was that man doing?*

By the time Francois reached them, the ensemble of dancers were bowing to their partners as the dance had finished. She placed her hand on Richard's arm when Francois appeared, not looking like a huffing bull any longer, but more like a gentleman with a whisper of a smile on his lips and mischief in his eyes, making her wonder again, what was he up to?

"Miss Lorrance," he greeted warmly. "Sir," he nodded coolly to Richard. "I believe you accepted my invitation for the next dance."

She stared at him speechless. She'd never granted that, however, to deny him was bad protocol as well. Aggravated, because she wanted more time with Richard, she slowly acquiesced by withdrawing her hand from his arm and gave it to Francois's proffered hand. "I do not recall this," she halfway snarled as they turned on the dance floor while she watched Richard retreat to the sideline and out of the corner of her eye.

"You can't have all your dances consumed with one man," he contradicted. "It'd raise too much awareness."

"And more than one with you is acceptable?"

He chuckled. "We've not been together but one dance all night. I think we'll be not be led to the altar over two."

Her eyes narrowed even though the strings began to sound and the dance partners bowed and curtsied to each other. "You can't expect me to believe you interrupted my dance for my wellbeing."

They stepped forward together for the first steps of the dance.

"No, more for my own wellbeing."

"How so, might I ask?"

They spun. "Who was that man?"

"Why?"

He shrugged slightly, before they returned to the first form of the dance. She bit her inner lip. He almost acted as if he was jealous, though considering how they'd been acting in bed, she shouldn't be surprised. Her stomach flipped. That was something that ate at her, though, now that Richard was finally back...

"He is a surgeon. Colonel Richard Peregoy," she replied at the next meeting.

She caught a flare in his eyes, which quickly vanished. *He'd heard of Richard? How?*

"Union quack, I see," he muttered.

"He's a well-qualified surgeon, sir."

The dancers turned and it was on that turn, as he opened his mouth to speak, he faltered, crumbling on the injured foot, stopping the dance sharply.

"Too much tonight, you think?"

He nodded.

Grinding her teeth, she stood and, looked for Richard, who was absent, but she found Will. He came over and suggested they move off the floor. Once to the side, the musicians started again and everyone returned to the dance, regardless of the missing dancers.

Will knelt before Francois and took a brief glance at the ankle, hardly straying his eyes off him. "Perhaps you need to refrain from dancing."

Francois nodded but hissed, "I can't just sit. People will be talking and, in the end, my true self will be exposed."

Ada glared at him. "Precisely why we shouldn't have come!" She turned her attack on Will. "You knew he'd be here, so again, you'll do anything to keep me away."

"Ada," Will started but she'd hear no more. If they were to leave, and to be honest with herself, she knew they'd have to since even she could see the ankle was red and slightly swollen, she'd see if she couldn't find Richard in search of Reginald Amherst, to apologize for their leaving.

So here was the price for demanding she be allowed to work on the Confederates and knowing Will. Also, she'd bet it was God's way of reprimanding her for sleeping with the enemy. The anger surged through her veins. *Dammit, he could find his own way home! Damn slave-owner!*

"If my name ever goes into history, it was for this act."
—Abraham Lincoln's remark for issuing his Emancipation Proclamation

Chapter 31

FRANCOIS ADJUSTED HIS SHOULDERS ONE more time, peering into the darkness and wondering, for once, if he'd made the right decision. Though, it wasn't really up to him. The choice was plain and clear—stay in New York with Ada and end up ruining her life, Dr. Leonard's life and destroying what freedom he'd ever have, imprisoned in a Yankee cell. Or, agree with the surgeon and leave for the South. Bracing for the next step, he shook his head, unable to forget the last encounter with that fiery abolitionist who'd saved his life.

"Yes, come in!"

Her bark at his scratches to her door made him want to laugh. She was still mad about leaving the ball, which floored him as she didn't want to go there in the first place. Yet he definitely got the hint of her anger on the ride back when she said nothing to him, virtually jumped out of the carriage when it halted at the house, and slid past the front door before he steadied his cane to step off the vehicle.

"Miss Ada, are you all right?" he asked once he entered her bedroom. He was surprised to see her brushing her hair with a vengeance, still dressed in the ballgown. The maid standing next to

the dressing table, looking confused and distraught at being without a task. He gave her a smile and nodded for her to leave.

"I am fine."

A short simple answer wasn't good, he decided. "My ankle feels better, having sat for so long on the ride."

Her gaze narrowed at the reflection in her looking glass. "Really? How convenient."

"I didn't know you had such a desire to stay. You, in fact, didn't want to go, if I recall correctly." When she didn't answer, he mulled it over and decided to try his theory. "Unless, that officer you danced with held more meaning for you than wearing the Yankee blue. Heavens knows there were plenty of those there tonight."

She threw the brush down and spun his way. "That officer is the man I hadn't seen for a long time. He will be my husband, when all is said and done, but instead of being able to see him, you come like a bull, determined to take me away!" Her face was red, her eyes on fire and her shoulders straight, like steel. That energy attracted him and that surprised him.

"What was his name again? I seem to recall hearing it before."

"Colonel Peregoy to you, sir. A surgeon with the Army of the Tennessee."

Now, the memory blossomed. His sister, upon her return to the family last fall, told a story of a doctor in Tennessee, one who had tried to lure her away from the man she loved. Francois snorted. The woman's anger now had her pacing.

"Ah, yes, I recall hearing of your hero." He poured a glass of wine. "You might want to rethink your desire."

"How could you possibly know of him? Your fated army was in Virginia."

Her quick defense of him instantly set off a series of questions in his head, that all seemed to zero back to the same conclusion. It was this man's letters he had seen her cling to and no doubt the same person he found her writing voraciously too. And he was the same one Cerisa claimed nearly ruined her marriage…

"That man is not what he appears to be," he answered.

"Whatever do you mean?" Her voice contained a sharp edge. "He is of rank and a good surgeon!"

"He is not the type for you to waste your time with!" Now he was angry.

She laughed harshly. "Stay away from Will, Dr. Leonard," she corrected. "He has never cared for Richard."

"You shouldn't either. He is not worthy." The hair on the back of his neck bristled as his blood raced through his veins wildly. Cerisa's story of this surgeon's forward advances to her came crashing back into his memories. And if he recalled correctly, the man was married!

"You say that just because I've allowed you to be too close to me!"

He could barely hear from the pounding of his heart as madness started to take hold. "I've made love to you, not once but several times!"

She laughed. "I should have never seen to your care, nor taken you back."

"My, how we get so snippety when you know damn good and well you couldn't turn down the chance to practice real medicine," he roared back.

That stopped her pacing.

"Ah, I see I hit home with that." He stepped closer to her but refused to touch her. "Now, you throw me aside, as if I was no more than one of those poor souls you want to save."

She inhaled deeply, her face turned red with anger and before he knew it, she slapped him across the cheek. Stunned, he quickly overrode that emotion and pulled her close, probably rougher than he needed to, and kissed her soundly on her lips. Again, she surprised him, for a moment after he locked her in his embrace, she fought back and bit his lip hard. He yelped, releasing her.

"So now I see what you do with your slaves. You're no better than any other Silas Marner!" She spat the worse example of the slave-owner from that Yankee abolitionist's novel, "Uncle Tom's Cabin", only making him want to laugh.

"You think that's all I am? All the South is? Yet you've never been there. Go look at your factories here. No better than what you protest, and in some ways, worse! We take care of our investments!" Why was he arguing a system that even he was now questioning? Being pushed into a corner, he realized he fought like a caged lion to get out.

"How dare you! Get out! Get out, I say!"

"As you wish, madam, but hear me well. That doc you've set your cap for is not worth it. From what I've heard, he hardly sleeps alone," he jabbed as he reached for the door handle. And as he started to turn it, he heard the whiz past his ear, making him duck as it reminded him too clearly of a bullet. Instead, it was her hairbrush and it crashed into the door. He cast her a leaving glance over his shoulder and found her standing straight, breathing hard, her eyes still aflame. She was so angry and so alluring, it took all his strength to walk out that door.

Virginia
Six days later

Christmas had come and gone. The weather had turned bitter cold but the further south they sailed the warmth fought to take the edge off.

"She's all I got available." The trader wrestled the lead rope in his hand as he led the spirited equine to the pen. "Ya know, horseflesh pretty damn hard to get these days. She'll cost ya a right sum."

Francois looked the mare over. "I'll take her."

"You ain't even know how much she is!"

He looked at the grizzly bearded trader. The man didn't look like he'd seen civilization in years, though from the looks of Virginia due to the war, there wasn't much civilization left…

"It's like you said. Not much selection about. Tell me, how did you get such a young, spirited animal?" he asked as the horse danced on her hooves.

The man shrugged. "Got men looking to make a buck or two, or," he spat. "Runaway from the show, if'n you get me, huh?"

Soldiers who'd fled the conflict. He had heard about this prior to his capture. Men who got letters from home, begging them to return, and those who no longer had the stomach for the bloodshed with little to no pay or food or ammunition…

"How much?" He wanted the horse and to get away.

"You got Yankee gold?"

"I told you that. Yes."

"Three hundred."

"That's outrageous!" He'd managed to get some money out of the family's bank account in New York. He was shocked it wasn't frozen, considering they were Confederate, but he didn't waste time questioning his good fortune.

"You want her or not?"

He snarled, digging the Yankee bills out of his pocket.

"Saddle and tack be another hundred," the greedy old man added.

Francois bit back the swear word.

"Here," he stated, sticking the script into the man's hand, then slapped another hundred on it. "And the tack as well."

The man grinned, exposing his missing teeth, and he

turned to go get the tack, handing Francois the rope. Francois watched the man leave so he turned toward the horse, reaching to pet her withers.

"Tres bien," he muttered. "I will call you Rose. You're as pretty as one, but I see you still have thorns," he commented, having watched her prance to break free, the wild look still in her eyes though he noticed she'd calmed somewhat.

He'd wished he didn't need to get the animal, but so far, his trip hadn't cost him much, just his life—if caught. He saddled her as quickly as he could and then stuck his foot in the stirrup to pull up and sit in the saddle. Settling into the seat took a little more work as she twisted underneath him, jerking her head to try to free herself of him, but he clung on. It'd been a while since he'd ridden but he refused to let her dump him. His window of opportunity was tight, getting away without attracting more attention from the Yankees. Finally, he got her to answer to his control, getting her to move to his cues.

Once he got her under his command, he made her bolt down the road, and out of the coastal town. They rode southwest, skirting as much of the tree line that still remained, after years of warfare. Trying to find the Army of Northern Virginia was going to be rough, because he was trying to get to them before the Northern Army did the same. He'd heard the new commander of the Army was General Grant. It was a name he was too familiar with, since Grant had invaded the lands close to home and stolen Vicksburg from the Confederacy, thus sealing the Mississippi River to Yankee control and splitting the South in two. He'd spit over the man's name now, except the spittle would only hit him with the speed Rose could go when he urged her.

Cutting through a copse of trees, he came upon an unexpected surprise. Sitting around a struggling fire, was a woman, all bundled in layers from what he could tell. Near her was a bulging carpetbag, a linen tied bag, stuffed with something and a little dog, laying against her skirts and eyeing him carefully. What was she doing out here? Virginia wasn't safe with two large armies hell-bent on warfare.

Slowly, he made Rose walk up to her and grew more concerned when she didn't raise her head.

"Ma'am? Are you all right?"

She pulled her head up out of the crouched position and glared at him. Wisps of amber hair escaped the scarf wrapped around her head. Her pale skin had a touch of sun on it, with a spattering of freckles across her nose. Her dark blue gaze glared at him, letting him know she didn't trust him, nor did he think she'd trust anyone, other than that dog next to her, which she pulled closer, despite the canine's small barks meant to ward him off.

"No, sir, I'm not 'all right'," she answered, with a defeated tone. "This war, this awful war, has taken everything from me, leaving me with what you see here." She laughed awkwardly, leaning towards hysterical.

He frowned. It wasn't in his nature to leave someone like this, but the longer he remained, particularly with a mount, endangered himself and her as well to the depravations of the Union Army that he feared wasn't far behind him.

"I'm not sure how I can help you. Have you any family?"

Her cheeks flushed as she stood, shaking her head. Holding tightly to the lead she had on the dog, she gave him a look that penetrated his soul. "This, kind sir, is my family now. My father and brothers went to the army and died. My mother, at a loss without my father, came down ill, and with all the docs at the war, she got no help, died. Then the Yankees came, demanding food and whatever else they could find, only to torch my home afterward. So no, I've got nothing."

He shifted in the saddle, toying with his next words as he pulled an orange out of the saddlebag. "Here, take this. Brought it here, but I think you need this more than me." He bent forward and handed it to her, and she grabbed it, instantly yanking at the skin like a soul who hadn't eaten in days.

"Look, don't suppose you've seen the Army of North Virginia? Lee's Army?"

Her brows furrowed. "You must be mad."

"Perhaps. But I just escaped my capture by the Yankees and want to return to the fight and get them out of our land, so people like you can be safe and get your property back." He gave her a smile, hoping.

She nodded. "I'd like that. Most disrespectful group I've ever seen!"

He searched his pockets and found a solid silver coin. It was the only one he had. "Here, its real silver. Might get you a trip to Richmond. When you're there, find my father. He's a senator, Mr. Pierre Fontaine. Tell him his son, Francois, sent you. You'll be okay."

She held the coin, twisting it one side to the other and even took a bite on it, checking its validity. "I thank you for this. As to the army you seek, I saw them yesterday, traveling that way. With the number in their ranks, you should reach them by nightfall."

He peered in the direction she pointed and could see a flurry of hoof prints in the dirt field. He tipped his hat. "Thank you."

"That man will fight us every day and every hour till the end of the war."

—General James Longstreet's prediction on Union General US Grant

Chapter 32

Washington DC
January 1864

"THERE, HOW ARE YOU FEELING today?"

The pale young man blinked, swallowing the broth she fed him and managed a weak smile. "Still wishing I could just die, ma'am."

Inhaling to build herself stronger, Ada fought not to grimace. The boy was an amputee, missing both legs from the knee down. He'd been a farmer's boy, one whose whole future had been destroyed by the war.

"Please, don't wish that. The Lord has bigger plans for you." She tucked the blanket in tighter and moved to the next patient, praying for relief from the dismal thoughts that plagued her. Yet the next didn't, as the man was too ill to do much more than swallow his broth.

She walked back into the kitchen area and threw the metal cups she'd been using into the washbasin with such force they banged loudly, just like her temper.

"My, rough day?"

She gritted her teeth. Will always seemed to show up when she least expected it. She'd returned to duty two weeks ago, after her forced furlough over the holidays, minus her rebel patient. That outcome should have improved her feelings, but alas, it did not, especially on how that came about.

"No, just normal. Battered and sick men wishing to be anywhere other than here." She replied, ignoring facing him.

"Ada," he said softly, taking her arm and turning her toward him. "I'm sorry but I'm not sorry. You know as well as I do, that man was no good for you. Beneath you, truly."

She widened her gaze, laughter forming in her throat. "Which one are you referring to? Or do you mean both?"

"Ada…"

She was furious. How dare that Southerner just accuse her of treating him like he did his slaves! If it wasn't such a turnabout on fair play, she might have laughed, but a slap across his cheek erupted instead. How dare he!

Her pacing returned, infuriated at the entire evening. Richard had surprised her, showing up unexpectedly, and it was such a surprise. His deep brown eyes sparkled when he smiled, and he'd done a lot of that as they danced. She'd managed to get two out of him before that malcontent she'd been treating stormed over to her, claiming a dance. Shocked, she couldn't speak fast enough, but Richard conceded, giving her a knowing wink as he walked away. She hadn't even gotten out of him how long he was in New York or where he was staying.

Then, Francois's collapse required them to leave. He'd no doubt injured his foot again, and it made her want to scream. She man-

aged to get them out gracefully, but she was irritated. It shouldn't have surprised her that the man actually came to her room, but any intimacy between them was dead in the water to her. Oh, her body churned, deep and low, but she squashed that idea as quickly as she could. Her exam on his ankle told her he needed rest and ordered it done. Whatever else he argued, she never heard as she'd blocked him out of her thoughts…

By the next morning, she'd woken refreshed, her anger dissipating through the night. She went down to breakfast, fully expecting Francois to be there, though with him not, she decided she'd go see him. Wrapping a biscuit in a napkin, she stood, though James came to her side.

"Is there something wrong, milady?"

She frowned. "No. I thought I'd take this up to Mr. Fontaine, since he's not here…"

"No, ma'am, he won't be. He left last night."

She stopped in her tracks. "I beg your pardon?"

"He came down, rather late, saying he needed some air." The butler shrugged.

Ada stood stock still, her mind racing. A Confederate was on the prowl in New York City. Whatever was he doing? "And he didn't return?"

"Uh, no ma'am."

"We need to search for him!"

"No, Ada, we do not." It was Will. He waved the butler away and took her arm, leading her back to the table. "I told you I'd find a way to get him returned. I have fulfilled my promise." He stole the biscuit she'd been carrying and took a bite.

Stunned, she glared at him. "You sent him back to prison?"

"Ada, please. Let us not go further…"

The rest of the day was a blur. The longer she mulled in her mind what had happened, an incredible loss swept over her. It was like she missed him. She shook her head. He was a slave-owner!

He represented all she hated! But her arguments fell on faint ears, because somehow, along the way, the man had managed to find a way into her heart. Perhaps all the lovemaking might have added to it, and she should've stopped that, but how? He had seduced her and she'd devoured him, like a starving woman looking for love.

That realization only made her mad. In retaliation, she kicked Will out.

"...don't be irrational. You knew we needed to be covered for that indiscretion," Will said softly.

Wiping her hands, exasperated and tired, she cocked her head. "So you told him to run away in the night, after making sure he'd aggravated me so badly, I wouldn't notice anything till morning, when I finally cooled down, right?"

"No, of course not. I'm not that good at orchestrating things and you know that."

"Yes, so I've noticed in your practice." The words slipped from her mouth before she could stop it. Her mouth dropped open and she covered it with her hand as the color washed from his face but his eyes inflamed. "Will, I'm so sorry. That's really not what I meant."

Color flooded back into his cheeks. "You knew that was a dangerous game we were playing. I got my end covered at the prison. You left too many threads open, going to balls and rallies with him."

"No one knew he was a rebel," she retorted.

"Regardless, he is back where he needs to be."

"In prison?"

"No. The South." And on that note, he wheeled to his right and walked out of the army hospital.

Ada sank to the chair, all energy sapped. Her heart fell into the pit of her stomach and she wondered if she'd ever see him again. With a snort, her other half snapped back, "Only if you see him on the battlefield…dead."

A flood of emotion slammed into her. Grief, anger, frustration, irritation, lack of sleep and a broken heart, all rolled into one. She bent over and cried for the first time since the war began.

Virginia
Clarks Mountain

Francois shifted in the saddle. His ankle wasn't hurting, but then, he'd been in the saddle all day. Rose needed a rest from him and he needed to relieve himself. With that in mind, he slowly swung his leg over the saddle and tried to lower himself to the ground without a big impact on his feet. Success was there for a moment, for he wasn't as cautious when he tried to clear himself of the horse tack. A shot of pain raced up his calf. He did note it wasn't as sharp as before, or perhaps he was deluding himself. With a snort, he ignored that thought and grabbed the stick he'd adapted as a cane, he steadied himself before he limped to the bushes.

It was there, right as he readjusted his trousers to close, that he heard the cocking of a gun.

"Don't move."

He scanned the landscape but it was dead until he saw the gleam off a rifle muzzle. When he remained still, there was a rustle of the winter-dead plants as the soldier revealed himself. Francois hoped for a Confederate, and with the appearance of a mud-covered ragamuffin, with a gingham shirt and beat-up shell jacket, the guardsman fit any regiment in the Confederate Army to a T.

"Where you be goin', boy?"

Francois couldn't help but chuckle. The soldier was younger than him! "Back to my unit, the 9th Louisiana."

"The Tigers?" The boy's voice held a bit of longing at the edges.

"Yes. I'm Corporal Fontaine, returned from Yankee capture."

"Oh, we heard you all was a comin'!" The boy screamed with glee.

That intrigued Francois. There was a release from being shot? "Yes, well, sir, perhaps you'll point me in the right direction?"

Ada finally could expel the breath she'd been holding for a long time. "It's affirmed? We are finally leaving?"

Will laughed. "I find it rather interesting how you get excited to return to the front, when the bulk of the army would rather leave."

She grabbed more supplies and put them in the box. "You know me too well. I grow tired of this stagnation. I want to see us win!"

He grabbed her hand. "You seek that so the bloodshed will stop? Or is it to punish every slave-owner?"

She shot him a narrow gaze, yanking her captured wrist free.

"Ah, both, I'd gather."

She continued to stare at him before she snapped out of it and returned to packing. How was she to explain the bitterness she held for Francois's words, and his abandoning her? Thankfully, she wasn't with child, and for that, she was grateful, but it didn't cover the loneliness the nights had brought. Nor the driving pain of reporting to work as a nurse to a ward full of men sick and dying and her unable to truly help. She'd been pulled aside once for redressing a wound without the doctor's permission, which had made her want to scream but to stay, she bit her tongue.

Her time with Richard was too short as well. He was at that dance, smiling and chatting, but by morning, he, too, was gone. She threw the instrument in her hand into the box a little more forcefully than needed, out of her sheer frustration.

"I need to stay busy and needed," she confided, hoping that was enough to quiet him. "Here, I have no say, have minor chores to do and am prohibited from truly helping. At least at the warfront, men like Waxler are too busy with the numbers and commanders drive to win despite the sacrifices, that I have more freedom."

Will touched her shoulder, his palm resting there with a slight squeeze. "I understand." He straightened, tugging his frock coat to even the crease lines from wear. "I, too, am reporting back. Apparently, there's been a few skirmishes on the Rapidan, so we are needed." He smiled. "Cheer up. Perhaps that secesh will end up in our ward again."

She started. How had he known her thoughts had strayed to that sinner?

"I am almost wild. I do not think that I will ever be fit again to associate with respectable people. I have not spoken to a lady for two years [for] I have been in the woods since I left home."

—Soldier, Louisiana Tigers
Winter 1863-64, Virginia

Chapter 33

March 1864
Clark Mountain, Virginia

FRANCOIS FLEXED HIS FOOT, FINDING it remarkable how well it had healed. He could stand now, for longer periods, and no longer needed the make-shift cane. Just as the trees had blossomed and the birds chirped, he found himself reborn.

"What's got you grinning like a loon? Thinking of that doc again?" Wiggins prodded.

"Hardly, outside of gratitude. Just thinking how my ankle isn't in pain anymore."

"Good!" Wiggins punched him in the arm. "But you can't run too good no more. That's a problem, I'd say."

Francois growled. "Doc Murphy said it was a good thing I found a good surgeon, because most would've chopped it off. I'll walk fast and make it. Can't think I made it this far only to be killed cause I can't run."

Wiggins laughed. "Yep, that's how them Yankees fight. Just walking right up to the battleline, waiting. Guess when we turn their asses back to the North, they'll walk, too."

"And tell me again, how'd you get out of that jail?"

Wiggins stopped his laughing and gave him a stern look. "They exchanged us. Just too important to have locked up, that's all."

"And you didn't take that oath?"

Wiggins spat on the ground. "Only oath I took was one to get the hell back here, so I could beat their asses, drive 'em off our lands!"

They both laughed, but Francois's was cut short when he turned his foot the other way without thinking and hit a sore spot that still echoed pain. He inhaled deeply. Doc Murphy had given him a good prognosis, after that attempt of running during the snowball fight.

Most of the boys hadn't seen snow, so when it fell on the Virginia countryside last month, the tedium of winter camp cracked. They ran outside, laughing and tried to lap up the falling snow or fell into the minor accumulation, reveling in it. Soon, a snowball zoomed through the air, and before they knew it, the group had split to two sides waging a war with snowballs as bullets and cannonballs.

Francois jumped in as a participant, ignoring the first signs he was in trouble. A minor ache, a twinge that shot upward was nothing and he continued to play until he arched his back to avoid being hit and tried to run away. At that moment, his ankle finally gave. It took Wiggins and another soldier to haul him to the hospital tent, by then wrapped in pain.

"Son, you can't be pushing yourself so," the doctor scolded him. He put Francois's foot into a pan of snow, so cold he virtually jumped off the hospital bed, with Murphy pushing him back down. "It will bring the swelling down. Wait."

Steeling his shoulders, he did, trying to accustom himself to the icy pain. "Will it need to come off?" It was a fear he couldn't ignore.

Murphy frowned. "No, I think you're still manageable. But I think your days of running are through. I'll inform your commander you need to be sent home."

Home? No! Vague images of Emma with Jack invaded his once cleared mind and he struggled to fight it back. He'd come here to fight and forget her, and almost had when he was with Ada, but even that, too, had ended. Alone, he was in trouble, unless he remained with the Tigers.

"No, sir. I beg of you no. I'll find a way to fight. I am a Tiger," he insisted.

Murphy stared hard at him, as if deciding, only to break the hardness with a gentle, "Son, while I might regret it, I see it'll do no good to tell you Tiger boys to not fight. I'll have your duties changed, so no more damage, all right?"

It was that decision that changed his rank to Company First Sergeant and mounted on the very horse he purchased. He still shook his head over it, because now he was with the commanders and issuing orders down the line.

Wiggins laughed. "Think you can ride and issue orders?"

He shot his buddy a glare but the smile Wiggins had made him join him with a chuckle.

"Here, think I got something of yours." Wiggins handed him his fist and dropped into Francois palm a small object. With a frown and curiosity, he stared at the object. It was his small painting of Emma. His heart skipped a beat, making breathing harder. He clutched it tightly.

"Where did you get this? I thought I had lost it."

"You did," Wiggins replied. "When those Yanks whipped us off to prison. Remember how that guard kicked your hand? You dropped it but I snagged it. Kept it as you were too fevered and then, you disappeared." He shrugged. "Now, I get to give it back to you."

He stared at the image. She was so pretty and he fondly recalled how he loved her. He still did, but his heart now belonged to Ada.

"Thank you." He put it back in the inside breastpocket of his jacket.

In the distance, the bugle called and both men looked at each other.

"Time to drill!" Francois prodded his buddy. Wiggins just snorted as he gathered his gear.

"Yeah. Time for you to act like ya know somethin'."

Francois grimaced. During the winter break, the change in his status hadn't bent Wiggin's mood. They still were friends, as well as could be, Francois thought. But with the coming spring, as the whole countryside woke from her winter slumbers, he feared that would change.

Biting back a groan as he rose from seating, the echo of his ankle pain a constant reminder, he went to his horse and mounted. The war was coming. Why did that doctor, who hated him and the South, keep sneaking into his thoughts?

May 4, 1864

The sky was blue. The air buzzed with the awaking insects, though Francois consciously noted the volume was decreasing. What did the bugs know that the humans didn't?

As the spring settled in, the anticipation of a battle increased daily. The cavalry mounted daily for reconnaissance and reported back with more and more frequency.

Francois inhaled deeply, checking his supplies and the readiness of his gun.

"Francois! Did you hear?" Wiggins called. "They say the Yanks are on this side of the Rapidan River!"

"Uh huh," he murmured, not facing his friend but stroking the neck of the mare in a vain attempt to calm her down when it was his own heart he needed to relax. His horse was tense, picking up his tremors of tension as well as the level raised in the camp. "Ole Bobbie Lee knows."

"Well, *First Sergeant Fontaine*, what's his plan?" His formal slant on Francois's rank irritated Francois.

"I don't rightly know." He pulled the bridle strap through to attach to the buckle. "Lee rode out. Apparently, the Yanks got a new general. The general is trying to figure his next move."

Wiggins spat to the ground. "Thinkin' its going get ugly here, real soon."

Reins in one hand that gripped the saddle and his other reaching for the back of the seat, Francois pulled himself up, grinding through the dull pain of his foot in the stirrup. Shifting into place on the leather seat, he glanced down at his friend.

"From what I've gathered, we're going to stop them on Lee's terms, his favorite system of outreaching the North by audacity and shock, so we'll push through that wilderness to reach them. You watch after yourself. I won't be far off."

Wiggins nodded and turned to head back to the Tigers. Francois's gaze held a twinge of black at the edge of his viewing field. It was an odd feeling, as if this dense forest of shrubs and trees that made up the wilderness not only gave the south the advantage to start the battle on their own terms, but also as if it was haunted by the men who'd died there in another battle a year prior. Ghosts who warned them to leave.

The sound of leaves rustling caught his attention, breaking the morbid thoughts and making him look to his left.

"Ah, Edward, you were here before I heard you," Francois laughed. "This isn't the place to act so quiet. No master here going to whoop ya for causing a noise."

The tall, bald-headed slave snorted. "Some habits just ingrained, sir." But his grin told Francois the man relished in surprising him.

"So, considering your stealth, what'd you gather up ahead?" Francois had been amazed. Edward, the slave Captain Anthony Knox had brought with him to the front to serve as his servant, had been more or less taken in by the command and served many, including Francois. Though, upon his return, after being exposed to the abolitionist Ada's demands, doubts slowly began to eat at Francois's soul on slavery and it irked him to no end.

Edward shuffled his feet, looking down, an annoying trait born of slavery. "Looks like those Yankees gonna come through that wilderness to get to us."

Francois shifted on the saddle, fear knotting his stomach, knowing the man was right.

"You're a good scout, Edward." Francois tilted his chin upward. "Tell me, do you find it hard, being told what you can and can't do?"

The man looked into the woods, on the side of that backed to the Rapidan. "I do what I need to do, the rest I try not to think much on."

"So, how come you're still with us and not hightailn' it over to those Yanks to claim your freedom?"

This time, Edward turned to look at Francois and gave him a half-grin. "Sir, this is my homeland too. Yanks ain't givin' away land here, nor are they racing to let my type fight the real fight much. Here," he patted the gun butt in his waistband. "I get to carry a gun and fight to save what is mine."

The man was thin enough that Francois wondered how the gun hadn't slid down his trousers, but said nothing. His argument was sound, but he knew that'd irritate those abolitionists further.

"Well, you best be careful with that. Don't shoot that foot. I can tell you, that is a necessary piece of flesh to use now."

"Rightly so, sir, rightly so. Massa Knox showed me how to use it." He grinned, stroking the grip as he talked. "Why you be fightin', sir? I heard the Fontaines had enough to buy out of this mess."

Yes, why was he here? It was a question that loomed more and more until he switched it off. "For the country, Edward. For the land." He twisted his mouth. "Tell me, Edward, do you wanna be free?"

"Yessir. Mighty bad, sir. But we got work to do first." He nodded, tipping the corner of the hat he'd just jammed on his head and stepped away.

"You shouldn't talk to them that way, Francois," Wiggins whispered from the other side.

Startled his friend had returned, Francois twisted in the saddle. "Just an honest question, considering he's carrying a gun and all."

"Probably right to do, but don't let others be catchin' that. They might take offense."

Francois shook the thought from his mind as Wiggins disappeared again into the thicket, leaving him alone and back to dismal thought of the ghosts here. Lee would never entertain the US government would not fight because of ghosts so therefore, neither would he. Holding his grip tighter, he heeled the horse to take off toward command and prayed for better news.

Ada counted the crates again, satisfied that the number was correct. She put her paper and pencil stub down and stood back, wiping her forehead. The spring heat was setting in, and inside this army tent, what little breeze there was barely made it through the open tent flap. She'd have to get the opposite side open or she'd become a patient instead of help.

"So all is in order, I take it."

She spun, smiling at the sound of Will's voice. "Yes, thankfully. All here and in good shape. Considering how long it sat in those wagons, waiting to cross on that rickety bridge, I'm pleasantly surprised."

Will laughed. "Yes, well that pontoon bridge did well. Easier to cross the river, especially with the depth it's turned, thanks to the winter snow. Who knows, this General Grant might be more than we expected."

"I believe so. Those diehards, who are so quick to dispel a western general, despite his abundance in wins, are going to eat crow, I think."

"He's a drunk, Ada, or so the story goes."

"Ah, but didn't Lincoln commend him anyway, and a promise to send the same brand of whiskey to all the Federal command, if that's what made the man pull victories?" She snorted, then straightened to a serious face. "I think what makes him imbibe is the lack of his wife. Didn't you notice, while we waited for spring, and all the officers' wives were here, how not only their husbands perked up, but so did many of the men? Signs of civilization and society we hope to keep."

"Always the forward thinker, especially from a woman who entertains thoughts of love with a man not of her station," Will opined, as he looked her inventory sheet over.

"Will, please."

"Actually, I came with news," he stated, putting the sheet down. "The medical post has had a few adjustments."

She raised her brows, curious. "Major Waxler resigned?"

Will laughed and shook his head. "No. But, the general's move against the rebels down here has sparked a few arrangements, such as a medical post will be set here, with access back to Washington available if needed. We'll be the closest, in dire need and for the worst cases. The final stand, as it were."

"As a hospital? But all we have are tents. Before, they've commandeered houses for our needs." Her mind, though, rapidly began organizing the layout of the hospital, to make her suggestions to the major.

"Yes, but as a tent-hospital, we are more ready to move if needed. Also," he cleared his throat, pulling his collar a little, as if he couldn't breathe. "I was given promotion to Colonel."

She blinked hard, shocked. "Will, that's great! You accepted? You hate the paperwork a promotion like that involves."

He came to her, taking her hands in his. She could see the merriment in his eyes. "You are correct, yet you know me too well. My skills at the table are not as good as yours, but I do know how to write reports. My promotion puts me over a small contingent of doctors and nurses," he added, looking at her deeply.

She inhaled deeply. "Which means?"

"I have you under me. Don't you see? I can allow you to move up, be closer and help in the way you're better suited for."

Ada frowned, still quiet as her thoughts raced. "Let me see if I understand you correctly. You got a promotion, and under that, you've managed to be put in charge of a contingent to remain here, in an army field hospital of sorts, and with me under you, so you can let me practice as a doctor?"

Will nodded voraciously. He looked like a child who'd successfully stolen a cake from the kitchen, bartered it for sale to buy a pony, and had money left over, as well as the cake. She stared at him, stunned. What had he done? Who did he know?

Slowly, the weight of being underestimated as a doctor, started to fall right as her knees turned to jelly. She might have fallen if a soldier hadn't pushed his way into the tent, gasping for breath.

"Colonel Leonard," the boy sputtered. "Major Waxler wanted you to know the battle is about to start!"

Ada saw Will tighten so she quickly took the soldier's arm and sat him on the crate next to him. Pouring him a cup of water, she said, "Thank you for informing Dr. Leonard. Please inform Dr. Waxler we are ready."

The boy gulped the water, nodding his head. As he bolted out of the tent, Ada inhaled and turned to Will.

"I will make sure we are ready. You just manage your new role, but remember, you are a surgeon too. From the scores I've seen cross that pontoon bridge before us as well as after, we'll have a slew of casualties."

Will's jaw tightened. "More so than you think. From

what I've heard, Grant will make Meade throw everything at them. The word is, many think the man is a butcher. Pray, Ada, pray."

"Had there been daylight, the enemy could have injured us very much in the confusion that prevailed."

—General US Grant, Evening attack, Battle of the Wilderness,

May 6, 1864

Chapter 34

May 5th
The Wilderness

THE TENSION THAT HAD SPARKED the day before now exploded. The Federals were across the river, arriving on the Confederate side at two spots. From what Francois had heard, Lee ascertained the new Union general would try to lure them out onto the open fields to fight, where his numbers numbed the Southern forces, so Lee directed his troops to attack in the worst place possible. The wilderness that lay between the river and the Union advance to Richmond. The area was vast and dense, with scrubs and mismanaged greens making army advances—and retreats—a mangled mess. No clear paths appeared, just sporadic attempts through the vines, starter trees and low-lying growth. Only sheer determination would be the driving force and the Confederates had it, but what of the vast number of Yankees, city boys for the most part, who never dealt with this?

Francois rubbed his forehead, trying to wipe away the sweat that threatened to stream into his eyes. It was a hot and muggy day, or so he thought, knowing all too well that in comparison to home in the Deep South, it wasn't as harsh but still miserable. His ankle throbbed dully and he bent to adjust the stick he'd shoved into his boot as a way to offer support for the injury that refused to heal. Doc Ada had never told him it would be perfect, or when it might be doable, and for that, he commended her, because to lie to him would've served no purpose. All he could do was groan and bare it.

"Too bad you ain't done that prior to here," Wiggins had whispered late one night. "That might've sent you home, if it'd been last spring." He chuckled.

Francois had laughed with him, both knowing full well that unless he lost the foot, going home was never an option for him. Somehow, his time here had helped eased the heartache over Emma, only to be replaced by Ada. A woman who was enamored with another man, but even without that, she despised him because of who he was. It had made him truly wonder if the peculiar institution was worth all this, knowing damn good and well, his father and many other Southerners would argue the war was about more than slaves, yet for what he saw transpire in the North, the Southern argument seemed more hollow.

A bugle interrupted his thoughts and he adjusted in the saddle.

"Ya look just like a proper overseer," Wiggins snorted, spitting to the ground.

Francois looked at him, irritated by his comment.

"How many of that type do you know?" He frowned. "Thought you tried that on at one point."

Wiggins snarled. "Yessir, I did, when my pappy threw

me out. Young and stupid I was. Quickly found wrangling darkies was not for me."

"Would not be for me, either."

The conversation ended as the command came down the line to move forward into the thicket via the Orange Turnpike, guns ready to face the Union ahead. Rubbing the handle to his revolver, Francois nudged his mare into step, ordering the company to advance. They couldn't see a thing yet, but the rush to his senses and the pounding of his heart told him they were going to hell...

It started slow. One wounded, then three, before a lull and with the time passing, Ada paced between the beds. The minor wounds from going through a thorny thicket had bled profusely, covering the small gashes in the skin, some that she could almost not sew shut. Even now, at the edge, in theory, of the battle, she could hear the staccato of the musket fire with a periodic boom of an artillery piece hastily thrown together to fire, though it was like the sound of a lone wolf in a sea of bullets.

"Miss Ada, that might be all we see," murmured Maybelle.

Ada turned, all intent to glare at the girl for not addressing her correctly, not even as a nurse, but when she saw the fear on her face, she tempered her anger down. The young nurse had only returned to the hospital a month ago, when they were still in camp. Having the prior winter off had taken her courage down a few degrees, something that didn't surprise Ada.

"Nurse Maybelle, please take a moment and perhaps get a cup of coffee. You will need your strength. From the sounds from outside, I fear we are in for a long night," she replied, hoping she sounded more reassuring than she believed she was. She recalled how the return to the ghastly wounds had her gulping, after her trip up north for the holidays, but the groans of the men reminded her all too well her skills were needed. She hoped the nurse before her would rebound as well, or she'd have another patient and be minus a nurse…

"Ada."

She spun. Will stood before her, tense but on fire all at the same time. In his hand he held a medical bag. She frowned. He looked ready to leave.

"Dr. Leonard, where are you heading to?" She'd worried about him from the moment he got this promotion. He was a surgeon, adequate and better than many, but a paper-pusher he wasn't.

"I'm heading out to the battle. Men are falling at a rapid rate. We can't get ambulances through that thicket to get them back. Best to go assess them on the field, do what we can." He stepped forward. "I wanted to let you know that's where I'll be. Dr. Waxler will be back over you directly. I'm sorry."

Her stomach dropped. Licking her lips nervously, she nodded. "You be safe out there."

He gave her a grin and a wink. "Be ready. They are coming. Perhaps Grant's nickname of butcher is right."

As he slipped out the tent flap, she saw out of the other opening the incoming patients. Some carried, some walking but all bleeding and a horrible sight. Inhaling deeply, she yelled to the nurses, "Incoming wounded!"

Next day

Smoke filled the air, clogging it and making breathing harder. It clouded vision for many of the soldiers on both sides. Though relentless, they followed orders and loaded to fire again at the enemy whose forms were shadows. Spitting grime out of his mouth, Francois glanced over the area and toward the enemy. While the Confederates hadn't spared much, even Francois could see the ranks filling on the union side.

Up close, during the actual fight, the blue and the gray intermixed at times, unable to see others on their side or not. No one could see. The thicket made charging through or retreating a difficult thing to do. Uniforms were ripped, hats pulled off, skin scraped over and over again.

General Ewell pushed and all the men, particularly the Tigers, pounced as well as they could. At one point, Francois's horse whinnied painfully with a jerk to her right, almost unseating him but he fought to remain on, only to promptly get off to examine her. She'd been grazed by a minet ball, the bullet nicking her front withers near the saddle, and close to hitting his thigh. He yanked out his handkerchief and swabbed the wound. It wasn't deep but he gathered until this eased, perhaps she shouldn't be ridden. Well, not till the bleeding stopped, he reckoned.

A bullet whizzed past his head, the noise so loud, he jumped back a space. His blood started to boil. *That Yankee son-of-a-bitch nearly took him out!* Fury overrode common sense. He pulled his Enfield out of the gunstock on his saddle, loaded it and fired back. Then he pulled it back and reloaded it. It was madness. Falling in with the Tigers, Francois followed commands and loaded, held back, reloaded and advanced to fire again. His foot throbbed but he leaned more toward the better foot and ignored the pain. Even when his hat flew off his head, he didn't notice.

To hell with the Union!

But a subtle voice echoed deep. *Ada.* He was insane, he decided, picking up the rifle one more time when the enemy's fire hit him. It was like a thud, as if he ran into a chair, that ignited into a rippling pain that burned. Again, Ada was his last thought as he sank to the ground.

The incoming wounded were like waves of the ocean she'd seen once, years ago. A mess arrived like mad dogs that were looked at, treated and moved to their areas of either surgery or minor bandaging or taken out to the outside area for those deemed not able to be saved, like those with their stomachs ripped apart. Then there was a slowdown, where Ada could breathe and take a sip of water, only to be overrun again.

It wouldn't matter who was in charge, the Union medical department was understaffed for this huge endeavor of Butcher Grant. She decided after the third wave yesterday that the nickname was right, despite the fact General Meade was still in charge of the Army of the Potomac. Grant was here, and she determined that was all it took, for Meade would throw care to the wind to maintain his command.

"Here you go, Doctor."

She looked at the young orderly handing her a cup of water. "Thank you." She took a sip, staring at him. He was way too clean after now two days of battle. "May I ask who you are, sir?"

He gave her a smile and his cheeks flushed. "Private Jonathan Thorpe, ma'am." He bowed, which made her smile.

"Private Thorpe, how old are you?" She frowned. Not only was he too clean, he looked way too young and his voice squeaked of youth.

Thorpe swallowed. "I'm fourteen, ma'am." When her jaw fell open, he quickly added, "I'm the drummer boy for General Hancock's Corps. Got sent to carry the wounded in, so I kinda stayed to help out."

Fourteen. She wanted to gasp. *Way too young for this!* "Well, thank you for your help, Private. We always need the help around here." She smiled.

"More wounded!" Came the cry and she turned to see the oncoming stretcher carriers.

"Private Thorpe, go help them, please." As the boy scurried off, she put the cup down and returned to her makeshift table.

But she wasn't ready for the first patient.

"Will! What happened?" She raced with her bag in hand as he was escorted to a nearby chair.

"It's hell itself out there," he muttered, cradling his right arm.

She saw the blood-drenched frock coat sleeve and the rips in the fabric. "We gotta get this off you. Here." She pushed the uninjured side off first, hearing him grimace when it jostled the injured one. "What happened?"

"It's a disaster out there. Wilderness is the right name. All thick like a wild land and it tears at you as you try to get through it." He bit his lip when she worked to get the injured side off, and paled as she yanked gently.

The sleeve was torn and bloody so she ripped the fabric off. It was still too covered in blood and grime and fabric for her to see, so she found her cup of water, thankful the boy had filled it so it still had plenty in it, and poured it on his arm. He jumped with a screech but she ignored him as she turned his arm. A jagged gash ran down the forearm, similar to other gashes she'd seen. A bullet grazed the arm.

"You'll live. I'll get you cleaned…"

"No, no," he muttered but with urgency. "I need you to find another to go out there. If you think you have it bad in here, it's worse out there."

"Will, please. Let me take care of this."

He yanked his arm from her, surprising her with his determination. "I can get a steward to do this. You have severely wounded out there." He stood and walked away, a little swaying, but managed to get to a steward as Ada stood, her mind racing.

She went to the flap of the large walled tent that served as the hospital. Before her were roughly, she guessed, twenty wounded, carried or walked in by men who were worn out and tattered. This was the hospital tent closer to the Rapidan. She knew there was another closer to the front. Biting her bottom lip, she wondered how they'd all be sorted, when one of the doctors out there was gone. Stewards were needed here and there, just like the surgeons. Mulling the thought over in her head, counting the surgeons nearby, she pondered her decision until she saw one incoming soldier, yelping at every hop on his good foot as he leaned on the man helping him in. The wounded leg was in a tourniquet, but below the knee swung loosely.

"Get him inside immediately," she ordered the soldier helping him and got a nod in return.

That made up her mind. Turning, she raced back in, grabbing a bag and shoving bandages and surgical tools inside.

"Nurse, I mean, Doc Lorrance." Maybelle walked up her

eyes wide open. "We got wounded."

"Yes, I know. But Dr. Leonard has returned. Help is needed on the field. I'm going. He can help out as best he can here." And without giving it another thought, she grabbed the bag and raced out the tent flap and into the war.

"Richmond must not be given up. It **shall** *not be given up."*

—Confederate General Robert E. Lee to Confederate President Jefferson Davis, Seven Days Battle, 1862

Chapter 35

WILL HAD SAID IT WAS hell itself. It took no time at all for Ada to agree. The sun was setting, so she feared her time would be limited. She dove in and quickly found her first downed man. He was covered in dirt, sweat, blood and black soot. The moment she touched him, to roll him over to see the erupting wound, she recoiled. His skin was cold with death. Bile climbed up the back of her throat and she focused hard, swallowing it back down. He wasn't the first dead man she'd seen, nor would he be the last.

"Joey, go that direction, and I'll go this way. Let's stay in sight of each other, just in case," she suggested to the hospital steward. Joey Adams nodded and took his satchel of medicines down about twelve feet. She liked this steward. He had been in medical classes when the war broke, so what he did know allowed him the position of steward, not surgeon, but she figured after the war, he'd excel at medicine.

The ground was layered with the fallen. Some begged for water, and it didn't take long for her canteen to be almost empty. The air was also littered with the sound of gunfire and cannons exploding. They were distant, allowing her to believe that Will's fate wouldn't happen to her, but the war itself was a bit distracting. The further she went, the fainter the sounds of war became. Unfortunately, the noise of the wounded rose, and she heard plea after plea for help.

An eerie glow cast the skies a brighter orange than the sun as it set but she plugged on, trying to help the few she could until she heard the crackling noise, like a fireplace. It stopped her in her tracks as she scanned the horizon. She was in an area with battered trees, a blanket of fallen leaves and mud and a minimal number of downed men, most of them long since lost to this world. She realized she couldn't see Joey either, so she opened her mouth to call him when she heard that noise again, followed by a loud scream of severe pain.

Whipping her head around to the direction of the dying yell, the sound curdling down her spine she saw the bigger menace. Fire. Now, it all registered in her head. The crackling that she heard was fire and fear with its icy fingers, tried to wrap around her, but her inner soul, the one that drove her to medicine with the need to help others, stomped it down.

"Joey!!"

"Doc!" The reply she hoped to hear was closer than she thought.

"This way. There's fire eating the wounded alive!"

Francois heard the noise. It was a snapping sound, a hiss even, like a snake and he frowned, wondering how the hell a snake could live in this hell. Then a masculine moan, one laced in pain also echoed around him and the two combinations made him struggle to open his eyes, fighting the cloak of darkness that lured him to stay.

All he saw when he opened his eyes were fallen timbers and layers of old leaves. He did catch the odd fluff that lightened the grungy color of earth with snippets of blue, gray and white puffs, no doubt shredded pieces of uniforms and remains of paper cartridges. Among the littered ground were other soldiers of gray. Most were stagnant and that disturbed him enough that he fought to move.

Pushing with his arms, he raised his head and shoulders, slowly pulling himself up to a sitting position. But as his butt came into contact with the ground, he had a stabbing pain from his injured foot race up his leg. With a groan of frustration when he tried to move it and the burning sensation remained, he tensed but refused to lie back down. He looked down over himself and didn't find any injury outside the old one throbbing plus a few cuts and scrapes.

Trying to bury the pain, he switched his attention to the area around him, trying to rediscover where he was. The distant sounds and small tremors of cannon fire reminded him. The War. They were in the Wilderness. His senses came back in full. When he tried to rise, his ankle reminded him how that wasn't a good idea, so he dragged himself over to the closest inert soldier near him.

Concealed in torn up earth and decaying leaves, the body in the heap didn't move. His uniform was butternut, qualifying him for any number of units in the Confederate army. Francois nudged him.

"Get up, soldier," he barked, giving the body a sudden shove and when the soldier rolled back, Francois wished he hadn't. Half the man's face was ripped off, the remains blackened from the gunpowder. "Rest in peace," he murmured, crossing himself, adding a silent prayer as he moved on.

The next one was several feet away, also not moving. Betting that one was the same as the prior, Francois looked about. His body hurt from being dragged over the rough ground, and with the way it looked, it'd be pummeled by the next yard so he'd need help to get out of there. He spotted what looked like a long enough and hopefully sturdy branch and pushed himself closer to grab it. It took a minute but after he jabbed the end to the earth and used the pole to pull up from, he figured it was good enough to use. With a big limp, he staggered to the next body.

This one, though moaned.

Instantly, Francois fell to his knees, ignoring the pain, and worked to uncover the soldier.

"Wiggins?" Astounded to find his fellow Tiger, Francois fumbled for his canteen, uncorked it and gave it to him for a sip.

Wiggins took a swig, a grateful look in his eye. "That explosion just blew me away, as if I could fly." He snorted but halfway though, started to cough. Francois was horrified. Blood stained Wiggins lips and it was then, Francois saw the bloodstained teeth.

"We gotta get you out of here," he said with more determination. "Come on." He stood with his make shift cane but his buddy didn't move.

"No, no," Wiggins said, shaking his head. "I can't move."

"I'll get you a cane as well," he offered, giving the trees a look, searching until Wiggins grabbed his arm.

"Won't be no good."

Francois stared at him. Wiggins, looking pale even under the sunburn he'd gotten over the last couple of days, leaned back and pull his bloodstained and torn shirt apart. His abdomen had a blacken bullet hole that had ripped through Wiggins' clothing and skin to bury itself. Francois's heart dropped. Gut shots were death.

"I can't leave you here," Francois stated and then he whistled, hoping his horse would hear. *Where was that steed anyway?*

Wiggins laughed, but it was a short, gurgling sound. "You'd just be taking a body. I don't have long." He swallowed but the blood from the laugh coated his chin. "Gotta letter to the missus in my haversack. Will you get it her? Tell her I love her and will see her again."

The mare trotted up, surprising Francois, more so since he was staring agape at his friend. She nudged him so he took the reins, leaning on his makeshift cane and her to stand.

"You're going to be telling her that yourself," Francois snapped, bending down, still leaning on the cane while trying to help Wiggins up.

Wiggins moaned, though he tried to rise. All around them, the air grew hotter. Francois was soaked in sweat. The more crackling, only this time, it was closer. Peering over his friend's head, Francois saw the fire getting nearing them. Another scream filled the air along with the crying tones of others unable to move out of its path. It was that pending doom that drove him faster. He threw his cane down and devoted all his strength to Wiggins, though the man was sluggish and felt more like a sack of grain than an able to live man.

"Come on! We got to move!" he urged him as Rose danced on her hooves, the impending fire spooking her.

In that second, Wiggins's eyes rolled back into his head as he slammed to the earth floor. Near his body was his revolver and only a few feet away, a Yankee soldier dead.

Francois figured they'd both killed each other. The desire to yell, to curse at the war, overwhelmed him, but for what purpose? His friend was dead. Inwardly, he laughed. *Wiggins died an honorable death*, according to men like his father Pierre Fontaine, so his family should be proud. It made Francois want to retch. A dead son and husband did little good now…

Determined not to leave him on this field to burn, Francois dragged his friend closer to the horse, still holding on to the cane but in the end, dumping it to move Wiggins. *Damn, the man was heavy!* But the horse would have none of it. The flames roared behind him, Francois knew that, because the heat had him drenched in sweat and carrying another. But he was so close and she'd settled for a moment though he could see her head still high and eyes wide with fear. If he could only get that last step…

But it never came. He tripped. The weight of Wiggins now limp form and a vine or something in the leaves beneath them, caught his toe. He stumbled, bringing his friend down with him to the earth, Francois hitting a stump before he hit the ground. Dazed, his vision scrambled, he saw the faint form of Rose jumping back, tossing her head in the air as she darted away from the flames. He should go with her, but a slow blackness started to grasp hold on him, and his last thought was an image of Ada, the woman who had tugged his heart. She was also the woman who would shun him in a heartbeat. It was quite a problem, though apparently, one he'd never know how to solve.

The air was thick and hot. Even though she could hear the distant gunfire and artillery blasts, her biggest opponent was the embers of the encroaching fire that darted across the sky. Her woolen gown would protect her, as the fabric was too dense and the sparks would suffocate but true flames wouldn't. When her heart skipped a beat as fear wrapped down her spine, she shook her head and concentrated anew on her task.

So far, she'd seen a handful of wounded, mostly dead. One with severe damage to his body, covered in blood, all she could do was hold his hand as he cried out for his mother and, in his delusional thinking, thought she was that woman. It was a pretense that didn't last long. Once thinking he was with his mother, he gave her a brief smile—so angelic really—before he passed away. She closed his eyes as she laid his hand down, across his body, and fought against the tears that were forming. Crying over the senseless killing would serve no purpose, her medical thinking barked, so she picked up her bag and moved on.

The fallen she now came across were thinning, and the moans fading. As the heat gathered, she decided it was time to turn around when out of nowhere, a horse came trotting right up to her. Startled, Ada stood still. This animal was saddled but without any insignia on it claiming whose horse this was. No US stamped into the saddle blanket or on the bridle brass. What shocked her more was the equine came to a full stop before her without Ada doing a thing. Stunned, she tried to figure what to do. Ada hadn't ridden in years. The war had her ride in a carriage or walk, and her few times in the saddle were sidesaddle, even that was years ago. But if she could get on the horse, perhaps she could see quickly if the former rider was back there. She'd hate to leave anyone to the flames, though they were getting closer.

Giving the animal an eye over, Ada looked at her. "Well, girl, you wanna show me who you left behind?"

Cinching her medical bag to the strap on the rear of the saddle, she led the mare to a tree stump to mount her. Pulling every lesson she had in dealing with equines, which was very limited, she got the horse to sidle up to the stump, while she gathered her skirts, thankful she only had on a corded petticoat and petticoat, shoved her boot into the stirrup and pulled herself up onto the saddle.

Riding astride felt odd and she twisted in the seat, trying to find a way to situate herself when the mare started walking. Ada gathered the reins and forced herself to breathe. With a glance around, she didn't find any more bodies and she relaxed slightly, hoping the rest was clear and she could ride back to the army until she saw movement.

On the forest floor, a soldier with dark, almost black hair lay with a long stick next to him. Intrigued, she wondered who he was right as the horse came to a stop. The limb reminded her of a cane, and with the dark hair on his head, her first thoughts went to Francois. How dare she be looking for wounded and a man on the other side entered her thoughts. *Dang rebel!*

Then, he moved.

Instantly, she tried to jump off the saddle, only to remember all her skirts at the last moment. It was a jarring landing but she did get off and rearranged the skirts, which were eschewed badly. She got to his side.

"Francois?"

He popped his head up and gave her that seductive smile of his. "Why, Doctor, what a pleasant surprise."

She wanted to hit him but more sparks rained over them. The horse pranced and she feared the animal would bolt. On this uneven ground, she couldn't support him. "

"Come on. I need you to get up."

He rolled to the side and saw the dead man next to him.

"He's already beyond help," she murmured. "We need to go or end up like him."

Francois snarled but didn't' say a word. Instead, he grabbed for the dead man's haversack, grasping it tightly as he bent his healthy leg underneath him and tried to rise, but his face contorted in pain. "I need my stick!"

Scanning around them, she found the one he mentioned and grabbed it. "Here."

He jammed the end into the ground and with her on his other side, managed to get himself upright. But to move made him grimace in pain, so he stopped.

"Let me take a look at it," she suggested.

"No! Get me another stick," he ground out, his teeth clenched.

"I really think—"

"We don't have time to think," he growled and bent to get the broken branch next to them. As he started to jam it into his boot, she tried to stop him.

"I am not—" She was cut off as a tree, roughly thirty feet behind them caught on fire, lighting up like a torch.

The horse yanked back on the reins in an attempt to flee, breaking the grip Ada had, but Francois reached, fisting the whipping leather while teetering with the cane.

"Give me your apron!"

Confused but yanking the solid plain white pinner apron off, she handed it to him. He took the stained piece and put it over Rose's eyes. Without seeing the flames, the horse stopped pulling.

"Let's get the hell out of here!"

They walked with silence between them, dodging the lumps of dead men and horses and fallen timber in a mad dash despite his hobbling. Around the next turn, a colored man came running.

"Sergeant Francois," he said, putting his arm around Francois as support. "It be bad here."

"Edward, get us free of this!"

Ada frowned as they continued their escape. She couldn't believe, after all they'd been through, he had the audacity to bring one of his slaves to war with him. It nearly undid her. While she had silently pined away for his company, despite their differences, over the last month, she'd realized she actually missed him and wondered if he thought of her.

Now, all that meant nothing. She couldn't care for a man who stood for everything that was wrong!

If only she could convince her heart of that…

"I do not hope to gain any decided advantage from the fighting in this forest."

—General US Grant to an aide after his army's punishment in the Battle of the Wilderness, May 7, 1864

THE FIRE ROLLED ONWARD, EATING the badly wounded in its path as the sun started to set. Their cries for help etched permanent stains into Francois's soul like the fire that killed them. Angry he couldn't get Wiggins's body out of the impending inferno boiled inside him. At least, he did have the man's sack with the letter for his wife inside. The man's last wish was the very least he could do.

No one said a word as they slipped out of the battleground. Edward led them, though they weren't moving fast. Francois's leg ached enough that he had to stop at times. Neither the slave nor Ada complained, so he pushed forward, determined to beat the pain. But he noticed his angel, Ada, rarely looked at him. He'd seen her coming, afloat it appeared, but since Rose was there when he came fully to, he'd bet her floating was via horseback. He knew she was in turmoil over the slave. Her abolitionist side, no doubt, wanted him to run away, free, but then again, the man was leading them out of the flames, so her speeches remained silent. How long would that last, he wondered.

One thing he did know was that he was thirsty. He looked for his canteen and found all he had was Wiggins's haversack and it weighed way too light to be holding his. "Damn!"

Ada shot him a glare. "I don't see the need for such vulgar language."

Francois couldn't help but sputter a stilted laugh. "We're trying to get away from a fire, on a battlefield no less, during a war, and you're worried about my language?" He laughed again, only this time, he couldn't stop.

Edward gave him a questioning look, but couldn't contain himself either. It only took another moment for the doctor to join them. It was the laughter that made Francois finally feel alive again. As if he'd had his foot on the precipice of insanity—or worse. It was dark now and he bet, by the glow of the fire, they looked like specters. All seemed strangely right until the flames caught another screaming victim. The cry stopped abruptly as did their laughter when the severity of the time shocked them back.

"I'm parched," he finally squeaked out.

Ada picked up her canteen. Francois saw her hand shaking. He frowned, confused, until he saw the color escape her face.

"Here," she offered shakily. "All I've…." And she crumpled to the ground.

Francois threw his stick aside and hopped as fast as he could to her. Edward beat him by a second, stopping her head from hitting the rock beneath her.

"She looks ghostly, sir," the slave muttered.

Francois picked up the fallen canteen. "She doesn't have much left. Probably on this field a long time, looking for wounded, I'd reckon." He opened the water container and slowly tipped it toward her lips. A little went in but she was still out. "Ada, Ada."

She slightly opened her eyes but looked too exhausted to speak. Silently, he swore again.

"Damn! You're doing too much. Edward! Help me get her on Rose here. And we need to find a place to go. Not sure where either army is at this point."

"This way, sir. I found a shack, looks like an old slave shanty not far up."

"Away from this mess? We don't want any place near the fire."

Edward scooped her up. "Massa Francois, best if you get up there too. She's got all these skirts..."

The blindfolded mare wasn't happy to move but did Francois get her turned to mount. Up in the saddle, he couldn't help but sigh. The pressure off his leg was miraculous. Holding out his arms, he lifted Ada out of the slave's hold and onto the saddle. Adjusting her took a moment. Edward was right. All her petticoats and the skirt made finding her legs a bit harder but he got her on so his arms wrapped around her as he held the reins.

As they started moving, Francois inwardly groaned. With her snuggled up against him, he couldn't stop his body from responding to her, even through this fire. Every curve, her scent, sparked the memory of how she felt when he buried himself inside her. Grinding his teeth, he nudged the mare to keep walking.

Yes, this was hell itself.

Every ounce of energy was gone. Zapped. She couldn't think anymore, nor stand, it appeared. Ada realized she was not only exhausted but her throat was dry, the taste of sulfur on her tongue, since the air was filled with it thanks to the gunfire and smoke in the air. And now they were inside a dry, dirty room with no glass in the windows.

"Here."

A tin cup was in front of her. She took it and looked above to find Francois, leaning on the stick. Also, to the side, she glimpsed a black man bent over, the sounds of metal on metal grinding on her nerves. Curious, and won over by thirst, she took a sip. The favor shocked her. It wasn't just water, but tasted like vinegar, berries laced with honey and it quenched her thirst, enough so she downed the whole contents at once.

Francois snorted, giving her an amused look. "Now how do you feel?"

She blinked and sat upright. "Surprisingly better. What all was in that?"

"We call it a shrub, or switchel, I believe," Francois answered, with a small shrug. "Got a bit of vinegar, honey and whatever else can be found. Wonderful quench when lookin' for relief from the heat."

The black man turned, the knowing smile on his face answered who had made the concoction. He reached out. "Take these. I will make another."

She stared at the almonds in her hand. "And these. Where did you get these?"

The man didn't answer so Francois gave her a wicked grin. "You all in the North don't know our darkies like we do. Many of them have secrets that can help us in dire straits." He gave the other man a look. "Or kill us, if they like. On that, better white men acknowledge. It is the white trash and the ne'er do wells that need watchin', right Edward?"

"Massa Francois speaks the truth, Miss Ada." He grinned.

She blinked hard. "Why do you call him master? You know, you are free. You don't have to be on that side," she pointed to his butternut coat. Her goal to help him understand his freedom overrode the niceties they'd exchanged with her. She saw Francois tense.

"Oh, now, missy," Edward started slowly. "I heard of the freedom Massa Lincoln proclaimed. Ain't a secret here, but my home, my wife and family, is in Lous'iana. I ain't leaving without them."

"But you don't need to serve them here," she protested.

He rolled back on his heels, pan in his hand. She noticed he wore a belt and the buckle was odd. It was brass with a capital S and an upside down U next to it. *A stolen US buckle?* She knew both sides took from the fallen, but why upside down?

Edward only gave her a wink, as if he saw her staring at him, but he said, "Massa Francois, if'n you please."

Francois took the chair, the wood squeaking as he sat. "Edward, perhaps rank would be a better reference, considering."

The slave gave tight nod. "Sergeant, if'n you will."

Francois just shook his head as Edward kneeled down, still looking taller than Francois, and put his injured foot on his leg, pushing back the dirty brown trouser and dingy drawers, lowering the sock to expose the ankle. An ankle she was way too familiar with. It was swollen and tinged red.

She was up in an instant, at Francois' side, her wrist to his forehead checking for fever. He wasn't any hotter than she was, thanks to the springtime heat. But his injury looked angry. Edward scooped up the goop in the pan and pasted it onto Francois's skin.

"Ouch!"

"Only burns a second, sir. Give it a moment." He wore an infectious grin, as if he held a secret and that irritated her as he was stepping on her territory.

Under the hand she'd placed on his shoulder, she knew Francois tensed when the white paste went on but, given a moment, he instantly relaxed. Intrigued, she tilted her head.

"What was in that?"

"Oh, little bit of this, little bit of that. Tobacco, few leaves and such." Edward shrugged. "In about hour or so, the swelling will leave."

"Look here," she started. "I am a doctor and I will prescribe all—"

"Ada," Francois started, his speech returning back to the slow Southern drawl. "Rest. Later, if'n I didn't and only relied on you and what you got, we'd be no better than dead, because I couldn't move. There's a battle out there."

Fuming, knowing he was right, she turned and stared out the window. The sun had set but the night sky lit up bright with the flames they'd left behind. "That fire will be the deciding factor here," she spat back.

Edward shrugged and began to pick up his utensils. "Wait. He'll be better to move."

Ada leaned back against the table and crossed her arms, entirely aggravated and frustrated. How could there be a slave that didn't want to race to freedom? And one who had talents that would move him further into society? Medicine possibly? Confused, she found herself speechless.

In the far reaches of the view through the window, the pink color of sunrise began to show. As far as he could strain to see it, part of Francois jumped for joy. Sunrise in this dissolute land always brought the idea of hope, and hope right now was just a fragile thread poised to shatter once the armies got rolling. He downed that thought, and just relished in the slowly spreading rays of daylight.

He glanced back at his compatriots. Edward had slumped onto the floor to a sitting position, legs bent with his long arms leaning on his kneecaps, head back against the wall. Francois figured the man wasn't really asleep because he swore he saw the glimmer of his eyes at times. The push he had last night, for the need to make Edward refer to him by rank surprised him probably as much as it did the slave. It was a right call, but Francois realized his exposure to Ada and her argument on the peculiar institution probably was the cause. The woman was a force, that was for sure. He turned his view to find her.

Ada had fallen to the raised pallet that barely passed as a bed. She'd grumbled and fought against it all the time, but her body demanded she rest. Dedicated physician, Ada drive to help was strong, but time and draining energy won. He knew she didn't understand Edward's lack of enthusiasm for being free, and Francois had bit back the chuckle because he knew many of the southern slaves that had family or other ties, would not leap and fly to the north when all they knew was in the South. Oh, there were plenty that would run he had no doubt, but then there were the ones like Edward. Oh, those abolitionists would have their hands tied in more ways than one…

Suddenly, as if his stare had stirred her, Ada moved, her eyes snapping open. Admitting to himself that perhaps, his admiration of her sleeping form and how he longed to touch her was evident across his face as she glanced at him, once she looked clearly at him he doubted it. Then, she sat upright, a frown on her face.

"Are you all right?"

He laughed. "Yes. Good, actually."

She stood, shaking her skirt in an attempt to rid the wrinkles that formed during her sleep. "How is your ankle?"

"You're worried about my ankle?" After the wayward thoughts he'd been having about ravishing her body, her response was a little depressing.

She gave him a peeved look as she moved closer and bent to take a peek. "I'm a doctor…"

She'd just reached the ragged hem of his trousers when he bent, pulling her upright and closer, then he kissed her. She was surprised and at first, didn't respond. Truth was, she was rigid in his arms but that lasted only a moment, for as long as it took for him to seduce her with his lips to open for him. It was a heady moment, to feel the softness of her lips, the strength yet feminine feel of her body and to taste her again. He'd thought he'd never see her again. Probably would've been better if he hadn't. She always sent his mind into disarray, for she was a siren and a wildcat all wrapped up into a woman whose skills surprised him as she did her best to save lives, regardless of their sides.

He growled into her mouth, every sense alive and wanting. He hardened and the intense pressure to touch her everywhere grew until, somehow in the dark recess of his mind, he was reminded that Edward was there as well. With the greatest reluctance, he broke the kiss.

She stood there before him, with shortened breath and lips swollen from his kiss. Her darkened gaze started to clear as confusion and perhaps disappointment, he hoped, took control. He released her from his embrace and she stepped back, still staring intently at him. Neither said a word. Then, she blinked. That action cleared her eyes and all that remained were the bruised lips.

"Good morning," he offered.

He couldn't decide if she was glaring or concentrating. Instead of a direct reply, she dropped again to check his ankle.

"Amazing. The swelling is virtually gone." She gave him a puzzled glance, her doctoral shield back in place. "Again, how does it feel?"

He shrugged, managing to tamper the passion that soared and almost crashed with her switching to his injury over his attentions. "Sore, a little stiff, but with the stick, I can manage fairly well."

She stood. "It looked rather awful last night. Being off it over the last few hours was good, but I'm surprised it's gone down this much. I'm very curious what he put on it."

"You'll have to ask."

"It's a poultice of herbs, mostly, some of them I mentioned," the black man stated as he rose. He gave her a lopsided grin. "Little bit of this, little of that, mixed with mud."

"Mud?" She pursed her lips and frowned. "Now, I think you've started the day off with a fib."

Francois laughed. "No, I reckon you'd find he isn't." He bent and whispered low, "It's magic, or so it's believed."

Edward chuckled.

"Magic?" Ada huffed. "If they're full of magic, why didn't they just whisk themselves free?"

Again, her pushing that agenda. He sighed. Her abolitionist tendencies, of making all white Southerners friends with the Devil, came out in full force. He'd need to squash this quickly.

Grabbing his torn frock coat, he nodded to Edward, who also started to collect the few items he had in the saddlebag he'd brought in. Francois turned to Ada.

"We need to go. Bettin' both sides will be itchin' to fight this morning, and we're in the space between. Need to get to the side, and you out of danger." He stuck the LaMott revolver he'd taken from Wiggins into his waistband and shoved the cartridge box and caps into his bag.

Ada stood there for a moment, a puzzled look on her face. In the beaming sunlight, she looked almost angelic. Almost. Until she thought of another insult to throw at him and his country over her frustrations about Edward staying here. He saw her lips quiver, as if she was fighting for the right words.

Edward, who had stealthy slipped out the door, walked back in, leaving the door open. Francois could see his horse just outside, fully saddle. He whispered a silent prayer of thanks, because he was the one betting she'd be stolen by morning.

"Massa, your horse is ready."

Francois nodded. Ada, though, snarled.

"I will never forget the joy of the wounded when they were brought into our lines. One of them cried out, trying to raise himself from his litter. 'All right now! I shall not die like a dog in the ditch!'"

—Union General Regis de Trobriand at Marye's Heights & Fredericksburg, 1862

Chapter 37

WHAT HAD BEEN HELL YESTERDAY was a nightmare in the morning. The stench in the air nearly made Ada retch as the smell of burnt trees mixed with dying bodies, burnt remains, sulfur and horse manure, illuminated in sunlight. Smoldering lumps of weeds, sticks and heavens knows what else made her ill. She grasped her middle as if to stop the nausea that would be horrible to spill when sitting on top of a horse, and possibly on Francois, who sat behind her.

"Little rough, wouldn't you say?" he asked her softly.

She could only nod, still afraid of opening her mouth for fear of what might happen.

Slowly, they walked through the battered land. Edward walked next to them. The pressure of Francois against her definitely changed the focal point of her senses. His solid torso was an added comfort yet it sent tingles through her. Cradled in between his legs, she couldn't help but feel the slight bulge that nudged against her, despite the woolen skirt and petticoats. Her cheeks heated when her core registered his body. She blinked hard and tried to take her mind off him.

Looking into the distance, she swore she could see the red, white and blue of the Federal camp. In disbelief, she gulped. "We're heading toward the Union camp? Do you think that is wise?"

"I need to get you back to safety."

"At what price?" Her voice peaked, at virtually a yell. Her safety at the price of his? "You didn't do well last time you stayed at a Federal prison."

That comment got Edward to glance at them.

"I can't just leave you here," he began.

She grabbed the reins out of his hold and pulled back to stop the mare. "No!"

"Missus Ada, hollering out here not a wise thing," Edward warned. But neither she nor Francois heard him.

Francois tried to take the reins back.

"Ada, please, let go!"

"No, let me off! I'll walk back over…"

They managed to shift enough on Rose and tug her mouth to where the horse started to side-step, a little faster with each step. Just as the mare started to hop, trying to dislodge her riders, Francois got Ada's grip off the reins and managed to slow the horse some.

"Ada…"

She twisted as well she could in the saddle, infuriated, and slapped his cheek with all her strength.

2nd Lieutenant Jeremy Hillsdale inhaled deep and suddenly wished he hadn't. One would have thought the morning smells after a battle would have been familiar now, but it was the added enhancement of burned human and horse remains took it to another notch and his stomach threatened to upheave. It was bad enough he with two privates were sent to help find the surgeons in the field who'd, as his commander grumbled, *'wandered off to find those poor bastards'* — the wounded who'd fallen in the fields. So far, he'd found the one and his orders were to return with him immediately, but it was harder than he imagined as the man literally stopped at every lump on the ground.

"Doc, we need to keep movin'," he stated and spat into the ground. "Or we're gonna be in a mighty heap of hurt when those Rebs start this morning."

The surgeon glanced up from the stack of leaves and debris, a mixed look of relief and frustration on his face. "Been out here most of the night. Don't hear those howls of pain anymore…"

Or the screams of pain being burned alive! That still made Hillsdale tremble.

"…I guess we're done." The surgeon stood. "For now."

Grateful, Hillsdale nodded, the mood to take a gun and fire at the enemy growing out of desire to kill those sons of a bitch who'd started this war! He waited anxiously as the doctor mounted his horse and they with the two other soldiers turned to go.

They barely walked a few yards when Hillsdale heard the voices. Living people and they were yelling, but not for help, more like arguing. He motioned his entourage to stop so he could hear better and find them. Tilting his head in the direction he thought it came from, he heard them again. One of them sounded like a woman. He frowned. *What was a woman doing out here in hell? Unless she was a nurse…*

Slap!

That spurned him to send his horse at a trot toward her, with the rest following suit. Over the crest in the land, with its fallen timber mixed with standing trees and shrubbery, he found a woman on horseback with a man sitting behind her. They were arguing, yanking on the reins, sending the horse to dance with minor hops in its steps. Hillside knew that animal's fright was rising and those minor hops would turn to bucks. The black man on the ground was scurrying out of the equine's path.

The white male rider's cheek was flaming red from the slap. Hillside gathered he was secesh from the color of his clothes being mud-spattered butternut. Yet the girl was dressed like a nurse for the US Army, with her navy dress and tinged white pinner apron. Though, she could be a civilian…

"Whoa, hold, sir!"

The threesome stopped, obviously surprised. Hillsdale smirked. Coming in with prisoners might make this expedition worth the while.

But all his wild musings came to an abrupt stop when the surgeon piped in.

"Ada?"

The woman's eyes narrowed then. What little color in her cheeks paled. "Richard?"

Ada froze. What was Richard doing out here? She hadn't recalled hearing he was in the area, let alone searching for survivors. Her heart, though, jumped at seeing him. He did look rather dashing in his uniform, even with it as muddy as everyone's. As he approached, the usually warm wickedness she normally saw wasn't there. Recognition yes, but the warmth was lacking. Then again, she was sitting on a horse with the Rebel. She wondered if he recognized him...

Francois, though, recognized him as his whole frame tightened against her. She tried to relax against him, hoping he'd do the same but both failed.

"I thought you'd returned to the Army of the Tennessee," she started, trying desperately to recall what he had said. "It's a surprise to see you here, in Virginia."

He smiled, breaking the tense look on his face. "A pleasant surprise, I hope, considering. I was at the last minute re-assigned to Grant's command." He looked at Francois. "Are you not the man I met at—"

"He is," she interjected, praying Francois would not say a word and expose his Southern drawl. *The uniform, though...* "It's a joint venture, as it were, trying to find the wounded."

"Well, come to me," Richard offered, extending his arms. "Let the Rebels find their own."

"Ada," Francois warned, his voice low.

She pulled her confused focus off Richard to the man on the front horse behind him. An officer. And she noticed his hand was at his side, where his revolver was.

"Richard, this man is wounded as well. Don't allow Captain—"

"2nd Lt. Hillsdale, ma'am," the mounted officer claimed but he didn't move his hand.

"Lieutenant, then. I'd appreciate if you'd move you hand away from the gun," she directed at Hillsdale.

The two soldiers behind him moved closer. She hadn't seen them, but they were not mounted. They carried rifles. The air was tense and her worry increased. Edward, she saw out of the corner of her eye, had stepped back. What was he doing?

"Gentlemen, please," she started.

"Yes, Ada, explain what I'm seeing here," Richard said. "You are on the horse with this Rebel, obviously in dire straits. We cannot allow that type of behavior."

Her heart fell into her stomach as her eyes shot wide open, but she forced a laugh to try to lighten the mood. "You know me, Richard. Arguing is a pastime of mine."

Richard laughed, followed by Francois. The officer gave a chuckle and when they all bent over with the contagious jovially, no one saw Francois pull his LaMott pistol out and aim it at Richard. The click of the hammer locking back caught everyone's attention.

Ada gulped. "What are you doing?" she mouthed but he ignored her.

"I think it's time we leave."

Hillsdale steeled. "Soldier, drop your weapon."

Richard acted fast. He reached up, grabbing Ada at the waist and lifted her off the saddle, making sure he hit Francois's leg. Startled, Ada screeched as he flung her to the ground. Francois roared, bending in the saddle, his face painted in pain, his trigger finger squeezing. As Richard yanked her to the side, she saw in the confusion, with the horse prancing, the foot soldiers ran forward right as Hillsdale pulled his gun. The black man was gone.

Angry, Francois twisted in his pain and pointed the gun at Richard.

Shocked, Ada cried, "Francois, don't!"

But the gun fired, along with two others. Smoked filled the air and she froze. It took a moment but reality rang in her head, so she struggled to see and found Hillsdale's gun smoking as it fell loose of his grip as he fell off his saddle, his leg bleeding through the powder blue wool trousers.

One of the soldiers was on the ground, his eyes opened and vacant of seeing ever again. The other soldier was so caught in the vines that littered the ground that he fell to his knees.

Richard was reeling, trying to clear the gunsmoke to make it to the fallen officer. Ada had to blink hard, her ears still ringing from the gunfire, when she saw Edward, standing to the side, tucking his long-nosed revolver into his belt to hold it. The slave had shot a white man, a Federal soldier, her mind stuttered. The side that fought for his freedom! Befuddled, she slowly became cognizant of the moans and they came from more than the Federals. She heard Francois and ran to him.

His side had a red stain from blood, the clothing torn by a bullet. She raced to untie her medical bag.

"Can you move? I need you off that horse," she told him, freeing her supplies.

"No, no, Ada," he muttered low. "We got to go."

"Ada, don't! I need help here!" Richard begged.

"Give me my gun!" Hillsdale bellowed. "You shot me, you worthless bag of Southern shit!" He bent, trying to reach the fallen piece.

"Perhaps, sir, I oughta just shoot you."

Silence fell except for the sound of Richard ripping material. The rest looked up at the black man.

Hillsdale glared. "To think the fight is to free your black asses! Why the hell did you shoot me?!"

"Ain't right, firing at a wounded man and involving a lady in your fight."

Hillsdale swung back to Francois. "I'll see you hanged for this!"

Francois sat on the horse, patting her neck in an attempt

to calm her while he worked hard to breathe. The pain in his side was smart, like a slice went through him. He recalled his aim at the bastard Ada was so enamored with. How he longed for her to realize that man wasn't worth the spit it'd take to shine a shoe! But Rose moved, moving his aim off the doctor and more on her, so he managed to shift and he guessed, from his position, he downed the soldier on the side. From all the looks of it, Edward shot the Federal officer. He counted in his head the circumstances and realized, firing and killing at this close range, when all were on a 'mercy mission', being brought in as prisoners wouldn't go well. He doubted they'd make it to the Federal camp. Silently, he swore.

"Ada," he called. "Come with me."

"You're not going anywhere!" Hillsdale barked, even as he flinched at the doctor's ministrations. "I'll have you hanged!"

She looked at him, her eyes wide and wild. He could see the battle in them—to come with him or stay with that Yankee braggart? His shifted. "They will hang us, since Edward shot them too. We can't stay."

He could see her breathing hard, indecision plain as day.

"Ada, I need you to stay!"

Francois glared at the Yankee doctor. "I know you, sir, and I know your type."

"Oh, and what type is that?" Richard snapped as he tore the linen wrap and started to make it a tourniquet on his patient in an attempt to stop the bleeding.

"Heard about you through my sister, who was the last lady you tried to favor. You might recall her. Cerisa Fontaine."

Richard stopped for a second in twisting the lever that tightened the wrap. "I recall a lady by that name, though I didn't recall her last name being such."

"No, because she was wed. But that didn't stop you from trying to seduce her, did it? Or the fact that you have a wife."

He heard Ada gasp. The color drained from her face. He hadn't meant to tell her the truth of the man this way, but they needed to go and her indecision required he either shoot the man or tell her. He might just shoot him anyway…

"Wife?" Ada piped.

"Ada," Richard started.

Ada felt her heart rip. In the back of her head, she remembered Will constantly saying Richard Peregoy was no good, yet he never told her why. *Did he know of this? That there was a Mrs. Richard Peregoy?* Her breathing became hard.

In the far distance, gunfire rang and then an artillery piece boomed.

Still trying to take it in, she stared at him. His mercurial smile was gone, the warm brown eyes more begging than seductive. Somehow, she knew he had lied to her. The vacancy, the sporadic letters, the long courtship that was sparse, and no marriage even hinted at. And then to discover he had tried to dally with another woman? The pain was like a knife jabbed into her heart. She was going to be sick.

"So that's why you never mentioned marriage. Nor made yourself available to take me to meet your family or anything else."

"Ada, please, now is not the time to discuss our future," he pleaded a bit sternly.

She shook her head, unable to believe him.

"Doc, we gotta finish to go. The battle has started," Hillsdale stated, trying to right himself.

Out of the corner of her eye, she saw Francois pull up onto the saddle, shifting till he was secure. "Ada, we need to go!"

Edward, still to the side, managed to reload his weapon.

Ada couldn't move. Richard stood and walked over to her.

"Ada, please. I need you to stay."

As the truth started to make sense, she snorted. "Why? So I can continue to work, slaving away as it was, in a hospital, helping all I could, for you to tempt me later? For a promise of later that never came? And never would?"

"You can't be serious about going with a Rebel! Good grief, he's a slave owner, for Christ's sake!" He snarled. "Oh, I remember lovely Miss Cerisa and her family. If you go with him, you'll regret it. The story of his lifestyle will make you sick. Sick!"

As he threw the jabs at her, she realized she was stepping away from him and right towards Francois. Granted, Francois was what she despised, but he hadn't promised her the world, nor lied about what he was. She glanced up to him. The Rebel nodded.

Another volley of cannon-fire rained to the side of them, getting closer.

She could see his side bleeding through the bandage she hadn't secured, being pulled away by Richard's denial. Suddenly, Edward was at her side, handing her her bag and offering her a leg up.

At this point, the wounded Hillsdale had thrown his hands in the air. He'd ordered the other soldier to grab Richard's mount and they waited.

"Miss, if you go with him, your safety is in danger," the commander warned her.

As she settled into the seat, this time behind Francois, she looked at the Federals, refusing to believe what was happening. Instead, she looked at the man she had thought she loved, the one she'd waited for and suddenly, found him not what she wanted. Instead, the man before her was a better option.

"Good bye Richard."

"We have now ended the sixth day of very heavy fighting [and] the result up to this time is much in our favor. I intend to fight it out on this line if it takes all summer."

—General US Grant wired to President Lincoln, May 11, 1864

Chapter 38

IT WAS A LONG AFTERNOON. The ride was long, troublesome and he was too tired, too much in pain and too hungry but he was thankful. Despite everything, the woman who sat behind him, arms wrapped around his stomach, was now his.

That, he realized, was a bit presumptive on his part. He had ridden off with this lovely vixen despite the fact that he was a Southerner and a slave owner. The bit that vermin had hinted at, about his 'lifestyle', irritated him. He'd stopped that practice well over a year ago. The history that lasted years, though, and plagued his conscience now, was because of her. So he did his best to wipe it from his mind, for they were still in Virginia and heading south without another thought.

The silence over the last few hours was deadly. Periodically, he felt her shudder against him and he was sure she was crying. All he could do was be steady for her, but said nothing. They'd left the Wilderness right as both armies went at it again. He directed them South, not to either army, and no one complained. He hadn't given the direction much thought, until now. Location and food rang high in his thoughts. Though water was first, as his canteen was empty.

Edward must have thought of that, too as the colored servant skirted ahead only to return not long after, the wool cover of his canteen dripping.

"Sergeant, there's a creek up ahead. Water still clear."

"Thank you, Edward." Clean water was such an oddity nowadays, he thought. So much blood from battles often spilled into water source, making camp life hard. With a sigh, he stopped the horse and slid off while Edward stood close by to help Ada down. He watched, hoping she'd look at him or at least say a word but she did neither. What was going through her mind? He could only imagine the hearsay and wild thoughts prompted by that lowlife back there.

He dipped his canteen in the water, every move hurting. His body was racked with pain and to add the scrape on his side nearly made him collapse but he didn't. Thankfully. Breathing hard, he scooped up a handful of water and splashed it against his face, relishing in the coolness. With some stiffness, he rose and took the canteen to Ada, with thoughts of giving her his and filling hers but when he did the exchange, her dull expression changed. Her eyes caught on fire and without forewarning, she swung and slapped his cheek again, sending his hat to the ground.

Stunned, he stared at her.

"How dare you!"

Francois breathed deeply, picking his hat off the ground and ran his fingers through his hair before jamming the hat on his head.

"You should be mad at him," he finally blurted. "You just don't like me being the one to tell you the truth!"

But she was pacing.

"Why didn't I know?"

He picked up her canteen, headed toward the water and he refused to answer her. Edward stood to the side, his soaked wool-covered canteen sweated on his twill pants while he chewed on the long grass blade.

Francois wiped his mouth after another sip and screwed the top back onto her canteen. "I believe you were given hints."

"Ha!" She stormed away.

"He is vermin, the worse you've met. Be thankful you learned before it got worse." Once the words were out of his mouth, he realized she didn't want to hear that. He braced for another slap.

"Where the hell are we?"

He chuckled. "Good question. Virginia still, but south of the armies. Out of range, I reckon."

"Yes, sir. The battle is raging thata way," Edward added, pointing in the direction from which they'd come.

He nodded.

"And so where we headed then?"

"Gotta find you a way home," he muttered.

"Home? Pennsylvania? I can't go there!" She sounded appalled.

"Why not?"

"Because...because...I just can't. The ride wouldn't be safe, you can't escort me and simply leave me there!"

He could see her eyes fill with tears. Problem was, he wasn't sure what prompted it—her anger and loss of that pompous ass, or a true fear of returning home, yet why would the thought of going home make her beg him not to take her there?

As if to remind them they weren't far from the war, artillery fire echoed in the distance. Again, Francois took off his battered hat and ran his fingers through the dirty strands of hair on his head.

"Ada, what do you want me to do? If I can't get you back to your home, where do you want me to take you? I will not leave you out here, with two armies that plan to defeat the other. I can't return you to your side, because you won't go." Now he started to pace.

Ada's blood was boiling. Had been burning since earlier, when they'd clashed with Richard. Even the thought of him made her anger inch higher. And now this one, who knew, who kept it from her and then exposed him without her having a place to run. Add onto that the slave who killed a soldier and a Rebel who shot and wounded another Federal officer. Just what was she to do?

"You haven't left me very many options," she quipped back. "I've witnessed too much. Helped, apparently, too much. To return to my side will bring not only imprisonment and perhaps death to you. Edward, here, had a chance as a freedman in the North, but his shooting that Union soldier ended that. I suppose," her mind churning at the thought, "you could point me in the direction of Pennsylvania and I could try to get there on my own."

"What?!" Francois roared. "Not for all the saints would I allow that!" He stormed up to her, grabbing her shoulders, staring into her face with fire in his blue eyes. "There's a war going on out there. You've seen the bloody side, but let me tell you about what happens before that. Commanders ordering men forward, cannons loaded, guns primed. When we aim, nothing in our path can cross it without hellfire on it. All horses are taken by both sides, as well as guns, ammunition, food, saddles and anything else. For a lady, alone, to try to pass, even a doctor, you are inviting hell!"

"Well you can't go!" she snapped back. "You're not healed enough, even with *his* concoction on it! And they'd probably shoot you for taking me as well! And as to him," she pointed to Edward. "I saw his belt buckle. Even I can determine that was stolen from a Yankee, probably a dead one at that. He's killed a Union soldier while standing by your side, news that will flood the camps as half the men don't give a hoot about freeing the slaves as a reason for fighting. But you've opened up a new conversation and they'd like to be the deciding vote, meaning Edward would be shot. Defending me loses all rights with him by your side." Now her blood was racing. "So then what? If we can't go north, where?"

He didn't answer, which only irritated her more.

"And furthermore," she spat, spinning on her heel to face him. "Why in the world do you even care about my safety!?"

"Because I love you," he answered softly.

She glared at him. Despite the somewhat desperate look in his eye, she decided he was just throwing more roadblocks at her, though without telling the truth.

"Harrumph!" She walked away then spun around, a madness breaking through her walled nerves. "You must be mad to think that!"

Was he mad? He must be. Where the hell did those words come from? *I love you.* Most assuredly, the war was taking a toll on him mentally…

He saw Edward bending to select another piece of grass to chew on, smiling subtly as he did it. *Damn slave!* Though the man's infectious grin made Francois snort. This was mayhem at its finest. He'd gone to war to forget Emma and was successful, only to find his heart now beat erratically for another lady. One who could chew him up and spit him out like he was milkweed. The irony made him want to laugh.

Yet, despite all the musings in his head, his heart still beat madly for Ada. While he might be the type of man she saw worth destroying, he couldn't help that he'd seen her bright side, how she helped everyone with a natural strength and beauty that attracted him, soothed him and filled his heart with joy. He still remembered how she felt, the warmth of her skin, the response to his lovemaking and those heart-stopping kisses… It'd taken till now for him to truly understand just how deep his feelings for her ran. But, did she love him? Could she love a scoundrel who was a Southerner, who owned slaves and fought for the Confederacy?

"Yes, perhaps I am mad," he answered but as he took a step closer, the need for her bloomed in his heart. He took her hands and pulled her to him hard and fast. "Could you love me? I am what you see. I am not married, but I am a Confederate, I do own slaves, my family is Southern but I do have the money to support us." He scanned her eyes. "Come with me. And you'll never regret it."

She stared hard at him, chewing the inside of her bottom lip, her body rigid and cold, refusing to grasp his hands.

"And what if I don't return the affection? Then what? You'd leave me in the middle of hell?"

"Ouch, that smarts." He jerked back to emphasize. "I said I love you. I did not require you to return it just for me to protect you. You won't let me take you home. I can't imagine you want to return to that jackanapes, especially when he could easily turn the tables on you again, but this time, by implicating you in the death of that man and the injury to the officer. Hell, he could be dead now, too." He came back to her. "Here, I do have some pull. It's my homeland. I have the access to funds, US currency even. My father established several connections around the world through his lifetime. In other words, the options are better with me over dealing with that vermin and the piranhas you have in the Union Army, from what I saw."

Ada continued to roll her lip between her teeth to the point that it hurt as she considered his offer. He claimed he loved her. It was an irksome admission yet it tugged at her heart in a way she hadn't expected. Actually, she first thought that was because Richard had hurt her so and her heart still bled at the vast hurt he had caused. But this wasn't that. She had found herself thinking of Francois during their time apart in winter camp, even though she did her best to lie to herself it wasn't anything more than caring for a patient. Granted, she'd never slept with a patient either and that was a mark against her, she decided.

Now, he offered to protect her from the beasts he believed would wound her. He was right on the mark for most of it. Returning home was hard because not only Will lived there but so did Richard...and, apparently, his wife. Of course, Waxler was still there, too. Inside, her stomach curdled and her heart ripped another tear. To go back to the Union forces would make her subject to their investigation over the field if it came to light. Everything was making her head pound painfully.

More cannon fire and rifle shots sounded in the distance. The war wasn't too far away, and from what she'd gathered in camp, this new commander, Grant, had only one goal and that was to defeat Lee's army, regardless of the costs. It was those costs, in the terms of wounded, that ate at her soul.

"My duty is to help those soldiers," she moaned, torn.

"Yes, but as I recall, that call to help didn't specify only men in blue."

She glared at him. "So, now you'd throw me in with the traitors?"

He threw his hands into the air and tried to step away, finding a jab of pain reminding him to be careful. "Ada, I don't know what you want! Talk to me, because the battle is moving this direction."

Edward sat, leaning against a tree. The black man looked asleep. That irked her to no end. He'd stayed with the Confederate side, killed a man fighting to set his kind free and now, took a nap as she battled with Francois over what to do.

"All right!" she yelled, frustrated at the whole affair. "You're in no shape to take me anywhere north. He," she pointed towards Edward, who now gave her a hooded glance. "Proceeds to nap, after he's killed a man fighting to set him free. And me?" Her vision blurred, burning her anger higher. *How dare that man bring her down to this!* "Yes, you are correct. I am here to serve. My skills are to help the wounded and dying. The color of the uniform doesn't make a difference."

Francois's lips curled slightly and if he did smile broadly, she'd get on his horse and leave him! Perhaps he heard her thoughts, and stopped the smile. His brilliant blue gaze sparkled but the rest of him was deadly straight.

"Good."

"Sir," Edward called, standing upright, yanking the milkweed out of his mouth. "Considerin' what is happenin', I see a lot of fire, hell is rolling through the land. Both sides won't be counting on us, if we ain't there." His brows shot up. He was suggesting they not return.

Francois stood, thinking. "I think you are right." He took a few steps till he got the twinge in his ankle and stopped. "Many out in that field are dead and burned."

"Most not able to tell friend or foe," the slave added.

"True. It'd take days to try to figure it out, that is, if this battle ever wanes." He glanced at Ada. She sat on a tree stump, toying with her skirt, an absent look on her face. It was a look he'd seen often on the faces of men unsure of their next step in this mess. He hadn't viewed it on hers, her mission so clear cut that was until she'd met him, he decided.

"Did they know you went looking for casualties?"

She nodded. "Took a hospital steward with me but lost him in the journey." She snorted, which turned into a twisted laugh. "So, my body might be part of that burned wreckage, too, because I doubt Richard would relate it was me there with him and you during that gunfire. Will, Dr. Leonard, has never liked him and would probably bring charges against him for losing me to you."

Francois couldn't help but smile. He strongly doubted Leonard wanted her with Richard. Himself, perhaps, but…

"A perfect point for revenge, my love, but now isn't the time for such contrivances. Let's mount and head toward the southwest."

Edward brought Rose to them and the mare waited for them to mount with the slave taking the lead. Francois felt her body melt against his back and he relished in the moment. He'd take her South, perhaps home and they'd figure from there. All he knew was his heart swelled with joy to have his love with him.

The question was – would she ever love him?

"I see no prospects of peace for a long time. The Yankees can't whip us and we can never whip them."

—Confederate soldier's comment, after Stone's River Battle, December 30, 1862

Chapter 39

A week later…

W*HAT SHE WOULDN'T GIVE FOR a bath!*

The last six days had been a walk and duck game as they'd plodded southward. They managed through the countryside, sleeping in ruins of once great mansions, now long deserted by their owners. The remains of their estates and ravaged crops pillared their trail. Water was ready to find, though she could barely swallow some of the murky liquid pillaged by animal droppings, dead carcasses and fallen timbers, leaving her thirsty and cranky. The two men had finished sharing their remaining foodstuffs, which accounted for nothing due to the Confederacy's lack of supplies.

Ada's mood swung downward and threatened to explode, but anytime she thought of leaving, she found there was really nowhere to go. Better to travel in numbers, the men reminded her, than disappearing at the hands of the minions traipsing around the fields and towns. Besides, what did she have to go home to? Richard? He'd lied to her and he didn't have anything to say when she'd confronted him.

So, she picked up the pieces of her heart and ran, as it were. Only problem with that was Francois. His role as savior was deflated when he told her he loved her. *Love*. She still shook over it. She sat next to him a few times on the back of the horse and the comfort against her was relaxing and exciting and like home. It confused her so she pushed it from her mind, deciding all this was too overwhelming.

Plus the War kept showing up everywhere they went. She laughed. Of course, it did. She still had her nurse's outfit on, minus the apron, and it looked rather ragged. Just like Francois's outfit… She closed her eyes, trying to block the sunlight that was trying to force her to see the truth about them when she did everything in her power not to.

Inhaling deeply, she placed her mask of indifference back on and turned to face him.

"So where are we today?"

Francois and Edward were next to the mare they rode. Edward lowered the mare's hoof while a concerned Francois looked on. Both glanced at her.

"Middle Tennessee I reckon," Francois answered. "Hard to tell after a while, considering how the land is so badly beaten all along the south." He spat to the ground.

Ada couldn't help but smile. Her refined secessionist now sported a rough beard and hints of a mustache. It was more than the whiskers that had appeared a few days ago. Edward refused to let his grow, using his bowie knife to keep his head shaved as well as his cheeks. At first, she wondered why Francois allowed his to grow but the man stated he plainly didn't think the black man would let him use the knife, then the two men laughed. She failed to get their humor, so dropped the question.

The last four days had been hard. They might have

escaped the war in Virginia, but he was right—traces were everywhere. Remains of burned homes, torn railway ties with some bent in odd twists, which both men agreed were 'Sherman's neckties'—a telltale sign of Union General William T Sherman's campaign through the South to take Atlanta and then upward into the Carolinas, but to her, they were signs of the devil. She noticed the black man's brows shot up at the sight, while Francois grew more and more agitated at the Federals with every step they took that showed the destruction of the South.

She did cringe at each sight, a shudder that didn't fade easily anymore. Shaking her head, she got up off her make-shift chair and asked, "So is Rose okay?"

"She'll be fine, if we all walk for a spell." Edward spat to the ground and patted the horse's side.

Ada gulped. Walking would take them forever to get to… mentally she paused. "So we'll be walking to where?"

Francois couldn't help but snort. "Good question. Thinking the route we're on now will take us back to Louis'ana. Home."

She stopped. "Why would I want to go there?"

Francois stopped, his own thoughts questioning him the same. Why did he want to go back? And drag her with him? Edward hadn't questioned, so Francois guessed he was from there, a rather rude presumption, he gathered, but it was what it was, since his owner was part of the Tigers. In reality, he hadn't really planned to return, yet that was the direction they were taking.

Did he want to return? To see Emma, with her baby and Jack? Memories of their smiling faces, hers especially, used to drive a spike into his heart. Now, at the wisp of the memory, it was a dull heartache, annoying but livable. Had the War done that? Or Ada?

"Wasn't exactly what I planned when we left the battlefield, but it is familiar." He shrugged. "Even if they thought we were alive, it'd take more than a whim to get soldiers out west to look for me or you or even Edward, so it's safe ground for all of us."

Now, she was pacing. That was a somewhat irksome trait of hers, he mulled.

"I can't go there. I mean," she stopped and glared at him. "Why would you want to take an abolitionist home to your slave-owning plantation?"

Her snarl at the end was sharp. "I wasn't thinking that way. Look, doctors have been scarce since the War began. You might find some place that'd let you practice."

She didn't say anything, just concentrated more on lifting her skirts as she walked over the terrain. "Surprised you didn't suggest you could marry me, considering."

That stab he should've expected. He'd made his declaration on his feelings, yet through this trip, he'd left her alone. Considering she hadn't replied the same, he figured she wanted him nowhere close. So he kept a distance, even though it was eating him up inside. With her asleep on the saddle blanket and his coat, he couldn't keep his eyes off her.

"I would love it if you married me."

She frowned but laughed. "I should think not."

He wanted to fume but he stomped that fuel down and did his best to give her a hurt expression. "Oh, madam, how you wound the heart."

She laughed. The sound of joy actually rekindled his heart.

Edward had moved ahead to scout but now came back at a somewhat hurried step, his face void.

"Sergeant, you might wanna come see. You, too, missy."

Puzzled, Francois murmured for Ada to stay just behind him as he pulled out his LaMott and checked the cartridge. "Lead the way."

The slave led them through a copse of trees. On the other side was another gangly sight of one downed horse and two slumped bodies. The stench was underlying, as the slow decay started. Francois continued scanning the area. One saddled horse but two riders didn't make sense. Then he heard the shallow moan and Francois shot a glance in the direction it came from. It was to the right, far away. There lay another body, only this one moved. Francois started that way but Ada over reached him, getting there first.

It was a dark-skinned man, wearing a Yankee uniform. Blood ran from his mouth. His eyes had a terrified look and his shirt and waistcoat was in disarray. Francois saw why. He was gut shot and his reaction was similar to many who ripped their clothes to shred, trying to find their wound, fearful it was fatal. Ada shook her head, confirming he was dying as she saw the wound.

"Soldier, Francois Fontaine at your service. What happened?" He opted out of telling the poor soul the secesh were here again, especially since his first rapport with them was fatal.

"Carrying dispatch," he grinded, before he started to cough up blood. "For..." His eyes rolled to the back of his head and he was gone.

Ada moved the boy's hat over his eyes and bowed her head to pray. Francois inhaled and waited a minute before he took the boy's dispatch bag.

"What are you doing?"

He snorted, flipping the opening flap back. "Looking to see what's in here, of course." He rummaged through the pages. "To General Schofield, Army of the Ohio." He raised his brows. "There's also letters here." One caught his eye and he pulled it out. It was labeled to Jack.

"Brig Gen Fontaine?" Ada queried. He didn't realize she was off to his side, veering over his back.

"Yes. My brother."

"Your brother is in the Union Army?"

"Yes," he snapped. *What the hell was a letter going to Jack out here? Army of the Ohio?* The return on the post was his sister's writing. He'd recognize that curve on their surname anywhere. *But why was she writing him and not Emma?* The letter was marked three days prior. Finally, curiosity took control of him and he ripped the seal and scanned the letter.

"That isn't your property to open!" Ada cried but he ignored her.

"...Jack, it's been worse since you left. Emma hasn't been herself and then the spring rains have brought on a dire case of the fever. Please, if you can, send us a doctor. With your promotion, surely you can do that, right? The babies are in trouble if it gets to them. And Mama looks like she's a touch unwell. In my condition, I'm in no state to care for her and the rest. Please help! With love and affection, Cerisa"

A rock fell into his stomach. Yellow fever. Rarely did they get hit with it at Bellefontaine. What had happened?

"What's wrong?"

He refolded the letter, a scowl on his face. "Illness. That's my family. My mama is apparently sick. Fever. And my sister writes that most the physicians are at war, meaning only a small handful left. Our family doctor has fallen ill as well, and he isn't a young man." Jabbing the walking stick into the ground, he stood, still clutching the bag.

"You can't take that!"

"Why the hell not? You all up North have no problem taken our what's ours."

She gasped. Francois shook his head in disgust. He'd been nursing a wounded heart for too long. First Emma and now this vixen, who had his heart but acted as if it were nothing more than a patient, feeding it when needed but nothing more. *To hell with them!*

But that silent feud in his head over his heart brought a reality to light. Ada was a physician. She could help.

"You need to return it!"

He frowned at her words. "To who? A dead dispatcher?"

"No, of course not." She huffed. "I could take it to the Union."

"On what? Rose can't be ridden at the moment."

She growled. That made him want to laugh. But reality was, he needed her help and she deemed the Union more important to get dispatches. He toiled over the idea in his head before he blurted out the solution.

"Look. Edward could, in theory, take these to the nearest authorities – Union or Rebel depends on who he sees first. However, I need help for my mother. Will you help?"

She stopped mid-pace and stared at him. His fiery abolitionist looked perplexed. He'd be taking her into the heart of slavedom on a mercy mission to save his mother's life. Would she?

How dare he! First, he claimed to love her, then ignored her and now, after illegally opening mail not meant for him, he was begging her to help his slave-owning family! She wanted to scream, but her medical side jumped into the fray.

"You get him to take it to the North, I'll go help." Of course, she would, regardless of the mail's ultimate drop-off. She gulped. She'd argued against the world she was riding into, could she stay quiet enough to help the woman before they drove her out of town on a rail?

Francois took her hands, kissing the back of them. "Merci."

She wanted more than her hands kissed but she held back the retort and started to look for the mounts these soldiers had. "Where are their horses?"

"I see only one downed horse, so I'd reckon whoever shot them, stole them. But let us see if we can find them."

As he turned, using a limp to step, which made her insides clench, Edward appeared and in his hands were the ribbons leading back to the two saddled horses behind him. He wore a grin, like a Cheshire cat she imagined, finding the rides.

"Sergeant, for you and the missy. You head on back, get your folk well." The black man jammed the hat back on his head and grabbed the dispatch bag. To Ada, he said, "Don't you be worrying about this. I'll make sure this gets through."

Francois growled but the tall slave stopped him. "Its what's to be, sir. You'd never know about your folk if it weren't for this, but as Miss Ada says, I am free, to the Yankees, so me appearing with news be fine, plus I see about pay." He winked. "Remember, I'll be back. Got my wife and young'uns still here."

"Where are they, so I can check on them too?" Ada asked. If fever was sweeping through Louisiana, no one was safe.

Francois snorted. "Edward lives in my parish, if I gather right?"

"Yes, sir! When I heard you are a Fontaine, figured as

much."

"You know him by his last name?" Ada's father was the doctor of her town, but she doubted anyone would act as Edward was, like he lived just down the street.

The black man smiled big. The sun gleamed off his bald-head, making him look very jovial. "Everyone in Louisiana knows the Fontaines."

"I am to watch over you as a parent over his children; and you know that your general loves you from the depths of his heart."

—US General George McClellan to his army, March 17, 1862 prior to the Peninsular Campaign

FRANCOIS SHIFTED IN THE SADDLE again. It'd been an uncomfortable afternoon, after Edward left, laughing his merry way to the northeast while he and Ada had headed further south. He knew she wanted to know about his family, though she hadn't asked formally—yet. It was coming, but he wouldn't answer it yet until the tension between them cooled.

He swung around to find her several feet back. "Ada, is something wrong?"

She shook her head. "No, nothing."

But the yawn she stifled brought the trip closer to home. He'd pushed them for the first two hours, then for a fast click on the last one. At a walk now, the rhythm must have been calm enough for her to ride halfway asleep. Add they hadn't eaten, thanks to the growl in his stomach, he pulled on the reins making the horse halt with hers not far behind.

She rode up next to him, a frown on her face. "Are you all right? In pain?"

"I'm well, stiff but more from being in the saddle, not my

foot." He laughed and swung out of the saddle, making sure he landed on his better foot though a wince still escaped from his mouth despite him clamping it shut. Biting back the curse word, he limped to her and lifted her off the saddle.

"I can get down myself," she stated, straightening her skirts.

"I am a gentleman, and it is my honor and duty to assist you." He grinned at her with a wink.

She laughed. "Next time, perhaps you'll save your strength. Sounds like we are heading into a nightmare."

"Fever comes yearly," he mumbled, tying the horses. "But to reach the outer planters means it's pretty fierce. My mother has had a lot to contend with, so I worry about her. And my sister, Cerisa. If I recall correctly, she was with child." He pulled the saddles off and tossed her the blankets. "Let me see if I can scare up anything for dinner. Doubtful anything is still in these woods but I'll double check." He tipped his hat at her after he checked that the LaMott was still in his leather belt.

For once, she looked strong yet vulnerable, a delicacy all wrapped into a beautiful body, clad in a ragged dark wool dress. His hunger for her was growing stronger while she fretted over a scoundrel that wasn't worth a pot to piss in. Anger mixed with his desires and so he turned, determined to find a rabbit or something, and prayed his frayed nerves would cool along with his desires.

The fire crackled and added warmth to a night that had chilled, leaving her close to shivering. Perhaps it was exhaustion catching up to her. The remains of the roasting rabbit, the skinny, pathetic creature he'd bagged on his hunt, sat on the bayonet, propped between two sturdy sticks. She chewed the cornbread he'd made, still trying to decide if it was horrible or good.

"You be taking quite a while to tell me if you like tonight's cooking."

She giggled. "It certainly is a different fare than I'm used to, that is for sure. Army food is not great but…" she looked at him above her tin cup. "Roasted rabbit and this is certainly unique."

He laughed. It was a genuine laugh and very invitingly warm. It sparked tingles that spread to her groin and into her breasts, surprising her enough, she was sure she blushed.

"I figured it was worth it to try. You put up with Edward's cookin' just fine, though it wasn't much more."

"No, but I was used to salted pork fat and hard crackers." And it was awful, but she'd not tell him that.

"Well, we're about done with the hardtack, probably need it to chew in the morning. Salt pork be done. In the field, with minimum supplies, you make do," he replied. "Cornmeal, a little fat and smidgen of water, can make something fine to go with roasted hare."

"I'll remember that, next time I find myself in that position." She looked at him and found him staring at her with dark blue eyes. A heated gaze, one that again set off a flash of lightning through her nerves. Made her bite her bottom lip as she shifted on the stump she sat on, though she couldn't peel her gaze off him, that was until he put his tin plate down and put dirt on the fire, killing half the flames.

"Can't leave it burning too long," he told her. "If either army is nearby, it'll be a beacon. We don't want to draw that type of attention."

She could feel the cold seeping through her clothes

already but nodded. "How much farther do we have to go?"

He frowned. "Another day's ride. We're in Mississippi, if I figured right. On our descent, we'll need to skirt around Vicksburg, since it's now occupied by the Yankees."

She bit her lip from making a comment on that. With her, she could pass them as Federals—maybe. She cupped her tin cup, trying to trap the warmth the metal had picked up from the dampened fire.

"We'd better get some sleep," he gritted out, beating his saddle blanket pillow rather fiercely, as if the stiff wool soften any.

Ada still sat her knees bent up under her skirts. She tried to hug them without letting go of her cup. She was saddle sore but her exhaustion couldn't calm her restless spirit that seemed to scream at full volume. *How dare he think he could just upset her entire life, truth or not, and exclaim he loved her yet ignore her like she wasn't even there!* Maybe he heard her heart yelling because he tossed and turned. Good, she snidely thought.

Finally, he turned back to her. "Ada, it's time to sleep."

Now, she got angry. Her brows shot up as she quipped, "I see. Now you're ordering me like I was a slave or worse."

In a flash, he squinted his eyes as he tossed the blanket aside forcibly, as if he was mad at it, and leaped to his feet in a stance to stomp the three steps to her, even if it was awkward. He reached down, scooped her up and kissed her hard.

Shocked and surprised, she opened her mouth as if to protest, yet wasn't this what she had wanted?

Francois had had enough. She'd badgered, berated and accused him for way too long on the slavery issue. His gratitude for her saving his life, for re-awakening his heart, for coming with him to save his family and his covering her life with his wasn't enough for this hell-bound abolitionist who had enough troubles on her own for being involved with a scoundrel and trying to practice medicine in a world that rejected women's aid. Damn it, she even had him rethinking his home and it was run with slaves and if that was the only. He wanted to growl, especial when his growing desire for her, a need that ate at him, had finally reached the pinnacle of being denied. He'd shut up her whining with a need to groan! So he kissed her and kissed her hard.

Her lips were surprisingly pliant, even opened for him slightly and he took full advantage, delving into her mouth. She tasted too sweet for him to only kiss her once and sit back down. Their meal had been anything but desirable, but she was an ambrosia he couldn't stay away from. Like a starving man, he devoured her, wrapping his arms around her, with one of his hands inching up to steady her neck and head as he bent her backward in his seduction.

Her body responded to his advances, as her arms snaked around his shoulders, her fingers knocking his hat off, allowing her to comb though his hair. She returned his kisses with equal frenzy, as if her hunger matched his. He tightened his embrace, squashing her breasts between her corset and herself and that he needed to correct. He released her lips long enough to trace down her neckline with his teeth skimming her skin while his fingers pulled all the hair pins he could find out, tossing them the ground as his remaining hand held her steady. When her mane plummeted down her back, the silky strands danced across his skin and he groaned with hunger.

His manhood strained against the fabric that tried to contain it, but the beast inside craved to be freed and to take her. Quickly, he undid the hooks on her bodice closure, instantly thrilled that medical staff didn't have all the damn buttons that he'd rip off now to get to her. He squeezed in her waist to undo that busk at once, opening the dress down the front. With a gentle tug, he got the bodice peeled back, her arms freed of the sleeves and a gentle but firm yank at the tie at her waist under the dress loosened the petticoats. All it took was to lift her by the waist and all fell to a pool at her feet. He grinned.

She stood before him, looking angelic in a way, clad in a worn white chemise, with her pantalets underneath. With her hair loose, she looked wild and so seductive, his cock throbbed madly.

"You are beautiful," he murmured. He moved a step closer. It was like Christmas and he wanted his present now!

Ada hadn't expected his advance, so her senses were at first overwhelmed by him. This tall, dark and ruggedly handsome Creole had scooped her up and kissed her with such intensity, she should've been shocked but instead, she nearly melted in his arms. She'd been craving his attention, his affection so badly that she nearly was breathless, yet all she'd gotten was his guarded company. What had happened to change that, she did not care to ask, because the heat he stirred in her was begging for more.

She dug her fingers into his long hair, relishing in the luxury of it as his tongue played with hers. When his lips left hers, to descend down her cheek to her jawline and then down her neck with his teeth skating lightly along the path, sending tingles of excitement racing through her, she nearly came undone. Quickly, she discovered he must have read her mind as his fingers nimbly undid her bodice closure and in one gentle push, weaved through her dress to the ties of her petticoats and unlaced them. Before she knew it, her gown and undergarments shimmied down her hips to puddled on the ground.

"You are beautiful."

A flush of heat covered her body, her cheeks the hottest of them all. Despite her past with him, even with Rich, at that moment, she could feel the true admiration he had for her. The tent at the apex of his thighs was the other indicator. His voice had seemed gritted, as if he was strained and, in an effort to help him, she stepped out of her fallen fabric straight to him and started to unbutton his waistcoat.

He gave her a wicked smile. "Take care, love."

Her hips nudged against his cock when she reached up to push his jacket and waistcoat aside. "Oh!"

He winked. She stared into his eyes, hoping he didn't mean for her to stop and at the color of those sapphire blue orbs, now deep blue like the Union blue, and hooded, she realized he begged her for more. Now, she applied the skills her doctoring had taught her and unfastened his trousers in a blink of an eye, shoving the suspenders out of her way to free his hardness. The silken stiff cock sprang free and into her palm.

Now she gave him a wicked grin. "Perhaps he needs an inspection."

Francois snorted but didn't move. That thrilled her, because she knew he didn't know what she meant. So without giving him another moment, she sank to her knees and licked his swollen head.

He nearly jumped. "Ada…"

But she cut him off by wrapping her lips around the crown and laving his head with her tongue. Her hand closed gently around the rod and slowly she started to rub it up and down. She could hear him gulp as his hips moved with her strokes. With every thrust, she began to lower her lips, taking more and more of him inside her mouth. His skin was as soft as satin but his erection was as hard as metal, pushing deeper and deeper. Before she knew it, he was hitting the back of her throat and her hand had fallen to his scrotum, giving the balls there a slight squeeze when he entered her. He moaned loudly, his hands on her head, fingers through her loosened locks as he took her by the mouth.

Inside her own body, she could feel the fire in her lower belly roar, the lava slickening her core, waiting. It built her excitement and her lips locked around his member, her tongue licking him when suddenly he whipped his member out of her touch.

"No, no, I want *you*."

He put his blanket stretched near hers. In a moment, he finished stripping his trousers the rest of the way off and threw them and his shirt to the side, giving her full view of his sleek body. The war had refined him, making him leaner and harder. For a man who claimed to be a planter only, she doubted back before the war that his abdomen had been rock hard nor his chest and arms muscular, though his legs might have been that sinewy from riding. The soldier's color was established, with a slightly sun-kissed face and hands but the rest white. He was a handsome man. How could he still be unmarried?

She never had the chance to ask, because he brought her to the ground with him, kissing her as he shed the rest of her clothes. She was beneath him, with him between her legs, his manhood nudging at her dripping wet slit to her core. As he knelt above her, she licked her lips and begged, "I need you in me!"

That enticing, seductive smile inched back, grabbing her attention until he slid into her. She mewled. That sound seemed to set them off, as if it was a whistle starting a horse race. He plunged in and out of her core, her hips meeting his every thrust. His hardness seemed to go deeper every time until she could swear he was hitting her womb and opened her mouth to say such when he upped the speed, making her race to meet his every more. It didn't take long, as the pressure built and the need increased ten-fold. Every time his hips came back, his member almost escaped and she panicked, racing to keep him there. Slicker and slicker she became as she hugged him with her core walls. Then, suddenly, the stars exploded as she erupted inside.

Making love to Ada seemed like heaven, Francois decided as he nestled next to her on the blankets, near the dying fire. They were both breathing hard and he enjoyed watching the hardened tips of her breasts rose up and down with each inhale and exhale.

"Marry me."

She snorted and looked at him, her hair mussed from their wickedness, making her look wild and feral.

"Why do you want to marry me?" She propped herself up on one arm. "And why would I want to marry you?"

He laid back and sighed. "Well, to start, we are in a compromising position."

"There's a war on. Besides, who will see us now?"

"Oh, don't be so blind by the darkness, my love. Down here, there are eyes everywhere." He chuckled. "Besides, you could be with child."

That thought made her heart skip. In New York, she had been attractive enough to him that she wondered and had counted when her last menses was, though that was often unreliable a measure. Yet, she had no trace of their intimacy to worry about. "Perhaps, though I wouldn't waste time on that. Ladies always have their ways of covering that."

He snarled. Of course, he took that the wrong way. Let him…

"And you're down here alone, un-properly escorted. A slattern, perhaps?"

She frowned. "How many of those do you know of?"

He shrugged innocently.

"So why would I marry you?"

He smiled. "I'm from a good, old family. I do have money to care for you and children. I am a man of my word and a good soldier."

"Truly?" she propped herself up on her elbow. "You're a Southerner, therefore a Confederate. Your money comes from the backbreaking work of people you enslave. Which makes the good somewhat debatable."

"You have spunk, my dear. I like that. As to our riches, slaves are only part of the equation. We are traders and international merchants. No, I think you won't find another."

"No, that is a given." Somehow now, he sounded different. She didn't like it. "And nothing for me? I'd be a wife in name, nothing more?"

He flipped to his side, facing her as he nudged her to her back, his eyes again dark and determined, his face carved in fierceness.

"I want to marry you because I love you. I have stated

that repeatedly. I'm willing to throw myself, to beg for your mercy just so I can have the right to do this for the rest of my life." He held her hands above her head and kissed her like a drowning man.

It was intense, the heat rising again. He pulled back and stared into her eyes, the plea for an answer all over his face.

How did she feel? Could she love him? A southerner, a man who stood for everything she fought against? As she stared into his gaze, her heart answered for her.

"Yes."

"The campaign is the severest one ever endured by any army in the world."

—Officer of the 139th Pennsylvania reported

Battle of the Wilderness 1864

Chapter 41

"AND LOOK! WE ARE HERE!"

Ada glanced up from the saddle. She'd spent the better half of the day for the last two trying to find a way to feel comfortable. Inwardly, she wasn't the least unhappy about it. Ever since she'd agreed to marry him, a huge weight that had hunkered over on her, keeping her confined and miserable, was lifted and she found happiness. Perhaps love. That part scared her, especially since she had thought she loved Richard, only to discover what a scoundrel he was.

But Francois had been playful, seductive and made her feel joyful. And the last two nights, he'd made mad passionate love to her, the type that had sent her to the heavens and back. She sighed softly as warmth, more than the heat of the sun, embraced her. As to her seat, though…Not only was she not used to horseback riding this far, her body was sore all over, and, she finally admitted to herself, the worst was her thighs and seat thanks to Francois.

Traveling like this, though, was killing her neck. Sleeping on the grown was not comfortable. Finally, he had wadded up his uniform jacket and let her use it as a pillow while he'd insisted he was used to the ground as a mattress. He'd fallen asleep so easily and she would've too, except for the annoying hard thing that jabbed her ear. Finally, she gave up and wheedled her fingers to find the source, discovering a miniature portrait of a beautiful lady. Her stomach fell. Who was she? Her heart lurched. While he'd pounded how awful Richard was, then made love to her, wanting her to marry him and now this? Who was she???? Needless to say, she didn't sleep well.

"All I see is a river and land," she grumbled, again adjusting her seat.

He laughed and steered his horse back to her. "Still sore?"

"Of course not."

"You, my dear, are a miserable liar. I assure you, it will improve," he claimed, siding his horse up next to hers and leaning over to give her a kiss. "Think of it as a glorious way to become so unsettled."

She glared at him but the kiss managed to bury her worry about the portrait and to bring her a feeling she was slowly becoming accustomed to—happiness. It made her spine tingle and her nipples ripple, as if he was licking them. Richard had never had this prolonged an effect on her. Of course, Francois could be lying to her too.

"You, my dear secesh, may be correct, but I'll be happier tending patients than treating myself," she stated, searching for a neutral ground.

He leaned closer, to the point his breath warmed her neckline. "I'd be more than happy to take care of you."

She blushed, she was sure, and sat up straight, the pull on the reins grabbing her mount's attention. "I'm sure you would. Now, tell me, how do we cross this to get to your home?"

"This way." He motioned his horse and she followed down the slope to a cabin. With a quick dismount, he grabbed his cane and went to the door, battering on the wooden plank. "Charlie! Charlie Bloom! You best be home, boy!"

The door opened and an older black man peeked out. "Mista Francis?"

"Oui!"

Charlie whooped and hollered along with Francois. Ada watched, her mind spinning. The elder man, a former slave she bet, greeted Francois like they were old friends. It was warm and the smiles appeared genuine, but it was the last thing she expected. Her abolitionist nature had the hairs on her neck bristling.

"You still got that old ferry?" Francois asked, not even paying attention to her.

"Why, now, Mista Francis, you come banging at my door, then not introduce me to the missus?"

Ada blushed, pushing a loose hair back behind her ear. Francois laughed.

"The future missus, old man! Miss Ada, meet Charlie, one of the best ferrymen in the parish!" He gave her a wink. "Charlie, Miss Ada is a doctor, so be mindful."

Charlie walked up to her, took his hat off his head. "Right nice to meet you, ma'am. Charlie Bloom, at your service." He bowed.

"Glad to make your acquaintance, Mr. Bloom."

He stood, smiling wide. "Now, don't be letting Mista Francis let you think he's all in charge. He thinks he's the man, and he is, but don't let him badger you none."

"Charlie!" Francois shouted.

"I won't. Thank you." She liked the old man.

"I take it, you be heading home, sir?"

"Oui. Can you get us across without raising no ruckus with them Yankees?"

Charlie shoved his hat on his head and started toward the river.

Francois mounted his horse, sliding his cane into the straps off the pummel as she rode up.

"Former slave of yours?"

He wouldn't look at her right away but she saw him purse his lips, as if trying to find the right words.

"Ada, we're heading into lands of my family. Southerners. Yes, there's an illness plaguing the land, and a sickness brought by war and famine. What I'm asking is for you to leave your abolitionist's views here, tucked away until this is all done. No point making the people you've come to help refuse because you want to damn them for their lives as they know it." He finally looked at her. "If you would, please."

They hadn't talked about this, as if the subject was like walking on eggshells for their upcoming marriage. She had agreed to come to help, medically speaking. Could she keep her tongue quiet on the depravity of slavery? With a deep breath, she nodded.

"Merci," he whispered. Then he gave her his handsome smile. "Now, let's go, before Charlie heads out without us!"

He tried really hard not to smirk when they landed on the Louisiana side of the Mississippi River safe and sound and with the horses. He paid the old man with a Confederate bill he had, with a silver coin underneath, the coin worth far more than the paper the currency was written on, then turned to his horse. Ada gave him a slanted gaze.

"I thought Louisiana and Mississippi were occupied, and the Union controlled the river," she said. "So how did a wayward Confederate and a doctor, with two horses, manage to cross without issue?"

He eased into the saddle, happy to relieve the pressure off his foot. "That's why I went to ole Charlie Bloom. That man can make magic happen!"

"Uh, huh, I see. Back to that magic again." She inhaled and looked around. He couldn't help but watch her. She was so beautiful, even in a dirty and frayed dress with her hair straying from the few pins she still had, something else that made him want to laugh. He'd sown into her so much, removed all those clothes and pins to get to her, he was sure she was missing some due to him. He was a lucky man. Of course, she hadn't said she loved him, but she liked him enough to agree to marry him. He'd get her love later.

"Francois, how close are we to your home?"

He frowned, trying to collect his thoughts from his current desire for her back to the overall plan. "We'll pass the town if we head down this path," he said, pointing to the trail that swung right. "Bellefountaine is straight ahead, about an hour, give or take."

"A town you say? Perhaps there might be an apothecary still functioning there. Supplies might be good, if there are as many sick as you've claimed," she stated bluntly.

He shifted in the saddle. At this point, he couldn't tell how many that might be. Their bustling plantation no doubt lacked a good number, thanks to his brother Jack, but he swallowed that bitter pill. A quick look at his beloved made his decision, because she'd be meeting his mother and he doubted his future wife would want to look like the ragamuffin she did, thanks to the hard traveling. "Yes, ma'am. Your wish is my command. Though, we have a stop to make first."

He veered them to the right side of the town and out, looking for the outcroppings he knew were there. Ada, riding next to him, scanned the area and sighed.

"So this is the rich South?"

He grimaced. "The soil is where the money is. It's rich and fertile. But this area, its not farmed but settled by yeoman farmers and craftsmen." He swallowed hard, memories of the 9th flittering through his mind. "Many a man from the Tigers lived in this area, if not right from New Orleans itself."

"And there are sick here?"

He shrugged. "Probably, though my mission isn't to find the ill." He glanced at her. "One of my good friends died while we were fighting in that wilderness area, he was too wounded to move. Died before my eyes. Made me promise to give his belongings to his missus." He fought the shudder that built up inside him as his mind replayed that day in his head, with Wiggins begging him to check on his wife. A deed he didn't want, but was obligated to perform. After all, the man put up with him trying to adjust to soldier life from that of planter.

Up ahead, a small group of women dressed in black, stood conversing, or mourning, Francois decided, as the priest wearing memorial vestments stood with two young boys carrying the holy pieces for a funeral mass, stood in front. There was no coffin, no sign of burial and that twisted Francois stomach.

"They look as if in mourning. Did they just return from the cemetery?" Ada asked softly.

"No," he answered, his tone sharp. "I'm afraid this is the

scene for most of the South. Bodies not found and if so, not able to get back to loved ones to bury."

He saw her shudder and a layer of his own uneasiness eased. She might be familiar with death from the hospital, but for a family to not be able to do a full burial, the pain was tenfold. He slid off his horse, taking his time to land and protect his foot. With a yank, he had cane in hand, maneuvering it to help her off as well. It was improper to ride up to the party, though to hobble could be worse, except his mind was set and therefore, he managed to make it to one of the boys, whispering, "Who is this memorial for?"

The boy looked up, his vision glazed, as if he was vacant. Francois inwardly groaned, believing he'd had to help the priest to several of these lately. "Its for several, sir."

Francois grinded his teeth, then bent lower. "Is there a Mrs. Wiggins here?"

The boy nodded and pointed. "She is the lady in the middle, with that purple ribbon on."

Francois turned and saw the lady with the purple cockade that showed well against her died black dress. He waited while the priest finished his prayers and blessed them all before he limped over to her.

"Mrs. Wiggins?"

The short woman looked up, her deep brown eyes liquid in tears and a sea of red. Her skin was pale, traces of the black stain of the gown stained her neckline as the high humidity made her glisten. Wiggin's wife was a short petite lady, with black hair and rosy cheeks. The strains of the war were evident in her lean face and tight stance. *How he wished he wasn't here with this frightful task.*

"Yes, I'm Mrs. Ronald Wiggins."

He took his hat off. "Mrs. Wiggins, I have bad news. I'm

Francois Fontaine, a member of the Tigers and friend of your husband." He saw her shiver. *Damn, how he hated this!* He pulled a small, brown paper-wrapped parcel out of his frock coat and handed it to her. "I was with Ronnie, when he was killed in Virginia. It was a tremendous battle and he gave his all for the country he loved. He asked me to give you this."

Ada was at their side and as his friend's wife broke into tears, Ada touched her arm with a squeeze. "I'm so sorry, Mrs. Wiggins."

The woman's wailing stopped and she looked at Ada with accusatory eyes. "Your accent. You're a Northerner!"

Ada's eyes widened, not prepared for the attack, just like Francois wasn't.

"Yes ma'am. I'm a doctor. I'm from Pennsylvania."

"Murderer!" she screamed.

"Mrs. Wiggins, please," Francois started but she cut him cold.

"Ronnie wrote to me about you two. How you were wounded and captured but she saved you." She glared at Ada. "And while you might heal, you also are one of them 'free the slaves' folk! One of the reasons my husband died! Died! All for you wanting to set the darkies free! How dare you!"

Francois scooped his free arm around Ada's side, trying to take her out before she said something that'd make this worse. "Mrs. Wiggins, she is to be my wife. I understand you're upset, but I must ask you to refrain."

"I'm a doctor first!" Ada declared, in a chance to defend herself.

"Liar!" Then Mrs. Wiggins started to laugh. "Fontaine is the family? Well, Miss High'n Mighty, enjoy that little fun you're marrying into!" Her laughter escalated as did the tears.

He could feel Ada tremble. She'd never thought she'd be attacked like this. Still trying to walk out of here, having completed his task of delivering Ronnie's last request, he tried to bow and added, "We are sorry for your loss, ma'am."

"Get out! Get out!"

Ada sniffled as they rode away, trying to blame the flowering trees for making her nose itch, instead of the confrontation she'd just had. With a wipe of her handkerchief, she grimaced. The embroidered linen square looked dirty, wrinkly and so unappealing that under normal circumstances, she'd toss it into a fire pit, only to realize she probably appeared no better. They were going to his family's home, and even as just a doctor alone, she hated to look so bad. As his fiancée, it was worse. Not only would her credentials be questioned, as always, but so would her loyalty, her sanity, perhaps her social status as she no doubt looked no better than white trash, one they'd figure he'd bedded and now, she with child, so he needed to wed her. It all made her angry. Because, outside the frumpiness, all those appraisals were wrong!

Ahead, she saw the outline of a few buildings. "Does it by chance have a hotel we could clean up in?"

"Yes, though its been ransacked by the Yankees. Now, I do know a place we could clean up that will be in better shape."

That puzzled her. The hotel was in pieces, he claimed, but there was another place? A former mistress's place? She shuddered at the thought. "You know this lady well?"

He was silent as they walked down the main street. Few

people were out, a couple waved, calling out hello to him and his return. She kept expecting he'd stop but he didn't till they got to the last building and pulled his horse up in front of a store with the placard outside claiming it was Antoine's Barber shop.

"This is what you're looking for." He lifted her off the saddle.

Antoine was an elderly white man with white hair and whiskers and spectacles perched on the bridge of his nose. "Francois, boy, tres bien! You've returned in one piece!" He eyed the cane, eyebrow rising in question.

Francois laughed. "Yes, all in one piece, thanks to this lovely lady. Antoine, let me introduce you to Miss, no, Doctor Ada Lorrance."

Antoine's frown deepened, as if disbelieving, before he broke into a large smile. "A doctor? Only you Francois, would claim such!"

"No sir, I'm not fibbin'."

Antoine offered her his hand and then clasped hers in his two. "Pleasure to meet you, miss."

Ada stiffened, as usual when her title was scoffed at. "He is correct. I am a surgeon, sir. From Pennsylvania."

The man stopped cold. "Francois, you brought us a Yankee?"

Ada raised her chin, readying herself for another assault when Francois stepped in.

"Yes, Antoine, that she is. She saved my foot from meeting with the head surgeon's saw. Got badly hurt in Virginia, captured by the Union and left to rot in their hospital until she was given the permission to tend to me and the others of the Tigers. She brought me back from death and my body intact—twice, in fact!" He stepped closer to the apothecary. "She has come to see to the sick, since the fever is here. Now, we need some supplies."

Antoine gave her another glance. Her skin itched as he assessed if she was worth his time, or perhaps she had lice at this point but regardless, his look made her cringe. He finally asked her what she needed, but she never felt better until they left.

Was his, and the widow's, attitude what she'd have to face here all the time in the South?

LaJoyce heard the hustling in her main room, her girls yipping with excitement, and she raced in to find out what was happening. She was not prepared for what she saw. Standing in her door way was a strapping young man, a little disheveled looking in his rather worn Confederate uniform, bronzed in the face and wild black hair, but the devilish look his sultry blue eyes always gave him away.

"Francois!" She leaped right for him and he caught her, his cane crashing to the ground.

He laughed as he hugged her tight, though at a bit of an angle. "LaJoyce, I'm so glad to see you!"

He lowered her and she noticed the walking stick and picked it up. "I'd hoped you'd come back, right as rain."

He snorted, taking the cane from her. "You know, nothing keeps me down long."

She grinned, her heart thudding wildly. Her own fears he'd be killed now faded as she squeezed his arms again. He looked leaner and a touch older with the sun-kissed skin showing age lines. But he was still hers…

A rather loud grunt came from behind him. LaJoyce gave him a questioning glance before she bent to peer around him. There stood his companion, in a dark colored gown, covered in yellow dust and God-knows what else. Her hair was perhaps blond, though it was dull and wisps flew around her face as it escaped the pins that held it so fiercely tight. The woman's jaw was locked, her lips narrow and the angered stare told LaJoyce everything.

"Good afternoon, Miss ?" She gave the girl her welcoming grin. The woman didn't return it.

"Dr. Lorrance."

LaJoyce laughed and turned to Francois. "Oh, my, look what you brought home! Though didn't think you would, considerin'." She chuckled.

Francois shook his head softly. "LaJoyce, Dr. Ada Lorrance is a physician and my fiancée."

LaJoyce's smile broadened at his announcement. She opened her mouth to speak, but he didn't give her time to respond, throwing in a request.

"We need baths. I brought her home to tend to mama and the rest of the ill."

That reality check refocused her. "I'll have those made immediately." She turned toward the girl, who didn't look as harsh anymore since he came to her defense. Good, LaJoyce thought.

"Ma'am, or shall I say Doctor Lorrance, if you would be so kind, I have a couple of my girls having fits with this fever. May I ask you to take a peek at them?"

Ada sank into the tub, rubbing her eyes and letting herself just succumb to the warm waters. She didn't have long, knowing the water would chill, despite the sitz bath sitting near the fireplace with its green wood burning. But she was determined to allow herself the luxury of reclining in it, even if it was only a second. She slid down the back of the metal tub, her knees bent so her entire top half would sink under the water, a task not easily done.

"Doctor Lorrance! Doctor!"

She shot up out of the water. "What!" she cried, gripping the sides of the tub to pull up and get out but the black lady who greeted them was standing in the room, motioning for her to stop. LaJoyce was what Francois called her. She wasn't tall, but her large bosom kept her from being small, also. The dress she wore wasn't exactly the type for society, or none Ada knew of. The low neckline that displayed the swell of her breasts was hardly suited for teatime. She stared at Ada with a sparkle in her eyes and a grin that was anything but malevolent.

Ada sunk into the cooling water. Being naked in front of another woman was very uncomfortable for a conversation. She couldn't help but squint.

To that, LaJoyce laughed. "Oh, my, yes, I did put you in a tight spot. Here," she said, unfolding the linen towel and holding it above the rim of the tub.

Ada sat, still trying to decide. At the moment, she couldn't see the woman but this was highly improper.

"Missy, Doc Lorry, please. You'll catch your death if you stay in that cold water, then I'll have to deal with Francois over it." She shook the sheet.

Goosebumps were already popping up on her shoulders. With great reluctance, she tucked her legs beneath her and rose, grasping the towel by the top. "Thank you."

LaJoyce walked to the side. "I expect you want some answers and I have a few questions of my own I'd be looking for, so now was a marvelous time to get to know you."

Ada frowned. She'd never been around a woman with such boldness as this woman. Her skin prickled and not from rising out of a cold tub. The woman waited so she shimmied into her chemise, asking, "You are right. I do have questions, like who are you?"

The black woman's grin grew larger. "My name is LaJoyce. I've known the Fontaines for many years. Some of them very close. Yet, let us get this right. I am in charge, here."

"And we're where?"

"At La Bonne Jeux," she answered with a smile.

"A house of ill-repute." Ada shuddered. Francois brought her to a whorehouse?

"Now, you wipe that foul look off your face," the woman stated, as she went to the armoire in the back. Ada could see an array of silks in various colors hanging inside it. "You act as if my place isn't worth your time, but believe me, you needed that bath and a change of clothes if you think you're going to Bellefountaine, illness or not."

"I hadn't begun to start…"

"Of course not, because I stopped you." The woman yanked a dark dress from the back. It was a deep blue dress, trimmed in white and black. "Yes, this will do. Put this on."

Shocked, Ada stepped back. "I have a dress."

"Yes, so noted, and worth the rag bin, for sure." LaJoyce put the dress on the chair. "Perhaps this might help you understand. Your man is heir to one of the wealthiest families in this parish. The Fontaines have been here for nigh on a century, generation after generation. They're Creoles, you know, meaning they're French."

Ada bit her tongue. She knew what a Creole was.

"You may be a northerner and think yourself all righteous, but here, to make acquaintance, you need to follow the rules. Now, the illness has only touched the edges of their lands. Mistress Fontaine is the matriarch there and she will expect her children to behave in good manner. Manners I hope were instilled upon you in your upbringing, because you'll need it for the test God will rain on you. Now, put the dress on."

Francois sank in his own tub, letting the heat work into tired bones and muscle, relishing in a novelty he didn't know was one until now.

"Darlin', need you to sit up, raise that pretty chin for me."

He smiled, his eyes shut. "Yes, Clementine, you have my whole attention."

The girl giggled as she lathered the shaving soap on him and he tightened his jaw as she started to shave the whiskers. He heard the door whisk open, a rustle of skirts and his Clementine was gone. He snorted. "I wondered when you'd get here, you vixen." He reached for LaJoyce, but she stopped him.

"Tsk, tsk, let us get this gone, I tell you." She picked up the razor knife and started at his jawline. "Talked to that missy you brought in with you. Thinkin' of marrying her?"

"Yes," was all he could get out while she shaved.

"Well, as much as I'd hate to lose a good stud like you, you best prepare her for your family. From what I hear, it wasn't a pretty sight with Miss Emma when she found out."

He cringed a bit at that memory. "Always sounds worse than it was. You know that. Say, speakin' of Miss Emma, what is going on at Bellefountaine?"

"Ne'er you mind. Stick to what you need to do first. Or that pretty little strumpet could take that foot of yours after all, before she turns you in. Yankees still rule the roost here, if you'll recall."

Francois blinked hard. LaJoyce was too good at her job of reading clients, mostly men and their desires, or so he thought. But she had Ada figured well. The problem was, how to explain the Fontaine wealth, and his part in it. God help him!

"There is no enthusiasm in the army for Gen. Grant, and, on the other hand, there is no prejudice against him. We are prepared to throw up our hats for him when he shows himself the great soldier here in Virginia against Lee and the best troops of the rebels."

—Col. Seldon Conner, 19th Maine

Chapter 42

FRANCOIS STOPPED THE HORSES AT the gates to his family's home, letting the blood that raced through his veins come to a calm. He was home. After the mad dash to get away from here last November, he'd returned. But was he ready to?

"Francois?"

He grinned a lazy, lopsided smile as he turned to face his fiancé. "We are at Bellefountaine, my lady. Home to the Fontaines for the last century. A group of Frenchmen who'd wandered to this land under the French regime, got rich under the Spanish and maintained their wealth under the Americans. Welcome to the family." He bowed his head.

"You don't make it sound so good with that tone."

He inhaled. She was right. "My dear, we are slave-owners, the very type of you people you scorn. Fever or not, the darkies are here. Now, keep in mind, my brother, Jacque, is a Union officer, and was stationed here for control of the state of Louisiana, since the loss of New Orleans to the

Yanks. My sister, who is a bit like me, and ran away years ago, returned from her adventures towing a Union officer husband back with her. A general, if I recall correctly." He turned to face her. "Both sides are here and learning to live together, as best as any divided family can. Please, do us all a favor and keep your abolitionist views quiet. While I love you, they may not, regardless of their views. Agreed?"

Her gaze was tense and her jawline steeled but she did nod. The last thing he needed was her ranting about the number of blacks here. Though, then again, they may not have that many, considering...

He reached across and took her gloved hand to squeeze. "You know, I'm honored you'll marry me."

"You saved me from a life, worrying over someone who is not worthy of that, so I thank you."

It wasn't the answer he'd hoped for, but it was an answer. And he knew she yearned for him like he did her, all signs their lovemaking demonstrated that. Love would come, that he kept telling himself. With a grin, he nudged his horse forward.

"Bertrand! Bertrand!" he yelled when they reached the front of the house. He scanned the building he grew up in and saw wear and tear in places he didn't remember, like the front doors had the paint peeling away, the stairs up to them were worn and bare in areas like he'd never seen. One of the window sashes sagged and the shutter to the far left first floor window was missing a lattice. Puzzled, he dismounted, forgetting about his foot until the last second and caught himself. *Where the hell was Bertrand?*

The front door swung open and the head house slave ambled out at a pace that equaled Francois's gait.

"Massa Francois! Sorry, I didn't hear you at first," the old man said, taking the reins for his and Ada's horses.

Francois saw his doctor tense the moment the butler spoke but, thankfully, she kept mum. He reached for her, steadying himself on the better foot. As he lifted her off the saddle, he whispered, "Thank heavens ladies are so light!"

She batted him with the fan LaJoyce had shoved in her hand when they left. "Next time, I'll dismount by myself. *Harrumph*!"

He laughed. "Bertrand, ole boy, where is everyone?"

"Well, sur, after Massa Jack said his piece, some here and some ain't. Then the fever hit. Mighty bad, sur. Mighty bad."

Ada looked at him and then reached for her medical bag. Francois took her arm and as he started into the house, asked, "Where is that brother of mine, Bertrand?"

"Well, sur, he be gone. Massa Jack is gone."

Francois stopped. Jack left? Now? He went to the front parlor, hoping to find his mother there but found an empty room.

"Perhaps they're in their rooms?" Ada suggested, a slight annoyance in her tone, as if that was the better solution than a parlor.

Francois growled and turned to leave the room when a whirlwind in green brushed right into him.

"Francois!!"

"Cerisa?" He held her tightly. Her stomach bulged between them and he caught she was barefoot. "Still carrying that child?"

She ignored him. "I'm so glad you're here. It's been a mess ever since Jack left."

"Bertrand said the same. What do you mean, he left?"

Cerisa caught her breath, then seem to notice another person in the room. "Apparently, Francois has lost his manners. Welcome to Bellefountaine."

Ada nodded. "Thank you."

Francois added, "Cerisa, my fiancée, Ada Lorrance. Ada, my sister, Cerisa."

"You brought a fiancée back from the war?" Cerisa started laughing. It was an edgy laugh, one that grated on his nerves. "This family doesn't do well being single during this rebellion, do we?"

"Where the hell is Jack?" Once the swear word was out, he regretted it but he was in no mood for her laughter. If Jack was gone, where was Emma?

Gripping as best she could around her pregnant middle, Cerisa stopped laughing. "He was called back to the war."

"What?"

She shook her head. "He got orders to head to the western theater. Tennessee, I think."

"Why didn't your husband stop him?"

She snorted. "You can't really think Pierce could stop the War Department, do you?"

"He's a general, for Christ's sake!" His anger escalated. *How could Jack just leave the family like this?*

"Yes, Emma was pretty mad, too."

The man he was mad at ran into the room.

"Cerisa, what is—" he turned and saw Francois. "Francois, you're home." He looked his brother in law up and down. "Returned fairly unscathed."

"Ha!" Francois mumbled as he paced, his steps emphasized with the sound of the cane on the hardwood floor.

"He brought a fiancée, as well," Cerisa nodded.

Pierce turned to face Ada, smiling broadly. "Good afternoon! Welcome to the latest warfront here at Bellefountaine!"

Ada stood, unable to move, truly believing she was seeing a theater over real life. These people had embraced and embroiled within seconds and she stood to the side, like the audience of a bad play. She realized her hand gripped around the handle of her medical bag so tight, her fingers and wrist now hurt but she found she couldn't relax. This was the family that madam had told her to be prim and proper for? *Poppycock!*

"Excuse me!"

All three heads turned. Francois looked mildly surprised. The woman just grinned and the other man's eyes widened.

"I hate to interrupt your argument, but I am a doctor. I understand there's a fever here?"

"Yes, there is. Been spending the better part of the week trying to keep my expectant wife clear of it," Pierce offered, pulling the pregnant woman's arm into the crux of his arm. "Which has not been an easy chore."

"With Mama down, how can I ignore the demands of the house," Cerisa answered firmly, leaning into her husband, but the strong lines that outlined her features told Ada that the general would stand no chance.

"Where is Emma?" Francois asked. It was his tone that bothered Ada. It was a touch more concerning than she liked.

"She's gone, too."

"How do you mean, 'gone'?" His question hinged on worry and that now got Ada's hackles up. Her fiancée seemed way too interested in his sister-in-law, if she understood him right.

Cerisa shrugged. "Surely you remember those two could be rather," she rolled her eyes, as if trying to find the right words. "Argumentative at times."

"Wait, please." Ada's temper was rising fast with this family's unconstructive bantering. "Mrs. Fontaine is sick?"

"Yes ma'am."

Everyone turned to find one of the servants at the door. Ada didn't even see the ebony skinned young girl enter the room. She stood rather tall for the childlike features. Perhaps she was in her early teens, Ada guessed. The girl was thin but not starved, with long limbs and barefoot. The one thing that immediately grabbed Ada's attention were her light almond blue eyes.

"Would you take me to her?"

The child nodded and turned with Ada in tow. She could hear Francois still arguing with his sister, so she said nothing but left. With his quick worry over this Emma, Ada realized she must be the woman in the mini portrait she discovered in his coat pocket. Inside seething, she needed to get herself busy before she did something drastic. What that'd be, she wasn't sure, as her emotions rolled inside her stomach, making her mad and upset all at once. *He exposed Richard for the scoundrel he was, but from the look of it, was he any better?*

It took Francois a shove by his sister to realize Ada had left. He gritted his teeth and reached for his cane, which Cerisa took instead.

"General, get hold of your wife," he barked, anger surging. *What the hell had he just allowed to happen?*

Pierce leaned back against the server, crossing his arms. "I believe this is a discussion for brother and sister."

"Cerisa! You're in no state for bickering with me like this!" He stumbled and cursed the injured foot, the pain searing up his leg.

"And you bring home a northerner to wed," she shot

back. "You didn't tell her, did you?"

"Cerisa, don't get yourself so worked up," her husband warned.

"Pierce, please, not now!"

"Tell her what?" Francois narrowed his gaze but his sister wouldn't back down.

"Mon Dieu!" She threw her hands into the air. "It will come out. It always does!"

"Jack stopped all that," Francois shot back.

On that note, Cerisa laughed. "And all that evilness just washed away!"

"And who are you to say it was evil?"

"Wicked, and you know it was!" She was fuming. Pierce finally unslouched and went to her, taking her by the arm.

"The doctor told you not to get so riled up, my dear," he cooed.

"Fiddlesticks!" She turned to give her brother a look as Pierce walked her toward the stairs. "Tell her, Francois. If you have any feeling for her, tell her now, or lose her forever!"

Ice slithered down his back at his sister's last remark. He'd worked so hard to try to win Ada's hand and had succeeded only to now have the family secret destroy it? He closed his eyes, trying to cool the rush of nerves that came when it hit him—She was on her way to check on his mother. *Saints preserve him!*

As they walked the halls back, Ada enjoyed the relief from the heat and humidity by the breeze that blew through the open floor to ceiling windows that surrounded the house. The wrap-around porch also dropped the temperature slightly, enlightening her on how these Southerners could withstand the driving heat that dominated their part of the country.

The servant who took her back intrigued her. The girl had turned her over to another servant who appeared out of nowhere. The boy was quiet as he walked on his soles down the hardwood floors. His coloring was as light as the girl's. Mulattos were not foreign to her. Many of the runaways she heard from in the Underground Railroad tended to be lighter than their ancestors were when they arrived from African ages ago, and their stories on how they were related to their owners by blood, often caused a stir of sympathy and anger, but what was this boy's story?

He turned and she almost missed it, being so caught up in her musings, and then he stopped in front of a double door. When he opened it, she found herself in a spacious bedroom, with the windows shut and the mistress bundled in the bed. The older lady looked flushed and miserable.

"Oh, Isaac, please fetch me some water," she called.

"Mistress Marie, you got a visitor," he piped back, then he zipped out the door, and hopefully, Ada prayed, for that water.

"Oh, my, please excuse Isaac," she said softly. "He's uncomfortable being around the sick."

Ada swallowed but moved in quickly. "Good afternoon, Mrs. Fontaine, I'm Dr. Lorrance."

The woman looked at her with a surprised glance. "A woman doctor? Now, where did Cerisa find you? I realize we are short of physicians, due to the unpleasantness, but..." Her eyes closed tight as Ada put her wrist to the woman's forehead. She was hot, her skin clammy.

Quickly, she went to the washstand and found a pitcher with some water. The clay pitcher was cool, the rag wrapped around it cool as well. She put her medical bag near the bed, rolled up her sleeves and dampened another linen into the water. Wringing out the excess, she put it on her patient's forehead, right as the woman's eyes opened.

"Please forgive me. I have had better days," she moaned.

"Place your worries aside. You'll return to those days shortly." She began to loosen the bed linens that were tucked in around her. "You're like an oven, roasting away all waddled like that. Let's let you cool."

Isaac appeared with the bucket and she motioned him to bring it next to her. Before he slipped away, she called, "Isaac, I need you to open these windows."

"Mistress Marie always says—"

"Yes, but this is for her comfort, so please do as I say."

The boy ambled to the window and started to open them. Cooler air invaded the room and she relished in it. "Anyone could get a fever in here this way. Now, the bad humors can leave!" She wasn't sure who she was telling that to, or if it was just a reassurance, but she did.

At the doorway, another colored person arrived. A young woman, her hair pulled back tight and her cotton dress clinging to her with no shape without petticoats and corset. The dress didn't hit the floor so Ada could see her bare toes peek out. Her apron, though, was clean yet not a pure white, no doubt, Ada figured, from being used so often. Yet she, too, was a mulatto, her eyes appearing crystal green.

"Miss Ada, my sister Gemma."

The girl came in. "We're so glad you're here," she stated boldly. "Doctors been scarce, and Miss Marie wouldn't take one with the quarters sick. 'Fraid she's been ailing a while."

Ada smiled, plunging her hands into the bucket. Her skin tingled from rubbing Francois's mother down. The two colored servants got busy helping her, opening windows, re-dipping the cloth for their mistress's face.

"Anyone else sick?"

"Got a handful down in the quarters. Think they've hit the worst of it," the girl shrugged.

"Has Mrs...." She stopped, not knowing the proper name for Francois's enceinte sister.

"Has Mrs. Duval been here? No, her mama not allow it, being big with child." The girl sighed as she expunged the excess water off the strip of cloth. If Ada was guessing, she bet the girl was attracted to that Union general the girl was married to. She wanted to laugh. Youth...yet, the thought stuck her, was she that far off? She shook that thought aside and refocused on the ailment.

She pulled out a mortar and pedestal, with a paper packet, opening it carefully and withdrawing a couple of twigs. They were dry, so they pulverized easily with a couple of stiff grinds. She poured the contents into a cup and added water. Stirring it swiftly, she came back to her patient and lifted her slightly.

"Drink this. Slowly," she added, doing her best to barely tip the cup to Marie's lips so it could trickle in. The woman drank it with only once coughing. "There. A little willow bark will help with that fever." She watched patiently as the woman fell back asleep. Ada smiled. Sleep was the best way to get over yellow fever, she figured.

"Hmmm," she hummed, checking on her patient again. "I think, if you'll stay with her and keep doing what I've been doing of dabbing her face with the wet rag, I could go to 'the quarters' and take a peek."

"Uh, Mrs. Fontaine wouldn't allow that," the boy stated bluntly.

That surprised her. "And why not? Isn't she in charge of watching over the..." she stumbled, trying to find the right phrase. "Help?"

"Joe Johnston would have retreated after two days of such punishment."

—Ulysses S. Grant surmised, familiar with the CSA General in the West, May 7, 1864 Battle of the Wilderness

Chapter 43

FRANCOIS SAT IN THE LIBRARY, pouring another glass of wine and sank back into the chair. Coming home had turned to hell. He'd expected a marvelous event, not this. Perhaps seeing Jack? Emma? His nephews? Nope, they were all gone. As to Emma, that was probably good. Nothing like bringing another woman home and having to contend with hell.

Fact was he was here because they were sick in Louisiana. Sick of the Yankees, sick of the War, sick of the occupation but also physically sick with the yellow fever that ran rampant through here in the summer months. Reason his family had their retreat in New York. But the way it looked now, from what he'd seen of the war, he wasn't sure he'd ever see that home again.

As to Ada, his thinking stopped. His heart was heavy. He'd gotten over Emma, so he should congratulate himself. Ada was perfect. A beautiful lady, one with a head on her shoulders he should be wary of. Despite everything, he'd fallen for her. She didn't like him being a Southerner or a slave-owner, but she'd saved his life in more ways than one and was a passionate demon in bed with him. He'd saved her from wasting time on that scoundrel, yet, was he bad enough to be one as well? He poured another glass.

The doors to the room slammed open. He glanced up, halfway expecting her and she was there, breathing fire and brimstone, if he could read her face right. He girded himself up for the attack.

"You, you heathen!"

Now, that curse startled him. He relaxed a little. "Hardly, my dear. I'm a good Catholic, born and raised."

"That is not what I meant!" She flew in and stopped before the desk. Mildly, he wondered if her witch's broom was stuck in the furniture or on the ground?

"How is Mama?"

"Your mother is well on her way to recovery. The fever broke just before I left for the quarters." She paced, flushed and furious. Yet to him, she was so alive, it ignited his passion. "I go down there and find a flock of mulatto children, all with unusual eye color. Green and blue are hardly normal colors for the coloreds!"

"How do you know? Did you become an expert on this? Yankee schools teach you that cockamamie stuff?"

She whirled, her skirts swishing as she turned. "How dare you! And I thought you were more enlightened!"

That made him get up, hobble around the table and take her by the shoulders, forcing her to sit. "Ada, mulattos are pretty much prevalent down here. Millions of reasons why, majority of which you'd despise and the rest denied. But it does happen."

"And with a great deal of regularity here! How many of these did you father? They carry your blue eyes," she snapped.

Inside, his heart broke. He'd lose another again to the

family tradition. "Yes, one was mine. I was a young man. Not supposed to go play with the pretty little lady next door, so..." he shrugged, realizing that sounded bad to even him. "As you might bet, blue runs in the family, too. Slaves of that color fetched a pretty sum, or so the family claimed."

"You fathered slaves for profit?!"

"I guess you could view it that way," He was going to hell, and he knew it.

"Ah, no wonder Mrs. Wiggins laughed at me for agreeing to wed you! You realize I don't share well!"

"You're not sharing. Haven't in a long time. We don't even have slaves here, thanks to my brother Jack. He freed them all last year."

"I beg your pardon?" She frowned. "I don't believe you! They call you massa and—"

"Yes, they do. Some habits die hard. Look, Jack freed them and gave them a parcel of land, plus for those who stayed, he paid them. Not a bad situation, considering. Some did leave, but the bulk stayed."

"Well, of course. You can't go traveling anywhere here as a freeman!"

"Yes, they can and they have." He ran his fingers through his hair as frustration threatened. "They were slaves but given their freedom. Jack's offer was good and here, they were still covered by us on anything that'd go wrong. Yes, there are still the remains of that time, but they're given a chance. Creoles handle this situation differently. Having freed servants isn't a rarity."

She stood there, heaving to breath but the corset restrained her. "How could you?"

For a long time, he never given it a thought. It was done. Now, though, a voice, deep inside him, croaked the same question. Started when he was with her, maybe before when they waited for a fight, but the reality was hitting when he started to heal and listened to her. He couldn't pinpoint the exact moment, but it did make him question.

"You simply don't dispute the family rules," he stated. *Or how the family accumulated their wealth.* "We're around them all the time. We grew together. I knew her well. I told you I was young and she was pretty."

She walked right up to him and slapped his cheek hard. He wasn't ready for that, nor its sting, yet he probably deserved it. Fire glowed in her eyes, her cheeks were flushed, turning her into a breathing volcano and that passion, those flames, made his heart thud wildly. A mild maid was not in her repertoire. *No wonder she fought, and won, her arguments with the Union Medical Department.* He wanted to pull her into his arms and kiss her.

"Doc! Doc Ada!!"

They both turned to find Isaac barging in, gulping for air from running.

Instantly, she threw her anger aside and went to him. "Yes, Isaac, what is wrong? Mrs. Fontaine all right?"

"Yessum, ma'am," he stuttered between gulps of air. "But there's Mes Jenny calling for ya."

"Miss Jenny?" She wasn't sure if she was a servant, but she guessed so. "Take me to her." She swung a glance toward Francois. He grabbed his cane and ambled after her.

The boy took them to the front of the house as Francois tried to recall the Jennys he knew, and outside his servants, all he could think of was the shopkeeper's wife. She'd been with Mrs. Wiggins. What was going on?

They got to the entrance hall and there stood Jenny Miller. She gripped her reticule and looked worried or scared, he couldn't determine. Her husband, Benjamin Miller, ran the mercantile in town, the gathering place for most of the parish. Francois picked up his speed to catch up to Ada, finding his step easier as they went, that or he just ignored the pain.

"Mrs. Miller, good afternoon," he greeted. "To what do we owe this visit?"

"Mr. Fontaine," Jenny nodded but turned her attention to Ada. "It's been told that you are a doctor. I'm hoping I'm correct. Can't always get the truth out of these darkies."

Ada flinched. Granted, darkies was the usual term, but the tone was insulting. Yet her medicinal ear got the urgency, too. "I am. How can I help you?"

The woman outwardly sighed with relief. "Fever is flying rampant through the parish. I'm worried about my husband and several others are concerned over their families as well. Could you come and see about us? I understand you're Mr. Fontaine's wife, or to be, and we don't have much in Union money left to pay. Confederate ain't worth the paper it's printed on," she snarled, but then she switched back to pleading. "Please?"

Ada nodded before she could think. Doctors didn't decide help based on the political standings of their patients, just their health was the issue. "Yes," she answered, calling for her medical bag.

She wasn't ready for the onslaught that hit her. For the next four days, she had her own medical practice brought on by necessity, being the only doctor in town. The remaining physician had succumbed to the illness after the first day of her taking charge and she truly believed it was because the elderly man had been run ragged between the town and farms that scattered across the land.

"Dr. Ada."

She turned, too exhausted to think, it was just automatic for her to do. There stood Fanny, one of Francois's former slaves. In her hands, she held a pitcher and she handed it to Ada.

"Take it by the handle. It still be mighty warm."

Ada did and took a whiff, crinkling her nose. "Pine?"

Fanny snorted. "Helps with the parched achy throat. A cup of that and tablespoon of honey will solve that complaint."

Ada sighed, a slight wave of relief flittering across her shoulders. "Thank you. It's sorely needed."

"Yessum. I'm familiar with this sickness. Visits yearly. Most these folk scatter like the wind during the summer, that river they use so much ain't nothing but a cesspool at times like this." She leaned in. "Most us slaves know what to take to stave it off, though this year, with us being free, some think they're too good for old slave remedies." She snorted and walked off.

Ada couldn't help but laugh. She'd guess the woman was close to her age and had a tinge darker skin than the bulk of the other servants from Francois's house she'd seen. Plus the girl's eyes were light brown. She also seemed a bit standoffish, but then again, Ada had whizzed into Bellefountaine, proceeded to jump in helping with the outbreak while arguing deeply with Francois, so with that and her Yankee accent, she noticed several acting cool towards her. That was until they realized she could help them.

She grabbed a cup and took a drink of water, her thinking returning to her intended. Since their fight, she'd been pulled away, rarely being at Bellefountaine for longer than sleep, and even that wasn't long enough. Francois always nodded to her, arranged for her supper to be delivered to her bedroom and had breakfast ready in the morning.

He drove her to the farms and quarters, got her whatever supplies she needed. But they rarely talked outside the immediate need of her work and the patients. It was like they were skating on a pond with a thin layer of ice, both acting in unison for fear anything more would crack the surface and they'd be swallowed.

Even now, he brought her a fresh canteen of water, as if he knew she needed to slake her thirst.

"You look exhausted," he commented. "How are you feeling?"

She gave him a partial smile. "I'm doing fine. I think several are on the road to recovery. Hideous disease, burning from the inside out."

He nodded. "Thank you for being here to help."

His soft comment touched her deeply. "I truly appreciate that."

The warmth in his eyes and his handsome appearance, still a little rugged with whiskers struggling to show but debonair still, made her heart pang, tugging to making her realize love for him whispered inside her. At night, exhausted from working continuously on her patients, her dreams whipped up the distinct memories of making love to him. She swore he kissed her when she slept, but woke to find absolutely no evidence he was there, and her heart wept.

But the swirl of romance instantly dissipated when she went to breakfast and saw the light-colored children with blue eyes that showed the depravity of his life. Again, her emotions chilled as she began to build a wall around her heart, to keep from being hurt again—which worked, until he helped and his smile made it crumble.

She realized he was staring at her and she refocused as he opened his mouth to say something when the sound of pounding hooves grew louder and louder.

"Doc Ada! Doc Ada!" the rider yelled as the horse skidded to a halt.

"Whoa, whoa!" Francois grabbed the reins, leaning on the cane as he fought to stop the horses. "Isaac, is Mama sick again?"

The boy jumped off the horse, yanking the hat off his head as he went to Ada. "Miss Cerisa is bellowin'!"

Ada frowned then she opened her eyes wide. "The baby is coming."

"Now?" Francois asked.

"Yessum," Isaac sputtered out. "Aunt Fanny sent me, sayin' its time. Miss Cerisa is callin' for ya." The kid wrangled the hat in his hands. "She's in pain, bad."

Ada nodded. "Tell her I'm on my way."

Isaac gave a bob of his head and jumped back on the horse, riding away.

Ada turned to Francois. "Time to go."

Francois went to get the carriage as Ada inhaled. She'd been avoiding any conversation on marriage and children with him, considering their argument. And while the arrival of a baby was exciting, it also brought her back to her engagement. What if he brought up the subject of marriage again?

And worse. She was late. What if she carried his baby now? She swallowed hard.

"When Grant arrived, we began to see things move. We felt that everything came from a plan."

—Union Officer with the Army of the Cumberland, after the battle of Chickamauga, 1863

PIERCE PACED, HIS SPEED INCREASING on every moan he heard coming from the bed where his wife lay. She was in labor and with every contraction, she withered in painful bouts, contorting in positions he didn't think possible, considering the bulge of her pregnancy.

"Where's Mama?" she spat out. "Get me Mama!"

"Miss Cerisa, your mama is still sick with fever. She can't come," Fanny told her, wiping Cerisa's brows with a damp rag.

Cerisa didn't seem to hear her. Drowning in her own perspiration, she shook her head. "No, no! Pierce!"

Fear snaked down his side. "Yes, my love."

"Push on me, help this child come!"

He frowned. "You know I won't do that." He shot a questioning glance at the servant, who replied with a small but sharp negative shake.

"I thought we sent for Francois's doc." If the woman really was a doctor, she could fix this, he swore.

"I sent Isaac. Miss Marie knows this too well, better than me, but she's still weak from the fever."

"I'm not blaming you or anyone," he snarled before he realized his tone was laced with anger.

"Miss Cerisa, Doc Ada be here real soon. She'll help you."

Cerisa laughed. "That abolitionist will probably love to see me in pain, being a planter and all."

Pierce took her hand. It was clammy, but he ignored that. "No doctor would deny helping you. Wait."

That made her laugh harder. "Oh, yes, I can wait." She crumpled in pain, her fingers wrapping around his so badly, he feared they break as her grip was so strong. "Can't you see? I can wait."

Pierce prayed to God this child came. He was beginning to inwardly swear they'd be no more babies when he heard the noise of boots in the hallway and sighed.

"We're here!"

Pierce nodded. "Great. You brought the doc, right?"

"Yankee humor escapes me," Francois muttered right as his intended barged into the room.

Ada stormed into the room, ignoring both men and reached the bed within seconds. She touched Cerisa's head and then took her hand, feeling for her pulse. "Hi, Mrs. Duval. Here you've got a child wishing to come into the world right now."

The woman looked relieved. "Yes. Wanting to come pretty bad. Or maybe I want her to."

Ada grinned, heading to wash her hands. She couldn't bring herself to touch the girl until she'd washed the dirt and grime from the road and helping fever patients. With a glance at Fanny, she said, "Did you bring any cloths?"

"Oh, yes ma'am. Right over here, next to the bucket of water Eisha brought."

"Good. You helped with these before?"

Fanny shook her head. "No. Sorry. The sight of blood makes me sick."

That made Ada smile. "Yes, it does take some getting used to. But I may need your help. How is Mrs. Fontaine doing?"

"Last I saw, she was sleeping."

"Best thing for her." She wiped her hands and looked at the two men standing to the side, both looking a little befuddled. She'd help them on that. "Gentlemen, I need you to leave."

"No! I will not leave my wife—" Duval started when she cut him off.

"General Duval, yes you will. She is in good hands." She nodded to Francois. "He'll fill you in on how that is. Now, scoot!"

Duval growled, but kissed his wife's forehead and left, his boots clipping down the hall in quick time, a sound she hadn't heard in a while, with Francois's quick, gaited step not far behind.

"Ouch!"

She inhaled deep. "Fanny, how long has this been going on?"

"Water broke about mid-morning, I reckon."

Too long ago, as far as Ada could tell. Cerisa's energy was waning and that could be dangerous in this heat and with fever too close. She racked her brains, trying to recall something that might help this child come when the memory gushed into her sigh. She smiled. "Fanny, go put some blankets out on the floor. And fetch that water and cloth closer."

"Yessum."

She went to the bedside and maneuvered her arms underneath Cerisa's back. The girl had drifted to sleep after the last contraction but the next would wake her. Ada nudged her upright, instantly startling Cerisa.

"What are you doing?" she grumbled, before her face contorted again, hit with another labor pain.

"Come on, push!"

"Push into what? My baby can't breath coming out with me sitting on the bed!"

Ada liked to hear her fiery manner. It'd bring her back to full strength, perfect for what was to come. "You're right. Fanny, please assist me. Now, on the count of three." She looked at Fanny, who was on the other side of Cerisa. "One, two, three!"

They managed to get the girl upright and walked her to the nest of blankets on the floor.

"You want me to lay there?" Her voice was incredulous.

Ada shifted herself in front of Cerisa. "No. What I want you to do is squat and push with all your might!"

The cocktail tasted marvelous, Francois decided, but Duval would have none of it. Francois shrugged and went to pour another, deciding he deserved the break as his ankle was sore, his emotions drained and life as he knew it was gone.

"Perhaps when it is your turn, you'll understand," Duval stated.

Francois stopped halfway through his pour. "My turn?"

"Yes. When you wed Ada."

When he married Ada....truth was, he wasn't sure if that'd ever happen. After their heated argument, they'd operated on neutral grounds. She saw the area's sick and he helped her in travel, anything she required, trying to be resourceful and quiet, hoping to win her back that way. Memories of that night, when his past exploded into full color for her, replayed over and over in his mind, constantly reminding him of a time that was horrific to an anti-slavery advocate. But time and the war had changed him. He no longer was comfortable with what he did, though he still cared for the offspring he made, despite the outcome. Now, he viewed the dark man more as an equal, having fought with the few, seen the ones in the Union hospital work and even the freemen here, like old Charlie Bloom, who worked as hard as the whites to live and fight. He couldn't correct the damage done, but he could strive to not repeat it, nor to support it. But would Ada believe him?

"Yes, well, that day may never come," he finally vocalized, then downed the second drink in one gulp.

Duval snorted. "You should've explained the situation before you arrived."

"Yes, I was told that by LaJoyce."

Duval stared hard at him his eyes narrowed. "Considering what I heard and how you handle yourself, I was somewhat surprised you appeared with a white lady on your arm. Could've sworn your penchant was for ebony."

That made him shift. He waggled his tight lips, considering that notion in his head. "Yes, I see why you'd say that. I have enjoyed the pleasures of those ladies. But Ada..." He smiled. "She managed to grab my attention in more ways than one." In too many ways, he remembered. Now, those may only be memories. *Damn!*

Duval went and poured himself a drink, downed it and slammed the glass down. "You fought with the Tigers?"

Francois frowned. He knew he did.

"I just wish I could trust you," he muttered, before he returned to his pacing.

Francois's frown remained. *What the hell was that about?*

"Come on, Cerisa, push!"

Cerisa bit her lip, her face turning red as she squatted above the blanket beneath her and forced a push.

Ada was on the floor, near her, waiting. She thought she could see the crown of the baby's head. If she'd only push harder.

And it happened. Cerisa screamed as the child slipped out and onto the bundle of material. Ada reached for the infant, pulling him aside and taking the knife she'd placed on the side of the blanket and cut the cord still connecting them right before Cerisa stumbled. Fanny raced in to get the new mother as Ada stood with the baby all still covered in afterbirth. She spanked the child, trying to get him to clear his breathing with a good squall and the babe answered her with one, making Ada grin. She took the baby to the washbasin to clean her up as Fanny helped the exhausted Cerisa to bed.

"Mother, your new darling baby boy." She handed the swaddled infant to her mother.

Cerisa looked drained but Ada could see her color return as she looked at her child. Fanny picked up the bloody rags with a nod to Ada, which she took as the mother was cleaned.

"He's so beautiful," Cerisa cooed as she cradled her baby. His blue eye stared in wonder at the woman holding him. It was the perfect scene, Ada thought. *One she could replicate with Francois*...she cut the thought off.

"Yes, he is." Ada brought her a cup of water to sip from. "Now, we need you to rest so you can get on your feet. That baby will need you."

Yet Cerisa had the child at her bosom, nursing. "Perhaps you and my brother will have one soon."

Ada swallowed. Right as she started to think it might be very soon, her womb clutched and she doubled in pain.

"Are you all right?" Cerisa asked, worry showing in her eyes. "You've been too busy with the sick. You need to rest, too."

"I'm fine." She grimaced, barely able to ignore the pang of sadness as the monthly cramps took control.

"Have you and my brother made up?"

She spun. "Of course!"

But the question didn't leave Cerisa's brow. "He should have told you before. I'm sorry."

That unnerved her that his sister apologized for his transgressions. She started to pick up her medical supplies. "It's not your worry."

"But it is." She turned the child to her other breast, cradling him closely. "My family is a very old one, patriarch of the parish, so we're pretty well known. My brother might have added to the sins of my family, but, strangely enough, he's always cared for our slaves. In many ways, he's kept in contact long after they've left."

Memories of his half-sister, the mulatto in New York, Jaquita, appeared in Ada's mind. He did seem to care for her. "Regardless, it was a surprise to see."

Cerisa rolled her lips in. "Our oldest brother, Jack, didn't participate. Instead, he ran away to West Point and is an officer in the Union Army now. For a while, he was stationed here, in charge of the occupation. He freed our slaves and gave them the opportunity to leave, or stay, and the monetary backing for either. A good portion stayed."

Ada nodded as she listened, but the other worry about him kept into her thoughts. "And who is Emma?"

"Jack's wife. She's a Virginian. He wooed her across the South. They got separated for a bit, and she believed he was dead when she got here, pregnant with his child. Francois offered to marry her and make all well. I think, from what I heard as I wasn't here, he fell in love with her. But Jack appeared, all well and good and determined to get his Emma back. Emma loved Jack, so for them, all was good. But Francois couldn't handle it and left to join the war."

"He didn't go to fight to keep slavery?"

Cerise laughed and kissed her child on his head before she answered. "No. He went to run away from seeing her every day and knowing he couldn't have her."

Ada sat back, varying her thoughts and emotions from confused to ecstatic to angry. After their fight, they'd been together yet they hadn't talked outside mundane things. It'd been like walking on eggshells barefoot. But the other memory now exploded in her head.

"And who is that girl?"

Cerisa frowned, though Ada saw the flicker in her eyes. "What girl?"

"The one he carries a portrait of? In his coat?"

Cerisa closed her eyes. "He never told you? No, apparently not. That is Emma."

"Excuse me?" Ada's cheeks inflamed, she could feel the heat.

"Francois thought he loved her, so he went to war to forget her but must've taken the portrait." She smiled. "And then he met you!"

Ada started tapping her foot. "I'm supposed to believe that? That he's over her? She's married to his brother!"

"Yes, it was a bit black, you could say." She leaned forward, wincing from the childbirth, but looked at her tightly. "He came back, thrilled to have you with him. He does love you. And it's way more than with Emma. I see it in his eyes and the way he acts. Maybe, you might consider giving him a second chance?" Cerisa eyed her. "Heaven knows, we could use your help around here and I think you could badger him into seeing how things could be. Would you consider that?"

Ada drummed her fingers softly over her leather medical bag. She loved him and having his child did sound beautiful. But how could she forgive him for all he's done?

"The edge of the conflict swayed to and fro with wild whirlpools and eddies. At times I saw around me more of the enemy than my own men; gaps opening, swallowing, closing again; squads of stalwart men who had cut their way through us, disappearing as if translated. All around, a strange, mingled roar."

—Colonel Joshua Lawrence Chamberlain, 20th Maine, Gettysburg, July 1863

Chapter 45

3 days later

THE HOUSE HAD FINALLY SETTLED to near normal. Francois breathed in the clean river air and sighed. The baby was healthy, Cerisa recovered to a nice rosy, new-mother glow, his own mother was now well and Ada was buzzing around, taking care of the three. It was his own heart that beat with a skip when he saw her, hoping she'd give him a glance, one that he could view as time for him and he'd scoop her away, to beg for his case, but alas, she still skirted him. Would it never end?

It was a lovely afternoon, a day he could almost think there was no war as Pierce wore civilian clothes and no gunfire was heard. His ankle was less bothersome so the cane was in use less and less each day. As the birds chirped outside the parlor window, he swore he'd find a way to talk to her and try to sweep her off her feet…

Instead, his mother called the family to come to the parlor for tea. He could never refuse her.

"Mama, it's so good to see you well at last." He gave her a kiss on the cheek.

Marie blushed. "Glad you have left that awful unpleasantness. And that you brought the most enchanting mademoiselle with you to wed." She smiled at him and Ada.

Ada shifted on the settee, her cup of tea rattled softly in her hand. Francois went to sit next to her, giving her a wink as he mouthed his apologies for his mother being so blunt. Yet before he could say a word, Pierce escorted his wife and baby in, settling Cerisa near her mother.

"Oh, let me see that boy!" Marie held out her arms.

Cerisa gave her son to her and sat down. "We've decided on a name. Gustav Pierre Duval."

"Simply wonderful! We will set the baptism for this Sunday." Marie grinned broadly, kissing the baby on the head.

"Which will work out well," Pierce said, still standing. It was then Francois noticed his uniform was back on.

"What are you trying to say?" he asked.

"What have you two decided?" Pierce shot back, nodding toward Ada.

"That's a rather blunt question," Francois shot back. There was an edginess to the Yankee that he didn't like.

"Are you staying?" Pierce asked Ada. "Because if you want to return north, I can help you on that."

Ada's mouth dropped. Francois leapt up, ignoring his ankle screaming. "Why would she leave?"

Ada's heart stopped when the Union general before her gave her a ticket home. Home to what? A man who'd betrayed and lied to her? To a job duty where the commanding staff ignored her skill set? To a war of hell and pain? Of men she couldn't help and a multitude demanding nursing help? Or stay to marry Francois, who had slept with slaves, had a mulatto child, and was in love with his brother's wife, making her feel second place, like a fill in. Her heart pounded, her head ached and had been for the past week. Here was a ticket out. Yet her heart was tugged in another direction…

She faced Francois. He'd been quiet but she knew he was doing everything to help her here. Though they're still at odds…

"Don't leave," he begged. "I love you."

"No," but she nodded, her heart struggling to beat. "You love this Emma more than me."

"No, no," he said quickly, dropping to sit next to her again and taking her hand. "I did at one time. Drove me to the war. But then I met you." He smiled.

"And what of your brood of slaves?" The words came out with anger twisted around each letter. She shouldn't have put it that way, because his eyes flared in reply.

"I don't have a 'brood of slaves'! Merd!"

"Francois, do not use that language in this house!" his mother demanded.

His nose twitched. It was rather cute and almost made her giggle, that he was still under his mother's rules over cussing.

"They are all free! Jack set them free. That should make you happy!" he got up and walked away only to turn and come back. "I'm sorry I did not tell you of the family before. I apologize for my former misbehavior. Jack, Cerisa,

Emma and now you have reprimanded me for doing as I was told. It was wrong, I understand it now." He took her hand, and dropped to one knee. "Please, accept my apology. My sins you now know and will not continue. Please." He kissed her hand. "I love you."

Her heart beat wildly. Her fingers burned from his touch, sending lightning bolts through her, her body begging for more. She licked her lips, her mouth too dry to talk. So, she nodded. "Yes, yes, I believe you. You've been working so hard to get into my graces and you've won. You've been the only one not discrediting my credentials as a doctor, which won me in the first place, made me look past your gray uniform." She smiled to the point of hurt. "And even here, you've been my supporter. Thank you."

He kissed her hard. She vaguely heard the room explode in claps and a baby wail over them, but what she truly felt was her blood racing, the taste of him and the rock hardness of his body next to hers. Slowly, her upbringing made her pull back. Ladies don't act like slatterns, she reminded herself, throwing themselves at men. But, oh, how she wanted him!

Apart, he gazed into her eyes warmly though he asked, "I won you over by believing you're a doctor? Obviously, you are! You saved my life! But what of your heart? Any chance at having it?"

She giggled. "Of course. I love you!"

"This is wonderful!" Pierce boomed. "We shall have a priest here shortly."

Francois's whole soul sang joy at winning her hand. But his brother-in-law's talk of a quick marriage made him leery.

"Perhaps my bride might like a wedding," he suggested.

"Now? Nah. There's a war going on!" Duval exclaimed.

"Tell us why are you in uniform?" Francois asked, noting Cerisa's face paling at the comment as she clung to her baby tightly.

The man inhaled. "I've been called to duty back east. I must go."

"Pardon moi?" Marie asked.

"What?" Francois threw out.

"I have my orders. I do have a command. But I was reluctant to leave until all was situated here. Leaving my wife at her home is good, but to cover her and my son, I needed to know she had protection. You're a rebel. With me gone, you're in charge. If the Union army comes here, I needed to know they were protected. I wasn't sure with you having served in the Confederate army and a Southerner. But if you marry a Yankee doctor, then I feel the balance here is good."

"You're merd!" Francois shouted back.

"You," Pierce said, looking at Ada and ignoring Francois. "I'll put in good word for you in command and get you 're-assigned' to here. Your medical services are greatly needed and it will be incoming Yankee money, which is far better than the Confederate script that isn't worth a hill of beans."

"Cerisa?" He begged of his sister to say something.

She sighed. It was now he noticed her eyes slightly puffy and red. "I cannot win against the Union Army. But, if you two are here, Gustav and I will be safe."

He rolled his eyes. But Ada took his hand. He stared, hoping and praying she loved him enough to stay. He'd been a fool about Emma, but this lady had stolen his heart. If she left, he'd surely die.

"Please tell me you'll marry me," he pleaded desperately.

Her eyes watered. Damn! He hoped that meant out of love and not hate. When a tear fell, he wasn't sure what to do.

"You, Francois, are everything I despised. You're a slave owner, you took rights where there were none, fathered without regard and loved another you could never have. I should run, but you also managed to show me you *could* change, that you do have a heart, and in doing so, won mine. So yes, I will marry you."

His heart skipped a beat. He wanted to jump in joy. "Yes! Mon Dieu, thank you, ma chère."

"We will be fine. Both protected from the war, in a way." She smiled. "Now, kiss me, knowing I love you heart and soul."

His stomach flittered at her words. The warmth of her smile and the fire in her eyes ignited his own and he took her into his arms, kissing her hard and deep. He'd gone to war to forget love, only to find his real true love was a lady made of steel and fire. He'd love her to hell and back!

Author's Notes

THE AMERICAN CIVIL WAR IS the pivotal point in the U.S. History, the effects still riveting us today. It is a time period that yells at me through my characters my muse creates, mixed with real life people from. I am driven to write their story. But as a historian, I am compelled to write these stories with as much accuracy as I can.

The War itself had been brewing for decades. The country was divided by industry and agriculture; old money verses entrepreneurs and new money. Politics debated and were influenced by established power and new congressmen. Yet the straw that broke the camels back was slavery issue. Every Congressmen, every president fought to make compromises, knowing well that the divide between the North & the South was deepening and tempers were flaring. Every one in office did their best to not have a war break out under their watch, so they would not hold the blame, yet nothing was ever solved and the volcano would erupt with blood.

The Abolitionist movement had started decades before the war. It swayed the North, an area no longer using slave labor, to swing its way. They were the South's annoying pest, one the planters couldn't eliminate. So why didn't the Abolitionists get slavery ended? For the simple fact that there were different chapters of abolitionists and they did not get along. Slavery was costing the South heavily on a financial end, but the abolitionists pushed to get the owners to free their people, even give them money to start a new life but without a solution to labor. Labor was the issue, as the South had the highest exporting product for the United States: Cotton. It was labor intensive in a climate that was hotter than hades. But it was King Cotton that would kill the South's lifestyle in the years to come.

In this story, it is mentioned how the French viewed the peculiar institution differently than the English/Americans. Under the French and Spanish, slaves had to be Catholic and attend mass; all marriages were church marriages and not the fabricated spectacle the Americans did. 'Jump over the broom' was a slave marriage, not legal in any means, therefore if one of the couple had to be sold, the owner didn't regret it, unlike a church wedding, with the couple legally and religiously binded. Under the French, slaves didn't work on Sundays—not only was that a day of devotion, but it was also a day they could relax or hire themselves out, as some in Ste Genevieve and St. Louis did, working in the coal mining, and the money they earned, they kept. Planned right, the pay could allow a few to buy their own freedom. Once free, society treated them as Frenchmen.

In taking the reader back to the time of the War can be treacherous as words from back then have different connotations or use today. In the lexicon of the period, 'darkie' was used but African American was not. So use of the period correct terms is just a step to the past.

Ada's story of being a woman doctor is not that unusual. At the mid-19th century, Pennsylvania, Ohio and New York had medical schools that allowed women. In the South, there was one medical school that allowed a woman, and that was due to her being the owner's daughter, though her practice was small and set to the care of woman and children. Of the five woman doctors who applied with the

Union Medical Dept., all were allowed in as nurses only. Medical studies at the time were either by tutoring with an established doctor, though if he was a quack, they student learned the same methods. Schooling was way different at that time in that it lasted only two years and the second year was a repeat of the first year. Teaching surgeries were conducting in assembly-style setting, meaning most of the students couldn't see anything and even these were scarce as they had to have a cadaver to work on and robbing from the graveyard was highly discouraged. Many graduated with a set of medical books and a prayer.

During the War, with the lack of technology (no x-rays, labs), and a sad set of guidelines on how the human body worked, most gun shot wounds to limbs were treated with amputation with rare chances of reconstruction. Plus the influx of hundreds of wounded, coming off the battlefield often made doctors not take the time need to see if it was necessary and not a convenient way to move onto the next. The reuse of bandages and ill-kept equipment made any survivor lucky.

This story is Francois redemption, in an attempt wash his sins away. Not an easy task, especially with his heart set on a woman like Ada who stood for her beliefs. The two are at opposite ends of the war and despite it all love can win!

To read more about this period, below is a glimpse of part of the bibliography for this book, *The Better Angels.*

BIBLIOGRAPHY

The Medical and Surgical History of the War of the Rebellion, (1861-65). Surgeon-General Joseph K Barnes. (Washington: Government Printing Office), 1870.

Civil War Medicine, Challenges and Triumphs, Alfred Jay Bollet, M.D. (Tucson, Arizona: Galen Press, Ltd.), 2002.

Gangrene and Glory, Medical Care during the American Civil War, Frank R. Freemon (Urbana and Chicago: University of Illinois Press), 2001.

Mine Run: A Campaign of Lost Opportunities, October 21, 1863-May 1, 1864, Martin F. Graham & George F. Skoch (Lynchburg, Virginia: H.E. Howard, Inc.), 1987.

Soul By Soul, Life Inside The Antebellum Slave Market, Walter Johnson (Cambridge, Massachusetts: Havard University Press), 1999.

Lee's Tigers, The Louisiana Infantry in the Army of Northern Virginia, Terry L. Jones (Baton Rouge: Louisiana State University Press), 1987.

Hell Itself, The Battle of the Wilderness, May 5-7, 1864, Chris Mackowski (California: Savas Beatie), 2016.

Resources of the Southern Fields and Forests, Medical, Economical, and Agricultural, Francis Peyre Porcher, M.D. (San Francisco: Norman Publishing), 1991.

The Battle of the Wilderness, May 5-6, 1864, Gordon C. Rhea (Baton Rouge: Louisiana State University Press), 1994.

Masters of The Big House, Elite Slaveholders of the Mid-Nineteenth Century South, William Kauffman Scarborough

(Baton Rouge: Louisiana State University Press), 2003.

A Woman Doctor's Civil War, Esther Hill Hawks' Diary, Gerald Schwartz, Editor (University of South Carolina Press), 2nd Printing 1986.

Other books by Gina

Her Eternal Rogue
The Wicked Bargain
This Love of Mine
Great & Unfortunate Desires
A Merry Wicked Christmas
To Kiss A Lady

THE GLADIATOR
(ANCIENT ROME SERIES)
Love & Vengeance (Book I)
Love & Lies (Book II)

HEARTS TOUCHED BY FIRE
(CIVIL WAR SERIES)
The Wicked North (Book 1)
Unconditional Surrender (Book 2)
Rags & Hope (Book 3)

Author Bio

A *USA Today Bestselling* author, Gina Danna was born in St. Louis, Missouri, and has spent the better part of her life reading. History has always been her love and she spent numerous hours devouring historical romance stories, always dreaming of writing one of her own. After years of writing historical academic papers to achieve her undergraduate and graduate degrees in History, and then for museum programs and exhibits, she found the time to write her own historical romantic fiction novels.

Now, under the supervision of her dogs, she writes amid a library of research books, with her only true break away is to spend time with her other life long dream - her Arabian horse - with him, her muse can play.

Made in United States
North Haven, CT
25 January 2022